# Velvet

## TEMPLE WEST

Swoon Reads   New York

S

A Swoon Reads Book
An Imprint of Feiwel and Friends

VELVET. Copyright © 2015 by Temple West. All rights reserved. Printed in the
United States of America by R. R. Donnelley & Sons Company, Harrisonburg,
Virginia. For information, address Feiwel and Friends, 175 Fifth Avenue,
New York, N.Y. 10010.

Swoon Reads books may be purchased for business or promotional use. For
information on bulk purchases, please contact the Macmillan Corporate
and Premium Sales Department at (800) 221-7945 x5442 or by e-mail at
specialmarkets@macmillan.com.

Library of Congress Cataloging-in-Publication Data

West, Temple.
Velvet / Temple West.
pages cm
Summary: Orphaned before she was seventeen, aspiring designer
Caitlin Holte is saved from a supernatural force by Adrian, her "bad-boy"
neighbor who, she learns, is a half-demon vampire willing to serve as her
bodyguard, but unable to protect her heart when Caitlin falls in love with him.
ISBN 978-1-250-05708-2 (paperback) — ISBN 978-1-250-06361-8 (e-book)
[1. Love—Fiction.   2. Vampires—Fiction.   3. Demonology—
Fiction.   4. Supernatural—Fiction.   5. Bodyguards—Fiction.
6. Orphans—Fiction.]   I. Title.
PZ7.1.W437Vel 2015
[Fic]—dc23
2014049325

Book design by Ashley Halsey

Feiwel and Friends logo designed by Filomena Tuosto

First Edition: 2015

10  9  8  7  6  5  4  3  2  1

macteenbooks.com

Dedicated to Lara Croft.
Thank you for kicking such an incredible amount of ass.

# FIERY TORNADO
# OF DOOM

**B**y the suits and ties of Tim Gunn, I swear I will hunt you down and *eat you for breakfast*."

Above me, the flock of birds took off in a riot of indignant squawks while I sat horrified and covered in bird shit.

At least, I thought it was bird shit. I dabbed at my cheek with a hunk of rock moss, though a closer examination revealed nothing resembling feces, avian or otherwise. I briefly considered licking the moss to see if it was, in fact, bird urine—so I could be confident in my bird rage—but quickly ruled this out as totally insane. I sniffed cautiously at it instead, and it smelled pretty much like you'd expect: woodsy, and a bit like dirt.

Rain, then.

"I'm sorry, birds!" I called after them, fully aware that I looked crazy. "That one was my bad."

They just honked at me irritably.

Well, I'd tried.

This part of the mountain was deserted; quiet except for the understandably irritated pigeons and a musical breeze, which was picking up into a full-on wind. My sketchbook whipped open, pages fluttering back and forth wildly. I slammed the cover shut and wrapped my arms around it to protect the design I'd been working on for the past three hours. Above me, the scattered cloud wisps from a moment ago multiplied dramatically, spilling like ink stains across the sky. The sudden weather change was weird, but I'd only been here two days—as far as I knew, storms popped up like this all the time. The thought of trudging back to the ranch in the rain ignited the acidy rage-fire in my stomach, but the safety of my art supplies was more important than not wanting to be anywhere near my aunt and uncle.

That's actually why I was out here—Rachel, in a seriously misguided attempt to be comforting, had gone into mom-mode and hugged me. I'd dodged her outstretched arms and escaped into the woods to let my gut-response anger simmer back down to a nonexplosive level. Figured it was better to have a meltdown in the middle of the forest than the middle of their living room. After a mile or two along what seemed more like a deer path than an actual trail, I'd found this gigantic rock and climbed up to sketch, paying little attention to the time or, apparently, the weather, which was beginning to spit a misty rain.

Up until two days ago, I'd lived by the ocean my entire life so the rain was nothing new, but the forest was. I was used to being home with my mom, in our town, on our street, wrapped up in our tiny little bubble of suburban normal. Or, well, normal enough, I guess, until my parents died. Separately, of course, from the usual sorts of things, nothing too dramatic. Just life, being a bitch. My dad's death was quick, mostly painless, but I was so young when it happened that I didn't really understand for a long time that he was gone, and he was never coming back. My mom's was more recent—dull by comparison—but by the end she couldn't even speak to me, and she never said good-bye.

That was four days ago.

But I couldn't think about that now. My basic survival strategy was to keep my mind as blank as possible. Eat, sleep, sketch, repeat.

A low rumble of thunder echoed through the mountains, which was my cue to leave. Getting down *should* have been simple: walk to the edge of the rock and slide down the upturned roots I'd easily climbed up earlier. Unfortunately, a creepy, dense fog was sifting through the evergreens, cutting off the sky, making it virtually impossible to see where I was going. I'd just groped my way to the edge of the boulder, cursing the whole way, when the misting rain sputtered into a hard, freezing downpour. Moments later, a flash of lightning and roll of skull-pounding thunder exploded so close I could feel the vibrations through my fingertips. Rather than illuminating my way, it made the forest feel like an ocean, deep and pressurized and terrifying.

I wasn't that far from my aunt and uncle's property, but the trail completely disappeared in the swirling fog. I couldn't see a damn thing, but some primal, gut instinct told me to *move*. Swinging the messenger bag across my shoulders, I turned, blindly feeling around for anything I could grab hold of. My foot found the nearest root from the overturned tree and I started down, panic making me move faster than was wise. Fumbling in the dark, I lost my foothold at the same moment my fingers tore right through the moss that was keeping me anchored to the boulder. I screamed and fell, still a good six feet off the ground—but didn't hit. Where the ground should have been there was instead someone's chest, which I crashed into, hard.

My momentum knocked us both into the prickly brambles, but before I could do much more than finish my scream, the stranger rolled, pinning me to the muddy ground. I started to scream again, but he (it was a he, I could tell that much) clapped his hand over my mouth, looking around quickly as if expecting someone else to be there. The wind rose, shrieking through the trees, whipping at my hair. Above us, another flash of lightning rocked the sky, followed by a bloom of orange light that looked suspiciously like fire. The clouds gathered slowly into a broad funnel.

So, unless I was hallucinating—which seemed more and more likely—we were in the direct path of a giant, fire-spitting tornado.

Which was totally insane, because upstate New York does not *get* fire-spitting tornadoes.

The temperature plummeted and the stranger's breath bloomed in heavy white clouds. When he finally looked back down at me (perhaps because my struggles had transitioned from "Hey, you're heavy, get off" to "Hey, *there's a freaking* fire-tornado *behind you*"), I could only stare at him, all my words forgotten.

Because there was something wrong with him. There was something *very* wrong.

His pupils were pinpricks and his irises were liquid, like molten silver. A glowing white light cast the rest of his face into complete shadow so I couldn't make out what he looked like.

He slid his hand from my mouth to my cheek, and placed his palm against my temple. I wanted to scream, to say something, to *move*, but the words were all caught in my throat and I couldn't remember my own name, let alone how to move my arms and legs.

He leaned in close—way, way too close—and whispered, "I'm sorry—there's no time."

And then the pain began.

All the warmth crept upward through my body, away from my fingers and toes, crawling through my knees and wrists on fiery pins and needles. It gathered in my chest and pounded up my throat and into my skull, pulsing behind my eyes.

I was going to explode. I was going to splatter all over the forest like lava, or shatter like ice. And all the while, I couldn't look away.

Then he muttered one final word and quite suddenly, it was over.

My head cleared instantly. I could blink, I could *breathe*. The pain was gone, but with it went my entire sense of self. On some deep, subconscious level I knew I was still real—I knew I had a name and a family and a purpose in life, aimless as it was—but surface-level me believed that I'd winked out of existence. I didn't think I was dead, exactly. I simply believed that I had never *been*.

Hunched over me, the stranger flinched, once, and shivered, but I didn't think it was from the cold. In fact, the pouring rain was steaming off his skin like he was burning hot. Above us, the night-black clouds pushed closer, crowding out the sky. Looking around, as if expecting once again for someone else—or some*thing* else—to be waiting in the shadows, he scooped me up effortlessly and sprinted off into the darkness. I tried to grab hold of his shoulder, but none of my limbs were working. I was weak, pure dead weight, but he had no problem hauling me at a full run through the impossibly dark trees.

It could only have been a few minutes later that my aunt and uncle's ranch appeared out of the darkness. At the end of the trail that led into the backyard, the stranger stopped for a moment and looked down at me, eyes flickering from gray to molten silver. I tried to look away, but it was too late. I was caught in the light.

It could only have been a moment, but when I opened my eyes, I had no idea who was holding me, or why I was in the rain, or why I was outside at all. All I knew was that I wanted to be warm, and I wanted very much to fall asleep. The man kicked urgently at the front door until it opened.

I remember my aunt yelling, "Caitlin!"

And then I passed out, and didn't remember a thing.

# BACK TO SCHOOL

I couldn't delay by brushing my teeth any longer; I was about ready to gag on the foamy toothpaste and I could hear Rachel calling up the stairs for Norah and me to hurry. It was raining outside, and the Master ranch—where I was stuck living for the next year and a half—was on a road so rural it didn't even have a name. Honestly, "road" was a generous term—it was basically a dirt driveway, and its potholes were currently hidden under a foot of water. Rather than braving the weather on the ancient bicycles parked on the side of the house, Rachel had said she'd take us to school in the truck, which meant my mini-vacation from school was over. Apparently you can only use your dead mom as an excuse to skip algebra for so long.

I was nervous. And I felt stupid for feeling nervous. What was I, twelve?

To be fair, it had been a hell of a week. Funeral, freak storm, fever—my least favorite "F" words.

I stared grimly in the mirror: Dark circles puffed under my eyes, my skin looked pasty, and my lips were chapped. The big burgundy sweater I wore only made my face look more hollow. Skinny jeans, my mom's wedding ring on my right hand, my dad's wedding ring on my thumb, and an old pair of Rachel's boots. Definitely looked like I wanted to be a fashion designer.

When I'd shown up at the ranch, I'd spent the majority of the first three days locked in my new room marathoning episodes of *Project Runway* on Netflix. I'd brought my sewing machine with me to Stony Creek, but the pedal cord had snapped in the back of my grandma's station wagon on the move here, and I didn't have the money to fix it. I did some embroidery to pass the time, but it wasn't the same. I wanted to be a designer—I wanted to go to the Fashion Institute of Technology and open a store in New York. But our insurance was so crappy and Mom's medical bills were so insanely high that they obliterated any chance of going to college. When I graduated high school next year, I would be on my own, totally broke.

*Next week*, I told myself. Next week, I'd start researching internships. I'd make a plan. I'd work on designs, I'd figure out how to get money to fix my sewing machine. I'd use friggin' sheets, if I had to, to make a portfolio to show at the Fashion Institute. I'd find a way.

Today, however, I'd let myself feel as miserable as I wanted.

A hell of a week, indeed.

"Oh, good, you're ready," Rachel said, when I finally came down to the kitchen. "Come on, Norah!" she called up the stairs again. I could hear a muffled response as Rachel grabbed two brown paper bags and handed one to me. I was ruffling their routine, an extra mouth to feed and an extra body to transport. Joe, in his plaid flannel shirt with the sleeves rolled up, sat at the table reading an article on his laptop, completely unaffected by the morning rush.

Rachel had tried to get me interested in the ranch, and I might have been, but because she wanted me to like it, I didn't—which was immature, and I knew it was immature, but I didn't care. There were eggs to collect, a cow to milk, a garden to tend (though nothing was growing in mid-October), and, of course, the horses. There were eight, five of which were boarders owned by city people who came by once or twice in the summer to ride them.

"That's your lunch," Rachel said, pointing at my bag as she filled her thermos with steaming coffee. "I didn't know what you'd want, so I put in a little of everything."

I didn't say anything, but she was already at the foot of the stairs ready to call up one last warning just as my cousin came bounding down.

"Ready!" she announced, landing on the floor, grabbing her lunch out of her mom's hands and dashing out the front door, hair still wet from her quick post-barn rinse-off in the shower. Norah was fourteen, a freshman, and completely obsessed with horses. She got up at four a.m. every day to feed them and, I don't even know, muck out their stalls? My only source of farm terminology was *Black Beauty*, so I honestly don't know what she did for three hours every morning before school. Norah didn't like me and I was indifferent about Norah. I got it, though—I was invading her turf, soaking up all her parents' attention. If the circumstances were different, if I had met her even once before moving into her house, I think I would have liked her. Problem was, I *hadn't* met her before, and now we had a year and a half to butt heads.

"Have a good day, Caitlin," my uncle called as I slid on my jacket. I waved halfheartedly at him without looking back.

It wasn't Joe and Rachel's fault my mom was dead, I had to give them that. I was mad at them for other reasons, but not for that. I just didn't understand why they hadn't shown up once the entire time she was sick. They'd sent a few e-mails to ask for updates and to try and cheer me up with these stupid, animated eCards, but they never called, they never asked to speak to my mom, they didn't even show up for the funeral. I had to live with them because the lawyers said I did, but once I was eighteen, I was out of there.

Amid the scramble for seat belts in the truck, I managed to slip my earbuds in and spent the twenty-minute drive listening to angry pop music that simultaneously made me want to dance *and* punch someone in the face—both of which felt better than being depressed. Ever since the storm, my protective shell of anger had mostly given way to a listless sadness, and it pissed me off. Sadness wasn't useful. I guess anger wasn't really useful either, but it at least made me feel less pathetic.

Through the fogged-up window the rain-slick trees waved in the wind, beautiful and ghostly. Too soon, we arrived at the center of town and pulled into the parking lot of Warren County School. It was a squat brick building with ivy growing up the side of one wall, an arched roof, a covered picnic area with an adjacent covered playground, and an American and New York flag. I opened the door to the truck, Norah scrambling behind me to get out.

"Caitlin," Rachel called from the driver's side. I turned back to look at her. "Have a great day, okay, honey?"

I stared at her until her smile faltered and she looked away.

"Come on," Norah said, tugging on my arm. I shut the door and my aunt drove back into the rain and fog. Maybe I was a brat after all. Maybe I didn't give a shit. Maybe I really, really missed my mom and didn't want to be here.

Norah and I dashed under the cover of the sheltered walkway surrounding the building. "Mom told me to look after you," she announced after an awkward moment of silence. Her face was flat, probably trying to hide a scowl.

I decided to let her off the hook. "Just tell me where to check in; I can figure the rest out."

"First door on the right," she said, pointing I nodded and left her on the sidewalk.

Through the old, warped door, painted over many times and slightly too large for the frame, a cramped waiting room guarded a damp-smelling hallway. To the right, a tiny, feather-haired old lady sat behind her desk, hand shaking as she stamped a stack of papers. She hadn't noticed me so I dinged the old orange bell on the counter.

"I'm a new student," I said, as she finally looked up. "Should I sign in, or anything?"

She reached a trembling hand out to push a clipboard two inches in my direction and murmured, "Sign here."

I scrawled *Caitlin Holte* on the sign-in sheet and then waited.

Mrs. Goode, as her plastic, clip-on name tag stated, seemed to have fallen asleep.

"Mrs. Goode? Ma'am?"

She jolted awake, blinked a few times as if remembering where she was, then handed me a schedule and a hand-drawn map of the campus.

"Mr. Warren is in room three; he'll be your first period teacher." She smiled up at me from behind her enormous glasses. "Welcome to Warren County."

I glanced at the schedule. My homeroom teacher's name was Warren, and the school was named Warren—that couldn't be a coincidence. Maybe his grandfather was a town founder. Maybe people never left, like a horror-movie amusement park. I felt myself cringing—a year and a half in this place. A year and a half in the middle of podunk godforsaken nowhere completely against my will—and my mom's. I mean that literally. Mom's will stated that I should go live with my grandma, two blocks down from where I'd grown up. Then the state, in all their wisdom, declared Grandma wasn't a fit guardian. As if losing my mom wasn't bad enough, finding out two days after her funeral that I'd have to move in with an aunt, uncle, and cousin I'd never met before was so far beyond devastating that I pretty much existed in a state of perpetual rage. I wasn't upset, I wasn't *sad*—I was pissed.

And nervous. I hadn't had that first-day-at-a-new-school experience since kindergarten. It's not that I was worried about making friends, I just didn't want to be noticed or bothered, and in a town this small, anyone that hadn't lived here for three generations would be a source of gossip for weeks. I briefly considered skipping class to wander the town, but the little I'd seen was unimpressive and, anyway, I had zero cash.

I wandered back outside, pulling hard on the door twice to get it to actually close before studying the map. Mr. Warren was in room 3. Room 3 was ten feet to my left. I walked over and stared at the handle, knowing I had to open the stupid door eventually. Grabbing hold of the handle and expecting it to be warped and stuck like the office entry, I shoved too hard and pretty much fell into the classroom.

I pushed the door closed to cut out the cold draft that had swirled in after me, avoiding everyone's eyes. A few students were sitting, others were lounging backward on their desks. Mr. Warren, an older man in a blue collared shirt, sweater vest, and khakis, was leaning back in the chair at the front of the room reading through a Dean Koontz paperback. He frowned as I waited awkwardly by the door and I wondered what on earth I could have done already to disappoint him. But then he smiled and he stood up, holding out his hand.

"You must be Caitlin," he said as I stepped forward to shake it, very aware that everyone was staring at me. "Welcome. Have a seat anywhere."

I nodded, then tried to find an empty seat. Tried, but failed. One girl just straight up stood in my way.

"You're Caitlin Master?" the blond girl asked, standing half a head taller than me. She was built like a tank. I don't mean she was fat; I mean it looked like she could wrestle bears.

"Holte, actually," I said, trying to avoid this conversation.

"What?"

Something about her tone set my hackles on end. "My name," I replied slowly, in case she couldn't hear, "is Caitlin *Holte*."

Ah, there was the anger again, fresh and raw, making me invincible and careless. So what if this tank-girl could wrestle bears? So what if everyone was staring at me again? I'd never been in a fight before. Maybe actually punching someone in the face instead of just wishing I could punch someone in the face would make me feel a little better.

The girl stared. Behind her, Mr. Warren watched us curiously over the top of his book. The moment stretched, and I could feel the eyes of the other kids on us.

Then, mysteriously, she relaxed. "I'm sorry for your loss," she said solemnly. "I know your aunt and uncle. Nice people." She nodded at the other kids as if to say, "Come on, introduce yourselves."

They murmured their names and smiled at me, but I forgot them immediately, overwhelmed by the abrupt turn of the conversation.

After the last boy shook my hand, the tank-bear-girl said, "I'm Trish. Welcome to Stony Creek."

The final bell rang. Mr. Warren stood and called everyone to attention, so I sat in the nearest empty seat, which happened to be next to Trish. My hands were shaking, and the classroom blurred in front of me slightly. Ever since the storm I'd been having dizzy spells. I chalked it up to remnants of the fever I'd come home with. That, or the rush of unused adrenaline that spiked my system when I'd briefly considered getting into a fight with Trish. The dizziness passed quickly and I slunk down in my seat, wishing for a lot of impossible things. It would be super great if my mom could somehow be not dead, but I'd settle for someone pulling the fire alarm so I could get out of here. Alas, no such miracle occurred.

For the most part, the junior class stayed together because there were virtually no electives to take at a school this size. Appearing to be engaged with my homework, I spent most of the day dodging conversation with Trish and the few brave others who asked me questions. I was actually just sketching in the margins of my books. I figured that counted as homework, given my career aspirations. People got the hint pretty quickly that I wasn't much into chitchat, and with Trish's line about being sorry for my loss, I guess they all understood why. Pretty sure I was giving off a newly minted orphan vibe.

First, second, and third period passed by in a blur of information that didn't seem all that important for me to remember. Fourth was with a Mrs. Leckenby for art, which was mostly "sketching" with crusty markers and cheap tempera paint. I found a clipboard and tilted my paper toward me so no one could see the punk-rock/Victorian-crossover vest I was doodling. Frills and spikes, pale pink and black—

not the most original idea in the world, but I was understandably off my game, and Mrs. Leckenby didn't seem to care much what we made as long as we stayed quiet.

At lunch, everyone ate outdoors under the covered picnic tables. Trish stuck by me, but I was almost glad when Norah abandoned her fellow freshmen to plunk down her backpack at my table. She didn't say much, but she was trying, which was more than I could say for myself.

I was just about to take a bite of my sandwich when I saw him out of the corner of my eye.

*The* him.

The giant question mark in the back of my head. My *rescuer*, if Rachel was to be believed.

The night of the storm was a complete blank spot in my brain. I couldn't remember what happened, and it freaked me out that I couldn't remember, so I did my best not to think about it because I didn't want Rachel and Joe sending me to a shrink or, God forbid, a real hospital. From far away, Norah was speaking to me, or maybe to someone else, I couldn't tell, there was a strange ringing in my ears—because *there he was.*

"Caitlin! Snap out of it!"

"Is she okay?"

"I think so; she just does this sometimes."

"I'm fine," I said, still unable to tear my eyes away from him. "Curly-ish hair, expensive coat—what's his name?"

Trish looked over, saw the tall, dark-haired guy I was staring at, then looked back at me, clearly amused.

"That's gotta be a record. Adrian's so quiet it usually takes new girls a day or two to get all doe-eyed."

Norah leaned over to Trish and not-so-quietly whispered, "Caitlin got lost during that freak storm last week. Adrian found her. Probably saved her life."

"Oh, did he?" Trish asked. "He was out there just conveniently waiting to rescue you?"

"He lives down the road," Norah pointed out as she bit through a baby carrot. "I've seen him walking around the woods before. Our properties mingle."

"What's his name again?" I asked, trying not to stare as he ate his lunch at the picnic table kitty-corner from ours.

"Adrian de la Mara. Stony Creek's finest specimen of true manhood, unless you count Julian."

I asked, "Who's Julian?" at the same moment Norah countered, "Dude, they are so not from Stony Creek. We don't make men like that."

"Excuse me, we make damn fine men up here," Trish bristled, then frowned. "Although, you're right, they're not Stony Creek born-and-bred." She switched back to me. "And Julian is Adrian's older brother. Just moved here, in fact—Julian, not Adrian. Adrian's been here since, like, what—sixth grade?"

Norah said something in reply, but I was already lost in thought.

I'd had no idea that he was my age, or our neighbor, or that we'd be going to the same school. I guess it made sense that he'd been out on a sunny day, just like me, wandering around the woods. I mean, people did that, right? And it made sense that he'd seen me fall and had . . . had . . .

The details were foggy. Rachel said I'd been hallucinating pretty bad for a while after he brought me home. I didn't remember that, either.

And there he was. I don't even know how I recognized him—

one, because he was sitting with his back to us and I couldn't see his face, and two, because he was a dark gray blob in my only memory of that night before I passed out on the front doorstep.

"Keep your rescue on the down low," Trish warned. "Literally every girl here who's hit puberty would punch you in both ovaries if they thought Adrian had so much as smelled you."

Norah made a gagging noise and started packing up.

"All right, not *every* girl," Trish conceded, "but most. There's money down on who can get a date with him first. It's scary." She grinned and leaned in. "I may have put twenty bucks down that he's gay, but the others are holding out hope."

I'd only seen the back of his head, so I didn't know what all the fuss was about, but I guess the back of his head was . . . nice? His hair was dark and wavy and brushed the collar of his wool coat.

"Yeah, sure," I agreed as I absently waved good bye to Norah. "I'll keep it to myself."

Trish leaned in conspiratorially. "Good. Now, I've known you for a whole three hours and I have a good feeling about you, so I've decided to let you in on a highly classified secret."

I looked curiously at her around a bite of ham and cheese. She seemed eager to include me in the community, and I wasn't going to actively stop her from trying unless she got nosy about my personal life.

She grinned. "Every Halloween a bunch of us from all over Warren County have a party in this big old abandoned barn up on Black Spruce Mountain. There's a little initiation ceremony for people who've never been before, but don't worry, it's nothing embarrassing. And don't worry about your cousin seeing you there, only juniors and seniors are allowed in. I know that's really soon, but you should come—it'd be a good way to get to know every-one."

She mistook the look on my face for concern. "If you're worried about getting in trouble, just say you're spending the night at my house. My parents know I'm going and they'd totally let you stay over."

My mind chose that moment to go completely blank, and because I couldn't think of a good reason to say no, I shrugged yes.

Maybe it wouldn't be so bad. Maybe what I needed was a stupid party. Maybe I'd do something reckless; give in to the wild energy that more often than not took the form of rage, boiling deep in my stomach. Maybe I could let it all out for one night.

As the bell rang, I spotted Adrian ahead of us in the crowd, but again, his back was to me. Just as well. I had no idea what to say to someone who had apparently saved my life. Although really, who says he'd saved me? I probably would have been just fine out there. Might've taken a while to get back, but I would have been fine. Saved my life, my ass.

Fifth period passed with Mr. Warren again; he doubled as the history teacher. Sixth was music with Mrs. Leckenby and seventh period was study hall. It was weird because it was the end of the day and I felt I might as well go back to the ranch, except I didn't have a way to get there. Trish made herself my tour guide, dropping me off at the library. There were maybe a dozen shelves full of books, half a dozen mismatched tables, an ancient row of computers lining one wall, and a desk for the librarian. Most people had study hall at other hours, but there were a few kids scattered around. As I made my way to the nearest table, I felt the hairs on the back of my neck rise. I looked up slowly and to the left—

And there was Adrian.

Alone at a table, face stuck behind a really giant book.

Totally ignoring me.

The goose bumps on my arms faded as I took a few deep breaths. *Just say thank you*, I told myself. I could be nice to one person. I had the energy for that.

I found myself walking toward him. He must've heard me because he lowered his book as I stopped a few feet away, and for the first time, I got a good look at him.

Holy mother of God.

Now I understood why there was a bet going on. It wasn't so much that he was attractive—which he was—or flawless (this was a face that had never known acne or chicken pox or sunburn), as that he had a sort of *presence*. I could tell he was tall, but he also *felt* tall—like he was the archetype for all tall men, the original upon which the idea of tallness was built. His shoulders and arms were muscled, and I wondered what he did to look like that because he was sure as hell no farm boy.

He was currently leaning back in his chair, one arm flung casually around the back of the seat next to him, one boot resting on the table leg. He wore a cowl-neck sweater and expensive jeans—I could tell, because they were the type of jeans I would design if I were a menswear designer. Which I wasn't, but still, I had an eye for these things. The charcoal sweater had to be cashmere it looked soft as butter, and was beautiful against his slightly olive skin. There was some sort of hemp bracelet on his left wrist and an antique silver ring on his hand. It was tasteful, masculine, and confident.

Trish was right—he was totally gay.

"Hi," I said, but my throat was all froggy. I cleared it, awkwardly. "I'm Caitlin. Holte," I added, as if that would make a difference.

The librarian chose that moment to knock a stack of books to the floor, which startled me. When I turned back to Adrian, he was rubbing his forehead like he had a headache—or maybe he was irritated that his reading had been interrupted. I couldn't help but notice that his eyes seemed to be a dozen different shades of gray—darker on the edges and almost white near the center, with charcoals and silvers snaking back and forth. I'd had words that I'd intended to speak out loud, but my mind stuttered to a halt. In the awkward silence that followed, he remained leaning back in his chair, book open, obviously waiting for me to finish whatever I had to say so he could go back to what looked like very serious literature.

Finally, he filled the silence with a prompting "hi."

I snapped back, embarrassed. "Right. Hi. I just wanted to thank you, for the other night. The rescue and whatnot. I don't really re-member much of it, but thanks."

Before he could respond, I nodded good-bye, mentally smacked myself for *nodding*, and turned to go hide behind a giant shelf of books—but his voice caught me before I made it two steps.

"You have a ride home?"

Surprised, I turned back. "Yeah, my aunt's going to pick us up. For today, at least—I'm supposed to take a bike from now on."

For an eight-mile ride, each way. And the way back was purely uphill. With a backpack full of books. The last time I'd ridden a bike, I was eight years old with a scratched white helmet decorated in pink sticker flowers. Apparently Rachel and Joe needed the truck in the afternoons for the ranch, and there was no bus system to speak of. Norah was in good-enough shape, and the community was safe enough, that she'd been biking the route since she was ten, which made me feel like the laziest person on the planet.

Adrian regarded me for a long moment. "I can give you a lift to and from school," he said finally. "You're on my way."

I opened my mouth, then closed it, then opened it. "Sorry, what?"

"A ride," he repeated, with what looked like the hint of a smile threatening to take over the corner of his mouth. "I can give you one."

Of all the questions I could have asked, somehow this is the one that made it out: "What about Norah?"

He didn't even blink. "There's only room for two. I'm sure she'll understand."

We stared at each other for a long moment as my mind raced through the options. I didn't know Adrian—more importantly, I didn't *want* to know him (I didn't really want to know anyone), but I *really* didn't want to friggin' bike to and from school. And I could just picture the look of stunned horror on Rachel's face as Adrian dropped me off at the ranch. He was a bad boy—even if he wore cashmere sweaters and swung for the other team, he was definitely a bad boy. But I didn't understand his motivations, and I didn't trust him.

"I don't want to bother you," I said, stalling.

He shrugged. "No bother. Run it by your aunt and uncle and let me know."

I hesitated a moment longer, but the idea of freaking out Rachel was too great to turn down. Besides, it wasn't like I'd done a great job of keeping a low profile so far. "Yeah," I agreed finally. "Thanks."

He returned to his book, which I took as my cue to go. I sat in the opposite corner of the tiny library. From the few quick glances I stole through the gaps in the shelves, he seemed completely engrossed by his book. When the bell rang, he simply reached over his shoulder and put it back on the shelf without even looking, escaping through the door back into the fog and rain. I crept over to his spot and looked at the title, but couldn't read it—whatever it was, it was written in Latin. It looked strange and out of place in this forlorn little library, much like Adrian himself.

Yeah—definitely not from Stony Creek.

# 3

# DOES YOUR UNCLE OWN
# A SHOTGUN?

So are you going?" asked Ben, a fellow junior and a giant of a man. Or, boy. Boy-man. The dude was huge. We were outside eating lunch on my second day at Warren County—which, let's be honest, sounds more like a prison than a school—and all the upperclassmen had decided to sit together to discuss the upcoming Halloween party. As the new girl, my decision to go or not go was apparently a hot topic.

"Yeah, I think so," I told him.

"Where are you from, anyway?" asked a senior I hadn't met yet.

"Mystic."

"Where's that?"

I said, "Connecticut," but I was thinking, *Leave me alone, strange upperclassman.*

"Mystic," Trish said. "I like it. I'm gonna call you that from now on."

Two days in and I already had a nickname. Super.

"Did anyone call the Kellogg guys about bringing their sound system?" Ben asked, and the conversation steered blessedly away from me.

I was considering whether I could slip my earbuds in without anyone noticing when I heard Trish ask, "Hey, de la Mara, you're coming, right?"

Without meaning to, I looked up, right at Adrian. And for some reason, he looked right back at me, just for a moment. His gaze went immediately back to his sandwich.

"I don't know yet." He said it quietly, but his voice somehow carried so everyone heard. He was wearing a thick green sweater with a wooden clasp holding the neck closed. It looked cozy and expensive.

And it totally confirmed my suspicions.

"Aw, come on, man; you gotta go!" a senior protested. "You're graduating! And what you did last year at initiation was *sick*."

There was a general chorus of agreements. Around us, I could see the other tables quiet down as they caught on to the gist of the conversation, and that it was now revolving around Adrian. Freshman girls—all of them but Norah, anyway—were craning their necks to see him, which just struck me as funny. Did no one else see the obvious? Trish was definitely going to win the pool.

Aware that the entire student body was looking at him, he cleared his throat. "I'll probably show up."

Content with this answer, the normal buzz of conversation resumed. I turned to Trish. "What did he do last year?"

She leaned in. "Only juniors and seniors are allowed to go and I was a sophomore, but I heard it had to do with jumping off a balcony or something."

I stared at her. "He jumped off a balcony?" That sounded lame. And dangerous.

"Yeah, but, like an Olympian. I heard he did six flips in the air."

"Seriously?"

She grinned. "Guess we'll see this weekend."

The bell rang and we trudged off to class. History passed by quickly. We were going through the Industrial Revolution and Mr. Warren was showing us a series of documentaries. It was only my second day, but he was quickly becoming my favorite teacher. Music with Mrs. Leckenby was mostly painless, but a little smelly— the entire high school was stuck in one room and had to sing for forty-five minutes and the ventilation sucked. Escaping the choir room, I headed to the library and sat down in my secluded corner behind the bookshelves.

Looking forward to a nap, I'd just propped my feet next to a row of encyclopedias when I saw movement out of the corner of my eye.

"May I?" Adrian asked, nodding at the empty chair.

I shrugged. He set his backpack on the floor and took the seat opposite me. Now that I'd confirmed, in my own mind at least, that he was definitely not straight, my earlier nervousness evaporated— but that didn't make the growing silence any less awkward. As I sat staring at him, he finally cleared his throat and asked, "How are you?"

"Good," I said slowly, wondering where this was going. And then because he didn't seem like he was going to say anything else, I asked, "How are you?"

He smiled and murmured, "Good." And then the smile faltered and he rubbed his eyes.

I frowned. "Do you get headaches a lot?"

He looked up at me sharply. "What?"

I pointed a finger at his head. "You keep rubbing your eyes like you have a headache."

"Oh," he said, relaxing. "No, I don't get them often." He looked up at me again with a soft smile. "All better."

I smiled back awkwardly, but the silence stretched.

"So," I said, searching for a safe topic to break the weirdness, "I heard you had an impressive initiation last year at the Halloween Hoedown."

His mouth quirked up at the corner in a half smile, but he didn't say anything.

"I heard you somersaulted off a balcony about a dozen times," I prompted.

"Did you?"

"I did."

I stared at him, trying to get a read on his expression. He just stared back evenly. For a second, my conviction about him wavered, but then I looked at his flawless skin, the eight-hundred-dollar sweater.... Maybe in New York City he could merely be a meticulous dresser, but not here. Not in Stony Creek. Honestly, what was someone like him doing in a place like this, anyway? Trish had said he'd been here since sixth grade. Add that to the fact that he was a senior and had never gone on a date—no way he was straight. It felt safe to stare right back at him without worrying that he would consider it flirtatious.

Finally, he smiled. "I guess you'll just have to wait and find out."

I smiled despite myself, rolled my eyes, and settled back in my chair for my nap. I heard him open a book, but I was asleep after a few moments.

Half an hour later, the bell rang and I jolted awake to the sight of Norah hovering over me. Adrian quietly packed up his books to my left as I sat up and tried to remember where I was.

"Hey," she said. "Mom called the office. She and Dad are having a problem with one of the horses, so they can't come pick us up. I usually throw my bike in the back of Molly's mom's truck and she said she could take you, too."

Before I could respond, Adrian stood. "Actually, if you don't mind, I was going to take Caitlin home."

We looked in tandem at Adrian. Then Norah turned to me, obviously expecting an explanation.

"Uh, yeah," I said belatedly. "Tell Molly I said thanks, though."

"All right, well—see you at home." Norah was wide-eyed as she walked off.

As we left the library, snaking our way through the rush of students, it took about point-three seconds for everyone to notice that I was walking with Adrian. And I mean *everyone*: parents, students, even the faculty heading for their busted-up cars. I very much got the impression that Adrian was a big deal here—and Adrian deviating from the norm was practically unheard of, based on everyone's reactions. Distracted by our audience, it took me about six seconds to realize what vehicle Adrian was heading toward.

I stopped dead. "You're kidding me."

Ignoring me, he unlocked a helmet from the seat of a matte-black Harley-Davidson. I walked up to him, knowing and not caring that everyone had stopped to watch us.

"You drive a motorcycle."

"Yeah." He put his sunglasses on.

I couldn't stop staring. "You drive a *Harley*."

He handed me a helmet then settled onto the bike. "Yeah."

I took it, dumbfounded. This was not what I had expected when he offered to give me a ride, though it did explain why there wasn't room for Norah. The bike was huge, which made sense since he was at least six feet tall, but it meant the backseat, where I imagined I was supposed to go, was at waist level.

"Hey, Adrian," I said casually, testing out his name in his presence for the first time. "How do I, y'know, get on?"

He pointed at the back footrest. "Step there, hold on to my shoulder, swing over."

I stalled. "What if the bike falls over?"

"The bike will not fall over."

"How do you know the bike will not fall over?"

He stared down at me. "Because I'm on it."

Good point.

"When we're on the road," he continued, "lean when I lean. Don't ever lean the opposite direction. If there's some emergency, tap my chest. I don't have mics in the helmets, so we can't really talk once we get going."

I could feel dozens of eyes on us as I put my foot on the back pedal, used his shoulder to brace myself, and swung my leg over the seat ungracefully, wriggling into place behind him. The passenger seat was shallow and backless, which meant if I wasn't basically spooning him from thigh to neck, I would fall off. Not really wanting to touch him, but seeing nothing else to hold on to, I rested my hands lightly on the sides of his waist and leaned back so at least my chest wasn't plastered to his spine.

He stuck the key in the ignition. "You planning on staying on the bike?"

I nodded vigorously. "Yes."

He started the engine. "Then hold on. I don't bite."

I threw my arms around his waist, afraid he was going to take off with or without me, and could feel the vibrations through his jacket as he laughed. Kicking up the stand, he backed up the bike and pulled out of the parking lot. Even over the hum of the engine, I could hear the rabid gossip start up the second we were on our way.

It wasn't long before we were out of sight of the town and up in the winding mountain roads. I didn't know exactly how much I was supposed to lean, but soon figured out that as long as I held on to him, the two of us moved together by default.

I was actually beginning to relax when a sixteen-wheeler roared past going the opposite direction. I felt a rush of air flare against the bike, rocking it. Part of me wanted to slap Adrian on the chest so he could let me off, but I figured if I was going to die, crashing on a Harley with a man who wore designer jeans wasn't the worst way to go.

A few minutes later we reached the turnoff for the ranch, but Adrian kept going. I was about to yell that he'd missed it, but realized getting him to turn around at fifty miles an hour to look at me was not the brightest idea I'd ever had. We drove along for another ten minutes before he pulled onto the side of the road and we shoved our helmets off.

"The ranch is back there," I said, pointing over my shoulder.

"I know. I thought you should see this."

He nodded toward the sun, already low in the sky. Miles below, the center of Stony Creek was no more than a few pinpricks of light and chimney smoke. This late in the fall the forest looked like it was on fire in the brush of late-afternoon light. The breeze touched my face and for a brief moment I closed my eyes and just breathed.

"It's beautiful," I told him, looking up.

He smiled, and it was one of the warmest I'd seen from him yet.

He looked back down over the valley thoughtfully. "It grows on you. It's a small town, but it's in the middle of a big place."

Once again, I wondered what someone like him was doing way out here. The nearest city was almost two hours away, and while the town was, admittedly, picturesque, it seemed a strange place for a kid like him to grow up.

Glancing back, I saw his eyes were pinched shut. "I thought you didn't get headaches that often?"

"I don't," he said sharply, pulling his helmet back on. "Let's go."

When we pulled up to the ranch, I could see Norah spying on us through the kitchen window. Ignoring her, I handed him my helmet and swung clumsily off the bike, pausing a few feet away, not certain how to end our encounter. I settled with a safe "thanks for the ride."

He looked me over once. "It'll be colder in the morning, so dress warmly."

I guess that meant this wasn't a one-time thing. He started the engine and took off without a backward glance.

What an odd guy. Hot—but odd.

Sadly, it didn't look like Rachel had been around to witness the Harley. As soon as I closed the front door, Norah pounced.

"What was that?" she demanded.

I looked around innocently. "What?"

"You!" She pointed at the door. "*Adrian.*"

I walked into the kitchen and grabbed a Pop-Tart from the pantry, ignoring her, but she trailed after me. "He never lets anyone on that bike," she persisted. "I've heard a ton of girls ask, and he always says no." She paused, considering. "He's kind of rude about it, actually. You're here two days and he just *offers* to drive you home?"

I shrugged and bit into the pastry. "They're the last house on this road besides us, right? He drives right by, maybe he's just being neighborly."

She crossed her arms over her chest. "Then why hasn't he offered me a ride before?"

I smiled thinly. "Maybe he's got a thing for orphans."

I walked past my cousin, heading upstairs to my room. I might have to keep Adrian around. Gay or not, he was becoming a very useful distraction.

———

My bed was freaking tiny.

Every morning I'd roll over to turn off my alarm and fall half out before I remembered I wasn't home in my full-size tucked-in-the-corner-against-the-wall vintage brass-frame bed. I was in the attic of a creaky, converted cabin, sleeping on a secondhand twin with a lumpy mattress and musty blankets. Nothing like a sudden plunge toward the floor to wake a girl up.

Outside, thick clouds mumbled low over the trees. It would probably rain, and I wondered if that meant Rachel would take Norah and me to school.

And then I remembered—Adrian was picking me up.

No way my aunt would miss it this time.

Breakfast was its usual, awkward affair: Rachel and Joe asked me about school; I gave them intentionally short answers; we dissolved into hostile silence. Just as we were finishing up, I heard the unmistakable sound of a motorcycle making its way down the gravel driveway. Joe looked out the window, pulling aside the floral curtains with one of his massive fingers.

"We expecting company?"

"Not that I'm aware of," Rachel replied, turning to the window. Norah just glared at me.

Without saying a word I stood, grabbed my backpack, and left through the front door. I resisted the urge to glance back at the window, but Adrian could see the grin on my face plain as day.

He held the spare helmet out. "You're in a good mood."

I swung onto the bike behind him far more gracefully than I had the day before and wrapped my arms intimately around his waist for the benefit of my aunt and uncle.

"I'm using you to scare the crap out of my caretakers. Hope you don't mind." I waved at Joe and Rachel, who were staring gape-mouthed at the window.

Adrian glanced at them, too. "Your uncle own a shotgun?"

I smiled. "He owns three."

"Ah."

I laughed as he peeled out of the driveway. I think the kicked-up gravel was mostly for effect, as was the speed with which we rocketed toward the main road. I could have kissed him, he played the part so well. It was all petty, but I was feeling petty, and vindictive, and angry.

Underneath it all, so, so angry.

---

Lunch was such a strange time. I mostly tried to keep to myself, but it was impossible not to be drawn in when the conversations were this absurd.

"I could be slutty bunny," Meghan said, pouring a bag of Skittles into her mouth and chewing on them thoughtfully.

"You're not gonna be slutty *anything*," Laura replied. "You know how cold it gets in that barn? It's not like it's heated."

"What if I'm bundled-up slutty bunny?"

Laura stared at her. "That literally doesn't make sense."

All the upperclassmen girls were gathered around the lunch table discussing costume plans for the party. I looked at Trish and she grinned at me before turning on her megaphone voice. "What if we picked a theme this year?"

"Like what?"

"I dunno, like royal romance, or Disney characters, or fairy tales—"

"Only if we go with the originals," Meghan interrupted. "Like how Ariel dies to gain an immortal soul instead of killing the prince and his fiancée so she can return to being a mermaid." From the look of her outfit, Meghan liked fairy tales so much that she dressed like them—all at once. I could pick out bits of punk Cinderella, Snow White, and Sleeping Beauty in her ensemble.

When nobody responded, she said, "I guess I could be slutty Little Red Riding Hood after she slashes her way out of the wolf's stomach with an axe. I'd be warm with a cape. And sexy."

Laura threw an apple slice at Meghan. "Enough with the sexy and the slutty!" she demanded. "And the gore."

"I don't want to be a fairy-tale character," a senior whined.

"Okay, okay!" Trish said. "What about, like, mythical creatures in general?"

There was a moment of silence as people considered this. My mind immediately went into creative overdrive, thinking of half a dozen costumes I could create—and then I remembered that all my supplies were boxed away in my grandma's basement. My brief enthusiasm deflated.

Trish looked around. "So we're agreed?"

"Sure."

"Yeah."

"As long as I don't have to be an ogre."

"I bet I could be a slutty ogre."

Luckily, the bell rang before Laura could retort. Trish passed me funny notes during music and history, which honestly cheered me up quite a bit, but I was on my own for study hall.

Well, almost.

I came to a pause in the back corner of the library and stared at the one who had intruded upon my sacred place. "Is this your table now?"

Adrian was already settled in my corner nook. I hadn't been here a week, but I'd grown attached to this table. It was out of view of the librarian. I could play solitaire on my phone and no one would ever know. The heater vent was directly under my chair.

He glanced up at me from a very complicated trigonometry assignment. "Figured we could share."

"You're like some weird welcoming committee, aren't you?" I asked, sitting down opposite him. "Well, mission accomplished: I am sufficiently welcomed. Thanks for helping me freak out my aunt and uncle and for not asking me about my dead parents. I got it covered from here."

I kicked my legs up on the nearest shelf and rested my head against the back of my seat, closing my eyes. Adrian seemed intent on making a spectacle of the two of us, and I figured it was to keep up the appearance of his being straight. Maybe he sensed that I knew his secret. He'd keep me company if I was cool with making it look like we were interested in each other. I could deal with that.

"Do you want me to ask?" he said unexpectedly.

I was already half asleep, and didn't bother to open my eyes. "About what?"

There was a heavy silence. "About your parents."

I thought about it for a second—really thought about it, and had to swallow a couple times to get past the sudden, infuriating lump in my throat.

"No," I said finally. I risked a glance at him. "But thank you, for asking. No one's done that, yet. They assume that I do or don't want to talk about it, but they don't ask."

He nodded at me, as if he understood. As he went back to his homework, I leaned my head back and thought about my mom.

I missed her. It was simple, really.

I missed her so much, and it hurt. It just didn't stop hurting.

# 4

# WEIRD WORLD

The barn was massive, easily dwarfing the meager horse stalls we had back at the ranch. The little hoedown I'd been imagining was apparently a raging kegger, and the clearing around the barn was packed with trucks as far as I could see. It was ten thirty and pitch-black except for the pulsing, multicolored lights that seeped from the upper windows and through cracks in the massive barn doors. The road here was more dirt and gravel than pavement, and luxuries like streetlamps, sidewalks, and speed limits were not to be found for miles in any direction. I took a deep breath and Trish patted my shoulder.

"You'll be fine, Mystic. It's just a party. It'll be a hoot."

I snorted my disbelief and opened the passenger door. Stepping down, the slit in my knee-length dress rode halfway up my thigh. I covered it quickly with my cloak and muttered, "Shit."

This was going to be ridiculous.

"Come on!"

I'd gone straight home with Trish after school on the pretext that I was spending the night—which I suppose I was, but not until we'd made it through this party. I wobbled after her in the three-inch stilettos I'd splurged on after I'd gotten asked to prom the year before, as a sophomore. They were the only shoes that even remotely went with my admittedly half-assed costume. For now, they were extremely difficult to navigate across the pock-marked, improvised parking lot. When I finally caught up, Trish opened the barn doors and ushered me inside. I took one step and stopped dead.

Holy Halloween.

The place was packed. I recognized most of the juniors and seniors from my school, plus what must have been every other junior and senior in Warren County. There were *hundreds* of people. Someone had rigged up an intense lighting system that pierced the barn with shards of rainbow light. Three-quarters of the bottom floor had been turned into a haunted maze. Trish—who'd come as a Valkyrie—pulled on my arm.

"I just saw Meghan go into the maze. Let's scare the crap out of her."

And before I could protest, I was pulled into WEIRD WORLD—that was the sign above the maze, anyway. Glow-in-the-dark handprints were smeared down the cardboard walls, providing the only light, while fake spiders and cobwebs hung from the cardboard ceiling. With groups of other kids rushing past, giggling and screaming, it took all of ten seconds for Trish and me to get separated. Squinting in the darkness, I picked a corridor, which branched off in three directions, and headed right. Which seemed to be a really bad idea, because it was absolutely pitch-black.

I groped my way down the walls and slowly turned a corner, patting the toe of my heels blindly on the floor to preidentify things I would like to avoid stepping in. My feet must have activated a motion sensor, because a strobe light flashed on suddenly, blinding me. I was so startled I screamed and jumped back—and what I backed up into wasn't a wall.

A hand clamped down over my mouth and a muscled arm pinned my elbows to my side. A fun-house mirror reflected the intermittent strobe light, briefly illuminating the person who was holding me. He looked up through a curtain of dark, wavy hair, grinning.

It was Adrian, thank God, and not some random creeper—though I still wanted to punch him in the face for scaring me. Without Trish I felt strangely vulnerable.

"I'm a pirate," he explained, as if I couldn't tell from his costume. "Apparently we kidnap people."

I wriggled free and punched him in the arm, then immediately wished I hadn't because it hurt like hell.

"You scared the *crap* out of me," I said, shaking my hand to dilute the pain. "I could have stabbed you in your manly bits with my heel."

He rubbed his arm and glanced at my stilettos, but his mouth was quirked in a smile. "I'm glad you didn't."

The smile slipped off Adrian's face as he looked me over head to toe through the mirror, and if I didn't know he was trying to figure out what my costume was, I might have been offended—or flattered. My emotions were sort of all over the place.

"I'm a vampire," I explained, since it wasn't obvious. I hadn't had time to order crazy colored contacts or fake pointy teeth online, and the nearest costume store was eighty miles away. The only thing that said "vampire" about me was some bright red lipstick, a lot of eyeliner, the "cape" I'd fashioned out of my mother's old quilt, and the skintight black dress I'd made myself a year ago (also, coincidentally, for prom, and also now way too small in the chest region, since those had popped out of nowhere a few months back). With my sewing machine broken and no time to plan, it was the best I could pull together in less than a week. Well, that was a lie—I probably could have made something crazy out of tissue paper and Popsicle sticks, but I honestly didn't feel like putting that much effort into a party I didn't even really want to be at in the first place. I was a party pooper.

"So that's your theme?" Adrian asked, interrupting my thoughts. "Vampires?"

"We were supposed to come as mythical creatures," I replied with a shrug. "I picked vampire."

Okay, so vampire had been the best match for my extremely limited clothing options, but whatever. The motion sensor for the light must have gone back into sleep mode because the strobe cut off suddenly, plunging us into darkness.

From somewhere to my left, Adrian's disembodied voice asked, "Why did you pick vampire?"

I frowned, although he couldn't see me. "Why do you care?"

But there was no answer—he wasn't there. I called his name again, turning in circles, but if he could hear me, he didn't respond. I was instantly irritated. Way to abandon me in a scary-ass haunted maze.

Grabbing blindly for the wall, I picked a direction and started wandering again until I made it to the exit where Trish was waiting for me, though not before being almost trampled by a herd of freshmen who'd somehow snuck in and were now being chased out by football players from a neighboring district.

"Where were you?" Trish asked as I finally appeared. "It wasn't that hard."

"Apparently one of my hidden talents is getting lost in mazes. Go figure."

Trish nodded like that made sense, then pointed at a table stacked with the entire contents of the local liquor store. "Want a drink?"

I stared at the pile of alcohol.

I'd never been drunk before. I'd once had a half a glass of wine with my mom over dinner, but I'd never been to a party like this. I'd never been to anything *close* to this. The normal, I-have-life-goals-and-a-solid-future part of me was saying no. The I'm-all-alone-and-I-hate-the-world part of me said, out loud, "Why not?" I grabbed Trish's arm as she started to walk toward the table. "Just don't let me do anything stupid."

She grinned. "Hey, if you want to have a good time, I'm not gonna stop you."

There was a bowl of what someone said was Jungle Juice sitting in the middle of the table. It looked like fruit punch, which seemed safe, as I had no idea what any of the other bottles of alcohol were, and doubted I could drink anything straight. As soon as Trish and I had our red Solo cups, the music suddenly died and it went dark. A spotlight appeared on a pirate as he clung to the ledge of the second-floor railing. Seems the guys had also come up with a theme, as the majority of them were dressed in varying degrees of pirate garb. I'd seen quite a few Captain Morgans walking around with bottles of rum, looking very pleased with themselves.

The pirate dude waited for the noise to die down and finally raised his arms, yelling into a mic, "*Juniors!*" like he was the announcer in a stadium arena. I guess he was, in a way, because the place erupted into an absolute frenzy. Whatever was about to happen, everyone was very excited about it.

"Tonight," the pirate continued, "you shall all be *initiated!*" There was another round of screams and my stomach felt slimy. "Tonight," he continued, "you will prove yourself worthy to be called the *Children of Warren County!*'"

More screams. What was this, some sort of Satanic ritual? I was thinking about how far it would be to get to the door. And then how far it would be to walk back to my aunt and uncle's. And how I would explain my outfit. And my makeup. And why I wasn't at Trish's. Let's face it, I'd probably get lost and eaten by a bear. But that might be better than suffering through whatever public humiliation was about to come my way.

Trish glanced at me. "I see that look on your face. Come on, Mystic; just get into the spirit of things and this'll be a lot more fun. It's a long way back to Stony Creek."

I looked at her. She was right. It was a long way back to Stony Creek. I stared at my punch, and it stared back at me.

"What's in this?" I yelled at Trish over the din.

"Vodka, Red Bull, some other stuff," she yelled back. "That's the beauty of Jungle Juice, you never really know!"

It sounded awful, but I sipped, and couldn't actually taste any alcohol. It was mostly sweet, but tangy sweet, like pineapple juice. I downed the rest of it in a series of long gulps. I'd come here to let loose, after all. Vodka was certainly going to make that dumb plan happen faster.

The announcer-pirate waved for attention. "Juniors, the time has come. You have three phases of initiation. The test of the Holy Grail!" The guys cheered loudly. "The test of physical prowess!" More cheers. "And—*truth or dare.*"

This time it took a full minute to quiet the crowd down again.

"Form a line!" he said, then disappeared. On either side of the barn, horse stalls had been converted into drinking stations, and their doors were now flung open. In line, partygoers were handed a plastic, dollar-store "grail" and told to drink whatever was in it. Most went away coughing. Trish downed it in one gulp.

"Not bad," she told me. "Just red wine."

I stepped up to the table and a pirate handed me a cup. I tried to look into it, but he shouted that I wasn't allowed to peek. I took a deep breath, let it out, then drank. I almost spit on reflex and turned to Trish with a mutinous look. "That was *not* red wine."

"I know," she said. "It was tequila. But I didn't think you'd drink it otherwise."

Before I could respond, the flow of the crowd pushed us along to the next station. Guys were herded up the stairs to the second floor, girls formed a semicircle below them. A huge pile of hay had been stacked up against the wall, ten feet high and fifteen feet deep. One by one, half-drunk guys jumped off the second floor into the pile, some more gracefully than others, flattening it dramatically as time went by. I saw Ben and Jack from our class leap safely down, but I didn't recognize anyone else. It was kind of dumb, but strangely entertaining.

"What do the girls have to do?" I asked Trish, tugging on her arm as pirates flailed above us.

She grinned as another guy catapulted himself off the railing. "All we have to do is watch."

After a while, the line of boys ran out, and I was amazed no one had cracked their skulls or broken an arm, although a few had tottered outside to puke. After the last guy plummeted to the floor, picking himself up with a dazed look, the announcer-pirate hopped onto the railing and said, "Wait! Here for a one-night-only special encore, the one, the only, *Adrian de la Mara!*"

The place erupted with screams, the crowd cheering. And then the spotlight went on and there he was, standing in a loose linen shirt, pirate pants, and historically accurate leather boots, because of course he would have those just lying around. There was a ladder built into the wall that headed up to a tiny platform that made up the third level of the barn. Adrian bowed with a lazy smile, then began climbing. Nervous, I watched as he reached the ledge forty feet off the ground. He turned toward the wall, facing away from the crowd, and backed up until only the toes of his boots kept him from falling into space.

The cheering stopped. It was dead silent.

He bent his knees, arms out to either side.

And then he jumped.

His body catapulted toward the ceiling and then back again to the crowd, twisting in the air like a diver once, twice, three times; gliding through the multicolored lights, finally somersaulting into a landing that made the hay ripple in a fifteen-foot arc like he was some avenging angel come down for war.

But he was standing. And he looked totally fine. Which was not right.

How could he be *alive*, let alone standing? His head was bowed, and into the intense silence he looked up right at me, his eyes seeming to flash out their own light from the shadow of his face. All at once, the screaming cheers began, and they were deafening, reverberating off three stories of wooden walls so it seemed like a crowd of thousands. He smiled once, and the lights went out, leaving the barn in utter darkness. When they came back on, he was gone. Even though no one could see where he was, the cheering went on and on.

I turned to Trish. "How did he do that?"

She shrugged. "I have no idea! Isn't it great?"

Was everyone crazy? People shouldn't be able to *do* that. Why wasn't anyone calling an ambulance? I mean he had to have some sort of compound fracture, cracked vertebrae, shin splints or *something*. Trish tugged me over to the last station, but I snagged a cup of punch on the way. She just laughed at me as I downed it. Happy freaking Halloween.

"Ladies, ladies, please come forward," the pirate announced, mic in hand. "Since our gentlemen took the last round, we'd like to extend the honor of truth or dare to you. Please form a line!"

Trish pushed me gleefully forward. Since most of the other girls seemed to be as shy as I was, at least about performing in public, and because Trish was dead set on embarrassing me as much as possible, I somehow ended up being first. We were on the second story by the railing when the spotlight hit me.

"What's your name?" the pirate-announcer asked with a game-host smile, shoving the mic in my face.

I blinked, trying to keep his face in focus. "Caitlin."

Someone in the crowd yelled, "Go, *Caitlin!*" but I didn't recognize the voice.

"And what are you tonight, Caitlin?"

I blinked at the announcer again. "What?"

He held the mic away from his mouth and whispered, "What's your costume?"

"Oh. I'm a—" It sounded so stupid out loud. Let's be honest, it sounded pretty stupid in my head, too. But the drinks were finally working their way through my inhibitions, so I smiled at him, trying to put some sass behind it. "I'm a vampire."

I heard some of the guys cheer.

The announcer smiled encouragingly. "All right, Caitlin the Vampire: truth, or dare?"

I'd already decided. "Truth."

I may have been drunk, but I wasn't stupid. Dares always ended up being a thin excuse to do something vaguely or overtly scandalous with the even thinner defense of "but I *had* to." In seventh grade, the class perv, Kyle Hanson, dared the class nerd, Sean Rubatino, to touch my boobs. It was a dare, and dares were sacred. I didn't really have breasts to speak of anyway, so I let him do it, but we were both uncomfortable and I felt dirty about it for weeks.

"All right, all right," the announcer said to quiet the chorus of *boos* from the crowd of guys below. He pulled a crumpled piece of paper from a large glass jar. Unfolding it, he read, "When, where, and with whom was your first kiss?"

There was a chorus of *awws* from the girls and catcalls from the guys. How had this happened? How had I picked truth and still managed to embarrass myself? It was suddenly very warm in the barn with the spotlight and the press of bodies and the bright flush of embarrassment. I found myself gripping the railing to stay upright.

It only occurred to me much later that I could have named anyone from my old school and no one here would have known who he was.

"I've never kissed anybody," I admitted finally. Behind me, I heard Trish snort.

There was a moment of surprised murmurs before an unidentified pirate yelled, "Everyone kiss Caitlin!" Before I knew what was happening, another pirate pinned me to the railing and covered my general mouth area in a sticky, wet kiss. The awkward laughs around the room immediately transformed into gasps. Suddenly, the kisser was gone and I was being picked up, fireman style, and carried away from the railing and the spotlight and the humiliation. A door opened and slammed shut.

"*Out*," Adrian demanded.

Couples muttered and cursed, but didn't question him, scrambling to adjust clothing before hurrying out of the room. Adrian set me down on a couch carefully.

"Stay here," he told me, and started for the door.

"Adrian!" I called out, grabbing on to his arm before he could walk away. "He was just joking," I said, trying to smile. "It was a joke."

"No, it wasn't." He tried to get up again, but I pulled him back.

"If you go out there, it'll just make you look stupid, because everyone thought it was a joke, and you took it seriously, which makes it look—it makes it look like something it's not."

"I don't care," he stated flatly, and made to leave again.

"I care," I said desperately. "Please, Adrian, just drop it."

"Why are you trying to make this okay?" he asked, glaring at me. I didn't understand why he was so angry.

I fluttered my hands around in an agitated gesture. "Because it's not important. I just want to feel empty."

His eyes narrowed in concern. "Empty?"

Oops. I hadn't meant to say that last part out loud. "Full," I corrected myself, nodding. "I meant full."

I flung my arms wide to demonstrate *how* full, overshot, lost my balance, and stumbled backward. Luckily, Adrian caught my hands and pulled me forward before I could fall. I giggled, because the whole situation suddenly seemed really, really funny.

"Okay," he said, patting my back awkwardly. "What did Trish talk you into?"

"Just one drink." And then I snort-laughed because it wasn't true. I'd had *three* drinks.

"I should get you home," he murmured into my hair. But he didn't make any move to leave.

"Hey," I said, looking up. "Did you know there was going to be alcohol here?"

He met my gaze, an amused smile on his face. "I think that was implied."

"Somehow I didn't know," I told him slowly, the words lagging behind my brain. "I thought 'Hey, a Halloween party!' I forgot about alcohol. And here we are." I smiled up at him again, then leaned my cheek against his man chest.

Then the full implications of where we were hit me.

"Whoa." I looked around the room with grave concern. "People do *stuff* back here. And you took me in here and kicked everyone out." My eyes got big. "I bet people think we're doing stuff."

"We've been back here for a grand total of two minutes."

"So?" I scoffed. "I hear it doesn't take long for some people. Pigs," I muttered with an disgusted shake of my head. I got dizzy and planted my nose on his clavicle. "That's not love, that's just sex." And then the fact that I'd never, in fact, had sex, nor had I been in love, made me consider that it was possible I had no idea what I was talking about. "Maybe," I amended. "Maybe they're pigs. I dunno." I looked up at him. "Do you think you can do it in two minutes?"

"Okay," he said, flushing even in the faint light. "Time to go find Trish."

"Adrian," I said, suddenly desperate that he know the truth. "I didn't decide to be a vampire. I just didn't have a costume." I tugged at the cloak until it slid to the floor, then looked down and kicked off my heels. "I think this makes me look stupid," I mumbled, staring at my feet. "I think this makes me look really stupid."

My eyes watered as I tried to burn a hole in the floor just by staring at it; one big enough for me to fall through and disappear and go home. I was miserable. I thought being drunk was supposed to make you happy, but it didn't, it made you miserable, and sad. I hiccuped awkwardly and looked up at him. "It's not a cloak, it's my mom's . . ." I trailed off, momentarily forgetting what I was talking about. I caught sight of it again in a puddle on the floor and bent to pick it up, latching on to Adrian's pants to keep me upright. I stood and held it in front of me. "It's my mom's *quilt*. It's not a cape." I looked up at him, as though the coming information was still surprising. "She died. Eleven—" I interrupted myself with a hiccup. "Eleven days ago."

And I didn't feel like standing anymore, so I let my knees buckle, but Adrian caught me. After a moment, I put my arms around his neck and hugged him because I wanted to, because he was there, because he was warm, and for once the anger was gone and I was just wholly, completely sad.

"You're a good guy," I mumbled.

Before he could reply, the door burst open and a couple staggered in, completely oblivious to Adrian and me as they tottered over to a couch and did . . . stuff. Using one hand to prop me up, Adrian reached into his pirate pants and pulled out his phone, checking it.

"It's one thirty. You want to go home?"

I looked up at him and frowned. "I don't have a home. The ranch is not my home." It was very important that he understand that.

He nodded. "Do you want to go back to your aunt and uncle's?"

I flopped my face back on his chest. "I can't. I told them I was spending the night at Trish's. I can't go back looking like this."

Adrian smiled with the corner of his mouth, and it was adorable. "No," he said. "I suppose you can't."

"Trish won't want to go. She's having a good time. I don't want to make her leave because of me."

"Do you want to stay?"

I looked back up at him, miserable and dizzy. "No."

"Come on." He handed me my shoes and led me out the door and back into the party. Despite my paranoia, nobody paid any attention to us since truth or dare was still going on and apparently some of the girls had agreed to interesting dares.

I stopped abruptly in the middle of the crowd. "What about Trish?" In my inebriated state, it sounded more like "Trisssssh."

He glanced through the horde, but neither of us could spot her. "Text her that I'll bring you over before her parents are awake."

I thought about it a second. I didn't want to stay. I couldn't go to the ranch. I couldn't go to Trish's. "Where are we going?"

He smiled with the corner of his mouth again. "My home."

Little warning bells dinged loudly in my head. Or maybe that was the headache. "Won't your parents wonder about you bringing me home so late? Dressed like this?" I clutched my cloak around my shoulders and shivered like a crazy old cat lady.

"First of all, I live with my aunt and uncle," he explained. "Second, we don't even have to see them; there's a balcony connected to my room and we can get in through there. But they wouldn't mind either way."

"Are you sure?" I asked.

"Caitlin," he said, crouching down to make eye contact. "I won't take you anywhere you don't want to go."

I searched his face. He wasn't lying. At least he didn't seem like he was lying. I honestly don't think there was a way I would have known at that point, but his face looked like one of those sincere, non-lying faces.

I nodded. "Okay."

We slipped out the barn doors. I grabbed his arm so I didn't fall into the man-size potholes littering the dirt-and-gravel parking lot. He didn't seem to mind. Once we got to his bike, it occurred to both of us that I was wearing a dress.

"Hmm," I said, contemplating the logistics. "This will work. Just don't be staring at my business."

Holding on to him, I hiked my dress up and swung my leg over, the fabric bunched up to my thighs, the leather of the seat freezing against my skin. Adrian grabbed his coat from one of the saddlebags and put it over my shoulders.

"Won't you be cold?" I asked, already shivering.

"I'll be fine. I'm just worried about you. I forgot to factor in the whole"—he looked at my legs—"dress issue."

"I'm fine if you're fine."

He stared at my legs again. "I'm fine."

I shivered, waiting for him to get on the bike.

He cleared his throat. "Right."

I shoved my helmet on (did he always carry around a spare helmet?) and slid my arms around his waist.

It felt a lot different when he wasn't wearing a jacket.

Adrian had very nice abs.

I poked them just to make sure they were real, and he turned around to look at me strangely. I decided to stop poking him.

The headlight cut through the night as the Harley revved away from the barn, the beat of the music fading quickly behind us. We picked up speed until I was sure we were breaking the limit by a good twenty or thirty miles, or maybe it just felt like that because my eyes couldn't focus on anything.

God, it was cold.

My arms were fine because of the cloak and Adrian's jacket, and my face was fine because it was completely covered by the helmet, but my legs felt like they were being whipped with lashes made of ice. Overhead, the moon shone brightly through a few clouds and cast the road ahead into odd shadows, making the whole strange night even more bizarre. The woods on either side of the road were like zippers pulling closed behind us. If we didn't go fast enough we'd get eaten up in their teeth, crushed in cold leaves made of metal.

Sometime later, the silence hit me, and I realized we'd stopped. Adrian pulled his gloves off and put his hands over mine, presumably to warm them up. We sat like that for a while until I could move my fingers, then Adrian stood, removing his helmet. Still numb, I shoved my helmet off, too, and let it drop to the ground.

"Sorry," I mumbled.

He didn't say anything, just lifted me off the bike like I was a child. He carried me up some stairs, through a door, and into a warm, dark room where he set me down. I immediately curled into a ball and shivered while he closed the balcony door, then rustled through some drawers.

"Caitlin," he murmured a moment later, placing a hand on my arm. "When you can move, put these on." He tucked something next to my hands and then said, "I'm going to go downstairs to make some hot chocolate. I'll be back in a few minutes."

His hand left my arm, and a moment later I heard the door close.

I sat up. With the moonlight coming through the French doors, my eyes finally adjusted and I found a pair of drawstring sweatpants, some thick wool socks, and one of his deliciously soft sweaters. I buried my face in them and breathed deeply. They smelled like Adrian. It was a very good smell. I wobbled to the door and felt around for a lock, then switched it. I reached for the zipper on my dress, then paused, a thought finding its way to the surface of my sluggish brain:

I would be mostly naked, however briefly, in Adrian de la Mara's room.

I would be without clothing. In Adrian's room.

Naked.

I think I snorted.

Searching for any sort of sounds from the house and finding none,

I shimmied out of the dress and threw it on the bed, tried three times to unhook my bra (because let's face it, sleeping in a bra is pretty much the worst thing in the world), succeeded, threw it somewhere across the room with far more velocity than I'd intended, then reached for the sweater and pulled it over my head. I finally got around to the pants and fell trying to get them on. Then I had to sit still for a minute because my head was spinning. I was just pulling the socks on when there was a quiet knock. I made sure the tie on the sweatpants was tight so they wouldn't fall off and then opened the door. He looked to make sure I was dressed, then slipped inside, carrying two mugs.

"How are you feeling?" he asked, handing me a mug.

"Warmer," I admitted, tucking my feet underneath me on the bed. "What time is it?"

"A little after two." He sat in his desk chair.

"Hmm," I mumbled, then took a sip of hot chocolate. "This is yummy."

He smiled. "Secret family recipe."

"Did you try the punch?"

"No."

I looked at him, surprised. "Really?"

"Really."

"Why not?"

He shrugged. "I wasn't thirsty."

"I was," I told him, as if he didn't know. "I just wanted punch, not happy punch, but all they had was happy punch. And then the grail. And then more punch." I looked at him. "I was really thirsty." I took a sip of hot chocolate. "This is yummy."

"Thank you."

"Adrian."

"Yes?"

"Why are you nice to me?"

He smiled at me kind of funny. "Figured it was better than being mean."

I absorbed this, took a sip of hot chocolate, then stated again, "Adrian."

He smiled again. "Yes?"

"I won't tell anyone your secret."

He was merely a shadow sitting back in his chair. The smile slipped off his face and he didn't respond for a long time.

"What secret?" he asked finally.

"That you're . . ." I waved my hand around. "*Y'know.*"

He raised a brow. "Pretend that I don't."

I scrubbed my hand across my face, already regretting blurting this out. "That you don't like girls. I won't tell anyone."

The blank look on his face seemed, for a moment, to be frozen in place. Then, very carefully, he leaned forward. "You won't tell anyone that I don't like girls?"

I nodded vigorously. I would take his secret to the grave. Especially if he kept giving me hot chocolate.

"Why do you think I don't like girls?"

I made an incredibly unattractive *pbbbbt* sound with my lips. "'Cuz you wear *sweaters.* Your shoes cost more than my laptop. You've never gone on a date even *once.*"

Adrian stared at me. "So you think I'm—"

"Gay," I interrupted very matter-of-factly. "My gay best friend. Except not, because I don't have a best friend, and if I did, I think Trish would probably be it. You're my gay study buddy. Except not really, because school is meh."

Adrian dropped his head in his hands, and for a half a second,

I thought he was crying. But then he looked up at me and he was smiling.

"You are a funny girl, Caitlin Holte. And you should probably get some sleep."

I blinked at him and shivered. He frowned. "Are you still cold?"

"Kind of," I said, head lolling to the side. I was too tired to un-loll it. "I can't really feel my toes."

"Why didn't you say anything?" he asked, standing.

I blinked up at him. "You gave me pajamas."

"Here." He pulled me up and tossed back the sheet and blanket before setting me down again, swinging my legs onto the bed and tucking me in like I was a toddler. It felt wonderful.

"I'm stealing your bed," I mumbled sleepily.

"That's okay," he murmured.

"No, it's not." With my last bit of energy, I grabbed hold of his shirt. "It's your bed. Come here, to sleep."

I expected him to say no. He probably found me repulsive.

But he pulled back the covers and crawled in next to me. "All right."

I turned on my side, pressed my nose into his rib cage, and fell asleep.

# 5

# IT'S MY PARTY, I CAN CRY IF I WANT TO

I was warm. That was all that mattered.

I was warm and comfortable and sleepy. So when the soft *Caitlin* floated past my ear again, I wanted to ignore it, to snuggle into whoever it was that was next to me and fall back into the delicious dream I'd been rudely awakened from. But someone whispered my name again, and the stubborn part of my brain felt obliged to respond.

"Hmm?" I mumbled.

"So you *are* alive," the voice said. It sounded an awful lot like Adrian. Which was silly, why would Adrian be in my bedroom? Ridiculous. I was definitely still asleep.

"What are you smiling for?" he asked as I wriggled my head under his chin.

"You smell good," I mumbled into his collarbone. After all, it didn't matter what you told people in dreams. In dreams, if nowhere else, you should be honest. I pressed my cold nose against his warm neck and wrapped my dream-arm around Dream-Adrian's waist.

"Caitlin, you need to wake up now. It's four thirty."

"*Nurrr.*"

"Come on, Caitlin, up," he murmured. His hair tickled my face and I scrunched up my nose. Burrowing closer to the source of heat, I realized that my shirt was sliding off one shoulder—which was weird, because my pajama shirt wasn't large enough to slide off my shoulder. I reached up and felt the fabric at my neck and realized that it wasn't the heavy cotton I was used to; it was cashmere. I sure as hell didn't own any cashmere. In fact, I only knew one person who did.

Slowly, I opened my eyes.

It was dark at first, and I wasn't completely sure where I was. Then the hazy form of Adrian's face materialized above me. I was huddled, leechlike, along the right side of his body.

I blinked.

"You all right?" he asked after a moment.

I blinked again. He was still there.

And I still had my arm wrapped around his waist and my leg hooked around his knee.

Oh dear God.

"How do you feel?" Adrian tried again, starting to look concerned.

*Stupid.*

"Fine," I mumbled, my voice hoarse and froggy as I disentangled my limbs from his until we could both sit up.

"We need to get you back to Trish's," he said, scooting away, dragging his legs over the edge of the bed, walking to his desk, and . . .

. . . taking off his clothes?

I watched, absolutely fascinated, as he tossed the pirate shirt onto the back of his chair and pulled on a black sweater that clung to his body like Saran Wrap. He swiped a hand through his hair and scanned the floor, looking for something.

Maybe I *was* still dreaming.

I wanted to ask what time it was, why I was here, why I needed to go back to Trish's, why, why, why, what, where, when, how? but my tongue was all sloppy and I couldn't form any coherent thoughts.

He looked for something in a drawer, found whatever it was, and took off his pirate pants.

*Ohmygodhetookoffhispiratepants.*

He was dressed in nothing but a sweater and tight, black boxer briefs. Even in the dim moonlight, I could see that Adrian wasn't just in shape; he was *built*. Decathlete built. FIFA World Cup soccer champion built. Not bulky, really, but solid. Just muscles for days, lean and beautifully arranged. I was staring, and I didn't care.

I must be dreaming. Not only had *I* been mostly naked in Adrian de la Mara's room, *Adrian* had been mostly naked in Adrian's room. I mean, that made sense, since it was his room, but I was there, and *what the hell was happening?*

"I don't have any boots your size," he said, turning to face me once more, "but I stole these from my aunt. They're probably a couple sizes too big, but it's all I have."

He held up a pair of sandals, but I wasn't really looking at them, not when the image of his mostly naked body was burned into my retinas like a film negative.

"You're not really awake yet, are you?" he asked.

I blinked at him.

He stared at me and said, "Hmm," in a low, rumbly sort of way.

I blinked again, pinching my eyes shut and then opening them wide. The room came in to a bit clearer focus. Slowly, I sat up; the wide neck of his sweater slipping off my shoulder again.

"Adrian," I said, overpronouncing his name.

"Yes?"

"Your house."

"Yes."

"Your room."

"Yes."

I looked down at myself. I was practically swimming in the clothes I wore.

"Your pajamas?"

He smiled. "Yes."

"Time?"

"Four thirty."

"A.M.?"

"Yes."

I touched a hand to my head. "Jungle Juice?"

Adrian tried to suppress another smile. "Yes."

"Ah," I said, as if that one word summed up everything that had happened over the past five hours. A moment passed as we stared at each other. "I don't really know what to say right now."

"How about I go grab you something to eat while you think about it?"

"Okay," I agreed.

He left and I was grateful I had a moment to pull myself together.

How stupid did I feel? *You got drunk,* I told myself. *You got drunk and Adrian had to drag you all the way to his house so you wouldn't embarrass yourself. And then you* cuddled *with him.*

I scrambled out of bed, which was a bad idea because dizziness and gravity conspired against me, so I lay still until the world stopped spinning. I'd just managed to sit up again when Adrian opened the door.

"I'm not sure what your stomach can handle, so I made you a slice of cinnamon bread. Does that sound okay?"

He'd taken me home and put me to bed and made me toast. Thank God it was dark, I felt like I was blushing red and pasty white all at the same time. He handed me the plate and I took a bite. It was good. Lots of butter.

We stared at each other while I ate. When I was finished, he set my plate down on his desk and picked up a coat, slinging it over my shoulders and messing with the collar until it lay right.

"There," he said. "Why don't you call Trish and tell her we're coming?"

I nodded and looked around. "Uh—do you happen to know where my stuff is?"

I remembered taking off my clothes. I remembered putting on Adrian's pajamas. I did not remember what happened in-between.

"I think everything's on the floor over there." He pointed near the set of French doors leading out to the moonlit balcony. We both noticed at the exact same moment that I'd managed to fling my bra onto his lampshade. He quickly looked away as I slowly lowered my face into my hands.

"I'll, um—I'll wait outside."

Adrian slipped out the door once more and I quickly skimmed my bra off the lamp and tugged it on under his sweater, then found the rest of my clothes in a heap on the floor and dug through the pile to look for my phone. I flipped through my contacts and found Trish's. She answered on the fourth ring.

"Hey!" she said, yelling. I could hear music in the background.

"Hey. Are you still at the party?"

"Yeah! It's still going strong. Are you and—"

"Trish!" I whisper-yelled. I didn't want her shouting my name and

Adrian's name in the same sentence, not while she was around people that went to our school.

"What?" she yelled above the music. "I didn't hear you."

"Never mind," I told her. "Listen, I'm heading over to your house. Will you be there soon?"

"I'm leaving now," she said.

"Are you . . . okay . . . to drive?" I asked awkwardly. We were friends, I think, but new friends. It felt weird asking.

"Mystic, unlike some people I know, I only had one drink, and that was, like, six hours ago. I'll be fine. Thanks for worrying, though. I'll see you soon!"

"Bye," I said, and disconnected.

I felt my way to Adrian's door in the darkness and let him back in.

"Ready to go?"

I nodded and shoved the sandals on my feet, following Adrian out the French doors onto the deck, then down the stairs and across the lawn to his motorcycle.

It occurred to me that I must look really weird clinging to a guy who could easily make a living as an underwear model while I wore baggy sweatpants and borrowed sandals. Of course, I'd probably looked pretty okay while I was on here in stilettos with my vampire dress riding up my thighs, but still. Life was weird. I slipped my arms around his waist as he started the engine.

It was less cold this time, but it was still Stony Creek at four thirty in the morning at the end of October. Eventually, we pulled up to Trish's driveway and Adrian cut the engine. He pulled off his helmet and twisted to scan the road behind me.

"Trish'll be here soon."

A moment later, the headlights of Trish's truck splashed golden light down the road. She pulled up next to us and rolled the passenger window down.

"Hop in," she told me, then let her eyes wander to the other oc-cupant of the Harley. "Morning, Adrian."

He smiled back. "Morning, Trish."

Trish grinned, then looked at me and frowned. "What in the hell are you wearing, Mystic?"

I was glad it was dark—she couldn't see me blush. "Adrian let me borrow some clothes."

Trish grinned slowly at me. "I see."

"Well," I announced in a higher pitch than normal. "We better be going."

I scrambled off the bike ("fell" is more like it; Adrian had to grab hold of my arm to keep me upright) and shoved myself at the truck, pausing with the door half open.

"Thank you," I said, glancing up once, briefly, at Adrian.

He just smiled softly, looking amused. "You're welcome."

I nodded at him and hopped in the truck. Trish pulled into the drive and in seconds Adrian had disappeared back into the night. After we parked, Trish let us in the front door and we tiptoed up to her room. I sank to the floor wearily.

"So," Trish said, flopping onto her unmade bed. "You and Adrian, huh?"

Here we go. "Nothing happened."

"Yeah. Right. Adrian looked like he wanted to beat the crap out of that guy and dragged you away on his Harley because he wanted nothing to happen."

"He's a good guy," I told her a little more forcefully than neces-sary. "And it's not like that. Besides, *you* told me he was gay."

Trish snorted. "After seeing him with you the past few days, I have reversed my conclusion."

It was my turn to snort. "I think you had too much Jungle Juice."

Trish turned on her back, plunked her feet up against the wall, and let her head hang over the edge of the bed. "Firstly, he doesn't let anyone within spitting distance of his bike, but he voluntarily picks you up for school. Secondly, he does his crazy superman stunt off the hayloft and who does he look at when he lands? *You.*"

I thought I'd imagined that. Guess not.

"Not only that, he comes to your rescue—*again*, I might add—when that guy kissed you." She glanced down at me. "How was he, by the way?"

"A dream come true," I said dryly. "Lots of saliva to keep it smooth."

She laughed, then shuddered. "Gross. Anyway. After that, he hauls you back to the let's-get-busy room and I don't see you again until he's dragging you out the front door. Call me crazy, but that looks like he's pretty freaking *interested.*"

When she put it like that, it made sense. But she was wrong.

"Even if he wasn't gay—which he is—I think I'd know if he saw me as anything other than, like, his crazy little sister. I'm new to Stony Creek. I'm an orphan. I live with my aunt and uncle. I don't really belong here. Adrian's an orphan, he lives with his aunt and uncle, and the only place he'd blend in is a runway in Milan."

Trish looked thoughtful, then shrugged. "I still say he wants to get in your pants."

"It's not like that!" I replied more forcefully than I'd intended. "He's just . . . just not . . . not . . ." I couldn't even come up with what he wasn't, he was so not whatever it was Trish was making him out to be.

"Ahh," said Trish with a grin. "*There's* the reaction I was looking for. You *like* him."

I paled. "I do not."

"Yes, you do."

"I do not. I barely know him."

"Who," Trish said, "besides your aunt and uncle and Norah, do you spend the most time with in Stony Creek? And don't say me, because if that's true, it's sad."

I thought about it. "He lives near me, so he gives me a ride to school, and we're in the same study hall, so we talk."

Trish just looked at me.

"But sometimes we don't talk! Sometimes we sit. And read." She smiled at me and I frowned at her. "I'm making your point for you, aren't I?"

"I'm just saying, it would make sense if you liked him." She yawned and stretched. "Or maybe I'm full of shit; I dunno. See you in the morning." And she rolled over and fell asleep.

I crawled over to the air mattress we'd blown up earlier and slipped inside the faded *Beauty and the Beast* sleeping bag. My curls had deflated, and I was sure I had mascara all over my face, but that didn't matter. What mattered was that Trish had a point. We *were* alike. But so what? He'd graduate in eight months and go who knows where. I'd graduate the year after and go to New York. We'd probably never see each other again. Not that any of that mattered, because I was still convinced he didn't like me—or women in general—so the whole conversation was pointless.

Sleep pressed down on me like a weight, like a dozen feet of water and dark silence and I slipped into a dream, snuggled in Adrian's clothes.

---

Monday morning, the house smelled good, like pine and wood smoke and cinnamon. The rain outside drizzled down in tufts of mist as the wind blew lightly through the forest surrounding the house.

I was downstairs in the kitchen pouring myself a cup of coffee when Rachel walked in, smiling.

"Hope you had a good time at Trish's. You didn't say much when you got home."

I shrugged, already bristling. "It was fun."

Rachel had not given up on her attempts to be cheerful and welcoming. I hadn't given up on being really, really mad at her.

"I'm glad you've made a friend," she said. "Maybe you could invite her over sometime. Maybe to your birthday party?"

I looked up sharply. "What birthday party?"

"Joe and I were thinking you might want to have one here, and invite some school friends."

I poured creamer into my mug. "No, thanks."

I could feel the tension radiating off Rachel in waves. Or maybe that was my tension, it was hard to tell these days.

"Okay, well, have you at least thought about what you want? It's coming up pretty soon here."

I froze. For a second, for a *split* second, she'd sounded just like my mom. Or, like my mom a year ago, before her voice had gotten hoarse and raspy from intubation tubes and chemo. Rachel was her younger sister—her prettier sister. After my dad died, my mom had gotten slowly larger every year, then dramatically thinned out when she got sick. She was never really beautiful, but by the end she was downright scary to look at, with bags of loose skin pooling through the sleeves of her hospital gown and her head all dry and bald. Even with those differences, it was impossible to look at Rachel and not see her.

But my mom wouldn't have had to ask me what I wanted for my birthday. She would have driven me to our local craft store where we knew every employee by name. She would have handed me a cart and told me to pick out anything I wanted. I'd usually get a couple yards of a fabric I couldn't normally afford, or stock up on zippers, needles, elastics, pins, bobbins, seam rippers (I always managed to lose mine), pattern paper, backing, or any of the other thousand and one things you need to have a fully functional workshop. My freshman year, she'd surprised me with my own sewing machine—it was expensive enough that it had doubled as my Christmas present, but I didn't care because it was the best thing I'd ever been given in my entire life, and it meant that much more because it drove home just how much my mom *knew* me, better than anyone. Rachel, though— she had no idea what to do with me.

I slowly put the spoon into my mug and stirred, trying to stay calm. "I'm all good on the birthday front. Thanks, though."

Even from here I could see a vein beating in her temple as she struggled to keep her smile in place. "Come on, it's your golden birthday! It's not every day you turn seventeen on the seventeenth!"

"I don't need anything," I replied a little more sharply than I'd meant.

"Well, that's fine, because birthdays are about receiving things you *want*." She wasn't going to give up. "So what do you want?"

I turned to face her so fast that coffee sloshed over the rim and burned my fingers, but I didn't care. "I don't want anything from you." I'd said it quietly, but my voice was shaking.

"Caitlin, I know it's hard now that your mom's gone—"

"*No*—" I interrupted her, "you don't get to give me that talk. You don't get to pretend like you knew *anything* about her."

I knew I should stop, but after weeks of trying to choke it all down, I could feel it racing uncontrollably toward the surface.

"You weren't there," I said evenly, although my face was flushed red and it felt a billion degrees warmer than it had a second ago. "You didn't sleep for weeks in a chair by her bed. You didn't show up at the cemetery to pay your respects, you weren't there to help Grandma with the funeral arrangements or the medical bills or the service, you didn't even come to Mystic to help me pack up my stuff to move to your shitty town." I heard footsteps pause on the stairs, but I didn't care if Norah heard. "Just to be clear, I don't want to be here. My *mom* didn't want me to be here. So when I say that I don't want anything for my birthday, I don't fucking want anything for my birthday."

She blinked, mouth trembling, then set her mug on the counter and walked out of the kitchen.

Adrian had great timing—I could hear the hum of the Harley coming down the driveway. Abandoning my coffee, I grabbed my backpack and ran out the door. The bike was still running as I grabbed the helmet from his hand and swung on behind him before he'd even had a chance to put the kickstand down.

He frowned. "Everything all right?"

"Just go," I said, and crammed the helmet on.

He looked at me a moment, glanced at the house, then drove away. I spent the entire ride feeling stupid, feeling angry, feeling exhausted and drained and then angry again, and sad and desperate and hollow. I just wanted to sleep, but I had to go to school. Learn. Do homework. Bullshit, brain-dead work.

We arrived at school, and he parked the bike.

"I brought your dress," he said, swinging off the Harley.

"Damn it!" I muttered, setting the helmet down forcefully against the seat.

"What?"

"I forgot to bring your clothes."

"It's fine. I don't need them anytime soon."

"I know; but they're yours, and I forgot and I—" I couldn't finish the sentence I was so angry at myself. I didn't even know why I was angry, but I was, and it felt good.

"It's not a big deal." He smiled. "Hey, I heard it's your birthday soon."

I stared at him. "Are you *kidding* me?"

I grabbed the bag of clothes out of his hands and walked toward my homeroom. Before I'd gotten three steps, he grabbed my arm and spun me around, face set in a hard line.

"What's wrong?"

"Nothing. I'll bring your clothes tomorrow."

I wriggled out of his grip and walked to class, choking back tears.

By seventh period, I was composed. I managed to reach the library ahead of Adrian and went back to my little nook and moved the second chair to another table. A moment later, Adrian walked up to me, staring at the place where he usually sat.

"Are you angry at me?"

"No," I said, shrugging, but I could feel another wave of rage coming on.

He arched a brow. "You sure about that?"

"Don't mean to burst your bubble, dude, but not everything's about you. Bring a chair over, don't bring a chair over, I really don't care."

I flung open a book and leaned back. He looked at me and I felt something in the vicinity of shame crawling up the back of my throat, but I just stared right back and kept the cool look on my face until he nodded, backed away, and left.

I spent the rest of study hall trying not to cry.

When the bell rang, I walked outside and got on Adrian's bike like nothing had happened. He came out of the library a second later and stopped when he saw me sitting there. Slowly, he walked over and got on in front, saying nothing. The only sound I heard on the way home was the angry hum of the bike and the mutinous beat of my own heart. He pulled to a stop in front of the ranch and took his helmet off, turning to me.

"You might want to hide the clothes in your backpack. Your aunt and uncle might wonder otherwise."

I crammed the clothes in my backpack. Before I was done, he was already driving off.

# SEVENTEEN
# ON THE 17TH

My birthday was a week away. Adrian had started picking me up in his truck because the roads were too icy for the Harley, and even if they weren't, the wind chill made it miserable. We'd sit there in silence, sometimes with his phone plugged in playing music, but otherwise in silence. I honestly didn't know why he kept showing up—it certainly wasn't for my witty banter. I was low on banter.

Any day, the snow would start. I was waiting. Waiting for the weather to change, waiting for my birthday, waiting for it to stop hurting every time I opened my eyes and remembered that my mom was gone and I would never, ever, *ever* see her again. I knew it was possible to make new friends, to build a family from scratch, to "start over"—but I didn't want to. It was much easier to want nothing than it was to want something, and I was scoring major points as a beginner nihilist.

School dragged on. I dozed off in all of Mr. Warren's classes; I refused to sing in choir. I simply wouldn't turn in homework for anything but art, and study hall was just an extra forty-five minutes to sleep. I could tell all my teachers were upset, but I didn't care. Well, I didn't care until they called my aunt.

"Caitlin, can I talk to you for a minute?"

I'd just gotten home from school and Rachel was sitting at the kitchen table with her stacks of papers and her coffee. A second mug was already sitting next to her. It was much lighter, so I could tell it had been made for me. Warily, or perhaps just wearily, I sat down, sliding my backpack to the floor. I automatically curled my fingers around the mug, but didn't drink anything.

"Your principal called." She looked at me and waited.

"How is he?"

She frowned at me oddly. "Uh—good. Actually, he called about you."

I took a sip of coffee. Still hot.

"He said that your teachers have been concerned about your performance. That you've been sleeping in class and not turning in homework."

I took another sip of coffee. I liked coffee.

"Well?" she asked.

"Good coffee," I said.

"Caitlin."

"Nice creamer-to-coffee ratio."

"What is going on?"

I looked at her blankly. Had she not been present when I yelled at her the week before?

"What's wrong?" she said, reaching for my hand, which I yanked away. She looked hurt and I didn't care. "Why are you doing this? Why are you punishing us?"

I just stared at her, amazed that she still didn't understand. "My mom's dead," I said slowly. "You know that, right? She died. She's *gone.* So please, Rachel, please sit there with your very-alive husband and your very-alive daughter and explain to me, since I clearly don't understand—explain why I should care about something as trivial as *school.*"

Before she could answer, I stood up, slung my backpack over my shoulder, and shuffled upstairs.

Just as I reached my room, Norah came in behind me and slammed the door.

"What is *wrong* with you?"

I looked at her blankly.

"You don't *have* to be an asshole; you *choose* to be an asshole."

I could hear the emotion in her voice, I could see she was on the verge of crying in that angry sort of way you cry when you don't want to cry but you can't stop yourself, but I couldn't really register it all in that moment.

"Yeah," I admitted. She wasn't wrong.

But Norah was looking for a fight. "Stop making everyone miserable. Your mom died. It sucks. I'm sorry. But there are other people in the world besides you, and shit happens to them too, and they move on."

"Norah," I said, very quietly. "*Get out.*"

She might've said more, but I took a quick half step toward her and she flinched.

Would I have slapped her? Maybe. I don't know. If she kept talking, I might have. But she didn't, just threw me a disgusted look, turned around, and walked out, slamming the door behind her. In the resounding silence, I sat on my bed and stared at the wall. Gravity won and I sagged back against the covers and stared at the ceiling instead.

A few hours later, Joe knocked on my door. I must have fallen asleep, because the sound startled me.

"Yeah?" I called, not really awake.

Joe poked his head in the door. "Can I come in?"

I shrugged.

He left the door open as he took a seat at my desk. I could feel the anger seeping back in, the adrenaline pooling in my stomach, preparing for another fight. If he was there to make me apologize to Rachel, it wasn't going to happen.

"I didn't know your mother all that well," he began. I rolled my eyes. *Great. You didn't know her, but you're going to talk about her as if you did.* "But I do know why your mom and your aunt stopped speaking."

Despite myself, I looked up—this was a story I had never heard before. He shifted uncomfortably, a large and intimidating man in a too-small chair.

"Something happened," he continued, "a long time ago, before I even knew your aunt. Your mother had a hard time forgiving Rachel for it. Matter of fact, she never forgave Rachel. Your aunt is a very different person than she used to be. I know you don't want to be here, and I know you miss your mother—but as hard as it may be to believe, your aunt misses her, too. It wasn't Rachel who didn't want to visit you, or call you, or come to the hospital or the funeral. Your mother refused to let us come see you. We could have come— we *wanted* to come—but it would have been against her wishes. Rachel didn't want to do that, not when your mother was in so much pain already. It was a hard choice, and I know there are days she wishes she had just barged in there and tried to make things right." He paused, searching for the right words. "You are allowed to be angry. You are allowed to feel whatever you want to feel. But if you can, maybe try and cut Rachel a little slack. She lost her sister just as much as you lost your mother. And it may not look like she's in

♥ 72 ♥

pain, but she is. Maybe even more than you, in some ways, because she never got to say good-bye."

There was a moment of silence, then Joe stood, looked around my room, and let himself out.

I locked the door behind him, then piled the chair in front of it, and a stack of books, and my hamper. It wouldn't keep people out if they were determined, but it made me feel better, to put things between me and them. I crawled into bed in the dark and spent the rest of the night shaking, unwilling to cry when I knew the sound would carry beyond my door. If I started crying now, or yelling, or screaming, I wouldn't stop. So I clenched my jaw, ground my teeth until they hurt, until my throat ached. Eventually, I fell asleep.

———○———

I woke up on the seventeenth of November to snow. Big, fat, fluffy flakes of snow that had begun falling well before dawn. When I went downstairs for breakfast, there were no presents or decorations; no one even said "happy birthday," which was exactly how I'd wanted it.

We sat down at the table and everyone but me folded their hands as Joe said his daily breakfast prayer.

"Dear Lord," he began in his quiet, deep voice. "Thank you for Caitlin's presence here in our family. Thank you that she turned seventeen today and has become a beautiful young woman. Thank you for the snow. And thank you for pancakes. Amen."

The bitterness surged up and I tried to keep it from showing on my face. I was a beautiful young woman? Thank you for *pancakes?*

"There's plenty, so I expect you to eat everything," Rachel said cheerfully as she heaped my plate with food without asking me how much I actually wanted to eat. And just like that, I lost my appetite, anger curdling through my stomach. I forced half down my throat, not tasting any of it, because even though I didn't want to care about what Joe said, I did, and some part of me was trying not to hate Rachel. As usual, just at the end of breakfast, I heard the grumble of the diesel engine as Adrian's truck pulled into the driveway.

"I'll see you guys later," I said, standing up.

"Wait, you forgot to open your present!"

Rachel ran into the laundry room, dashing back into the kitchen with a box in her hand.

I could feel the anger rising up the back of my throat at the sight of the wrapping paper. *Be nice*, a voice in my head warned me.

"You said you didn't want anything, so we got you something we thought you could use." She smiled hopefully. I tried to freeze the blank look on my face instead of letting it slip into a grimace.

"I'll open it when I get home," I said finally. "I don't want to keep him waiting."

Rachel nodded and I walked outside into the silently falling snow. It was warm in the truck since the heater was blasting, so I settled into my falling-asleep-in-the-passenger-seat routine. Adrian drove, used to the silence by now, and we arrived at school.

In homeroom, Trish leaned over and whispered "happy birthday" to me. I smiled. It was hard to be mean to Trish, because she was Trish. She was basically the most genuine, kind, bizarre person I had ever met. She was supportive, didn't pry or expect anything from me, and sensed when I needed my space. If she were a guy, I'd probably date her. Or, if I were a lesbian. And if she were a lesbian. I guess we'd both have to be lesbians for that to work. Regardless, she made a pretty great friend.

The day passed quickly, although I got a few more happy birthdays, and a tiny chocolate from Mrs. Goode. After school, Adrian drove me home as usual.

"Hey!" Rachel called from the living room sofa when I came through the front door. It amazed me that she could keep pretending like we were totally fine when I'd already told her, to her face, what I thought about her. "How was your day?"

"Good," I replied. I was getting better at lying.

"Don't forget your present on the table!"

With Joe's plea pounding the back of my conscience, I pulled the present toward me, untied the big purple ribbon, and popped the lid off. There, pristine and expensive, were a pair of leather boots. Not the most fashionable things I'd ever seen, but they looked sturdy, water-proofed and thick-soled. I could probably wear these for twenty years. They'd certainly be warmer than my Converse.

Rachel came back into the kitchen and poured herself a cup of coffee. "Do you like them?" she asked, trying to keep the hope out of her voice, and failing miserably.

"They're great." And then an idea began to form in my mind. I smiled at her. "I'm going to test them out." I tugged the Converse off my feet and shoved the boots on.

"What, now?" Rachel asked as I laced them up.

"Perfect weather to test boots in." I stood up and headed out the front door without waiting for her permission. As soon as I was clear of all the windows, I headed to the back of the house where the trail led into the woods. It had been snowing all day and even the thickly wooded sections of the path were covered in snow.

Eventually, I reached the giant boulder I'd fallen from nearly a month ago. That night was still muddled. The place looked familiar, but almost like I'd seen it in a movie, or a photograph, and was only now visiting it in person for the first time. I started climbing, careful to test my footing before I advanced. Everything was white, pristine, and the snow somehow made the silence feel complete.

I hadn't really come here with a plan—I hadn't even really planned to come here. But now that I was, I found myself pulling my gloves off, and my hat. I unwound the scarf from around my neck and felt the frigid air snake down the back of my jacket. I took that off, too, tossing it to the ground. I sat in the snow, ignoring how it soaked my jeans, and peeled my sweater over my head, inhaling sharply as the cold air stung my skin. There was a pain to the coldness, but it was disconnected, somehow. I knew I should put the sweater back on, and the jacket, and go somewhere warm—but I didn't do that. Instead, I lay down on the boulder and noticed, looking straight up at the sky, that it had begun to snow again. The flakes got caught in my eyelashes, tickling me. I laughed, and I couldn't stop laughing, even when tears started pouring down my cheeks.

I'd been sad before—many, many times over the years. On the anniversary of my dad's death, on his birthday, on my parents' wedding anniversary watching my mom drink herself to sleep. And I was always sad on my own birthday because my dad wasn't there, and because I remembered him less and less. But this year—today—there was no one left to be sad *with*.

At least there were no more hospitals or fluorescent lights, no more rapidly mutating cells, no more IVs and blood draws and people poking at what was left of my mother. I wondered if I would ever get back up from this rock. There was nothing I really wanted to get up for. I started to shiver—snowflakes melting and running down my arms and stomach, but more took their place because it was still coming down, white flakes from a white sky on a white, silent afternoon.

Just as I was sliding into a nice little nap, someone grabbed my arm and pulled me off the boulder. I fell roughly to the ground, knees crunching in the snow.

"What the *hell* do you think you're doing?" Adrian demanded, glaring at me as he shrugged out of his jacket.

"What am *I* doing?" I asked, blinking rapidly. "What are *you* doing?"

How the hell was he here at the same time as me—*again?*

He put his coat over my shoulders but I knocked it off, turning to climb back up.

"Caitlin, you're freezing!" He grabbed me around the waist and his hands felt like fire on my numb skin.

"No shit," I tossed back. "Let go of me!"

"No."

I clawed at his hands, struggled and fought; trying to kick him, get him off balance so I could climb back up again, but he wouldn't let go and he wouldn't fall over.

"Why do you have to ruin *everything?*" I screamed, tearing my nails into his arms through his sweater sleeves, hating him more than I'd ever hated anyone in my life.

He just held me tighter, grabbing my wrists and crossing them over my chest so I couldn't scratch him. "Caitlin, stop."

"Just leave me alone!"

Using his superior weight, he forced me to my knees and followed me down; we bent forward, breathing heavily, unable to move.

"No," he repeated in my ear.

"*Why not?*" I sobbed, angry that he was stronger than me and bigger; angry that I couldn't break free no matter how angry I was.

He let me go and stood up. But before I had time to feel relieved, to feel happy, to feel blank, he grabbed my arm again and dragged me to my feet, glaring. "I saved you once, I can do it again."

"Save me?" I stared at him blankly. "What did you think I came out here to do?"

He shifted, looking suddenly unsure. "You're—you're standing half naked in the snow."

We blinked at each other before I wrenched my arm free. "I came out here to be *alone*, asshole, not to *kill myself*. It's *literally* my birthday, and I can *literally* cry if I *literally* want to." I huffed a stray piece of hair out of my eyes. "I can't cry in the house because everyone would hear, so I came out here to do it."

"Oh," he said, blushing. "Well . . . go ahead, then."

"I'm not going to cry *now*."

"Right." He had the decency to look embarrassed. He turned and walked off a few steps, then pivoted and turned back to me. "Except, why is your shirt off?"

I rolled my eyes. "I was hot. Sue me."

He frowned at me, eyes narrowed. "Yeah, that's not it. You were lying in the snow. Your fingers are blue. That's not normal."

I deflected with a question of my own. "What the hell are you even doing out here?"

He ignored me and scooped up my sweater. "Put your shirt back on."

I smiled at him. "Never seen a half-naked girl before?"

He held the sweater out to me. "I don't care about your modesty, I care that it's twenty-seven degrees outside. Put the damn sweater on."

I glared at him. "Don't tell me what to do."

"God, you *are* trying to kill yourself!"

"What moron tries to freeze themself to death?" I asked, truly incredulous, although my teeth were chattering so it made the question seem less than serious.

"Morons who are in denial about the fact that they're trying to kill themselves and choose a method that could look like an accident."

I stared at him. I shivered. He threw his arms wide, blue sweater already accumulating snow, and said, "Hit me."

"What?"

"I said 'hit me.'"

I blinked at him. "Why on earth would I hit you?"

He took six rapid steps until he was way up in my personal space. "If you don't hit me, I am going to throw you over my shoulder, carry you back to your aunt and uncle's, dump you in the shower, and tell them that you're suicidal and need help."

I glared at him, then hobbled for freedom.

"Stop, Caitlin," Adrian called after me calmly. I figure I got about five feet before he was just, all of a sudden, right where I had planned on putting my next step.

He stared down at me sternly. "I'm not kidding."

"Stay away from me," I managed to say between gritted teeth. The adrenaline was wearing thin and the cold was beginning to break through my mental fog.

"Why?" he demanded, backing me up against the boulder. "If you're going to let the snow send you into a hypothermic coma, does it matter if I'm here or not? You think your mom fought all those months in the hospital just so you could give up after she was gone? You think she'd be *proud* if she could see you right now?"

Something inside me snapped and I slapped him. And then I slapped him again. He didn't even flinch.

We stood there for a long time.

I deflated slowly. "I shouldn't have slapped you. You're an ass, but I shouldn't have slapped you."

"Why are you out here, really?" he asked finally.

I shrugged miserably. "She looks like my mom. Every time Joe does something nice it reminds me of my dad. I hate it."

My voice seemed to get stuck somewhere between my lungs and my heart.

"How did it happen? With your dad?"

I flinched involuntarily. I hadn't told anyone this story, except the police and my mom, and the words seemed even now like they were coming from someone else's mouth. I wasn't sure why I was telling him any of this, but the words tumbled out.

"We were out on his boat," I said, wiping at my face. "It had always been fine, nothing bad had ever happened—and then one time, a perfectly ordinary day, he started talking, but he wasn't making any sense. I couldn't understand what he was saying. And then he fell into the water, and he knew how to swim, but he wasn't swimming. The water wasn't even that deep, he could have stood up, but he didn't. After a while, I knew he was dead, but I didn't want to touch him—if I touched him, it would be real. A fisherman found us the next morning and called the police. Just your run-of-the-mill brain aneurysm. There was nothing I could have done, I was five years old, but I still feel like if I had just jumped in, if I had dragged him to shore, maybe he would've made it. But I was too scared to touch him. So it was my fault."

My eyes felt heavy. Everything felt heavy. "My mom shut down after that. She was just finally starting to seem okay again when she was diagnosed with bone cancer." I shrugged. "Now she's dead, too."

My knees gave out and he caught me, but I didn't care. Adrian could leave me here and eventually I would either get up or I wouldn't. But he didn't leave me. Instead, he wrapped his arms around my shoulders. He was warm.

"Everyone dies, except for me," I murmured. "I thought I'd come out here and cry about it for a little while."

We stood like that for a long moment: me leaning against Adrian, Adrian keeping me from falling over.

"Caitlin," he said slowly. "I need to tell you something. I think you need to know now. But you're not going to believe me."

I should have been more interested, but to be completely honest, I was falling asleep. "All right," I murmured into his collarbone.

Keeping one arm around my waist, he leaned back to look me in the eyes, searching my face, waiting until he had my attention.

"I won't die," he said slowly. "Ever."

I laughed tiredly. "Cool."

He frowned. "It's true."

I shook my head. "That's not true."

"I promise, it is."

"You can't promise something like that."

"Yes," he said simply. "I can."

He turned my chin with his thumb so I was looking directly into his eyes. They were gray, but more than gray. They were—

Silver?

They were *glowing*.

He murmured something, and with a snap, it all came flooding back, sharp and sudden, like some switch had been flipped in my brain retrieving repressed memories. The storm—the *fall*.

He searched my face. "You remember?"

"Oh my God." I stared at him, that whole night flashing before my eyes. "Oh my God. How did I forget that? How did I forget *you*?"

He looked uncomfortable. "I sort of suppressed your memories."

He was serious. He was completely serious. If it wasn't for his swirling vortex eyes staring me straight in the face, I would have thought he was trying to pull some really unfunny joke. That, and the fact that I suddenly remembered the night of the storm with full clarity. I'd fallen, he'd caught me, he'd *done something* to me, and then we were running, running away, and Adrian's eyes were burning silver.

"You *hurt* me," I said, remembering the blistering pain in my head, the burning behind my eyes.

He shook his head, visibly upset. "I didn't have a choice. I can't explain that now, but I swear to God, I did it to keep you safe."

"But—what *are* you?" I asked, staring unashamedly at his face.

He breathed in slowly, and let it out. "Caitlin," he began, shifting his weight a bit and resettling me in his arms. "There are a lot of things you should know." He caught himself. "There are a lot of things you *shouldn't* know. So I'm only going to tell you a few essentials, the first of which is that we have a—creation story, if you will. A myth."

"*We?*"

What the hell was he talking about? The conversation had very suddenly switched gears and I was not following.

"We," he confirmed. "My family and I. And our story says that we aren't really"—he grimaced again, looking almost embarrassed—"human."

I stared at him. "You're not human."

He shook his head.

I scowled. "You look very human to me."

He closed his eyes. "I'll just say it. I'm gonna have to say it sometime. All right. So, there are a variety of terms for what we are, there always have been and I imagine there always will be, but I'm what you might commonly refer to as a . . ." He paused and muttered, "Shit, I really have to say this." He took a deep breath and looked down at me. "I'm a vampire."

He looked apologetic as he waited for my reaction.

I narrowed my eyes, staring at him hard. "Did I hit my head?"

He frowned. "Not that I am aware of." Just to be sure, he grabbed my face and turned it, inspecting for lumps. "No cranial injuries."

"Okay," I said reasonably. "So I'm dead?"

He looked startled. "What?"

I stared at him. And then I smiled, and then I laughed. I laughed a lot. I laughed so hard I had to wipe my eyes on his sweater. I think I actually snorted at one point.

"I'm totally dead!" I exclaimed. I hugged him, and added an extra squeeze for good measure. "Oh, Adrian, you're so sweet. Thank you for all those rides to school."

He frowned. "You must be colder than I thought." He looked at the boulder. "Your clothes are soaked through," he said, indicating my snow-drenched sweater on the rock. "Can you stand by yourself?"

I smiled dreamily. I was dead! This was great! I could go say hi to my mom. Probably find my dad around here somewhere, too. Adrian wanted me to stand? Sure thing, my friend. I could probably fly, if I wanted to. I was about to hop around and flap my arms experimentally when he tugged his sweater off and handed it to me. To humor him, I put it on. It was toasty warm, and fell off my shoulder. Almost as toasty as Adrian standing in the snow without a shirt on. The boy was ripped.

He grabbed his jacket off the ground and slipped it on. I grinned at him.

"So you're a vampire, eh?"

"'Eh'?" he asked.

"I've decided to turn Canadian."

"I thought you were dead."

"They don't have Canadians in heaven?"

"I've never met any."

"Ha!" He was funny.

"Come here." He stretched his coat over me as I hugged my arms around his naked waist. "Good God, you're cold," he muttered when my hands touched his skin.

"Sorry."

He closed the jacket more tightly around the two of us. "Vampire is a misleading term," he started again. I couldn't believe he was still going on about this, but I was dead, so I figure I'd let him steer the conversation. Maybe this was some weird Heaven Initiation Ceremony and Adrian was my angel tour guide. I could live with that.

"You don't drink blood?" I asked.

"Well—yes."

"That's cool."

"That's cool?"

"Yeah," I said, looking into his silver, luminous eyes. He had probably been my guardian angel the whole time. I always knew he was too good-looking. "It's cool. The whole leaning-in-and-biting-the-neck thing." Strictly for demonstrative purposes, I stood on my tiptoes and softly nipped his collarbone with my teeth, since I couldn't actually reach his neck.

"Caitlin—*stop*."

His voice was strained. I looked at him again with a smile, but the expression on his face dropped the laughter right back into the pit of my stomach. I was dead; was it possible to still be scared?

"You're not dead, Caitlin," he said through slightly gritted teeth, "you're very much alive. So if you could just not move for a minute, that would be great."

I was confused. The light and the snow and the whiteness covering everything; the cold air and the heat of Adrian's body—wasn't I dead? And if I wasn't, why was he telling me all of this?

I shifted and he tightened his hold on me. "Just . . . don't."

His irises seemed to be swirling, which was a weird thing for irises to do. The grays mixed, melting into each other, re-forming like storms. I was just starting to get dizzy, to lose my sense of gravity, when he closed his eyes, tight. When he opened them again the irises were still silver, but they were motionless. He let out a breath and looked down at me.

"Where was I?"

"What was *that?*" I asked. "Your eyes went all crazy."

He stared at me pointedly. "I'm thirsty."

Ah.

"So if you would be so kind as to not bite me again, we might get through this."

He loosened his grip on me a little and rolled his shoulders. "As I said, vampire is a misleading term. We only drink blood because our bodies can't produce it. And it's not a purely hematic diet— I probably eat three times as much as your uncle." He smiled. "Great metabolism, ridiculous grocery bill."

"I bet."

He smiled, then frowned at me. "This all sounds crazy."

I frowned back at him. "Yes."

"But you're still here."

"You're holding on to me."

"And if I let you go?"

"You're the only reason I'm standing."

"Hmmm."

"And I still mostly believe I'm dead. So continue."

"Right. Well, my father—he's a demon. From hell."

I raised an eyebrow. "Bummer."

He smiled. "Some believe we were wiped out before the flood."

"The flood? Like Noah's flood?"

"That's the one."

"But you weren't?"

"I have no idea—this is all a story, remember? I wasn't there, no one left alive remembers. Some of us believe the story. Others don't."

"And what do you believe?"

He smiled a little, then let it slip away. "I'm still making up my mind."

I grabbed his face and turned it, inspecting for wrinkles. "How old are you? You're totally really gross and old, aren't you? Do you have kids? Do you have *grandkids*?"

He snorted. "I'm eighteen, no kids. And you're seventeen. No kids, either. Unless you have a secret love child I don't know about."

"No love children," I confirmed, and let his face go. "What about your family?"

He hesitated, but I was calm. Probably way calmer than he thought I should be. "Lucian is eleven. Julian is thirty-five."

I frowned. "I thought he was nineteen. And who's Lucian?"

"He looks nineteen. But he's thirty-five. Lucian is my little brother."

"And your aunt?"

"Mariana is one hundred and fifty-three. And she's not my aunt, she's my sister. Well, half sister. Julian and Lucian are my half brothers."

"Is your mom super old or something?"

"My mother is dead," he said flatly. "So is Mariana's, and Lucian's, and Julian's. They all die after they give birth." He cleared his throat. "But the rest of us can live indefinitely."

I stared at him. "Indefinitely."

"Forever," he amended. "Unless we're killed. But we're pretty hard to kill."

"So," I said slowly, mind racing with the ramifications, "you can't die."

"Nope."

"What if you get sick?"

"I don't get sick."

I stared at him. He wouldn't die. He *couldn't* die. "So I'm not dead. This isn't some bizarre hallucination."

"No."

I thought about it, then nodded.

He looked surprised. "That's it?"

I shrugged. "I can scream if you'd like. Maybe faint."

He smiled and shook his head. "There's more to tell you, but it's getting dark and we should probably get somewhere warm. I think you'll have to put your sweater back on if you don't want your aunt to freak out."

He let go of me. It occurred to me that I had basically wrestled with him half naked in the snow, and now that I was neither ambivalent about dying, nor delusional about already being dead, I couldn't decide if the whole thing was funny or humiliating. I skimmed off his sweater and handed it to him. He dropped his coat and we both put our clothes back on.

It was a weird moment.

His blush finally brought to the front of my brain a thought that had been nibbling at the back of my mind. I turned slowly and stared at him, horrified.

"Oh my God, you're not gay. You're a vampire. You're not gay, you're a *vampire*."

"I am not gay," Adrian confirmed. "Though your promise to keep it a secret was very kind." He cocked an eyebrow. "Does it disappoint you, that I'm straight?"

"I—what—no?" I stuttered, mind exploding with the implications.

Holy mother of Santa Claus. He wasn't withdrawn and secretive because of his sexual orientation, he was withdrawn and secretive because he *wasn't human*. I had slept next to a not-gay Adrian de la Mara in his own bed.

I had snuggled him against his will.

Trying, and failing, to suppress a smile, Adrian wound the scarf around my neck.

"My family has . . . resources," he explained. "I've always had nice things. I believe you made a comment about my shoes costing more than your laptop? All I can say in my defense is that everyone in my family is a bit fashion conscious. I adopted their tastes to fit in. As for why I've never been on a date, I think you can see why that might be difficult. I'm afraid Trish will lose the pool."

I choked. "You know about the pool?"

"I *started* the pool."

*Oh my God, of course he did.*

"One more thing," Adrian said as he stepped close to me again. He put his hands on either side of my face and looked me in the eyes with his burning silver ones and for half a second I thought he was going to kiss me. But his eyes began to swirl, and I realized what was happening.

"No-no-*no!*" I stuttered, remembering the vivid pain that had come last time he'd done this.

He kept his eyes locked on mine. "It's not like before, I promise. Just hold still."

I don't think I could have moved if I wanted to. His eyes flared brightly and he murmured in that lovely language I couldn't understand. All of a sudden I felt sort of calm and tired and warm. Tears ran down my cheeks again as I kept my eyelids open involuntarily. Then he blinked and I blinked and it was over.

"Feel better?" he asked, stepping a polite distance back.

I did a quick check. "Yeah, actually. What did you do?"

He looped his arm through mine and started walking back toward the ranch. "I transferred some of my body heat to you."

I stared at him. "You can do that?"

He smiled his half smile and it looked a little bit wicked. "I can do a lot of things."

Well, then.

We walked side by side in the quiet forest. Before I knew it, we were back at the house. When I opened the front door, Rachel looked frantic as she came and enveloped me in a hug.

"I thought something had happened to you! Are you all right?" She looked down at me and blinked. "Why are your clothes all wet?"

"My apologies, Mrs. Master," Adrian stepped in. "I forgot to give Caitlin her birthday present at school, so I was walking over here when we ran into each other on the road. We started a snowball fight," he grinned sheepishly, believably, "and I accidentally pushed her into a pile of snow."

"Oh," Rachel said, unsure of what to make of this.

"It was slushy snow," I clarified.

"Very slushy," Adrian confirmed.

"Well, come in! Dry yourself off. I was going to start dinner soon; why don't you stay?"

"Thank you," he said, stepping into the house and pulling me with him. "I'd really appreciate that."

"Just hang up your wet things on the rack there. Would you like some coffee?"

He grinned. "I'd love some."

Rachel smiled and went off into the kitchen. As soon as she was out of earshot, Adrian murmured, "Consider me your personal shadow from here on out."

"Why?" I whispered back.

He frowned. "I guess I forgot to mention that part."

I jumped at the sound of my aunt speaking. "Caitlin, get out of that sweater; it's soaked! Here you go," she said, handing Adrian a cup of coffee. "Do you want any sugar or creamer?"

"No, ma'am; black's just fine."

Rachel grinned at him. Of course he drank it black. And of course he said "ma'am."

"I'll be right back," I said, hobbling up the stairs as fast as my half-numb limbs would allow. I closed the door to my bedroom and leaned against it.

What had just happened? I shivered violently and realized I could think about it much better after I got warm. I tugged everything off and threw on dry clothes, then headed downstairs. Adrian was sitting at the kitchen table with his cup of coffee, talking to my aunt. When she saw me, she smiled.

"Why don't you and Adrian watch a movie until dinner's ready?"

"It's okay, I can help," I said, stalling.

"No, no; it's your birthday, you're banned from the kitchen."

Adrian smiled. "I'm up for a movie."

I narrowed my eyes at him, but there was nothing I could do and he knew it. We headed into the living room.

"What'd you say to her?" I whispered.

"Nothing much."

I gave him a look.

He shrugged. "Just that I was very happy you had come to Stony Creek, and I was having a wonderful time getting to know you."

I scowled at him and he smiled at me. I rolled my eyes. "Fine then. What do you want to watch?"

"It's your birthday," he said with a lazy smile. "Why don't you choose?"

I grabbed a random DVD from the pile, and popped it into the player, then headed for the armchair. Before I could sit, Adrian grabbed my hand and patted the seat next to him on the couch. I looked at him and shook my head no.

"I'm cold," he said. "I gave you all my body heat, remember?"

I snorted. "Way to play the guilt card."

But I sat next to him. He took the throw from the back of the couch and wrapped it around me, then leaned into the corner of the couch and pulled me against his chest in a very non-platonic manner.

"Are you crazy?" I whispered in his ear. "My aunt is right over there!"

"Do you want to sell the story?" he murmured, looking at the TV. "Wouldn't you rather have them wonder if something is going on between us than wonder if they should ever let you out of their sight because you might do something stupid?"

I gaped at him, fishlike.

"Besides," he said, settling into the sofa, "I still need to warm up. And if I remember correctly from the effects of a certain Halloween party," he murmured into my hair, "you *like* cuddling with me."

I was blushing too hard to think of an elegant reply. With the blanket on top of me and Adrian's chest beneath me, it was like a sauna, but in a good way. "Fine," I grumbled. Then I sat up again, remembering his earlier comment. "Wait—what was that about being my shadow?"

He shook his head. "I'll tell you tomorrow."

"*Adrian*," I warned.

"Caitlin," he replied, staring back at me evenly.

After a long moment, he very sternly pointed at his chest, then pointed at me, then motioned for me to lie back down.

How the hell was I supposed to resist that?

# SELLING THE STORY

I woke up to a variety of noises: the sound of silverware and glasses being set on the table, the drone of the movie sound track, my uncle speaking with my aunt, the bubble of a pot on the stove, and most vividly, the beat of Adrian's peculiarly slow heart against my left ear. I stretched, waking slowly, and rubbed my face into his chest.

"You're in a better mood," he observed, looking down with a small smile.

"I forgot how incredibly comfortable you are." I laid my face on his sweater again and almost drifted off. I could feel a chuckle trickle up through his chest.

"I think your uncle doesn't know what to do with me," he whispered a moment later.

I immediately popped up and looked first at Adrian, then at my uncle, then at Adrian again, horrified. "What do we tell him?"

He shifted underneath me, tucking the blanket around my shoulders. "We tell him that we've become good friends since you've moved here, and that we'd like to see where the friendship takes us."

"Does that mean we're dating?"

"It means your uncle can interpret that however he wants."

I frowned. "So, you're doing all this just because you don't want my family to worry about me?"

He waved his head back and forth in a so-so gesture. "There's more. But I'll tell you tomorrow. Enjoy your birthday."

I raised a brow. "That doesn't sound ominous at all." He smiled, but refused to elaborate. "Fine," I told him, "be cryptic." I hunched my knees up to my chin. "What about my aunt, though? She'll ask detailed questions. And Norah will repeat anything we say here to all her friends, so what do we tell people at school? Also, if this is all some weirdly elaborate joke about vampires because I wore a vampire costume on Halloween and it's my birthday, tell me now, and your death will be quick and painful."

He winked at me. "I can't die, remember?"

Before I could reply, Rachel called out that dinner was ready, so we stood and walked over to the table.

"Caitlin, how was your birthday?" my aunt asked, breaking the silence as she handed her husband a bowl of salad.

I almost choked on a crouton. Adrian patted my back helpfully. For half a second, I toyed with the idea of telling her the truth: *Well, Aunt Rachel, I went to school, I came home, I put on my boots, and I got naked-ish and cried on a large rock, but Adrian here just had to stop me, and oh yeah! he's a vampire and we're dating now. I think.*

"It was good," I lied.

"Adrian," my aunt began, "I can't tell you how nice it is to have you here. And I wanted to thank you for taking Caitlin to school; it's been such a help."

"No trouble at all," he replied, smiling warmly.

I was clearing dishes later, so I didn't notice at first when Adrian took Joe into the living room to talk. Over the dishwasher, Rachel leaned in conspiratorially.

"So," she began, trying to sound casual. "What's going on with you two?"

I'd known this was coming, but my face still turned red. Norah was rinsing plates in the sink and trying to listen without looking like she was listening.

I scrubbed at an imaginary spot of food on the plate I was holding and mumbled, "We're dating, I guess."

They both gasped and turned to each other with equal I-told-you-so smile.

"He's a very nice young man," Rachel said.

I peeked over at Adrian. "I'm not sure Joe agrees."

As if he heard me, Joe stood and walked toward us.

"Well, I better be going before the roads get too bad," Adrian announced, following him into the kitchen. I threw a tight smile at everyone as they wished him good night, grabbed Adrian by the arm, and walked him to the door.

"What did you say to Joe?" I whispered.

"Not much," he replied, tugging on his boots. "Mentioned the weather, the horses, what my intentions toward you are."

I paled.

He smiled, looking satisfied. "Don't worry, your uncle and I have an understanding."

"An *understanding*," I replied flatly.

He bent down and kissed me lightly on the cheek. "I'll pick you up in the morning."

He opened the door and walked back out into the night. I stood there in a daze as the engine to the truck revved to life. When I turned around, Joe, Rachel, and Norah were staring at me.

"Um," I said intelligently, "I think I'm going to go do some homework. If that's all right."

"Sure," my aunt said, smiling. "Good night!"

I headed upstairs, closed my door softly, and started a fire in my tiny little fireplace before wrapping myself in a blanket to huddle in front of the heat-spitting light.

I was now dating Adrian de la Mara.

I didn't really know how that had happened, but there it was.

I mouthed the words *Caitlin Marie de la Mara* as a joke—after all, it wasn't like we were actually dating.

Right?

I thought back to all the times he'd had headaches. Were they really headaches? Or did it have something to do with his weird eye thing? What did I even call the weird eye thing? And did I really have to call him a vampire? Because that was completely ridiculous. Had it all been in my head? Did I dream up the snow fight, the molten-silver eye trick, that little tidbit that his dad was a *demon*? Was this all just one incredibly detailed hallucination? Hallucination seemed more plausible than Adrian being immortal. I was totally in the middle of a fugue state, wasn't I? Maybe if I just slept, I'd snap out of it in the morning. That seemed reasonable.

———◦

The truck looked exactly as it had the day before. Maybe I was expecting it to turn into a giant pumpkin carriage or a flaming chariot, but it was just a truck, black, at least a few years old, with a couple of dings in the door. Probably the only thing of Adrian's I'd ever seen that wasn't brand-new and flawless. The driver's side window rolled down.

"Morning, sunshine," Adrian said with a big smile.

Who was this and what had he done with the brooding underwear model I'd known before?

"Hi," I returned, and climbed into the passenger side. "You're still a vampire?"

"Yep."

"Cool, yeah, just checking." Damn. Not a fugue state. "And we're still pretend-dating?"

Instead of answering, he just put his arm around my shoulders and pulled me against him, driving left-handed down the road.

I looked up at him. "I take that as a 'yes.'"

He smiled.

I settled into his arm, because why not? "So now's the part where I ask you questions, just FYI."

He kept his eyes on the road. "What do you want to know?"

What did I want to know? Everything. "How did you find me yesterday?"

He opened his mouth to reply, then closed it, glancing at me. "Before I say anything, please keep in mind that half of this is lore, the other half's myth, and the rest is bullshit that's been passed down so long no one really remembers the truth anymore."

I frowned. "That's more than a hundred percent."

"Shhhhhh," he said, exaggeratedly patting my hair. "All right, so, I am what I am because the thing that got my mom pregnant was a demon."

I was about to tell him I didn't believe in demons—not that I really believed in vampires either, but I *definitely* didn't believe in demons—but he saw my look and cut me off.

"That's just what we call them," he explained. "If you want to get into a theological debate, don't bother. I don't claim to know anything about heaven or hell or God or gods or afterlives or any of it. At least, not any more than anyone else can. We've been around long enough that *demon* has always been synonymous with *monster*. For all I know, he's really an alien, or a superevolved parasite. Whatever he is, he's not human and he's not what I am. What we do know is that he—and all of his kind—feed off human emotions. It's their only energy source, the only one they *need*, because for the most part they don't seem to exist in a physical state."

He paused, and then admitted, "As his offspring, I feed off emotions, too. Except instead of draining people of them, I simply"—he looked around, searching for the right word—"*absorb* them."

"What's the difference?"

He frowned, thinking. "Demons are basically leeches, slowly sucking out your life-force. Vampires are sponges, soaking up the energy you're already putting out—kind of like solar panels. We both get the energy humans emit, but one is a parasitic relationship and the other is merely commensal." He saw the blank look on my face. "One party gains while the other remains unaffected."

"Ah," I replied intelligently.

"You, though," he said, glancing down at me. "With enough concentration, we can actually pick you out from a crowd. It's definitely easier out here, where the population density is so low. The stronger you're feeling any particular emotion, the easier it is to find you. That's how I knew where you were in the woods."

"One, that's super-creepy," I interrupted, "and two, *how?*"

He frowned, thinking, then looked over at me. "Have you ever walked into a room and just *felt* that everyone was really angry, or sad, or whatever, without anyone having to say a word? It's not really like that at all, but that's the closest I can explain without diving into theoretical physics and emotional resonance and revealing that my alter ego is an unequivocal nerd."

I smiled at that. "I figured the nerd part out a while ago. But how do I know you're not just staying around me because you're hungry?"

He snorted a sudden, surprised laugh and glanced at me. "We're in a small town, but it's not *that* small—I get breakfast just passing people at school."

I sat up. "So, wait, if you were in the city, would you be crazy-strong or something, because there are so many crowds?"

He shook his head. "We're like batteries—we can only charge up so much."

I didn't really know how I felt about all this. Was he feeding off me now? Was "feeding" even an appropriate verb? I wanted a different one, mostly because I didn't want to think of him as some sort of animal. "Charging up" was much cleaner.

"I sense confusion," he said half seriously.

"Can you really pick out which emotion I'm feeling?"

"Sometimes. Sometimes all I can tell is tone. Dark or light. Negative or positive. Demons can only feed off negative emotion. Like Dementors."

A smile spread over my face. "Did you just make a Harry Potter reference?"

He shrugged, blushing. "I was a kid, too. I may or may not have read Harry Potter."

"How many times?"

"The whole series?" I nodded and he blushed harder. "Five times," he admitted finally. "I had a huge crush on Hermione."

I couldn't help it, I burst out laughing. "You totally have a

Gryffindor scarf, don't you? And an Elder wand and a Goblet of Fire." I grinned at him. "Tell me you have a Goblet of Fire."

His face was red, and it was adorable. "No goblet." He paused, then admitted, "I might have the wand."

I laughed again, suddenly liking him so much more. "Well, I'm glad you're not a Dementor. Although it's super-creepy to think that something like a Dementor exists. Which I'm not totally sold on, by the way. Maybe you got some sort of bio-tech contact lenses yesterday to freak me out, and you're really committed to an elaborate joke. I could be on a reality-TV show right now."

"Could be," he conceded. "And you're welcome to believe whatever you wish. My job is simply to keep you safe."

I looked up at him sharply. "Wait—what?"

But we were coming up on the school parking lot. He pulled into a spot and cut the engine, then looked at me.

"Later," he said. "I promise."

I scowled, but got out, shutting my door. Before I could even make it to the sidewalk, Adrian caught my hand.

"I'll see you at lunch," he said quietly. He bent and kissed me lightly on the cheek like he had the night before. All too soon his fingers left mine and he walked off.

I floated to Mr. Warren's room and hovered above my seat. What on earth was happening to me? I was one of the least romantic people I knew. I didn't get whimsical over a kiss on the cheek. I was probably just still in shock that Adrian wasn't gay. And the whole vampire thing. And that we were fake-dating, which I still didn't really understand, at all. Trish walked in and plunked down next to me.

"Ready for the quiz?" she asked.

"The quiz?" I repeated stupidly.

"On the last chapter of the novel?"

Yesterday, I would have shrugged and been perfectly happy failing. Today, somehow, I felt awake—I felt *alive*—and I cared. Maybe it was that everything Adrian had told me made me feel like the world was bigger than it was before. Maybe my life—my future—wasn't as closed in and cut off as I'd imagined. Maybe the cheek-kiss was affecting my brain.

I spent the next ten minutes skimming the last chapter, trying to remember what we'd read. When Mr. Warren passed the quiz around, I guessed on maybe half the questions and slunk off to second period.

An eternity later it was lunch and Trish and I walked to the picnic tables. Just as I was about to sit down, I felt an arm slide around my waist. I froze, blushing instantly. I guess Adrian was really determined to make the fake-dating thing look legit, even at school. I did not, however, expect to feel the brush of lips against my temple. Half the table was staring at us, and in the sudden, rippling hush, *everyone* turned to stare. The red flush covering my face was burning hot, even though a cold breeze was blowing the snow around in little flurries. Trish stood opposite me, lunch in hand, mouth hanging open.

I cleared my throat and that seemed to trigger everyone back into motion. When we sat, Trish kicked my shin under the table and gave me a meaningful look.

*Later,* I mouthed.

She scowled at me, but didn't say anything. I looked around and spotted Norah at another table. There was a crowd of freshman girls around her, craning their heads closer to hear. By the end of lunch, everyone up to the principal would have heard that Adrian and I were dating.

"Something wrong, sugar plum?" Adrian murmured in my ear.

I smiled my most demure smile and leaned close so only he could hear. "I am going to punch you in the left kneecap if you call me 'sugar plum' again."

He just chuckled.

Twenty minutes later the bell rang, and I would have dashed off to fifth period if Adrian hadn't caught me by the back of my coat.

"What is it with you and running away from me?" he asked quizzically, slinging an arm over my shoulders.

"Maybe you're hideous, and I can't stand the sight of your face?"

He looked thoughtful. "Mmm, no, that's not it."

I snorted. "Confident much?"

He leaned in close and murmured, "I'm not the one who talks in my sleep about sexy pirate men."

I paled, horrified. "I did not."

He grimaced at me in a way that clearly said, *Yes. Yes, you did.*

We stopped in front of my classroom and he leaned down and slowly brushed my cheek with his lips. I stumbled through history and music, walking with my stomach in knots to study hall. For once, I beat Adrian. I'd just settled in when he stopped and looked at the vacant chair opposite me.

"I take it I'm allowed to sit with you again?"

I tried to keep my face composed, neutral. "Yes."

He set his stuff down and took out a book.

"Nope," I said, placing my hand on the cover and sliding it toward me. "Questions first."

He looked around. "In study hall?"

"Do you seriously think I can concentrate on homework right now?"

He put the book away. "All right—what's next?"

We were pretty secluded in our little corner, but I leaned in anyway. "What did you mean when you said you were my personal shadow?"

He rubbed his eyes. "It means that you're in trouble." I frowned, waiting for him to elaborate. "For instance—that storm? Wasn't a storm."

"The storm was not a storm."

"It was a disturbance."

I snorted. "In the Force?"

He shrugged. "I mean—yeah, sort of. My father came back."

"From where?"

He looked at me, equal parts amused and uncomfortable. "From hell."

I blinked. "Oh."

"It's not a fiery lake or lava pit or anything like that. It doesn't seem to be a physical dimension at all." He glanced at me, then down at the table, twirling a mechanical pencil in his hands before clearing his throat. "My little brother, Lucian, he's only been with us for a year. When he was born my father took him. He grew up in hell until he was ten."

I stared at him, thinking he must be joking. "Your brother grew up in *hell?*"

"Yes. Or the dimensional plane we collectively agree to call hell."

I thought he must be joking, but he looked dead serious. "But, if it's not a physical, y'know, *place*," I asked, "how did your brother survive?"

Adrian started to speak, then stopped. "I—I've never been. Some of us have. It's been explained to me that it's a bit like when you're e-mailing someone a picture. The visual information—colors and shadows and lines—it all gets converted to ones and zeroes and compressed before it's transmitted. Apparently Lucian's body was like that—stored, indefinitely, as information. As an idea."

Well, that one was certainly hard to wrap my head around.

He smiled uncomfortably. "The more science progresses, the more we understand particles and light and time, the more it seems to wrap right back around into myth." He shook his head. "The point is, we found him—which was unprecedented—and took him back—which was even more unprecedented." He risked a glance up at me.

"So," I said slowly. "You're immortal. Your dad's a demon. You absorb emotions as energy. You can do freaky things with your eyes and make people forget stuff, your brother was stored digitally in hell, and for some grand, mysterious reason, I am being intentionally informed about your secret vampire society."

He thought about it for a moment, then nodded. "Yes. The point of all this has to do with Lucian—and you. Julian, Mariana, and I are all lost causes as far as our father is concerned. But when you invest ten years in a kid, like our father did with Lucian, you're gonna be a little pissed if he's taken away. We knew he was going to come looking, which is why Lucian came to live with us. We're remote, unlike most others of our kind, who prefer high-density population centers. If there was going to be any kind of altercation, the collateral damage would be minimal out here. But we had no idea that he'd be so *close* when he came. Usually, it's very difficult to pinpoint where you come through. When you travel between dimensions, you sort of upset physics. It literally agitates the fabric of the universe. Anyway—he opens a gateway, we get a freak storm."

I stared at Adrian. "So I just happened to be sitting right there when an interdimensional portal opened up next to your house?"

He nodded.

"Okay," I said, "but, so what? You rescued me, the storm's over, I'm safe now." When he didn't respond, I followed up with a prompting "I'm safe, right?"

He leaned in close, even took my hand in his and stared down at it like it was the most fascinating thing in the world. Whatever he was about to say, it was bad.

"Your mom had died only a few days before," he began. "You were, quite understandably, upset. If my father had come through in the city, he could have latched on to anyone, but there are so few people up here, and you were—*emotional* enough to draw attention. We could feel you, and we knew he'd head straight for you to strengthen whatever body he'd managed to create for himself. But I found you before he did. And I had to—"

He shook his head and sat back, a disgusted look on his face.

My stomach felt slimy. "What?"

His glance flicked up at me. "There's no good way to say this." He grimaced. "I had to drain you."

"You had to—*what?*"

He let out a long breath. "In order to keep you from being detected, I siphoned off your emotion—all of it. I had to make even *you* forget you existed. That's why you couldn't remember the storm, and that's why you were so weak. I nearly killed you, to keep you alive."

I stared at him.

He scrubbed a hand across the bridge of his nose. "The stupid thing is, that *should* have been it. You were safe, you were home, our father left, we scared him off. Even Lucian was safe." He looked tired suddenly. "Except Mariana had a dream about you."

I stared at him. "What sort of dream?"

He shrugged. "She didn't tell me much—she rarely does. They're abstract and open to interpretation and that can mess with things. All I was told was that it had something to do with our father wanting to locate you."

"But—it's just a dream. Right?"

He shook his head. "No. No, unfortunately, it's not just a dream. You'd already left residual emotional energy all over the place, like heat coming off pavement after a day in the sun. He still noticed you. Mariana's vision confirms that."

He glanced at me. "Since we go to the same school, it was my job to keep an eye on you after that, give you information as needed. My sister's vision could mean nothing, but that's rare. We don't know what will happen, we don't know *when* it will happen—but we do know it will revolve around you."

A pregnant silence followed his statement as we stared at each other. I was, apparently, at the epicenter of a crazy demon vision, and Adrian was my vampire liaison.

And I had no idea how I was supposed to feel about that.

The bell rang sharply, startling us both. I looked away, cramming books into my messenger bag, and walked to his truck in a sort of daze, weaving through the flood of students. It felt weird that all this mythical shit was going down, and yet life went on, looking for all the world like everything was totally normal. Trish certainly didn't know about any of this. Could I tell her? Could I tell my grandma? No. How could I tell them something I didn't even really believe myself?

"So," I said, finally breaking the strained silence after we were winding our way into the mountains. "Your father's secret evil plan is to—what? Kill me?"

There was another uncomfortable pause before he finally muttered, "Not exactly."

I looked over at Adrian. Finally, he cleared his throat. "We think he wants to impregnate you."

I blinked.

I laughed.

And then I saw that he was serious.

I spun toward him on the seat, not sure if I'd heard him right. "He wants to *impregnate* me? Like, with a *baby*, that kind of impregnate?"

"I understand you're upset—"

"That does not even cover the middle finger of what I am feeling—"

"—but please believe that nothing is going to happen to you while I'm here—while we're *all* here, my family and I."

"What about when you're not here?" I sputtered. "What about when I'm at home? Or when I'm asleep? What about *my* family?"

"This is not—he won't rape you, or anything," he said, struggling for words and looking awkward as hell. "He'll make you *want* him. It's—what they do. It's a game."

"This is not a *game*," I spat back.

He took in a deep breath. "Look, I've never heard of a demon going up against a forewarned human."

"At least give me something to work with here! How would I know who he is? What does he look like?"

Adrian looked at me almost apologetically. "Technically, he doesn't look like anything. He's more of an—*entity*. When he comes into this dimension, he either creates a body for himself or inhabits one. It's different every time. Technically, he could look like me, though I doubt he'd go for something so obvious."

I stared at him. "So I'm supposed to be afraid of all men for the rest of my life, including you."

"No," he replied firmly. "No. Not forever. And not afraid—just cautious."

"What if he *does* show up as you? How would I know?"

"He wouldn't have my memories," Adrian said with a shrug. "He's never met me, so he wouldn't know my speech patterns or habits. You should be able to figure out pretty quick that he wasn't me. And you can always call my cell—if it doesn't ring in his pocket, it's probably not me."

"What if you don't have your phone on you?"

"It's not a foolproof plan."

"Great."

"You're smart," he said, looking over at me sharply. "And gut instinct is going to count for a lot. Something feels wrong, *listen to that feeling.*"

He pulled onto the driveway leading up to the ranch. "The truth is, you're well protected. The only reason we're telling you all this is so you can keep an eye out. But that's all—you don't need to worry about anything except selling the story. You and I dating is believable. Your aunt and uncle believe it. Everyone at school believes it. It gives me an excuse to watch out for you. Just leave the rest to me and my family. We'll keep you safe, we'll let you know what's going on. I promise."

I snorted and leaned my head against the back of the seat. "Sure, sure. I won't worry about a thing." I stuck a finger in the air, frowning. "Remind me, why does your dad want me to bake his vampire baby in my bun oven? I mean, honestly, what's the *point* of getting me pregnant?"

He leaned back, looking somewhat deflated, as the house came into view. "It may have something to do with the type of person you are, the emotions you give off. And it may be payback."

I narrowed my eyes. "Payback for what? I sure as hell haven't done anything to him."

He parked in front of the house and sat there for a moment before responding. "We took Lucian back. We pissed him off. Getting a local girl pregnant right under our noses would be a characteristic revenge."

"But *why*? Why does he even need another kid?"

Adrian looked uncomfortable. "That's one of the things I'm not allowed to tell you."

"Well, that's bullshit."

He shrugged, looking grim. "I know."

I waited, but he didn't elaborate, and by the way his jaw was clenched, I doubted he was going to.

"Fine—don't tell me. But shit, dude, I'm *seventeen*," I protested, as if Adrian was the one that needed to be convinced that impregnating me was a bad idea. "Wouldn't he want someone older to seduce? Like a—*woman*. Or something?"

"Mariana's mother was fourteen when she got pregnant," he said, which made me feel zero percent better. "When you're immortal, the current cultural attitudes about motherhood don't really mean a whole lot. The younger the hosts are, the stronger and healthier they tend to be."

He shut off the engine and we got out, walking awkwardly to the front door of the ranch.

"I'd like to take you to meet my family tomorrow," he said as I dug my keys out. "Would that be all right with you?"

Did it matter, really, if it was or not? But all I said was, "Sure." Maybe they'd have more answers for me. Ones that Adrian apparently didn't have permission to reveal.

We stared at each other for a moment before I opened the door to the house and let myself in, locking both the handle and the dead-bolt behind me.

Everything was exactly the same, really. Nothing had *visibly* changed about my life, but I was now mulling over ways to ward off demon seducers and avoid showing up on the supernatural edition of *Teen Mom*. And I was pretending to date my stalker's vampire son. And I still had a shit-ton of algebra homework to do.

# 8

# MEETING THE FAMILY

"So, dumb question. If you're 'thirsty' and have to drink from a live person, how do they not turn into a vampire when you're done?"

Adrian snort-laughed, suddenly, like I'd made a joke. And then he realized I was serious. "We can't just bite people and they turn into one of us," he explained. "That's—that's not a thing. We're born, not made."

"Oh."

I felt kind of stupid. Although who can blame me? All the vampire lore I was aware of was pretty consistent on bitten humans turning into bloodsucking sociopaths.

It was the next morning and we were in his truck, going to school. I'd warned my aunt and uncle at breakfast that I would be popping over to meet his family before I came home for dinner. They hadn't said a whole lot, but I got the impression it seemed like I was getting engaged to Adrian rather than just dating him. Which was funny because I wasn't even really dating him.

Though by the looks of things, you couldn't tell it was all fake. I was sitting tucked under his right arm, one leg stretched out over the bench seat and the other resting on the floor. The snuggling-on-the-way-to-school thing was his suggestion—he said we needed to be comfortable with each other and act, convincingly, like a couple. I wasn't gonna argue. He was always ten degrees warmer than me, and in the middle of winter I would take practice-cuddling in exchange for additional body heat any day.

I played absently with the sleeve of his sweater. "So then how do you not just straight up kill people when you're snacking on them?"

"By *not* snacking on them as often as possible. Blood bags have been a modern blessing."

"Okay—dumb question number two: Why do you even *need* blood?"

"Because our bodies can't produce it correctly. It's kind of difficult to go about your day when your heart's not beating."

I absently traced his knuckles with my finger as I stared out the window. "I thought vampires didn't have heartbeats—I mean, you're one of the undead, right?"

I could feel his eyes roll even if I couldn't see it. "Quite alive, thank you. And any operational body needs a power source. Humans have the cardiovascular system. I'm more or less human, so I have a heartbeat. However," he conceded, "it's more efficient. My resting heart rate is about ten beats per minute."

"And mine would be?"

"Seventy-five." He paused. "Ish."

I looked up and gave him a dazzling smile. "I feel totally inadequate right now."

He smiled back, just as sarcastically. "At least you don't have to ingest other people's blood to stay alive."

I nodded. Good point.

"We drink blood," he continued, "because our bone marrow produces red blood cells that interfere with the hemoglobic process—"

"Whoa, whoa," I interrupted. "Just, hold on. In case you haven't noticed by now, I'm an art person. Your fancy science words mean nothing to me."

"Sorry," he apologized, looking sheepish. "I—I'm used to reading about all this in lab reports and case studies. I'll try to make it more—visual?"

I settled back into his arm. "If you produce a flannel graph out of somewhere, you will be well rewarded."

He smiled. He was smiling a lot these days. "No flannel graph. I do a mean shadow puppet, though."

I snort-laughed. "This is the weirdest conversation I've ever had."

"You're telling me. Anyway, listen up—there's a quiz on this later."

"Oh my gosh, you *are* a nerd."

He clamped a hand over my mouth, smiling. "*Lesson One:* human biology. Being mortal and clumsy, you trip over your own shoelaces and scrape your knee." I muttered something about being *clumsy, my ass*, but his hand muffled it. "Now, the platelets in your blood snag on the damaged blood vessels and explode"—he released my face to tap his fingers against my palm in an exploding motion—"releasing fibrin, which attaches to itself to form a net that your red blood cells can't get through, which is called a blood clot, and it keeps you from dying horribly every time you get a paper cut. Now I, being an awesome vampire, get in a really cool fight—bullets flying, explosions, the works. Someone stabs my shoulder—do I die? Nope. My vampire platelets are hyperactive. They actually pull the wound back together while my injury heals—and I heal very, very quickly."

I stared at his hand covering mine. "I still wish you had a flannel graph, but I gotta admit, that's pretty bad ass."

He rested his arm across my stomach and continued. "It is, and it isn't. We kinda got screwed over in the red blood cell department. Their shape is amorphous, constantly fluctuating between randomly mutating structures. And they don't contain hemoglobin. And they're about ten times the size of a normal human red blood cell."

I looked up at him, eyes narrowed questioningly. "And that's bad."

"It's bad," he confirmed. "The mutating shape prevents oxygen from bonding. Even if it *could*, there's no hemoglobin to attract oxygen in the first place."

"Science words," I warned. "When you say *hemoglobin* I just think of little Irish tricksters who live in caves, or *Lord of the Rings*."

"You mean *goblin*?"

"Yes."

He rubbed his hand over his face, but he was smiling. "Your brain works on a completely different level from mine."

"Apparently."

"All right, how about you just give me a signal anytime I get too technical?"

I thought about it. "You cool with a thumbs-up, thumbs-down approach?"

He nodded. "That would be acceptable."

I gave him a thumbs-up. He smiled.

"All right—take two. Because our red blood cells constantly change shape, they can sort of morph their way through the smaller blood vessels, but it takes longer. Slower surface circulation leads to a low oxygen supply—" I was starting to raise my hand in a thumbs-down gesture, so he said, "Okay, okay! If we don't drink blood, we look really pale. Regardless of our ethnicity or geographic location or exposure to the sun. And we feel cold to the touch." He paused and looked down at me in exasperation. "I am seriously trying here. Every instinct I have is telling me to use polysyllabic words to impress you."

I squeezed his arm comfortingly. "You're doing fantastic. But your information doesn't add up. You're not pale, and you're not cold. In fact, you're downright hot," I said, remembering how my cheek had burned against his chest two days ago in the clearing. I saw a smile spread slowly across his face at my choice of words, and I rolled my eyes. "Not *that* kind of hot." He arched a brow at me. I rolled my eyes again. "Okay, *yes*, that kind of hot. You know what I mean."

"That's because I'm very good about maintaining a consistent diet."

I frowned at his typical answer-that-was-not-an-answer, but before I could call him on it, we turned a corner sharply and the bright morning sun reflected off a metal switchback-warning sign, casting a glare onto myself and Adrian. A thought struck me and I examined his hand in the light.

"According to legend, you should be bursting into flames right about now."

He smiled, glancing out the window. "There's a little truth to that, but only a little. If we haven't had blood in weeks, our skin loses all its pigmentation—which is really weird if you're a dark-skinned vampire, by the way—so if we're outside in bright sunlight, we *do* burn. We just don't spontaneously combust."

"Glad to hear it—I'd never get your ashes out of these seats."

"Try Lysol. Works like a charm."

I smiled at him and he smiled back.

"Lesson Two," he continued. "Vampire biology. All vampires are born with type AB blood, which is a universal receiver. Basically, it doesn't matter who we get blood from, as long as we get it from a human."

"So, no drinking the blood of innocent bunnies."

"Correct," he confirmed. "The bunnies are safe."

"And all the bunnies rejoiced, and there was great joy in the land of bunnies."

He looked at me funny and I shrugged as if to say, "Deal with my weird; I'm dealing with yours."

"All right," he said, apparently moving on. "This is where it gets gross—and complicated." He paused. "It is also extremely weird saying all of this out loud, especially to someone who didn't grow up like me. I just want that to be on record."

I nodded very seriously. "Noted. Hey, can I call you 'Dracula Pants' in public? It's kind of like 'Smoochy Pants,' but funnier, because you're a vampire."

"No. When we drink blood," he continued, "our immune system destroys everything *but* the red blood cells. Our native red blood cells mimic the size and shape of the donor cells before they break apart the donor cells, exposing their hemoglobin into our bloodstreams."

I stared at him. He'd said "cells" so many times it was starting to sound like a made-up word.

"Normally, raw hemoglobin would be toxic, but our red blood cells safely absorb it and use it to attract and bond with oxygen like normal." He glanced over at me sheepishly. "That's the, uh, basic overview."

"So," I said slowly, honestly wishing he'd brought a flannel graph, "you drink 'donor' blood so your body can function the way a normal human body should, except with a bagillion more steps thrown in for supernatural kicks and giggles."

"Pretty much."

I frowned. "That's all way less mysterious than I was expecting."

He shrugged. "We've been studying our own anatomy for centuries. We may not know exactly where we come from, but on a basic physiological level, we understand how our systems operate. Anyway, all that was a roundabout way of telling you why we need blood. I believe your original question was how do we not kill humans when we get it?"

"Right. That one was the one. Yes."

"You don't sound very convinced."

"You just dumped a lot of information on me. How am I supposed to remember what my original question was?"

He blushed a little. "I can stop talking."

"Gee," I said, scratching my chin, "y'know, I think I'd really rather discuss foreign policy or the bacterial growth of yogurt—*of course I want to hear more.*"

He smiled. "Okay, well, this is all new to me, too—at least getting to talk about it with someone who isn't old and pompous and incredibly boring." He cleared his throat, blushing a little. I liked how easily he blushed. "Anyway," he continued, "people kinda freak out when you're trying to extract blood from one of their major arteries, so we kind of convince them not to, y'know—twitch around and stuff. In fact, I can persuade you to do almost anything I want, if the conditions are right."

I peered closely at his face. "You talking about the freaky eye thing?"

"Yes," he smiled. "But we call it compulsion."

I leaned back. "So, basically, you're telling me you can do Jedi mind tricks."

He glanced at me. "Well—yeah." He shrugged. "Closer to hypnosis, really. I have to be making direct eye contact, and the donor has to be physically weakened or otherwise susceptible to persuasion." He held up my wrist and ran his thumb across it. "We hypnotize them into a short coma so they don't make a mess." He blinked, then set my wrist back down carefully. "It's not just that we need it, though. We—*like* it. When it's weeks old, transported between God knows how many blood banks and hospitals—even if you're trying to be cultured and drink it from a juice glass, it's bland. But when it's fresh—"

He was still driving carefully, but his eyes had a slightly glazed look to them, like he was daydreaming. "You kind of just want to take more than you need."

A small smile played across his lips, and I think that was the first moment I truly believed what he was. If he'd shown a matching pair of fangs, I wouldn't have been surprised. Freaked out, but not surprised.

He blinked a few times, then turned to me, frowning. "You know it's weird that you're not more weirded out by all of this."

I shrugged as he pulled into the school parking lot. "Besides your freaky eye thing and the freaky storm thing, this is all just a story—you're telling me a very detailed, very bizarre story. It's hard to be scared by that, especially when it's sunny out," I said, pointing a thumb at the window. "Anyway, I'll see you later."

He smiled at me, but we were late, so I ran off to class.

As soon as I sat down in what had become my customary desk in Mr. Warren's room, Trish pounced.

"*What the hell, Mystic? You hook up with Adrian and what? Forget to tell me? This is why we have cell phones, e-mail! You could've tied a note to a friggin' pigeon and sent it to me!*"

Was it really only yesterday that he'd sat by me at lunch and basically announced to the whole world that we were an item? It felt like a week ago.

"I'm sorry," I said, trying to sound meek. "It all happened really fast." *Really* fast.

She looked at me slyly. "What exactly *did* happen?"

"Nothing *happened*," I said, knowing what she was implying. "He was just over at the ranch for dinner, and we talked, and voilà, we're dating."

She eyed me, obviously convinced I was withholding juicy details. "You're a bad liar, Mystic, but congratulations, you snagged a boy."

I mentally snorted. I hadn't snagged a boy; I'd snagged a freaking vampire. Well, it was more like he'd snagged me, but whatever, some snagging had occurred.

When I headed to lunch with Trish, Adrian was standing outside my fourth-period class. As we walked out, he slipped his arm around my waist, which was beginning to feel less and less weird.

We sat down and a senior started talking to him immediately, diverting his attention. Trish looked at me meaningfully over her carton of milk.

I turned so no one could hear. "What do you want to know?"

She peeked over my shoulder to see that Adrian was firmly engaged in his conversation, then whispered, "Details—when, where, *how*."

I gave her my driest look. "Two nights ago. At my aunt and uncle's. Because we decided it was best."

She shook her head. "You are the worst storyteller I have ever met."

"Are you looking for a good one, then?"

It was Adrian. A hush went over the entire lunch area. Adrian never spoke up voluntarily, let alone to tell stories—let alone to tell *romantic* stories. They'd all been waiting years for this.

Adrian put his arm around my shoulders. My first instinct was to smack him, but I realized two could play this game. I plastered a love-drunk smile on my face and twined my fingers through his hand with as much sugar-coated grossness as I could muster. He arched an eyebrow as if to say *challenge accepted*, then looked up at the waiting crowd.

"As many of you know, I'm not the most social person." There were a few scattered laughs, but no one could tell if he was actually trying to be funny or not. I only knew he was because of the half crinkle of a smile in the corner of his mouth. "For years," he continued, every single person hanging on to his every word, "I've been so focused on academics and getting into a good college that I hardly ever saw the world around me. That is, until I rescued Caitlin during the storm." He looked down at me like I was just *so* adorable. "After that, I couldn't stop thinking about her." He smiled happily. "And now we're completely inseparable."

There was a sort of letting out of breath as everyone sighed. Even Trish looked a little dreamy. I looked up at him and fluttered my eyelashes a few times as I whispered, "If you don't let me go right now, I'm going to bite you."

He grinned wickedly and murmured, "Go ahead."

I didn't even try to hide my glare.

"Although," he said, nuzzling his face against my neck so no one could hear him, "perhaps *I* should be the one making threats about biting." I felt the gentle scrape of his teeth on the side of my neck and—

"You all right, Mystic?"

I looked at Trish, startled, and squeaked, "I'm fine!" Adrian chuckled too low for anyone else to hear and let me go.

Fifteen minutes later the bell rang. I tried to run off to class again, and again, Adrian caught me by the back of my jacket, looking puzzled.

"You're really giving people the wrong impression with all this running away." He slung an arm over my shoulders casually.

*"We need some rules,"* I hissed.

He looked around at the milling students. "Really? I think the ad-libbing is going quite well."

He stopped in front of my fifth-period class, but I grabbed his hand and pulled him a few feet down the hall to the tune of giggles and whispers behind us. As soon as we were out of earshot, I let go of his hand and stared sternly up at him.

"If I want grossly affectionate public encounters, I will let you know. Until then—rules."

"All right," he said brightly. He planted a quick kiss on the top of my head and headed off, but there was a grin on his face that I didn't trust. Maybe he was just reveling in having an excuse to interact with people for the first time.

Maybe.

———◦———

"Lucian's the one that looks like my younger brother, because he is. Julian's the one that looks like my older brother—although he's in New York for the foreseeable future so he won't be there tonight. Mariana's the one that looks like my aunt but is actually my sister, and Dominic's the one that looks like my uncle but is actually my brother-in-law."

"Thanks," I said flatly. "Very helpful."

We were driving along the winding, forest-lined lane to Adrian's house. In a few minutes, I would be meeting his family, which was legitimately freaking me out. Would they be like Adrian, or would they be all pale and creepy and mean? Would there be cameras and lights and a D-list celebrity host popping out with a mic? "Surprise! You're on a dumb prank show where we convince normally intelligent people that mythical creatures exist!" I honestly didn't know which would be worse—if it was a joke, or if it was real.

We finally came around the last curve in the driveway and he parked—while I stared. Technically, I'd been here once before, but it had been the dead of night, and I'd been drunk, and sitting here now I was completely unprepared to come face-to-face with the embodiment of just how different Adrian's life was from mine.

A detached five-car garage stood to our right. Straight ahead of us, however, was a three-story—well, I think *mansion* would be the only adequate term. It looked like an architect's fantasy of a luxury ski resort, with one- and two-story wings spreading gracefully from the main hall. French doors were scattered at picturesque intervals, leading to little decks and terraces with manicured potted trees and shrubbery. Honest-to-God *shrubbery*. Their front door gave me the impression that it had once belonged on a Gothic cathedral, and the wrought-iron fence surrounding the property lent the whole snow-laden house an air of elegant impenetrability.

"You live in a castle," I told him, as if he was not aware of where he lived.

He glanced at it. "This was built ten years ago. It's not a castle."

"Fine then—mansion."

"It doesn't have enough rooms to be a mansion."

I looked at him. "How many rooms does it have?"

He shrugged and said, "A dozen bedrooms," as if that were the normal number of bedrooms that houses were supposed to have.

I choked. "And there's *five* of you?"

He smiled way too cheerfully. "Ready?"

*No,* I thought but slid down out of the truck and followed him through the snow to the house. Entering a code into the security keypad, he pushed the door open and led me inside.

The entryway was a good fifteen feet wide, made entirely of white marble. Straight ahead, a winding staircase branched off at the second story before continuing up to the third. Black-and-white marble busts of what I assumed were very important people were placed tastefully on white pedestals. It should have been kind of tacky and over the top, but it wasn't—it was beautiful. And intimidating as hell. Adrian slipped my coat off and hung it in on a mahogany rack.

"If you don't mind, Mariana doesn't like shoes inside the house."

I quickly tore my boots off. This place was rich enough to be holy ground.

"Come on," he said, leading me to the left through an archway. We walked into a vast dining room with a marble fireplace on the opposite wall. The furniture was dark wood, intricately carved; the candleholders were solid silver; the chandelier dripped with Swarovski crystals. Adrian pulled lightly on my hand and we came into a kitchen the size of my aunt and uncle's entire house. We passed through this, too, down a hallway, and to what I would have to call the most kick-ass library I have ever seen. The ceiling was at least two stories tall, maybe three. Huge overstuffed armchairs and couches were scattered around the room, and floor-to-ceiling bookshelves were grouped in spiral formations throughout the hardwood floor, which made it impossible to see from one end of the room to the other. As we walked, I realized there were rolling ladders lining the walls and

I had the sudden, crazy urge to climb on one and have Adrian push me around. I was therefore understandably distracted when the attack came. From above, something flew straight at me. I shrieked, jumping back into Adrian's chest.

"Boo," the thing said, coming to a halt inches from my face.

Adrian clasped his hands over my mouth, then tilted my head up to look at him.

"It's just Lucian."

I looked again. An eleven-year-old boy was hanging upside down from a pulley attached to the ceiling. His light brown hair stood out in wavy strands from his upside-down face, and his eyes were covered in an overly large pair of aviator goggles.

"How do you do?" the boy asked me, sticking out his hand.

"I'm—fine," I said, shaking it.

He looked at Adrian. "Her heart is fast."

"That's because you scared her. Normal people don't hang from ceilings upside down."

"They don't?" Lucian asked seriously. Adrian shook his head. Lucian sighed, flipped over, and landed gracefully—and barefoot—on the hardwood before walking off.

I looked at Adrian. "What was that?"

"Lucian is fond of this room." He pointed up. "The harness is attached to rolling magnets, which adhere to the steel ceiling. As long as you have the right weights up, you can roll around the whole library. Makes getting books down a lot easier."

I stared at Adrian, a gleeful look stealing over my face. "When can I try this?"

He rolled his eyes, smiling. "And you call me a nerd."

We came around the corner of a bookshelf into a sectioned-off area at the far end of the library. A massive fireplace was roaring merrily with a fire (as it should, being a fireplace). In front of this was a trio of white sofas with tall backs and plush pillows. A man and woman, looking to be in their early thirties, were perched elegantly on the right couch.

The woman, whom I assumed was Adrian's sister, Mariana, had bright, bright blue eyes and wavy brown hair in a chin-length bob. She wore an ivory cashmere sweater and black leggings, feet tucked under her as she pored through a leather-bound book and sipped on a glass of white wine. Her husband, Dominic—Adrian's brother-in-law, I think—had brown eyes and sandy hair that looked effortlessly tousled in a way that most people found impossible to achieve without the help of trained professionals. He, too, was reading a book and sipping on a glass of wine, although his was red.

My stomach dropped. I thought it was red wine. But maybe it was—

"Caitlin," Mariana said in a soft voice that had a hint of a French accent. She set her book and wineglass down on the coffee table to shake my hand. Dominic stood, too, and put his arm around her waist.

"Welcome," he said, voice sounding solidly American. "It's nice to finally meet you."

"Have a seat." Mariana gestured at the couch opposite theirs. "Can I get you anything to drink?"

My stomach did another little somersault as I shook my head. "No, thank you."

Adrian and I sat. Out of the corner of my eye I saw Lucian climb over the back of the other sofa and roll down until he was sitting with his legs crossed, goggled face staring blankly into the fire.

"To begin, please rest assured that your family is safe," Mariana said. Her voice was charming, smooth and light, and it reminded me, for some strange reason, of those old preparatory schools that used to teach etiquette and diction.

"We have informed the Council of our father's return to this dimension," she continued, "and either myself, Dominic, or Adrian will be scanning your house at all times to make sure nothing is—out of place."

I cast a quizzical look at Adrian.

"Sort of like emotional sonar," he explained. "We send out a wave and see what emotions bounce back. If anything unusual is going on, we'll know."

I nodded, then looked at the couple across from me. "I don't remember Adrian mentioning anything about a Council."

Dominic took another sip of wine, then set it down carefully, glancing at his wife before turning to me. "The Council is our governing body, founded several millennia ago by a woman named Adataneses. She was only human," he said, as if it was a bit of an embarrassment. "A midwife, actually—but she knew what we were. She was the first to take infant vampires from their dying mothers and raise them as her own. In those days, children who weren't retrieved by demons immediately after birth were often decapitated and burned alive by humans, thought to be demons themselves, or any of a number of other monsters. Adataneses began to save them. She created our entire society, the rules by which we live peacefully with the rest of the world. The children she rescued became the Council, and the Council continues to govern us to this day."

I guess he and Mariana were of the faithful variety—they spoke like all this was fact, not myth. I raised an eyebrow. "So—your dads are all demons. Like, holy water, Dante's *Inferno* demons?"

Adrian moved imperceptibly closer to me on the couch. For some reason, it felt like a warning.

Mariana smiled faintly, but it was not a friendly smile. "More or less."

I leaned back, shaking my head. "I don't mean to be rude, but do you expect me to believe all this? That there are *demons* out there?"

Mariana's gaze was ice-cold. "You should believe in evil, Ms. Holte. Call it what you will."

"However," she continued, "we are not concerned with your disbelief. We are concerned with the threat that has been placed against you."

Figuring I didn't have much to lose but a few pints of blood, I stared right back at her.

"Why am I so special, exactly? Adrian was a little vague on that point."

Mariana and Dominic exchanged a look. He stood, went over to the shelf, and pulled out a thin, embellished book.

"This," he said, handing it to me carefully, "is a copy of the *Matris Libri*—the Book of Mothers. The original is, of course, in the Council vault. Even so, please handle it with care."

I opened the leather cover slowly. The first half of the book was filled with faded charcoal sketches of women that had clearly lived centuries ago. The closer I got to the end, the more modern the women became. I reached the last page and Adrian pointed at the bottom right picture. "That was Lucian's mother." He pointed to the photo on the left. "And that was my mother."

A soft smile came over Adrian's face as he looked at the woman in the picture. Her dark, wavy hair blew in the breeze as she stood on a sailboat on the brightest blue water I'd ever seen, against the backdrop of a white city.

"That's Greece," he explained. "She was going to become a biochemical engineer, according to her college transcripts. She was only twenty when I was born." The smile on his face faded. Twenty when he was born—twenty when *she* died.

"From the information we've gathered about these women," Dominic continued, "they were all noted in their communities as individuals of great intellect, skill, and drive. Women that most likely would have become religious martyrs, political revolutionaries, scientists, and mathematicians. And you can see for yourself their beauty." He leaned back and swirled the wine in his glass as though this were all regular dinner conversation. "Genetics appear to be an important factor. One theory is that demons choose handsome, intelligent women in order to produce similarly handsome and intelligent children."

I didn't mean to, but I laughed. They looked at me sharply, and I felt bad for breaking the moment.

"If that's the case, you've got the wrong girl," I explained.

Mariana frowned at me, clearly disliking that I'd interrupted her husband. "And why is that?"

I blushed. "Look, I'm—I'm okay to look at, but I sure as shit don't look anything like her," I said, pointing at the picture of Adrian's mother. "Pardon my French," I added, in his direction. "I also happen to be failing every class but art. I mean, I'm decently smart, I could be getting As if I wanted, but I don't really care about school. I'm not a savant. I'm not *different*. I know how to sew better than anyone I know, but if the formula for whipping up vampire babies is an unfair amount of beauty and an absurd amount of intelligence, I doubt I'm a candidate."

"I am fascinated that you are so glib with your own life," Mariana said, covering my interruption. "But we are not. Something *will* happen concerning you. Please do not disillusion yourself on this matter."

I bristled, but bit my tongue. She folded her hands in her lap, posture perfect, movements careful and measured, more like a marionette than a human being.

"Since Adrian is the closest to you in age," she continued, "and has a plausible excuse to be near you, the Council has assigned him as your primary guardian until the danger has passed. We will all, of course, be responsible for your safety, but any questions you have may be addressed to him. Please understand that, for the sake of your well-being, there may be subjects Adrian will not be permitted to discuss. If you try to acquire these answers in some other fashion, there will be consequences."

She paused to take a sip of wine, eyeing me over the rim of her glass. I kept expecting Adrian to pipe up with some funny, tension-relieving vampire trivia—but he didn't. Finally, she set the glass down on the table and settled back into her spot on the couch, never breaking eye contact with me.

"I must stress," she began again, "that while your relationship with my younger brother must be convincing, it cannot be authentic. Our law forbids relationships—of any kind—between our race and yours. When the danger has passed, you and Adrian will"—she paused, looking at him—"how do they say it now? 'Break up'? Publicly, of course. After which, you may return to your accustomed life—and we to ours."

If the silence had been awkward before, it was ten times that now.

"Sure," I said, the information stuttering through my brain. And then I blurted out, "Does he have a name? Your father?"

Mariana's eyes narrowed marginally. "He does."

But she didn't elaborate—and neither did Adrian or Dominic. I'd definitely trespassed into restricted territory.

Mariana was a tiny woman, smaller than me, but I felt like she could burn me with her eyes from across the room, like an evil, petite Superman. Maybe she could.

The thought was not comforting.

"All right, so, you'll just—keep me updated, on stuff?" I asked, eyes flickering back and forth between Dominic and Mariana.

They nodded in unison, which was just about the creepiest thing I'd ever seen.

"Okay then," Adrian said, standing, "now that we've unnecessarily terrified Caitlin, I'm going to take her home."

"It was very nice to meet you, Caitlin," Mariana said with a smile that I'm not certain had ever reached her eyes.

I nodded awkwardly at them, mostly because I couldn't bring myself to return the sentiment. I turned to where Lucian had been sitting to say good-bye, but he was gone. Adrian led me off through the library again, back through the elegant maze that was his house. We reached the front door and he helped me into my coat.

"That went all right," he said finally.

I snorted in disbelief, lacing up my boots.

He grimaced a little. "Yeah, that was awful, I'm sorry. I kept wanting to say something, but you don't know what it's like here. I'm in such an awkward—" He paused, rubbing his hands over his face. "Let's just say this is all unprecedented. I mean, this *never* happens. Humans don't know our business. And Mariana and Dominic are rarely around your kind anymore, so they've lost their tact."

I'd actually never seen them in town, even to get groceries or fuel up their cars. They were like gods up here on the mountain, looking down at the little townsfolk. If these were the people he grew up with, a lot of Adrian's initial standoffishness made a lot more sense now.

We walked through the snow to his truck and the moment he opened the driver's side door something sprang from the cab, ramming him back onto the lawn. I screamed, on edge from the recent threats. But when I looked closer, I realized the attacker was Lucian, and he and Adrian were wrestling—not to the death, as it first looked, but for fun . . . I think. After a few moments, Adrian had him pinned.

"You didn't expect me there," Lucian said with a wicked grin, chest heaving from the exertion of fighting someone almost two feet taller and a hundred pounds heavier.

"You're right," Adrian said. "I didn't. Especially since I told you to *stay out of my truck.*" His tone was stern, but the expression on his face wasn't angry. If anything, he looked amused.

"I forgot," the boy said impishly.

"Yeah, I bet you forgot. Just like you 'forgot' to clean your room yesterday."

Lucian continued to grin and Adrian shook his head. "How about I forget you were in there if you go up and clean your room like Mariana told you to. Deal?"

He hauled Lucian to his feet. The boy shook Adrian's hand to agree to the terms and sprinted back into the house.

I smiled. "Cute kid."

"He needs to stop popping out of nowhere."

"It wasn't that bad."

"You forget I can hear your pulse."

Ah—right.

We got into the truck and he backed out through what I had mentally dubbed "the palace gates." I wanted to ask him so many things, but I felt uneasy. To be honest, Mariana and Dominic had totally unnerved me. They were so *inhuman.* Perfectly human looking, but their mannerisms and speech patterns were precise and slow, like beautiful, creepy-ass puppets. I'd initially thought Adrian was aloof, but he was a circus clown compared to his aunt and uncle. Or, well, his sister and brother-in-law. Geez, I was never gonna keep this all straight. It wasn't that far between our houses, so we were pulling up to the ranch before I could find the words to voice any of my thoughts.

"Sorry I dragged you away from dinner," I said as he parked the truck in front of the house. "You want to eat with us?"

He seemed to consider it, then shook his head. "I'd better get back. Gotta take my medication."

I looked up at him curiously. "I thought your immune system kicked ass?"

He laughed. "Sorry, that's what we say when we need to drink—" He shrugged awkwardly. "Y'know."

"Oh," I said, blushing for some reason.

He looked down, obviously embarrassed. "It's kind of an inside joke. Not that funny, really."

I should have kept my mouth shut, but curiosity got the better of me. "Does it . . . taste good?"

He looked up at me for a long moment, before his gaze slowly drifted down to my neck. "You can't imagine."

My pulse jumped, half in fear and half in . . . something else. His voice had gone low and liquid, and his eyes were burning silver.

"Hey, Cait?" he murmured, and though he hadn't moved an inch, it felt as though he were leaning toward me.

"Yeah?" I whispered.

He wasn't looking me in the eye anymore, just staring somewhere above my chest and below my jaw. The sound of my own heart seemed loud in my ears, and if *I* could hear it, so could Adrian.

His eyes flicked back to my face. "You should really get out now."

I blinked. "Yeah."

I scrambled to undo my seat belt and almost fell out of the truck. I could hear the click of the automatic locks snapping into place the moment the door was closed. Adrian peeled out of the driveway, back into the darkness.

# 9

# DEATH SLED

The Saturday before Thanksgiving was bright, the sun sparkling off the snowy ground and trees like flakes of diamonds all fluffed up into piles. I was standing at the stove in my sweatpants and one of my dad-sweaters cooking French toast and bacon and everything felt perfect, for once. Nothing actually *was* perfect, but it felt like it, and I was perfectly willing to ignore reality, if just for the morning.

As usual, Rachel was sitting at the table going over paperwork. I'd long since figured that, between her and Joe, she had the head for math, which is why she did most of the bills and financing for the ranch. I glanced over and saw that her mug was empty. If I offered to refill it, she might want to talk. But I was in a good mood—I could risk it.

"More coffee?" I asked, holding up the pot.

"Sure," she said, looking surprised. "That'd be great."

I walked over and refilled her mug before sitting down to eat my French toast. Rachel set down her papers and slid her reading glasses off.

"Y'know, Caitlin," she began cautiously, "you and Adrian seem pretty serious. Did you want to invite him over for Thanksgiving?"

I choked on a bit of French toast. "I'll invite him," I said, still clearing my throat, "but I think he might want to be with his family."

"Okay," Rachel said with her usual smile, "just let him know that he's welcome here anytime. We'd like to get to know him."

I nodded and munched my breakfast cautiously, wondering if she'd say more, but she simply slipped her glasses back on and returned to the paperwork. I finished breakfast without having to engage in further conversation and headed upstairs only to find that my phone was ringing, which was weird, because nobody ever called me. Unfortunately, I couldn't tell where it was ringing *from*. I finally found it in the pocket of some jeans that were buried in my hamper.

"Hello?" I said, nearly dropping the phone.

"Cait?" It was Adrian.

"Hey, what's up?"

"What are you doing right now?"

"Uh—" I looked around. "Standing in my room? In my pajamas?"

"Get dressed; I'll be by your place in twenty minutes to pick you up."

I immediately tensed. "What's wrong?"

"Don't worry," he said. "And dress warm."

He hung up and I stared at my phone. He could really be arrogant sometimes. Didn't even ask if I wanted to hang out. Just assumed I had nothing better to do. The fact that I did not, actually, have anything better to do, was completely irrelevant.

I ran into the bathroom for a quick shower and dressed in dark skinny jeans, an off-white sweater, my feather-print infinity scarf, brown leather gloves, gray knit hat, and birthday boots, which I was just lacing up when I heard Rachel call up that Adrian was here. I raced down the stairs.

"Adrian and I are going out for a while, we shouldn't be gone too long."

"Okay," my aunt said with an amused smile that made me blush for some reason.

I opened the door and just about ran into Adrian.

"Hi."

I was a little stunned by his physical presence and had to crane my neck to look up at him. "You usually wait in the truck."

He smiled and closed the door behind me. "I wanted to surprise you. Actually," he said, pulling a thin, black piece of fabric from his pocket, "the surprise hasn't started yet."

"What?" I began to ask, but then he was wrapping the cloth around my eyes and tying it so I couldn't see. I frowned in his general direction. "Just for the record, saying 'The surprise hasn't started yet' while pulling something out of your pants is super creepy."

"Yeah—I regretted it immediately but it was too late to switch to something else."

"As long as we're on the same page." I felt my face with my hands. "Is this a blindfold?"

"No," he said dryly, "it's a kitten. Of course it's a blindfold."

He prodded me forward, one hand on each of my arms. I walked like a zombie, hands out, legs stiff.

"This would be a lot easier if you just trusted me not to let you walk into the truck."

I rolled my eyes underneath the blindfold. "How do I even know we're going to the truck?"

"We are. Don't make me use my Jedi mind tricks on you."

"My eyes are closed, so you can't."

He let out a sigh. "Just let me walk you to the damn truck."

I looked up at him—well, tilted my face in what I thought was the direction of his—and frowned. "Fine." I forced my legs and arms to go limp. He pushed me forward gently and we reached the vehicle without incident.

"May I ask where we're going?"

"That would defeat the purpose of the surprise," he said, pulling down the snowy drive after we were settled.

"At least promise me this won't be embarrassing. Or dangerous."

"Would I do that to you?"

I, well, "looked" at him with a heck-yes-you-would expression. Or as much of one as I could muster with half my face covered.

"I only embarrass you when it's necessary."

I snorted. The truck bumped along the driveway to the main road.

"Adrian," I said after a moment. "Now that I can't awkwardly make eye contact with you, we should talk about our fake-relationship rules."

There was a moment of silence. Then, "All right."

"So, I guess Rule One would be that you're not allowed to fall in love with me."

"Oh, yeah?" he asked, sounding amused. "What about you falling in love with me?"

I scoffed. "Why would I fall in love with you? You're just a hot, closet-nerd vampire with a bazillion dollars and a Harley. There's absolutely nothing attractive about you."

"I'm repulsive, I know."

"Yep. Rule Two," I continued, "is that if we're gonna be smoochy or huggy or whatever, there should be a formula."

"A kissing formula?"

"No—well, yes. More like an algorithm or something. X number of displays of public affection per week, multiplied by holidays and special occasions, divided by well-timed lovers spats and what-not. We could make a chore chart."

"What is a chore chart?"

I laughed politely, and then realized he was serious. "You don't know what a *chore chart* is?"

I think he may have nodded, then realized I couldn't see him, and finally said, "No."

I leaned back, flabbergasted, then tried to figure out how to explain what I thought every American kid already knew.

"It's a piece of paper you stick to your fridge with magnets. It has chores, on a chart, for different days of the week. So ours can be that, except for PDA Mondays and Wednesdays you give me a peck on the cheek, Tuesdays are extended hugs, Thursdays are real smooches, and Fridays we have off—or something. We can give ourselves stickers."

I was blabbing on about the stupid chore chart, but I was blabbing because it was finally dawning on me that I'd be hand in hand, lip on lip with this guy for who knows how long, and I barely knew him, and the thing was, he *was* attractive. He'd be so easy to like. Even without the money and the Harley and the expensive sweaters, he was just a cool dude. And he was a nerd. He was a *huge* nerd. And socially awkward. I loved it. I didn't love *him*—but I could. I could see myself maybe falling in love with him, one day, and since that seemed to be strictly forbidden, and just a bad idea anyway, I needed rules. I needed a buffer between this act we were putting on, and what I was really feeling. I needed a frickin' chore chart.

"All right," Adrian said finally, "you draw it up and I'll bring the stickers." There was a pause, and then he asked, quite seriously—"Is there a certain kind of sticker I should acquire?"

I pretended to think about it. "Gold stars are always a good choice—very classic. Or you could buy Valentine's Day stickers. That would be appropriate."

"Got it."

I knew with absolute certainty that he would show up to school Monday morning with a full assortment for me to choose from. He was very literal and endearing like that.

"Any other rules?"

I was about to say no, but then thought of something else. "Just one," I replied. "Don't lie to me. This is my life, and it's very weird right now, and I need you to promise that you won't lie to me."

There was a moment of silence. Then—"I promise."

I stuck my hand out blindly in his direction, and felt him grab it. We shook on it awkwardly and I settled back in my seat, feeling as though I'd taken a step in the right direction of gaining control of my life.

We'd listened through two full playlists on his phone by the time Adrian pulled the truck to a stop. He unbuckled my seat belt and pulled me across the bench seat and out his door.

"I am capable of independent movement," I explained, in case he had any doubts.

"True, but it's more fun this way."

I tried to glower through my blindfold. "Can I open my eyes yet?"

"No."

I heard him crunch through the snow to the back of the truck. I turned in a small circle to follow the noise of his movements.

"You're cute when you do that," he called to me.

"When I do what?"

"Turn in a circle like that. It's kind of penguin-y."

"Great," I called back. "Just what every girl dreams of being told by their inhumanly attractive, immortal vampire protector: they look kind of 'penguin-y.'"

"You think I'm attractive?"

I heard something land at my feet and I flinched, lost my balance with one leg, slipped on a patch of ice with the other, and was halfway falling when I suddenly found myself suspended in midair. I had no idea how Adrian had gotten to me so quickly or so quietly but, well, it was Adrian.

I pointed at my face. "Now can I take the blindfold off?"

Adrian propped me up again. "Yes, you may."

I dragged the cloth off my eyes and blinked into the bright white snow. I didn't recognize where we were. Definitely not in town anymore. If anything, we were higher in the mountains. I couldn't even pick out a road, just the tracks of Adrian's truck through the snow.

And that's when I spotted it.

"Oh, *hell* no."

He grinned at me, looking very pleased with himself. "I figured that since so much has happened in the past week or so, you deserved a little fun."

"Adrian," I said desperately, "the last time I tried this I was five and I ran into a brick wall."

He patted my shoulder. "That's why you're not steering."

I found myself being dragged to the edge of a very long, very steep hill.

"I really don't think this is a good idea," I told him as he set the sled down and then made me sit. He settled himself snugly behind me and reached around my waist for the rope. "I mean, you're immortal and that's fine and all, but I'm a sad, pathetic normal person. I break."

"Y'know what I think? I think you have major trust issues. And I think that since I'm both your fake boyfriend and your real body-guard, it's time we tried out some trust exercises."

"I don't think—" but I cut myself off with a high-pitched scream as Adrian kicked us off down the hill. I wanted to close my eyes, but not watching the trees whiz by was more terrifying than blindly hoping we didn't crash into one.

"Isn't this fun?" Adrian yelled in my ear.

"No!" I yelled back, grabbing his legs so I wouldn't fly off. He laughed loudly.

"Just relax!"

"If I relax, I *die*!"

The thing is, I'm not easily scared. I went on the stomach-dropping rides at Disney World. I kissed a frog once, when I was a kid, because it seemed like a good idea. I only had a few nightmares after watching *The Sixth Sense*. But Adrian was steering like it was the bob-sledding Olympics and he was trying to break a speed record.

Finally, *finally*, the hill evened out and we slowed, trailing to a stop at the edge of a small frozen pond in the middle of the woods. I leaned back against Adrian and closed my eyes, trying to get my racing heart to calm the crap down. He put his arms around my waist happily.

"That was fun."

"If you weren't my fake boyfriend, I'd beat you with a stick."

"You mean, if I weren't a vampire, you'd beat me with a stick."

"Yeah. That."

"You had fun. Admit it."

I opened my eyes and stared up at him. "You have no real con-cept of 'death,' do you?"

He shrugged. "We were never in any danger."

I muttered about showing *him* some danger as he slid off a

backpack I hadn't noticed him wearing and pulled out two pairs of ice-skates. Well, the small, white pair were skates—the large black ones looked like meat cleavers.

"Lace up, Ms. Holte," he said, tossing the smaller pair at my feet. As opposed to when his aunt—sister—sister-aunt?—had called me that, coming from him, it almost sounded like a term of endearment. 'Ms. Holte'—I kind of liked it.

I laced the skates on unhappily, knowing I was about to make a giant ass of myself out on the ice. It was hard to be average around someone like Adrian. I mean, I could kick his ass if we were competing on *Project Runway*, but the odds of that happening were slim to none.

"You ever done this before?" he asked, helping me take the blade protectors off.

I stared at the pond. "I've been to a rink two or three times. Nothing like this, though."

He grinned. "Perfect. Come on." He led me to the edge of the pond, holding on to my arms.

"I don't suppose I should even bother asking if the ice will hold us?"

He put his arms around my waist. I held on tightly as he pushed us out onto the lake.

"It's been below freezing for almost a month. Plus, it's only five feet deep—I've tested it out in summer."

All of a sudden he let go, and I clutched his jacket desperately. "What are you doing?"

"Just trust me."

He peeled my fingers off his coat and held me at arm's length so that only our fingertips touched, then skated backward expertly, forcing me to actually pick up my feet and skate with him. I concentrated on his skates, waiting for him to suddenly let go and sprint away from me. He didn't.

"You're smiling."

I looked up at him quickly. "No, I'm not."

"Oh. My bad. I thought you were having a good time."

"Nope. This is one hundred percent awful."

He nodded and slowed, holding my hand over my head, skating around me in a slow, graceful circle. Then he stopped and raised his hand, forcing me to spin in a slow, clumsy circle.

I grimaced. "I told you I wasn't good at this."

"You're doing great," he said with what sounded like sincerity. I looked up to check and then stared, puzzled.

"Why are your eyes glowing?"

His mouth drew up at the corner slightly. "I don't know."

I looked down, suddenly embarrassed, and not sure why. He put his right arm around my waist and held my hand, pushing me backward. We gathered speed and I had no idea how he didn't trip over my fumbling skates, but somehow he managed not to, and soon we were gliding gracefully, arching around the pond, spinning together from one end to the other. Eventually we glided to a stop near the edge, his arms still secured around my waist.

And—it was kind of nice, actually, to be held. I mean, I hadn't really touched a lot of people recently. In the hospital, I wasn't allowed to have contact with my mom, because the risk of infection was too high, for her. After that, I just didn't really want anyone to touch me.

But it was nice, standing here with him. It was more than nice.

Suddenly, I was afraid to look at him.

"You're right," I mumbled at his feet. "That was fun."

His hands tightened around me for a moment, and I risked a

glance up. He was smiling lightly, eyes still burning silver. "Told you."

We looked at each other a moment too long, and both became aware of it at the same time. He cleared his throat, letting me go, and glanced up the hill.

"You hungry? There's lunch in the truck."

I nodded and we sat and switched our skates out for boots, but when I tried to stand again, he nudged me so that I fell over onto the sled.

"What?" I asked, confused. "Aren't we going back?"

"Yep," he said, and picked up the handle.

"What, are you gonna *pull* me up the hill?"

He frowned at me in an amused sort of way. "Caitlin, I don't think you've really grasped the fact that I'm not fully human."

And with that he started jogging, pulling me behind him like I weighed nothing. I thought about mentioning that I might be human, but I could still *walk*, and then I realized he was pulling me up the hill faster than I could have run it, and I would've had to rest many, many times.

When we reached the top, I hid my amazement with sarcasm. "Am I allowed to stand now?"

He reached a hand down to me in reply. I took it and stood, watching as he threw the sled in the back of the truck before pulling out a small cooler. We hopped up onto the hood and he produced a thermos from out of nowhere. Adrian was like a sexy, scary Mary Poppins.

"Your aunt said you like hazelnut," he said, pouring me a cup of steaming coffee into a little tin cup.

"I do."

I was sort of touched that he'd taken the trouble to find out. For as much vampire trivia as I'd learned recently, there was a lot about *him* I didn't know.

He pulled out sandwiches wrapped in cloth napkins, little bags of fresh vegetables, and apple slices. I felt like I was in first grade again.

"So you're a chef as well as a vampire?"

"God no—I can barely slap together a PB&J. Mariana made the lunch. She's a bit of a foodie."

Part of me was really amused that Mariana had deigned to make a meal for little old human me, but all I said was, "Oh, good. It would be boring if you were incredible at everything." I winked at him to let him know I was kidding. "Speaking of food, my aunt wanted to invite you over for Thanksgiving. I told her you probably wanted to eat with your own family. You totally don't have to come if you don't want to."

He leaned back against the windshield, one arm tucked behind his head, which made his shirt pull up just enough for me to see a slice of rock-hard abs. The wind ruffled his hair and he looked like he should be in *Vogue*'s winter issue.

"I'd love to, but Julian'll be in town, and we already decided we'd have a big family dinner. I'd invite you over, but we always drink during the holidays."

It took me a second longer than it should've to realize he didn't mean alcohol.

"When it's bagged, and there's a fresh supply sitting right across the table—" He shook his head. "It's just not a good idea."

"Sure," I said, a little more high-pitched than necessary, and took a sip of coffee.

"But that brings up a good point: what to do about holidays. I suppose it's a little early in the relationship to spend Christmas Day together, but what about Christmas Eve?"

What odd conversations we had. "Sounds good. I'm sure my aunt and uncle would love having you over. Well," I amended, "I'm sure Rachel would love having you over. I think Joe's still warming up to the fact that we're an item." He smiled and I blushed. "What about your family? I should probably spend some time over there, so everything looks equal."

He seemed to consider this. "How about we come over to my place that afternoon and your place that evening?"

I nodded and took another bite of sandwich. He set down his apple and hopped down from the truck. "That reminds me—happy birthday."

I looked at him funny. "My birthday kind of already happened."

"I know, but I ordered your present and it just came yesterday."

"You got me something?" I asked, mouth full of sandwich.

He just smiled and rummaged through the backseat of the truck, returning with a brown-paper-covered box wrapped up in a red bow. He set it on the hood with a heavy thud.

"Geez, what'd you get me, a bowling ball?"

"I would be frightened to see you with a bowling ball in hand."

"Hey! I am completely average at bowling."

He smiled. "Open it."

I felt weirdly nervous as I set my sandwich down and untied the bow. The lid popped right off and I pulled out one of a dozen framed vintage couture gown designs. Really, really *old* couture gown designs.

"Wow," I breathed. "Where did you get these?"

"Mariana was apprenticed to a *couturier* once upon a time. I found them in the attic when I was a kid living at her old place in Paris, and she said I could take them."

I looked in the corner of the sketch and found a date. "But—these are from 1923."

He raised his eyebrow, as if waiting for something to dawn on me. It finally did.

"Ha! Right. 'Cause Mariana's, like, a hundred and fifty years old. Got it." He smiled and took another bite of sandwich. "But wait, how did you know I was into sewing?"

It wasn't really a secret, but I also didn't broadcast it at school. All the sewing stuff I'd brought with me to Stony Creek was boxed up in my room, and as far as I was aware, he'd never been in there.

He looked a little uncomfortable. "When our father picked you as his next target, we researched your family—standard procedure. We learned that your mother was a seamstress and that you both donated quilts to the neonatal ward at the hospital."

"Oh."

I wasn't really sure whether that was reassuring or creepy. We finished up lunch and headed back to the ranch. Adrian was right—it had been a fun day. But his comment about researching my family just drove home the fact that I was an assignment to him. Maybe we were actually friends, too, but we certainly weren't anything more. That shouldn't bother me—I tried to convince myself that it *didn't* bother me.

But on some level, it did.

# 10

## HYDROPHILIC INTERACTIONS, SIBLING RIVALRY, AND CHRISTMAS SHOPPING

I threw my pen dagger-style at my chemistry book, because my chemistry book deserved it. I was sitting in the de la Mara's monstrous library on one of the many overstuffed couches, surrounded by bearskin rugs and spiraling, two-story bookshelves.

"What in particular do you not understand?" Adrian asked, rappelling down from the ceiling and hovering above the coffee table where my homework was spread out. He was wearing military-issue pants, fingerless black gloves, and a tight black T-shirt. I'd spent the entire afternoon trying not to laugh at how absurd he *should* have looked rappelling around a library in partial military gear. Somehow, he pulled it off without looking like an ass. In answer to his question, however, I pointed at the textbook.

"That. I don't understand that."

He looked over at me, his body completely parallel to the ground. "You don't understand the entire book?"

I looked sad. "Yeah."

He nodded contemplatively, then grinned. "All right," he said, grabbing me. "Up."

I yelped as he pushed off from the coffee table, propelling us twenty feet in the air. Coming to a stop, he grabbed on to the lip of a bookshelf, bent his knees (while I clung to his neck for dear life—he was the one strapped in, not me), and catapulted us across the library toward the door, landing gently. Setting me down, he opened a large steamer chest and pulled out a harness similar to the one he was wearing, except ten sizes smaller.

"Put this on."

"Why?" I asked suspiciously.

He looked at me like the answer was obvious. "We're going to study."

I'd recently had the epiphany that when Adrian said things that didn't make sense, it was faster to just go along with it—eventually he'd always come around to explaining himself. I stepped into the harness and pulled it on. He helped cinch the straps so that I wouldn't fall out, then grabbed a connected pair of cords hanging from the ceiling and attached them to the carabiners at my hips.

Still holding on to the cords, he looked down at me. "When you want to ascend, just jump and the line will recede with you. If you want to go down, release the tension by pressing this button," he said, pointing to a shiny black button on the side of the harness. "I'll be moving us around the room, so you don't need to worry about that. You ready?"

I blinked at him. "I think so?"

"Good."

He grabbed my harness and threw me in the air like I weighed nothing. I rose almost thirty feet before gravity finally slowed me down. Adrian got a running start and jumped off the back of a couch, climbing through the air like a militarized Peter Pan until he was hanging opposite me.

"This is fun," I said with a happy smile.

"You're studying hydrophilic and hydrophobic interactions, right?"

"Yep. Hey, can you do a somersault in these?"

I leaned forward hesitantly, and the harness allowed me to pivot. Suddenly I lost my balance and fell forward, hanging upside down, and instantly realized I should have asked Adrian if the harness would stay *on* upside down. Luckily, it did. He grabbed hold of my ankle and pushed me upright, looking amused.

"Are you having fun?"

I just grinned.

"All right," he said. "Now *hydro* means 'water' and *philos* means 'love,' so *hydrophilic* means 'water-loving.' That means if you are a water molecule and I am, say, a glucose molecule, I will be attracted to you because we're both polar."

He propelled himself forward and grabbed hold of the cords connected to my harness so that we were hovering a mere half foot apart. I knew he was only talking about regular old science-y chemistry, but his voice had this natural purr to it that made me want to make a lame joke about *chemistry* chemistry.

"*Hydrophobic* is the opposite," he continued, blissfully unaware of my inner thoughts. "It's 'water-fearing.' Although that's misleading—it should be hydro-doesn't-give-a-rat's-ass. If you're, again, a water molecule, and I'm an oil molecule, you have poles, but I don't. We don't repel each other, exactly; we simply don't bond." He pushed off from me and floated five feet away.

I frowned at the distance between us. "I think I like hydrophilic better."

He didn't catch on. Which was probably a good thing.

"Do you understand now?"

"Yep. But that wasn't the part I was having trouble with." Adrian stared at me blankly. "Thanks, though; I liked the three-D demonstration." I smiled and did another somersault in midair, managing to get upright again without Adrian's help. I grinned at him and pressed the release button on the harness, plummeting toward the ground at a frightening speed. Luckily, I landed on an overstuffed couch, let go of the button, and bounced, doing another somersault on the way up with a lighthearted "whoo-hoo!"

Adrian crossed his arms, a smile clinging to the corner of his mouth. "So you think sledding down a hill is a near-death experience, but you don't mind doing gymnastics twenty feet in the air?"

"If I fall here, I'll land on a sofa," I said in a reasonable tone. "If we crash on a hill, I'll hit a tree. Sofa. Tree." I looked at him, holding out my hands and pretending to weigh the options.

He grinned and propelled himself toward me until he could grab hold of my cables again. "Is there anything else you don't understand?"

Oh, the things I didn't understand. But I shook my head, because I was having way too much fun with the harness thing to do homework.

"Good," he said with a slight smile. "Now—we're going to do something I've never done before that I've always wanted to try." For about two-and-a-half heartbeats, I thought he meant kissing me. But he followed his previous statement with "Lucian's not coordinated enough, Julian's got a stick up his ass, and Mariana and Dominic would rather die than do anything fun. So—you ready?"

I frowned at him, intrigued. "You haven't told me what we're doing yet."

He looked around the library and held out his arms, smiling the biggest smile I'd ever seen him smile. "We're going to play tag."

And he dropped straight down like a rock, hit a sofa, and bounced back up, landing on a bookshelf and using it as a springboard to leap a quarter of the way across the library. I laughed, heading toward the same bookshelf. I was about to push off when I paused.

"Are these steady?" I called to him halfway across the room.

"They're bolted to the floor, each other, and the ceiling. Just try not to knock any books off."

I grinned. "Okay!"

Carefully planting my bare feet on the ledge, I grabbed on to a cast-iron light fixture affixed to the edge, bent my knees, and jumped. I probably weighed half as much as Adrian, so I didn't get very far, but enough to reach another bookshelf and leapfrog myself off that one as well.

Waiting for me to get the hang of it, Adrian clung to the side of a shelf until I was only one spiral-formation away. Grinning, he jumped to one of the sliding ladders on the edge of the room. I followed on a ladder fifteen feet to his right. We both ran along the bookshelves, holding on to the ladders as they slid. Once they picked up momentum, we hopped on and rode them around the room. Luckily the tracks curved at the corners of the library, so we didn't crash into the walls.

Right when he reached the gigantic fireplace at the far end of the library—where the curved tracks abruptly stopped—he sprang off the ladder and flipped through the air to land, spiderlike, on a bookshelf twenty feet away. I jumped, too, landing ten feet lower, intending to climb up and tag him, since it seemed like I was "it."

But all of a sudden he let go and fell. I watched in a sort of slow-motion horror as he neared, grabbed me, and pressed the button on my harness. I was sure we were going to hit the ground, but at the last moment he pushed against the bookshelf with his legs and, wrapping his arms around my torso protectively, landed on an overstuffed sofa—the same one we'd sat on for the disastrous interview with Mariana and Dominic.

I stared, dazed, at the ceiling, my heart racing furiously. And then I went limp and laughed so hard my stomach hurt.

"That's odd," I heard Adrian murmur from underneath me a few moments later.

"What?" I said, trying to limit myself to an occasional happy chuckle as tears leaked down my face. I wiped them away with the back of my hand.

"I don't think I've ever heard you laugh before."

I wanted to turn around and look at his face, see what he was feeling—and at the same time I didn't.

I shrugged, still smiling. "I haven't run around like that in a long time."

"Endorphins."

"Mmm," I said, which he misinterpreted as an invitation for a verbatim recitation of the word's definition.

"When you participate in physically demanding activities, your body produces endorphins. *Endo* means 'inside,' and *orphin* is short for 'morphine,' so it's like morphine that your body creates to bond to receptors in your nervous system and dull pain, which makes you feel good."

I wriggled around to face him. "You're a huge word nerd, you know that, right?"

But it was a bad idea to turn around. Bad because my arms were resting on either side of his face. Bad because we were lying down. Bad because I was lying down on top of him. Bad because we were alone. Bad because the firelight made his silver eyes bright and deep and beautiful. Bad because my heart was racing suddenly, and the temperature had skyrocketed about fifteen degrees. Bad because his hand had somehow ended up on my hip, and bad because I realized I was basically straddling him.

"Am I interrupting?"

I was so scared I actually jumped about five feet in the air, doing an involuntary backward flip and hanging upside down with my hair pointing everywhere as a strange figure stared at me from the end of the couch.

"Hello, Julian," Adrian called from where I'd left him. He put his hands behind his head and smiled at his brother and then at me, looking amused.

I awkwardly flipped right side up again and felt all the blood drain back down out of my face. I blinked a few times and then looked at what was apparently Adrian's older brother. He was barefoot, too, wearing expensive jeans and a linen shirt that was completely unbuttoned, revealing a chest and abdomen so sculpted they looked fake. He had medium-brown hair that fell in a perfectly tousled mess a few inches shorter than Adrian's. I couldn't tell what color his eyes were from here, but something dark. He was different from Adrian, but certainly lived in the same sphere of physical perfection.

He smiled, but it wasn't a very nice smile. "You must be the infamous Caitlin Holte."

"Hi—yes—I mean, I am."

I closed my eyes and tried to concentrate on slowing my heartbeat, which, in the company of vampires, was way more embarrassing than my inability to speak.

"Be nice," I heard Adrian warn his brother from the couch, although he sounded more amused than threatening. I pressed the button on the harness, lowered myself to the coffee table, and hopped lightly to the floor. Trying to salvage some of my pride, I walked over and held out my hand.

"It's nice to finally meet you."

He grinned and shook it slowly. "The pleasure is absolutely mine."

He raised my fingers to his lips and placed a light kiss on my knuckles, his focus entirely on me. I was close enough now to see that his eyes were a curious brown-blue, a combination I'd never seen before. They were absolutely gorgeous.

"Julian, now that you're back in subfreezing weather, do you think it might be wise to dress more—natively?" Adrian asked drolly from his place on the couch. Julian looked down at his bare chest.

"Oh, I suppose. I've been used to being naked for so long, I forgot what clothing felt like." He glanced at me. "They paint me as an angel most of the time. And as everyone knows, angels fly around the heavens rejoicing in the Lord in the nude."

I swallowed. Adrian rolled his eyes.

"You're a model?"

"Something like that," he replied with a smile. "I don't need the money, but I do so love promoting the arts."

"Such a sacrifice," Adrian commented.

Julian smiled. "I do what I can." He draped himself across the opposite couch and asked, "So what're you kids up to?"

The word choice struck me as funny—and then I remembered he wasn't really our age. He *looked* fresh out of high school.

"We were just working on some chemistry homework," Adrian said coolly.

Julian slowly eyed the two of us, the corner of his mouth tilting up. "Uh-huh."

"Actually, I need to go finish, so why don't you two catch up while . . . I . . . do that."

I ran out of words, so I hopped on the coffee table and pushed off, landing on the middle of the bookshelf and propelling away from the brothers as quickly as possible. That much gorgeous was not good for a girl.

After a few seconds, I found our previous study station and let myself down onto the couch. I contemplated taking the harness off, then decided against it. I might need another fast escape.

As I sat down, the clasps and knots bit into my legs uncomfortably. I sighed and stood, mulling over what to do. Finally, I jumped into the air, pushed the button to lower me just a bit, and hovered parallel to the coffee table where my papers were spread out.

After struggling through homework for a few minutes, I slowly became aware that all the hairs on my arm were standing on end. I looked up from my textbook and saw a familiar pair of aviator goggles peeking just over the edge of the coffee table. The boy that went with them was perfectly still.

"Are you breathing, Lucian?" I asked, half afraid and half concerned.

I heard a deep intake of breath from somewhere below the surface of the table.

"Now I am."

I peered at him curiously. "Why weren't you breathing?"

He peered right back. "I forgot."

"You forgot?"

"Yeah."

All righty. "Why are you hiding underneath the table?"

He blinked. "Why are you on top of the table?"

Smart-ass. Cute little munchkin smart-ass.

"Good question. Why don't you come out so I can see you and we can talk some more? The couch is probably a lot more comfortable than the floor."

I swiveled the harness so my body faced the couch, but kept my gaze locked on his face. Lucian was an unknown entity. And I doubted he had Adrian's control, or Mariana's and Dominic's maturity—or at least, their natural reservation. There was a good possibility he viewed me as a snack.

He blinked again and slowly slithered out from underneath the table to crawl onto the couch. He turned around and sat limply, peering at me with his head tilted to one side, wavy brown hair sticking out in all directions.

"Isn't that more comfortable?" I asked with what I hoped was a friendly smile.

He seemed to consider. "Yes."

"Now what's all this about not having to breathe?"

He did a funny one-shoulder shrug. "Didn't need this so much back then."

It took me a second before I realized "this" meant "body."

"Where were you before?" I asked, trying to sound casual. I knew the answer, but I wanted to hear it from Lucian. Just because Mariana and Dominic believed all this stuff about demons and hell didn't mean he did.

He stared at me from behind his big goggles, his eyes too dark behind the tinted glass to see what color they were. He replied without blinking, without breathing, without moving a single muscle but his lips.

"Where my father lives."

I shivered. It seemed like a crazy question, but I had to ask it. "Did you like it there? At home?"

He tilted his head slightly farther to the side and held his hands in front of his face as if they were alien. "I didn't . . . I don't remember . . . these . . ." His expression turned frustrated. "Everything gets in the way." He let his hands drop limply at his sides.

"But, you can do lots of great things with those," I said, wondering why I was trying to convince him that having a body and being a quasi-human were great things. "I mean, you can pick up stuff and you can hug people and you can play."

He seemed to perk up. "I like to play."

I smiled encouragingly. "You do?"

The boy grinned. "Adrian plays card games with me." And then he frowned. "Nobody else does."

"Do you like Adrian?"

He nodded. "Adrian doesn't tell Mariana when I'm in his truck or when I do things people aren't supposed to do, like hang upside down. And he tells me stories when I go to sleep. I like to sleep. I like dreams." He paused and tilted his head again in consideration. "I like to be awake, too." He smiled. "I like blood."

We'd been doing great up until that last part.

"Why is your heart fast again?" Lucian said in that half-dead monotone of his.

"Because I'm happy to be talking with you," I said, only sort of lying.

"Your heart goes fast when you're happy?"

"Yeah," I said. "Sometimes. Sometimes it goes fast because of other things." And before he could ask what other things, I asked a question of my own. "Why do you wear those goggles all the time?"

He blinked at me through the semitinted lenses before answering. "Light hurts."

"Really? Why?"

"I never used them before," he said, tapping the glass slowly with his finger, indicating his eyes.

Oh.

"Are you Adrian's girlfriend?"

I was a little shocked by the abrupt turn of topic and could only come up with, "I, um—yes?"

He frowned. "What's a girlfriend?"

My cheeks blushed. I did *not* want to be the person to explain this to him. "Uh—well, a girlfriend's kinda like a wife, but not. I mean, Mariana is married to Dominic, and I'm dating Adrian, which is sort of like being married to him, but . . . not."

It was a really bad answer, mostly because it didn't make a whole lot of sense, but Lucian simply nodded once. Then he asked, "Do you play with Adrian?"

"Uh—"

Just then, I heard the telltale whisper of magnets rolling across the ceiling and looked up to find Adrian clinging to a bookcase twenty feet above us.

"Hey," I said, grateful for his timing.

He hopped down to float next to me. "Lucian," he said to his brother, "why don't you go ask Julian how his trip was? He can tell you stories about New York."

Lucian instantly scrambled over the back of the couch and disappeared. Adrian turned to me. "Sorry about him. He's got the body of an eleven-year-old and the social skills of a toddler." Before I could comment, he asked, "How's the homework going?"

I scrunched my face. "It's going. Did you and Julian catch up?"

A dark look passed over his face. "You could say that." He rubbed his hands over his eyes and peered down at the table. I'd never seen him look tired before. "Family dynamics are a little interesting when your siblings are old enough to be your parents or great-great-grandparents. We didn't get along back then, but I at least *knew* Julian from when I lived in Paris. I didn't even meet Mariana until I came here when I was twelve."

"That's hard," I said quietly. "I'm sorry."

"You're sorry," he said with a short, sharp chuckle. "Julian's an ass, my sister tried to scare the shit out of you, my father's after you, not to mention psycho-Lucian—I should be the one apologizing."

Without thinking, I touched his arm and said, "Don't." He looked up at me. "Besides Trish, you're the closest thing I have to a real friend. You have nothing to apologize for."

He smiled in a painful sort of way, and sat up. "Need some help with the rest of this?"

I nodded, smiling.

I muttered angrily.

"What was that?"

"I said I hate money."

Adrian looked at me strangely. "You hate . . . money?"

"Okay, I don't hate money; I hate not having a job, and therefore not having money."

"That makes more sense."

I was sitting at my desk, staring dully at my laptop as I searched Craigslist for jobs. Adrian was lying stomach-down on my bed, checking my math homework. The door to my room was, of course, open. I thought Joe was going to have a heart attack when he saw us head upstairs. I'd very intentionally left my door as wide as it would go.

"What kind of work are you looking for?" He sat up and peered over my shoulder at the screen.

"I'm not really sure. I mean, my mom taught me how to sew and knit and crochet and embroider and all that, and I'm pretty good, but what jobs can you get with those skills? It's a dead art. And even if it wasn't, what am I going to find in Stony Creek?"

Adrian set his chin on my shoulder and said "hmm" in a deep, rumbling sort of way as I continued my search. The nearest job that I was anywhere near qualified for was over forty miles away.

"What kind of stuff do you sew?" he asked finally.

I shrugged. "All sorts of things. I made that blanket on the bed, with my mom."

"This?" he said, leaning back and holding up the green quilt. "Wasn't this your Halloween costume?"

"Yep. I also made the dress I wore that night."

He looked up. "Really?"

"I've got a few other things I made here, but most of it's packed away in my grandma's basement. I've got whole books full of designs I've never made because I can't afford the materials. The kind of fabric I like to work with is stupidly expensive."

"Can I see them?"

I shrugged and reached over to my nightstand, pulling out my journals and setting them on the bed next to Adrian. While he opened the top one, I turned back to the computer and glumly continued searching.

"Cait?" I heard him say a few moments later.

"Hmm?"

"Can I borrow these?"

I was preoccupied by the job postings. "Sure. I'm not doing anything with them."

"Why not?"

I jerked a thumb at the corner of the room. "Pedal's broken on the sewing machine and I can't afford to get it fixed."

A pop-up ad for Christmas-themed greeting cards appeared. I needed to update my malware protection. Which also required money. Which reminded me—

"I forgot to tell you, I'm going with some girls from school to Queensbury to shop for Christmas presents."

He frowned. "That's forty-five minutes away."

"Yes, and it's got a mall."

He frowned again. "I don't like it. Too many people."

I frowned right back at him. "If someone starts trying to seduce me, I'll pull the fire alarm and scream for the cops and throw holy water on myself."

He didn't smile. "It's not funny, Caitlin."

I also didn't smile. "I have to buy presents."

"I'll come with you."

"It's a girl thing!" I protested. "We said no boys allowed."

"What is this, second grade?"

"Adrian," I said slowly, my patience wearing thin. "I cannot stay cooped up in this house or your house or school for the rest of my life. I understand the danger, but I'll be with five girls in a mall bursting with security guards and video cameras. I'll have my phone. I'll have pepper spray. It'll be the middle of the day. Unless there's some critical piece of information you're withholding from me, nothing is going to happen."

He lay back against my bed, scrubbing his hands over his face.

I stared at him, puzzled. "Are your eyes glowing again?"

He sighed in an annoyed sort of way. "Yeah. They do that whenever you worry me, which is all the time." He sat up before I could respond. "Listen, will you promise me that you'll stay with all of them—*all* of them—at all times?"

I held up my right hand. "I promise."

He shook his head. "This is a bad idea."

I leaned my chin against the back of my chair. "If it makes you feel any better, I'm not above biting people. And screaming really loud."

He smiled a bit. "I know that first hand from sledding. The screaming part, not the biting part."

"It's not my fault if you steer like a maniac."

"Did we hit anything?"

I rolled my eyes. "Noooo."

"Thank you."

"Whatever. Now, did I mess anything up on my homework?"

He winced. "Only a few things."

I narrowed my eyes at him. "Be honest."

"Why don't we go get you something to eat before we tackle this?"

"Tackle it? I thought I was getting better!"

"You are; this is definitely better than last time."

"But it's not good," I grumbled.

"Caitlin, you're not going to magically understand algebra. It'll take time."

I sighed at him. "Y'know, maybe it's a good thing all this happened. Otherwise you'd never have felt obliged to tutor me, and I'd be failing."

"You wouldn't be failing—you'd just not be passing."

"You're so encouraging."

"You told me to be honest."

"Earlier, not now!"

"Come on," he said, dragging me out of my chair. "Snack time."

———

Thanksgiving passed by in a blur of food. As soon as dinner was over I waddled up to my room and passed out from all the turkey voodoo that makes you sleepy. Adrian told me the next day that it was called "tryptophan" and I told him "Gesundheit." The day after Black Friday, he drove me to Stephanie's, and only said, "Be careful," before kissing me on the cheek—in front of everybody, of course—and driving away. We loaded up into Stephanie's mom's Suburban and headed out to Queensbury. To my surprise, Jenny came along—she never said anything to anyone at lunch or raised her hand in class. I honestly forgot she was *there* half the time. If it was possible for someone to be more of a loner than I was, she was it.

When we finally arrived, the mall was packed, and it took us twenty minutes just to find a parking space. We headed in through the food court and I realized it had been over a year since I'd been shopping.

I actually really liked shopping. A mall was like a giant Pinterest board where I could soak in design ideas and simultaneously feel good about myself, knowing that I'd created clothing that was higher quality than what could be found in many of the stores.

It was good to be back.

"Welcome to Aviation Mall," Stephanie said cheerfully as we stepped inside. I didn't talk to her much (actually, I didn't talk to anyone much besides Trish), but she was the definition of cheerful. A little plump and shorter even than me, she always had a pair of woolen mittens hanging around her neck that gave her the appearance of a Good Christmas Spirit.

"Where to first?" asked Laura, another girl I'd barely spoken to since coming to Stony Creek. She was very practical and oddly stern, dressed in sensible winter clothes in various shades of brown. She already had a little spiral notebook in hand, and I would've bet money she had a list of every store she needed to go to with exactly what she wanted to buy.

"Why don't we just wander around?" asked Meghan—Laura's antithesis in every way. She was wearing a red plaid miniskirt over faded black skinny jeans, a pair of black combat boots, a red shirt with wide sleeves, and a black corset, half covered by the knee-length Victorian coat she wore. She was the one who'd wanted to be a slutty bunny for Halloween.

Stephanie looked back and forth between them, and I could sense her powers of mediation bubbling to the surface. "We could always split up and meet back at the food court for lunch?"

I panicked and said, "No!"

Everyone stopped and looked at me.

"I mean, it would be better to stick together. Safety in numbers."

"Uh, Mystic?" Trish said. "We're in a mall."

"I know, but, look, Adrian's really worried because I'm new to the area and I've never been here and he thinks I'll get lost."

Trish snorted and said, "He's probably right," while Laura muttered, "Overprotective, much?"

"Anyway," I started again, "I promised him I would remain with all of you at all times."

"I have stores I need to get to," Laura said, crossing her arms.

Meghan cocked her head to the side. "And I have no i-*dea* where I need to go."

I was afraid the two were about to have a showdown, which seemed to be a regular thing for them.

"Look," I said, trying to keep the peace, and my promise. "Why don't we make a list of the stores we know we need to go to, spend twenty minutes tops in each of them, and then if we have time, we can hit whatever other stores we want?"

There was a moment of silence as everyone considered this plan.

"Sounds good to me," said Trish finally. "Where should we go?"

"I've already made a list!" Laura cried, waving her notebook.

Everyone crowded around, planning the route we'd take through the mall. I didn't know what I wanted to buy, so I looked around, letting them decide. To be honest, it was weird not having Adrian around. He *had* become my shadow, and here in the enormous crowd with the Christmas music and crowds and constant tumble of voices echoing off the tiled floors, it was more than a little unnerving to know he was not within screaming distance. Which, in and of itself, kind of irritated me. I only had his family's word that I was even in danger, and here I was, letting myself be scared.

"Excuse me, miss, would you like to try a sample?" a young man standing next to a kiosk asked me, and I jumped because now I was thinking about Adrian's father looking for me at the mall and I just realized there were guys *everywhere*.

"No thanks," I said, turning back to the girls.

"It's free," he persisted.

"I don't wear perfume." I turned, but he touched my jacket and I flinched.

"It'll only take a moment." Were his eyes glowing? Did he seem way, way too persistent here?

I smiled tightly and said, "No, thank you," before turning back to the girls and urging them on.

"Where are we going first?" I asked, anxious to get away from the creepy salesman.

"Victoria's Secret."

"Victoria's—why?" I asked. "I thought we were shopping for Christmas presents."

Meghan smiled wickedly. "We *are*."

In a daze, I followed them into the store. I'd been in there once, a year ago, when my friends back home had made me go in as a birthday dare to try stuff on. Entering the store again, I was just as uncomfortable now as I'd been then.

"You look like you've never seen lingerie before," Trish said in her usual blunt fashion.

I crossed my arms over my chest, bristling. "I've *seen* it before."

Meghan held up a black satin teddy fringed with lace. "This is hot."

"Let me see that," Trish said. She pivoted to face me and held the hanger against my throat. "What size are you, Mystic?" she said, eyeballing the scrap of cloth against my body.

"Why does it matter?"

"Because you want to make it a very merry Christmas for a certain someone." She checked the price tag. "Ooh, maybe not that merry. Let's keep looking."

I stopped dead. "Wait, what are you talking about?"

Trish raised her eyebrow. "What do you *think* I'm talking about?"

My brain still wasn't working through the implications, and I didn't answer. Trish shook her head sadly. "We are in a lingerie store. Buying Christmas presents. Who would *you* buy lingerie for?"

I stared at her blankly. "My . . . aunt?"

Trish and Meghan burst out laughing.

"Mystic, I am sure as hell not talking about your aunt!"

"She means Adrian," Jenny said quietly. I hadn't even heard her walk up.

I turned bright red. I'm not sure I'd ever blushed that hard in my life.

"Oh."

The girls saw my reaction and it just set them off even more.

"So you've—never, with Adrian?" Stephanie asked, trying to sound tactful.

"Uh . . ."

"Mystic, I can't believe you've never had your way with that boy," Trish said, still laughing.

"My way? My way is not a way, it's a non-way. There is no way-ness happening," I stuttered.

Trish actually had to lean against a bunch of glass drawers filled with underwear to support herself, she was laughing so hard. People were starting to stare at us.

"The hottest thing that ever hit Stony Creek finally got himself a girlfriend, and they're not doing it," she said sadly, shaking her head. "Kinda makes you wonder what's wrong with the world."

"Wait, so how far *have* you gone?" Meghan asked.

"I don't want to talk about this anymore!" I threw my hands up and walked away.

From behind me, I heard Laura say, "As fascinating as Caitlin's nonexistent sex life is, I just want a new white bra," followed by Trish saying, "Nuh-uh; we're gonna get you something in leopard print."

I wandered toward a section of the store that seemed less threatening—pajamas—and pretended to check the price tags on cotton T-shirts and flannel pants. Someone cleared their throat and my heart jumped into my throat when I turned and saw it was a young man.

"We're having a sale on underwear today—"

But I ran past him before he could finish. Since when did guys work at Victoria's Secret? Was that even allowed? I spotted Jenny looking up at a rack of furry satin robes and headed over to her.

"Hey," I said, trying to calm myself down. I was starting to think shopping hadn't been such a good idea after all.

"Hey," she said back, then continued to stare at the robes.

"Where is everybody?"

She glanced over at the dressing rooms. "They kidnapped Laura and said that we couldn't leave until she'd tried on something color-ful."

"Poor Laura," I said, meaning it. "Are you getting anything?"

She was back to staring at the robes. "I need some socks."

"There you are," I heard Trish say from behind me. "I found something perfect for you, and don't worry, it's hot enough for de la Mara."

She grabbed my arm and dragged me toward the corner of the store. I was shoved into a dressing room with a single hanger in hand.

"Come out and show us when you have it on!" Meghan called from the other side of the door.

I looked down at what I was holding, wondering how I'd gone from talking innocently with Jenny to trying on lingerie. The hanger I was holding had a dark green . . . thing. I peeked my head out the door and whispered, "I don't even know how to put this on."

Trish rolled her eyes. "Just undo the hooks in the back; it's not that hard."

They shooed me back into the dressing room. I turned the hanger around and saw that whatever it was, it did indeed have a short row of hooks. Feeling completely stupid, I shrugged out of my shirt, knowing they wouldn't let me leave until they'd seen it on. After a few minutes of wrestling and muttering obscenities under my breath, I faced the mirror—and stared.

I'd never really considered myself an especially attractive or unattractive person, just somewhere in the everyday middle, and never once in my life had I heard the term *sexy* associated with the word *Caitlin*, but I would almost dare to use it now. The Green Thing, as I'd so cleverly begun to call it (because it was green), was basically a corset, sheer from the bosom down, with boning sewn into the lace. The back was—well, there *was* no back, except for the tiny row of hooks that met just above my rear end, leaving the entirety of my spine exposed. The bodice was covered in iridescent beads, tiny sequins, and surprisingly intricate lace. I basically looked like Tinker Bell, if Tinker Bell had been possessed by a Playboy Bunny.

Slowly, I opened the door. Trish, Meghan, Stephanie, Laura, and Jenny were leaning against the wall. When they saw me step out, they all stared.

"You have breasts," Trish said, sounding surprised.

"You look amazing, Caitlin, and that shade of green perfectly matches your eyes," Stephanie said in an encouraging sort of way. Of course she found something wholesome about lingerie.

"You do look curvy," Laura commented. In her hand, I saw a neon-pink bra on a hanger.

I grimaced. "They got you, too?"

She nodded sadly.

"Mystic, you have got to buy this."

I snorted at Trish. "No way."

Meghan looked at me like I simply didn't understand what was going on. "Did you look in the mirror?"

"Yes, but—look, I wouldn't ever wear this!" I protested. "Besides, there's no way I can afford it."

Trish looked at the tag. "You're in luck, Mystic; it's fifty percent off!"

"That's still fifty percent I don't have."

"Fifty percent that works *miracles*," Meghan countered. She grinned suddenly. "Besides, I bet Adrian would reimburse you. In more ways than one."

I turned bright red. "Guys, I can't spend money on myself at Christmas! I barely have enough to buy presents for my family."

Trish frowned at me and then nodded. "All right, all right."

I eyed her suspiciously, but she just looked defeated. A little too defeated. I headed back into the dressing room, closed the door, and looked in the mirror one more time. It did look good. But they didn't understand that Adrian and I weren't really dating. And even if we were, we wouldn't . . . do . . . what they thought we would do. He was a freaking *vampire*. How would that even work? I mean, I guess it would work like it would normally work but, just, no.

But it did look good.

I struck a few stupid "sexy" poses just for fun, then rolled my eyes at myself and took it off, putting my comfy, oversize blue sweater back on. When I opened the door, Trish and Meghan had their heads together, whispering intensely, but looked up when they heard me set the Green Thing on the return rack.

"Are we ready to go?"

"Actually, I wanted your opinion on something," Meghan said, grabbing my arm. She pulled me over to a table that held half a dozen dismembered legs.

"Do you like the diamond pattern better, or the fishnet?"

"Uh . . ." I wasn't an expert on hosiery. But the diamonds looked a little less hooker-y. "Diamonds."

"Really? Because I also kinda like the rosettes."

We stood there for another ten minutes talking over the specific details of each pattern until I was ready to pick up the mannequin thigh and slap Meghan in the face with it. Finally, the rest of the girls walked up to us.

"Okay," Meghan chirped brightly. "Thanks for your help!"

"Which one are you going to get?"

"None of them. I still can't decide."

I closed my eyes and let out a long breath. I liked to browse as much as the next person, but I had my limits.

"Let's go!" Trish said.

I was so eager to get out of there I didn't realize, at first, that I had turned left when everyone else had, apparently, turned right. For a few seconds, I stopped dead, looking around in panic as I blocked the walkway. The mall was packed, and I took shelter by a kiosk to stay out of the flow of rabid Christmas shoppers, trying to spot Stephanie's signature knit hat, but I was jostled roughly by a passing shopping bag.

"I'm so sorry," the man said, grabbing my arm to steady me. "I was trying to avoid that lady with the stroller and I ran right into you. Are you okay?"

"I'm fine," I said, backing away. He was cute, five o'clock shadow, nice jacket, shopping bag from an upscale store—and he set off my danger radar big-time.

"Oh," he said, looking down, "you dropped your list."

He reached down at the same time I did, and his hand brushed mine. I snatched the list of stores and stood, feeling ridiculously creeped out. Which was stupid, because nothing about this guy was overtly creepy. He was probably just a normal Christmas shopper trying to be polite and apologize for bumping into me. Adrian was getting in my head too much. And despite him saying I didn't have to be scared of all men, I *was* scared of all men. Which was bullshit.

"Thanks," I said, smiling politely. I was about to open my mouth to say more when right behind me, I heard someone exclaim, "Caitlin! Is that you?"

I turned, and there in all her petite, chic glory, was Mariana.

"It *is* you!" she exclaimed, taking my arm and leading me away from the shopper man. Her smile was tight, her words were rehearsed. She looked so gargantuanly out of place, stuck in among the humans. As soon as we were out of earshot of the man—who was staring after me strangely—Mariana whispered, "We discussed your trip and decided I should come along just in case."

I stared at her. "Was that *him*?"

Mariana shrugged, eyes constantly scanning the crowd around us. "I cannot tell. The number of people makes it impossible to determine if anyone is a void."

Another new term. Yay. "What's a void?"

"A being who does not emit emotional energy. Vampires cannot sense one another, or demons, just as demons cannot sense us. Crowds muddle our perception, which is why we did not want you coming to a place as populated as a . . . mall."

*My apologies, oh great Vampire Lady, for wanting to get some Christmas shopping done, at Christmastime. What an absurd thing for me to do.*

I raised an eyebrow at her. "If it *was* him, do I need to be worried?"

Mariana shrugged, which was not comforting. "I doubt he would try anything here, and I will be watching you for the remainder of your time. Just try not to draw attention to yourself."

I suppressed a smart reply. Draw attention to myself? Right, I would definitely do that, because I'm a moron.

Mariana melted back into the crowd just as Trish finally wandered back to me, craning her neck at Mariana's retreating figure. "Was that Adrian's aunt back there?"

Unable to think of a quick lie, I said, "Yeah—just ran into her. Crazy."

"A lot of people from all over Warren County come here. Though it would have been really funny if she'd seen you in Victoria's Secret."

She grinned at me while I shook my head—and then realized Mariana probably *had* seen me go into Victoria's Secret. We caught up with the rest of the girls and Laura kept us moving with her notebook of tasks, getting us to the food court by one thirty. Just as I was about to take my first bite of pizza, I thought I saw a man looking at me. I peered closer and realized that he was actually waving at someone behind our table who was walking over with a tray of food. But I soon found three other guys I swore were eyeing me creepily. Swallowing, I looked over at Trish's shopping bags.

"So what'd you get?" I asked to distract myself from my hyper-awareness of *men, men, everywhere men!*

She wrapped her tongue around a string of cheese hanging from her pizza. "I got my parents a record player because our old one broke, like, ten years ago, and my dad's got a ton of stuff on vinyl. I got Paul a new case for his rifle, I got Mark a new dartboard, and I got Jimmy a flask with his name etched on it. They're all in college," Trish said when I looked at her quizzically. "Paul's the oldest, he's about to graduate, and Mark's a junior. Jimmy's a freshman and he's getting married this summer. I told him he's crazy, and he just smiles and says he is in love. Speaking of love, well, let's just say I got Ben's present at our first stop."

Meghan and Stephanie made an "oooh" sound. I was confused.

"Wait, Ben? As in, our class Ben?"

"Yep. Finally got the guts to ask me out at the Halloween party." Trish smiled happily.

I still couldn't wrap my mind around it. "The big guy that never talks in class?"

"That's the one."

I couldn't believe she'd been dating somebody for close to a month and I hadn't known. She'd never said a thing about it. I made a silent vow to get my head out of my butt and start paying better attention to the one person who'd gone out of her way to befriend me.

"Geez, well, congratulations! Sorry I'm a horrible person for not knowing that."

She laughed and shrugged. "We're not exactly licking each other's faces off in public or anything. Anyway, what did you get?"

I shrugged unhappily. "I got Norah this old hardcover of *Black Beauty* because she's into horses, I got my aunt a new iron because our old one is about to bite the dust, and I got my uncle a bunch of wool socks." For some reason, no one thought that was a crazy gift idea.

"Yeah, my dad's always running out of them."

"When you're outside working most of the day, they get worn out pretty quick," Meghan agreed.

"They're nice. Like, Scottish wool or something," I mumbled. I still felt bad for getting him socks, but he said he needed them.

"What did you get Adrian?" Meghan asked.

I looked up sharply. "Shit," I said, realizing that I'd completely forgotten him. "I totally didn't get him anything."

Out of the corner of my eyes, I saw Meghan flinch, like she'd just been kicked under the table.

Trish smiled at me innocently. "I'm sure he'll just be happy to see you on Christmas. He seems like the selfless type."

"Yeah," I agreed warily. She was up to something.

"Is there anywhere else anyone wants to go?" Stephanie asked.

Laura shook her head. "I'm finished."

I felt bad not getting something for Adrian, but I couldn't think of anything last minute, and it seemed like everyone wanted to leave. Maybe I could scrounge something up in Stony Creek later.

We stood up and gathered our things before heading out to the Suburban. The sun had disappeared behind low clouds and it looked like it might start snowing again. We all crammed in, throwing our purchases wherever they fit.

"I can't believe I forgot to get Adrian something," I muttered to myself a few miles down the road. I thought I'd spoken quietly, but apparently Trish heard me.

"Well, Mystic, we thought that since you're so poor and all this year, and Adrian's so . . . *Adrian*, we'd buy his Christmas present for you."

All the blood drained out of my face. "You didn't."

Trish grinned. "We did." She looked incredibly proud of herself.

"*We?*" I asked in disbelief.

"Yep, all of us."

I turned to Jenny. "Even you?"

She smiled a very small smile.

Meghan turned around from the front seat looking smug. "And we're too far away to go back and return it, and it was clearance, so you *can't* return it."

I closed my eyes and concentrated on breathing.

"You okay, Mystic?"

When I was sure I wouldn't kill anybody, I opened my eyes. "Thank you, guys. I appreciate your . . . efforts . . . on my behalf." Either they missed the sarcasm or they chose to ignore it.

"Don't forget to tell Adrian we said 'Merry Christmas.'"

I smiled tightly. "I'll pass that along." Over my dead body.

"Look, guys, it's snowing again!" Stephanie exclaimed from the driver's seat. They all turned to stare out the windows at the falling flakes, and I took the opportunity to sink into the cushions red-faced.

"Do you really not like it that much?" Jenny asked. We'd ended up sitting next to each other in the back.

"It's not that," I said, letting out a breath. "It's just . . . we're not . . ." I waved my hands in the air as if that could explain the thing that we weren't.

Jenny nodded. "That's okay."

I smiled at her tiredly. "Thanks."

My thoughts were drowned out by the sudden blast from the speakers and everyone besides me and Jenny burst into song as "Grandma Got Run Over by a Reindeer" played over the radio.

When we pulled up to Stephanie's house, a familiar black truck was parked in the driveway.

Trish grinned. "Don't forget to tell him to have a Merry Christmas."

I flipped her a mostly friendly bird in reply, which she laughed at.

We piled out and Trish stuck the Victoria's Secret bag in my hand. Everyone overeagerly said good-bye and watched me climb into the passenger seat of Adrian's truck. I set my packages on the floor, the bright pink Victoria's Secret logo screaming for attention. Adrian started the engine and backed out of the driveway, but glanced down occasionally at my feet.

"What'd you buy?" he said with the hint of a smile on his face.

I blushed. "Just some socks and an iron and a book."

"I didn't know Victoria's Secret sold irons."

I crossed my arms over my chest in a classic five-year-old move. "I don't want to talk about it."

To his credit, I think he tried his best to suppress a smile, but he didn't quite succeed and it was enough to throw me over the edge.

"You wanna know what I got at Victoria's Secret?" I asked, ripping at the bag. I pulled out the Green Thing and held it in his face. "This! I got *this*. No, *I* didn't get this, they went behind my back and bought it for me! No!" I corrected myself again. "They bought it for *you!*"

"Caitlin," Adrian said calmly, "I can't see the road."

I took the Green Thing out of his face and slumped in my seat, shell-shocked.

"I take it shopping was a bit stressful?"

I kept staring in horror at the road. "They wouldn't stop talking about it. How am I supposed to answer those types of questions? You're the hottest guy in Warren County and now they know I'm *not* sleeping with you. They've taken it upon themselves to get us laid."

I heard something from my left and looked over. Adrian had one hand covering his mouth, trying not to laugh.

"You think this is funny?" I asked him in a low, dangerous voice.

He glanced over at me. "Cait, you gotta admit—"

"*I had to try this on,*" I said in the same low tone. "Do you know how hard it is to hook those tiny little infuriating hooks?" I didn't wait for him to answer. "*Really* hard. And now they expect me to actually *wear* it. For. You." He turned the corner into the ranch's long driveway. "How am I going to get it into the house?" I whispered in horror.

"Look, I don't care what you tell them. If it makes it easier, tell them that you wore it. Tell them that I liked it. Tell them whatever you want. In the meantime, you can put it in here."

He parked and handed me a brown paper grocery bag. I stuffed the Green Thing in it and scrunched down the top so there was no chance of anyone looking inside.

"Thanks," I mumbled, and opened the door.

"Oh, and Caitlin?"

I turned back to look at him. He grinned at me.

"Tell the girls I said 'thank you.'"

# 11

## 'TWAS THE NIGHTMARE BEFORE CHRISTMAS

Someone was playing the drums. The slow, constant rhythm echoed in my head, beating along to the blood rushing through my veins. My brain felt sluggish, I couldn't figure out where I was, and my limbs were like magnets weighted to the ground.

No—to the bed.

I was in a bed. The drums were in my head, behind my eyes. But it wasn't a beat, it was a . . .

*Beep.*

*Beep.*

*Beep.*

It was my pulse.

I wasn't groggy anymore, I was wide-awake and somehow completely paralyzed.

The *beep* accelerated, sharp and high. I finally wrenched my eyes open.

"Ah, there's our patient," a familiar voice called from far away. But the voice was wrong, distorted. The darkness peeled back just enough for me to make out two figures coming toward me, one with burning white eyes.

It was Adrian—and my mother.

She wore a starched white nurse's uniform from another era, and hung limply from Adrian's arms, her eyes milky and dead.

"You wanted your mother back," he explained. But it wasn't Adrian's voice. It was deeper, and echoed as if it were coming from far away. "Here she is."

"I love you, Caitlin," my mom whispered as the Adrian-thing laid her on my hospital bed, tucking her face gently against my neck.

I lay completely immobile, but the screams inside my head echoed the screams of my heart monitor.

"I want to come home, sweet pea." I could feel her cold, slimy lips against my cheek. "Don't you want me to come home?"

The shriek of the heart monitor abruptly stopped.

"I just need to build my strength, Caitlin. I need a way to come back. A little . . . snack."

My lungs unlocked and I screamed just as her inhuman teeth ripped into my neck. She tore into my windpipe until I was breathing my own blood, drowning in it, watching her filmy eyes roll like marbles in her head.

Adrian observed, passive.

It felt like hours later when I finally opened my eyes. I didn't just snap awake out of the nightmare, it was like I had to drag myself up through layers of heavy, damp curtains. When I could, I sat up quickly and ripped the covers off, feeling my neck.

It was whole, just like it should be.

I reached over to my nightstand and snatched my phone, searching through the contacts with shaking hands until I found the number I was looking for, actually dropping the phone once before getting it successfully to my ear. It picked up on the third ring.

"Hello?" Adrian answered, sounding groggy.

"Adrian?" I was shaking too badly to get anything else out.

"What's wrong?" he asked immediately. "Are you all right?"

I tried to collect myself. "I'm sorry," I said, voice trembling. "I had to make sure."

"Make sure of what? Caitlin, did something happen? *Are you okay?*"

"No," I managed to get out. "I just . . . I had a nightmare."

"A nightmare?"

"Yeah," I said, already feeling stupid for calling. "But I've never had one like that before."

I heard him let out a breath on the other end of the line. "You sure that's all? You're not hurt?"

I let out a breath of my own and tried to suck the next one in slowly. "No, I'm not hurt. I thought I was. I had to call you to make sure it wasn't real."

"Okay. Tell me what you saw." His voice had settled back down to its usual low rumble.

I drew the covers up again, suddenly cold, afraid to be exposed to the darkness.

"You were there," I said, my voice breaking as the first wave of tears hit. "And you were carrying my m-mom in your arms."

I pressed my eyes into the back of my hand and clenched my teeth. Finally, I put the phone back up to my ear, trying to breathe. "She said she wanted to come back."

I couldn't go on. Adrian let a couple seconds pass in silence.

"Where did she want to come back to?"

My whole body trembled. "Here. She wanted to be alive again. And then she bit me."

"She—*what?*"

"I had to make sure it was a dream."

"Damn it," I heard Adrian say, but he wasn't talking into the phone. "Okay. Caitlin?"

"Yeah?" I whispered, trembling uncontrollably as I turned my face into my pillow to hide my eyes from the dark room.

"I want you to turn on your light."

"No," I whispered, horrified, curling into a tighter ball underneath my covers. There was no way I was moving.

"Caitlin," he said in his reasonable voice, "nobody is in your room. I'm not in your room. Your mother is not in your room. Your mother loved you, and she would never, ever hurt you. Now, I need you to turn your light on."

"Please don't make me do this," I whispered into the phone, clutching it so hard my hand hurt.

"I need you to turn on your light," he repeated.

My heart was beating so fast I thought it might explode.

"I can feel your fear all the way from my house, but I can't take it away over the phone. I can't come over there. You have to do it. Turn on your light."

I stopped breathing. Just held the air inside my lungs until it hurt. And then I let it out slowly. "Keep talking."

"All right. Did you study for your history midterm?"

I took another breath and let some of my muscles relax. "Not really."

"You going to wear my Christmas present to the exam?"

"What?"

"My Christmas present. The Green Thing?"

"Why would I wear that to an exam?"

"Well," he replied in a smug tone, "it looked pretty effective."

I sat up. "Just what is that supposed to mean?"

"All I'm saying is if you want to pass, you might want to wear it to the exam. Are you sitting up yet?"

"Yes, but—" Then I got it.

"Turn on the light before you lose your nerve."

I reached out and switched on the bedside lamp before I could think about it too hard. The room flooded with a soft, gold glow.

"Anybody there?" Adrian asked.

I looked around, even peeking over the sides of my bed before I admitted, "No."

"Good," he said brightly. "Oh, and by the way, I don't actually think you should wear it to school. People might think you were trying to make me jealous."

I smiled wearily. "Yeah, well, they also might think I'm a hooker."

"Nah. Stripper, maybe."

I smiled. "What time is it, anyway?"

"About four thirty."

"Wow, well, my bad for calling at the buttcrack of dawn."

"Don't be. I was about to wake up anyway."

I frowned. "Why?"

"I usually wake up at five and do a few laps in the pool."

There was no way. No one in Stony Creek had a pool, not this high up in the mountains. But it was Adrian. Adrian defied most of the laws of physics. He could certainly have a pool in the mountains. He could have a pool in space, for all I knew.

"Right. And where, exactly, do you store this pool?"

"The east wing."

"Your house is absurd."

He laughed. "I'll pick you up in a couple hours. Call me if you need anything."

"Will do."

*Wouldn't* do, actually—now that the last dregs of the dream had been shaken off, I felt really stupid. I was seventeen years old. That was a decade too old to be having nightmares. I was fine. Nothing had happened.

A few minutes later, my eyes were heavy. I leaned my head back and drifted off to sleep.

This time, I did snap awake, to the sound of my alarm going off. My lamp was still glowing softly. No dead nurse moms or crazy-eyed Adrians. Probably safe to get out of bed.

A half hour later, I headed downstairs having showered and dressed. Snow was still falling outside, peacefully.

"So," Rachel said when she saw me, "which is it today? Are you going to Adrian's, or is Adrian coming here?"

I reached for a mug. "I'm not sure yet."

Her lips pursed. "You two spend an awful lot of time together."

"I hear that's what couples do."

"I know," Rachel said as Norah stumbled tiredly down the stairs. "Just keep in mind that there's more to life than boys."

Dual flames of irritation and amusement coursed through my stomach. Part of me wanted to say *back off* and the other part of me wanted to tease her for being worried. I compromised with "Duly noted."

"Joe and I just wished we saw more of you. Sometimes you leave for school and then we won't see you until dinner."

"We can come here today. After school, I mean."

Rachel smiled at me. "That'd be nice."

Twenty minutes later I was brushing my teeth when I heard Norah call out, "Adrian's here!" She'd taken it upon herself to announce his arrival every morning. Very loudly.

I shrugged into my coat, threw my bag over my shoulder, and headed downstairs. I felt a nervous tug in my stomach as I opened the door. Adrian was sitting in his truck, as usual, but facing away, probably on his phone or adjusting the heater vents. When he looked at me, it was him. Real, non-nightmare him.

"Your heart rate's up," he said as I climbed into the truck. It still unnerved me that he could tell that kind of stuff from fifteen feet away.

"I'm sorry," I said, rubbing my eyes. "I know it's stupid, but dream-you scared the shit out of me."

"Are you okay?"

For some reason, the look of concern on his face—the way he was turned to me, like I was a frightened animal—irritated me. A lot.

"I'm fine," I snapped. Why was I snapping?

He smiled at me a little, but for some reason it came across as patronizing. "How can I make this better?"

"It's all good," I said, sitting on my half of the cab rather than snuggling up under his arm like usual. "Just a dream. Not your problem."

He started the truck frowning, both of us very aware of the physical space between us. "Your problems *are* my problems."

"Look," I said, feeling the old, familiar anger starting to creep back in. "I'm sorry I called you last night. It was just a stupid nightmare; I'll get over it."

That definitely came out bitter.

He threw the truck in gear and pulled out of the driveway. "You are my responsibility. If you aren't well, that lands on me."

I laughed sharply. "I'm sorry I'm such an inconvenience."

He gripped the steering wheel. "That's not what I meant."

I turned to him and cocked my head to the side. "What did you mean, exactly? Ever since I got here, I've been somebody's *responsibility*—"

"Yeah," Adrian interrupted. "The state assigned you to Rachel and Joe, the Council assigned you to me—"

"I am not a fucking five-year-old!"

"No, you're not," he agreed. "But when people are willing and able to *help*, you don't act like they're trying to ruin your life."

"I didn't *ask* for your help!" I sputtered, instantly enraged by his condescension. "And I sure as *hell* didn't ask for Joe and Rachel's help, either."

He shrugged, and it pissed me off even more. "Pretending like you can take on the world on your own isn't brave, it's stupid."

"I didn't want *any* of this." I'd meant to yell that, but it came out as a whisper. My throat was hoarse with a wave of tears there was no way in hell I'd let show in front of Adrian. "I didn't ask to move here, I didn't ask to be targeted by your dad. And maybe I do need help, but don't you dare think for a second that my life or my choices are yours to *approve*. I don't need your permission. You are *not* my boyfriend, and you don't have any say over what I do or how I feel or how I deal with what I'm going through."

I sat back in my seat, crossing my arms over my chest as I stared out the window, trying to reel my anger back in. We didn't say anything the rest of the drive. When we parked at school I slammed my door and walked straight to homeroom.

"What was that?" Trish asked as we both sat down. "Looks like you and the Incredible Hunk just had a fight."

"I don't want to talk about it," I muttered, getting out my books.

"Well, it's nothing that his Christmas present won't fix," she said with a wink.

"Not everything can be fixed by having sex!" I yelled, so outraged that I actually stood up. Everyone stared at me.

"What'd I miss?" Meghan asked, strolling through the door. "I heard yelling and the word 'sex.'"

I slunk back down into my chair, embarrassed, but still pissed off.

"Caitlin's having trouble with the mister," Trish whispered loudly as she sat down.

"Has she tried using his Christmas present yet?" Meghan whispered back, also loudly.

"She says it can't be fixed by sex."

She looked astonished. "Really?"

Trish nodded.

"That must've been a big fight."

Mr. Warren walked in then. It was probably the only time I'd been grateful for class to start.

"Caitlin," Trish whispered to me. "You know we're just giving you a hard time, right? If you don't want to do the down-and-dirty with de la Mara, it's none of our business."

I nodded in her direction, but was still too angry to actually respond.

"Please stand for the Pledge of Allegiance."

We said the pledge and sat back down, and Mr. Warren began teaching, so there wasn't time for Trish or Meghan to comment anymore on my love life. The day dragged by slowly and I waited in a sort of anxious, angry tension for lunch. Fourth period rolled around, but Mrs. Leckenby was just giving a lecture about the history of modern art, so I didn't even have a project to keep my hands busy. When the bell finally rang, I loaded my bag slowly, feeling the beginning of a headache building behind my eyes. I wasn't angry anymore, but I was still frustrated with Adrian (and Trish and Meghan for that matter) and tired from my sleepless night. I walked out of the art room straight into Adrian's arms.

"Y'know," he said, pulling me away from the flood of students, "if we never fought, we'd never be convincing as a couple. Maybe this was well-timed. Come on," he said before I could respond. "We need to talk."

He let go of me and walked in the opposite direction of the lunch tables, stopping in front of a group of pine trees.

"I'm not your boyfriend," he began bluntly. "I'm your bodyguard. But I'm something else, too."

"And what's that?" I tried to load my voice with sarcasm to hide the fact that I would rather have been anywhere other than where I was, trying once again not to cry. I could see Trish and Meghan staring at us from the lunch tables. Actually, a lot of people were staring. Adrian tended to attract attention.

He moved so that he blocked my view. "I'm your *friend,*" he said, meeting my gaze evenly. "You may not believe it, but I enjoy being around you. It's not an inconvenience, in any way." He put his hands on my arms. "I have a few more things to say and I want to make sure you hear them. And to make our audience happy, I want you to hug me."

I didn't want to. I didn't want to touch him, because I wanted to touch him.

"Cait," he said in that stupid, soft way of his.

I hated that he had that effect on me. I stepped forward and put my arms around his waist woodenly, staring straight at his chest. He rolled his eyes, but didn't try to make me relax.

"One," he began, resting his chin on the top of my head and holding me tightly. "I'm sorry you got involved in all this. You're right, you didn't ask for it, and it's not fair. Two: I'm *not* sorry I got to know you. You make me feel more human, and that means everything, to me. Three, and please listen to this: There is nothing wrong with being afraid. I'm afraid every time I leave you at your doorstep and drive away. I'm afraid every time I fall asleep that whoever is on watch isn't going to be paying enough attention."

He tilted his face down and lowered his voice. "Fear is a good thing, sometimes. It keeps us aware of what's important." He smiled a little, but only a little. "Four: If the circumstances were different and I ever actually saw you in my Christmas present, I'd be in big trouble. Five: According to the chore chart, we're supposed to kiss today."

We actually had made the chore chart—he'd gone for the gold star stickers. Although we'd somehow managed to conveniently "forget" that Mondays were smooch days. He never brought it up, so I didn't, either. Except for now, of course.

He searched my eyes for a moment, then leaned down, hovering half a centimeter away, giving me the chance to pull back.

But I didn't.

So he kissed me.

Even while it was happening, I wondered if I could count this as my first "real" kiss—because in the end, it wasn't really real. It was soft and slow and perfect and it sucked because I wanted this, but not like *this*. He pulled me tighter against him and for a moment I stopped caring about whether it was right or wrong or real or fake, because it sure as hell felt *good*. The relationship may have been staged, but my full-body shiver was a product of natural chemistry, not a choreographed show for the benefit of the admiring public.

Speaking of the public, over the sound of my racing heart, I heard a few scattered claps and even a "You show him, Mystic!" from what had to be Trish. I should've felt embarrassed, and I probably would in a matter of moments, but for now, all unnecessary brain function had been shut off to divert power . . . elsewhere.

He paused, breathing deeply. I looked up and caught his eye and in that moment I knew, absolutely, that despite whatever bullshit story we had about ourselves, *this* was real. This kiss, this moment. And I didn't know when we'd get another one like it. I slid my hand up his chest and stood on my toes, tilting my face. His eyes turned, burning silver as he threaded his fingers through my hair and pulled me in again. Without thinking, I bit his lower lip softly between my teeth. His breath caught and he turned sharply away, his arms an iron vise around my waist.

"I'm sorry," I whispered, panicking. "I wasn't thinking. Are you okay?"

For a long moment, he said nothing. Then, he turned slowly, hair tickling my cheek, and placed a light kiss underneath my jaw. Another full-body shiver radiated out from where his lips met my skin, and I could feel every muscle in his body tense in response to my reaction. It was another long moment before either of us dared to breathe.

"I'm okay," he mumbled finally. "But you should probably not do that again."

"Yeah," I squeaked, blushing. "Okay,"

He deliberately stood up straight, his eyes pinched closed. When he opened them, they were his normal, multihued gray. He smiled lightly, though his arm was still tight around my waist. "So—are we friends again?"

I couldn't keep an insane little giggle from escaping. Friends? Well, if that's how "friends" made up, then hell yeah—"We're friends."

Adrian rolled his shoulders, letting out a deep breath, before glancing at the picnic tables. "I think pretty much everyone was watching. You want to go eat lunch in the truck?"

I leaned my forehead against his chest. Cue daily embarrassment.

"I take that as a yes."

I nodded into his shirt. He laughed and turned so that we were headed toward the parking lot. I could feel dozens of eyes following us from the picnic tables as I tried not to trip. Maybe going to his truck was a bad idea. Maybe they thought we were going to continue our little performance where they couldn't see us. I shouldn't care, but I did, but I also didn't. We rounded the corner of the building, away from prying eyes, and settled in the truck. Adrian turned the radio on and we listened to classic rock as we ate.

How could I go from being angry enough to slap him in the face one moment to mushy and breathless the next? I had *allowed* him to kiss me. I shouldn't have, but I did, and I liked it way, way too much, and it was going to kick in soon that we might be friends again, but that's all we were, and then this was all going to hurt.

We continued to munch silently on our lunches. I swallowed a bite of my sandwich.

"I owe you an apology," I said, finally working up the courage to say it out loud.

Adrian stared at me blankly. "For what?"

I toyed with stem of the apple in my lunch bag. "For blowing up at you this morning. You were just trying to help. I just get pissed off so quickly and take it out on whoever's near—and you happen to be near most of the time."

He took a bite of his own apple, looking thoughtful. "Y'know, I feel like we spend a lot of time apologizing to each other."

I barked a laugh, feeling suddenly tired. "We do, don't we?"

"For what it's worth, apology accepted—if you accept my apology for blowing up right back at you. I know I keep to myself, but there's a lot going on with the Council and my family that I don't agree with, and there's nothing I can do about it. So—I get it."

"Apology accepted," I said, smiling. "Oh, shoot."

"What?"

"Well, you might need to accept another apology. I promised my aunt we'd go to the ranch after school. She said she and Joe miss me."

He sighed dramatically. "I don't think I can forgive that."

I snorted. "If you can't forgive that, our cover story is headed for some serious trouble."

He smiled. "I'd be happy to come over. Besides," he said, tossing his apple core into his empty lunch bag, "I like your house. It's all cozy and full of people."

I frowned. "Don't more people live at your house than mine?"

He stretched, putting his hands behind his head with a sigh. "Technically. But the de la Maras live their separate lives in their separate rooms. Julian's always off somewhere, Lucian is barely housebroken, Mariana's devoted to Dominic, and Dominic is devoted to his work. Our concept of family is pretty much nonexistent."

I let that process in my brain for a long moment, then said, "I think Lucian really looks up to you." Adrian gave me a puzzled look. "We had a nice conversation while you and Julian were catching up the other day."

"I bet that was interesting."

I searched for the right words. "It was . . . educational. He mentioned some of the things he liked, and you were on his list. He said you told him stories."

Adrian looked embarrassed. "Lucian has trouble sleeping. It's like he doesn't know how to shut his brain off. He actually stayed awake so long that he fell into a coma. We didn't realize when he went into his room at night, he just stared at the ceiling until someone came to 'wake' him up. But if I tell him a story, he relaxes enough to let his mind wander and eventually drift off. One time he had a dream about the story I told him, and now he gets excited to fall asleep, so he can dream."

"He seems like a good kid," I said, remembering the way he'd first introduced himself. Yes, he'd been upside down, but he'd shaken my hand and said, "How do you do?" very politely.

Adrian closed his eyes and leaned his head back against the seat. "I don't know about 'good,' but he's definitely a kid. Doesn't know right from wrong, has almost no sense of morals or responsibility, doesn't understand the concept of private property. He can't be around other kids because he'd just take things from them that he wanted, and if they resisted, he'd probably get violent. And that would be bad for so many reasons."

"He did mention that blood was one of his favorite things."

Adrian shook his head. "He drinks more than the rest of us combined. We're trying to get him off of it gradually, but he's having a hard time adjusting back to this dimension."

I remembered him holding up his hands and looking frustrated, saying that his body got in the way. "I don't know if he really understands the concept of love," I told Adrian, "but if any part of him is capable of it, he loves you." I wasn't trying to make him feel better, it was just the truth. Well, I guess I *was* trying to make him feel better—but it was also the truth.

The bell rang and we climbed out of the truck. Adrian walked me to my fifth-period class, hugged me once, tightly, and let me go.

I watched him walk away, a rush of contradicting feelings flooding through me. Finally, I headed into my own classroom.

This would be so much easier if he were unattractive, or boring, or dumb.

But he wasn't. He was incredible.

# 12

# AS I LAY ME DOWN
# TO SLEEP

The paralysis was familiar. The setting was not.

I struggled to open my eyes, and when I did, a harsh white light glared down at me from overhead. I squinted, and realized I could move my neck, but everything else was nonresponsive. Whatever I was lying on, it was white, cold, and looked similar to the marble in Adrian's foyer. An altar, maybe? It didn't seem to extend much beyond the length or width of my body. Beyond that, everything was dark. I was also wrapped in my mother's quilt. And—as far as I could tell—I wasn't wearing anything *other* than the quilt, which scared the shit out of me.

Something tickled the arch of my foot, and if I'd had control over my reflexes, I would have jumped or kicked, but I couldn't. It scuttled around to my ankle and it felt like it had legs—

Lots of them.

I knew it was a dream. But I could *feel* the quilt around me and

the marble beneath me and the thing crawling slowly and intentionally up my leg and it might have been a nightmare, but it was real.
This was too clear, too vivid, to be anything else.

Something moved out of the corner of my eye. It was a cockroach,
and it crawled across the marble toward my shoulder. The thing on
my leg wriggled its way under the fabric and over my knee. The cockroach disappeared into my hair, its antennae flitting against the back
of my neck. I let out an involuntary sob, and then bit my tongue,
breathing heavily as tears spilled down my cheeks.

When I opened them again, worms were crawling over the sides
of the marble. Huge, fat, mucous-covered worms. I had no idea how
they were climbing up, but they were, in waves. The centipede
thing had made it past my thigh and was currently wriggling across
my stomach. I was going to puke.

"You know, Caitlin, you're not being very helpful," my mother's
disembodied voice said from the darkness. I whimpered as a worm
slid between my toes. "Why don't you want to help?"

*"What do you want from me?"* I screamed, and then closed my mouth
immediately as a centipede scuttled over my jaw, running across my
lips. I shook my head violently and it flew off.

From the bright light overhead, a dark shape slowly descended.
I watched in horror as it neared to within three feet and stopped,
suspended by hundreds of IV tubes. Finally, I could see that it wasn't
an *it*—it was my mother, wrapped in a copy of the same green velvet quilt that was tucked around me. She was also quite obviously
dead. As I watched, patches of her hair fell off and landed on my face.
I shook them off violently, but strands got stuck to my eyelashes.

Her jaw moved to form words. "You let my bones change, Caitlin. You let this happen."

"You're not my mom," I whimpered as the cockroaches began

flitting against my arms and crawling against my rib cage. A legion of centipedes had found their way under the quilt and were congregating over my stomach restlessly.

"You let this happen," she said again, inhumanly loud and deep in the darkness. "You let the worms eat my body."

"I was sixteen!" I screamed up at her. "What was I supposed to do?"

The plain, milky eyes flickered white and burned down in my direction.

"Feed me."

The bugs went into a frenzy. I clenched my teeth together so hard my jaw ached. I would not scream.

"You let the worms and the beetles and the crawling things destroy me. And now it's your turn."

She smiled at me, sick and dead.

And then her body disintegrated in a flood of centipedes, beetles, cockroaches, and worms. I barely had time to close my mouth before they landed, covering me in a seething mass so thick I couldn't breathe.

I came awake more quickly this time, and I think it was because I had literally been holding my breath while asleep. I shoved the blankets aside and scrubbed my hands over my body, trying to get rid of the bugs. I swore I could hear them scuttling against my sheets, crawling in my hair, my clothes.

It took a full minute before I realized there was nothing there. I turned my lamp on anyway to check. Nothing. And yet I could still feel thousands of little legs slithering across my skin. I even picked up my pillow to make sure there was nothing behind it. I reached for my phone to check the time.

It was two in the morning.

"I know girls don't like to be told this, but you look tired."

I'd climbed into the truck and immediately used Adrian's shoulder as a pillow, which was far more comfortable than it had a right to be.

"I had another nightmare," I mumbled. I could feel the muscles in his arm flex as he gripped the steering wheel.

"Same dream?"

"No. This one had worms."

"Worms?"

I nodded against his sleeve. "And centipedes and cockroaches."

He grabbed my shoulders and pushed me up for a moment so he could tuck me under his right arm. I leaned the back of my head against his chest and almost zonked out right there.

"Was this the same place?" he asked, starting down the driveway.

"Nope." I held on to Adrian's arm like a second seat belt across my stomach.

"Why didn't you call?" He didn't sound angry, just concerned.

"What could you have done?" I mumbled, on the edge of sleep. "They're dreams. I just have to"—I interrupted myself with a yawn—"to get through it." I looked up at him. "But these aren't just nightmares. I know they're not real, because when I wake up, nothing about me has changed. But they're real while they're happening. I don't know how, but they are."

I expected him to tell me I was overreacting, that I was being stupid, that I needed to calm down. But he didn't.

"Cait, if it happens again, I want you to call."

"Why?"

"Just humor me."

"All right," I mumbled, and turned my face against him arm, falling immediately asleep.

I stumbled through classes the rest of the day and used Adrian as a pillow again during study hall. He insisted we spend the afternoon at my place and I didn't argue (possibly because I fell asleep again once we got inside the truck). When we got to the ranch, I drank a couple cups of coffee and perked up enough to get through some homework. By the time dinner hit, the caffeine was wearing off; Adrian had to keep nudging me under the table to make me stay awake. As I said good-bye to him at the door, he gave me a hug and whispered in my ear.

"Remember, call me if it happens again."

I nodded into his shoulder. He kissed my cheek and let me go, heading out the door. I went to my room, started a fire in the fireplace, checked Facebook, and played three games of Bubble Guppy Explosion.

Finally, I ran out of energy. After brushing my teeth and throwing on some sweatpants, I stared at my bed. Somehow, it seemed ominous. I climbed unhappily under the covers. My room was warm, my bed was soft, my limbs were heavy.

But I was terrified to fall asleep.

It only felt like a few minutes later that I opened my eyes. The fire was still going, so I must not have been out for very long. I blinked several times, but I was tired and the room stayed dull and blurry. I closed my eyes again, shivering against the cold air.

I reached for the blankets to pull them up further over my shoulders, but couldn't find them. Half awake, I sat up and groped toward the end of the bed with my hand. But there was nothing there. Irritated, I finally opened my eyes completely, and realized that I hadn't kicked my blankets off—my bed was made, and I was lying on top of the covers. I looked down.

And discovered I was wearing the Green Thing.

What the hell?

I kept blinking, but my vision wouldn't clear. I felt groggy, not just tired, like I was drunk—or drugged.

I leaned a hand against my forehead, brushing a loose strand of hair—then frowned. My hair wasn't in the usual, wavy mess; it was curled and hair sprayed, and longer than it should be. I blinked a few times, and my eyes felt odd, so I brushed my fingers over my lashes. They were stiff and gritty. I was definitely wearing mascara, maybe even fake eyelashes. I licked my lips and they tasted like cherry.

Something was not right.

The floor creaked. I looked up, heart hammering in my chest. The door handle twisted, squeaking the tiniest bit, sending a shock of adrenaline through my system. Slowly, barely discernible in the dark room, it opened.

"Caitlin?"

I stared incredulously at the figure in the doorway.

"Adrian?" I whispered, trying to keep quiet. "What are you doing here?"

He stepped forward into the firelight, looking concerned. "You called me."

I stared at him with the same confused expression. "I did?"

He took a cautious step forward. "Yeah. You told me to come over immediately."

I shivered. "I don't remember that."

"Cait, you're freezing." He came around the side of the bed and sat on the edge of the mattress, feeling my cheek with the back of his hand. "You're like ice." He immediately wrapped his arms around me and chuckled, which didn't seem right. He wasn't much of a chuckler. "You didn't have to wait for me like this. I would've found you under the covers, too."

He rubbed my back lightly, comfortingly. I closed my eyes and let the heat from his body warm me as I tried to sort out everything in my head.

"You know, I'm kind of surprised you called," he said, voice a low rumble. "I mean, after the way you almost bit my head off yesterday, I didn't expect this. But I'm . . . glad."

I looked up at him, intending to ask what he meant, but his eyes melted into a deep, warm silver, and I forgot the question. His fingers stroked up my spine. His other hand tilted my face. "You're so beautiful," he whispered against my neck. I frowned and he laughed softly. "You don't believe me?"

"I'm not beautiful," I murmured. What was going on?

Something. Something was definitely going on.

He sighed a little. "You're right, you're not beautiful." Then he ran his fingers lightly down my jaw, my throat, and traced my collarbone with his fingers, very slowly. "You're absolutely"—he pressed his lips against my neck in a delicate kiss—"*sexy.*"

I was about to say "Huh?" but when I turned my face in his direction, I turned right into his mouth. I was about to pull away and apologize, but he murmured, "I want you."

I sat frozen. He pulled back a fraction of an inch to stare into my eyes. All I could see was liquid, dancing silver, beautiful in the darkness.

"You do?"

He didn't answer. Well, he didn't answer verbally. My stomach burst into a thousand butterflies as he pressed his lips against mine.

We stayed like that for a few moments: Adrian holding me, the flames leaping in the fireplace, the only sound was the beat of my own heart in my ears.

Finally, I kissed him back.

He immediately wrapped his arms around my waist, pulling me closer. I ran my fingers through his hair, tangled them in the curls, crawled on his lap, and kissed him again. He leaned forward, lowering us against the bed, pressing his lips against my throat in a kiss. I lay perfectly still, afraid to move, when he brushed my collarbone with his mouth, fingers running lightly over the beading on the Green Thing—

—which I had not been wearing when I fell asleep.

"Adrian?" I murmured, fighting to hold on to logic.

"Hmm?" he rumbled, hovering over my skin.

I blinked, trying to collect my thoughts. Finally, I had it. "When did I call you?"

I felt his hand trace the sheer lace pattern down my rib cage as he said, "Not very long ago. You sounded insistent."

I tried to concentrate, I did, but it was hard when the slightest touch of his hand sent shock waves across my nerves. I blinked again, fighting the haziness in my mind. "What did I say, exactly?"

He traced the pattern down my waist and across my stomach. "That I should come over because you had a surprise for me."

His fingers had gone all the way down to my hip. I was rapidly losing my train of thought. "How come I can't remember any of that?"

His hand froze.

I looked straight at the ceiling, feeling a cold, slimy fear percolate in my stomach, waking me up. "And how did you get in?"

He sat up stiffly and I peeked at him. His eyes continued to burn silver in the darkness. "One way or another, Caitlin," he said in the voice of my dead mother. "I will return." I watched in horrified fascination as his two canine teeth descended into curved, snake-like fangs. "Give me what I want," it hissed—whatever it was, it wasn't Adrian anymore, or my mother, but something else entirely.

But I whispered, "No."

He glared at me and then, without warning, snapped forward, fangs flashing in the firelight. I flung my arms up to protect my face. I expected the attack to continue until I was in excruciating pain, until I was dead or defenseless.

But it didn't come.

Slowly, I opened my eyes and peeked toward Adrian.

But he was gone.

I let my arms drop to the bed. He was gone, and I was alone, pajamas twisted, the blankets everywhere. The only light came from the barely glowing embers in the fireplace. I let out the breath I'd been unconsciously holding and slumped forward, drawing up my knees, hugging my arms around myself.

The nightmare was over.

---

Adrian put the truck in gear and started down the driveway, motioning for me to use his shoulder as a pillow, like I had the day before. I shook my head violently.

"Caitlin," he said slowly, "what's wrong?"

I stared straight out the front window. "Nothing's wrong."

He reached a hand toward me and I jerked away.

He grimaced, but didn't touch me. "There was another one, wasn't there?" When I didn't answer, he ran a hand through his hair in an agitated gesture. "Was it like the first time?"

I shook my head, but didn't look at him.

"Okay. But—I was in the dream?"

My eyes watered. I nodded.

He looked at me closely. "Did I hurt you?"

My lips trembled and I covered my mouth with my hand and shook my head.

I could feel him tense, and I wasn't sure if it was because I was once again on the verge of tears or because he sensed that I was somehow evading his question.

"What did I do?"

I leaned against the door and covered my eyes with my hand, trying to hide the few tears that had managed to leak out. My throat felt thick and froggy and I mumbled, "I don't want to talk about it."

"I can't help if I don't know what's going on."

"Please, just let it go," I whispered.

"What could I have possibly done that made you this upset?"

I huddled in my corner of the seat and drew a knee up, letting my tears soak into the fabric of my jeans. I was trying my best to be silent; my stomach actually hurt from trying not to make any noise.

The truck slowed and stopped. I was not ready to go to school. I didn't want to be around people. I opened my eyes in narrow slits and saw that we were not in the school parking lot. In fact, it looked like we were just pulled off to the side of the road.

Adrian put the truck in park and leaned back.

I didn't want to be at school, but I didn't really want to be alone with him, either.

"Caitlin," he said after a few moments. "I don't know exactly what happened in your dream. Nightmare," he corrected himself. "But I'm not going to apologize—because it wasn't me. I'm not trying to be mean. I just want you to understand that whatever happened to you last night wasn't real."

I knew it wasn't real. It hadn't actually happened, none of it had, not in any of the dreams. But in a sense, it had. Because I remembered it. I felt it. I lived through it as much as I was sitting here, living through this. But I couldn't explain that to him.

I heard the creak of the leather seat as he moved, and I tensed. When he spoke, his voice sounded nearer, but not threateningly close.

"Please look at me."

It was a request, not a command. I pulled my sleeves over my thumbs and scrubbed my eyes again, glad I wasn't wearing mascara, and then slowly turned toward him.

"Adrian—it wasn't worse than the others because I thought it was real. It was worse because I woke up and knew that it *wasn't*."

He looked at me sadly. "I don't understand."

I stared at a scratch on the seat instead of meeting his gaze. "I know."

He didn't answer, just took my hand in his. I wavered, and then let my forehead fall against his shoulder. He carefully put his arm around me. I breathed in the scent of his jacket.

"This has got to stop," he murmured into my hair.

I continued to breathe in his smell, familiar and grounding. He hadn't smelled like this in the dream.

"I can't stop them." I'd tried, every time.

"You can't," he said after a moment. "But maybe I can."

I looked up at him.

His eyes had been flaring a soft silver for the past couple minutes and I hadn't even noticed. He met my gaze. "First, I need you to trust me. Completely. Can you do that?"

He wasn't trying to trick me or mess with emotions. I don't know how I could tell, but I could. I nodded.

"Good. Second, I need you to tell Trish that you're spending the night at her place tonight."

I blinked. "Why would I do that?"

"Because that's going to be your alibi for coming to my house. Trish will cover for you."

I tensed. But he'd asked me to trust him.

"Stay with Trish for the afternoon. Before dinner, I'll pick you up, and Trish will tell her parents that you felt sick, so you went home."

I swallowed. "And then?"

"And then you'll eat dinner at my place. We'll do some home-work. And you'll sleep in one of the spare rooms."

My stomach felt tight with fear. "And then what?"

"And then, after you're asleep, I'll see what happens."

I paled. I didn't like this plan at all.

But he wasn't finished. "If you seem to be getting too upset, I'll wake you up and siphon off the fear and see if I can figure out where it's coming from."

I liked that a little better. Actually, I liked that a lot better.

"Okay."

He seemed surprised, but pleased. I glanced at the dashboard clock and grimaced. "We'll be late."

"I'll tell them we had engine trouble."

Adrian and Caitlin, boyfriend and girlfriend, showing up late, to-gether. I'd get grief from Trish about it, especially when I told her what the plan was for the evening.

---

"You want me to do *what*?" I frowned at Trish. She'd heard me per-fectly well. "All right," she said, "but could you at least tell me why?"

I sighed, knowing that I'd have to tell another lie that made it sound like Adrian and I were more than we were.

"Look, we just want some time alone, and we can't do that at his place or my place or school. We're both stressed out and we just want to be by ourselves for one night."

Trish looked at me skeptically. "This from Miss Sex-Doesn't-Solve-Everything."

I couldn't leave her thinking anything would happen, because then she'd ask for details I'd be unable to give. "Believe what you will, but we honestly just want to spend some quality time together. Alone. Can you do that for me?"

"Oh, fine," she said, giving up. "But if anything does happen, I want *details*."

I smiled.

The bell rang and we headed off to math with Mr. Cliff, which I was not looking forward to. I'd gotten my homework done, but I knew at least half of it was just flat-out wrong. As we settled in, Mr. Cliff smiled at us, which was a bad sign.

"Congratulations, juniors; today you have the privilege of taking a pop quiz."

I didn't like Mr. Cliff very much.

Since science came right after math, and Mr. Cliff taught both classes, we stayed in the same seats for two periods, which was strangely exhausting. All we had to do was a stupid lab about wheat germ DNA, but I was so tired that Trish did most of it.

Fourth period with Mrs. Leckenby was a welcome break. We were starting on a new clay project, so I could just sort of mindlessly work with my hands for forty-five minutes without having to do much thinking. Lunch came and went with the usual chitchat. Norah came by and started a conversation with us about Christmas plans. She managed to worm out of Adrian that I'd be spending Christmas Eve at his place, and I knew that she'd be informing her parents as soon as we were home.

In history, Mr. Warren was midway through a unit on westward expansion. He handed us back tests from the week before, and I was surprised to see that I'd gotten an A. Out of the corner of my eye, I saw Trish do a little victory jig in her seat—apparently she'd gotten a good grade, too, which made me happy.

Music was as painful as ever. I felt bad for Mrs. Leckenby—the choir only had a few talented singers. I was mediocre at best, Trish was downright awful, and most of the others just mouthed the words without actually producing any sound.

When the bell rang after Study Hall Adrian gave me a hug and said, "See you later," before walking to his truck and driving away with a little dorky wave. It was adorable, and made me smile.

Trish found me outside the library. "So we're going to my house and hanging out until you have a mysterious stomachache and have to leave before dinner?"

"Yep."

She nodded. "Sounds good."

We drove to her house and holed ourselves up in her room. I realized I hadn't been here since the night of the Halloween party.

"You want anything to drink?" she asked, slinging her backpack down. I hesitated, and she saw it. "I'm gonna get a soda anyway, so it's not an inconvenience or anything."

"I'll have whatever you're having."

"One mystery pop coming right up."

She disappeared and reappeared a moment later, holding two store-brand colas.

"Heads up," she said, and tossed one in my direction. I caught the ice-cold can just before it crashed into her desk. "Mystic," she said, flopping onto her bed, "I got a question for you." I grimaced. Her questions generally revolved around me, Adrian, and Victoria's Secret. But she surprised me with "What was home like?"

I blinked, trying to see if there was any way that question could be interpreted sexually. Maybe by a great stretch of the imagination, but probably not.

"Why do you ask?"

She shrugged and popped the top of the can. "I just don't know much about you is all. I mean, I do, but I don't. I didn't want to push you when you first got here, but I feel like we're friends now."

She smiled at me and I smiled back, then shrugged. "Not much to know. Grew up in Connecticut in what I thought was a small town, until I moved here. Mystic's a metropolis compared to Stony Creek. I loved the ocean and our house. Sewed a ton of shit with my mom, watched the *Bachelorette* with my grandma every week. Pretty simple life, really." I popped the top of my soda can. "Speaking of not knowing a whole lot about people, what about you? You have what, two brothers?"

"Three," she said with a look that clearly said three was too many. "I already told you Jimmy's getting married this summer. Crazy bastard," she muttered and took a swig of cola. "He's just a freshman. But when he's home, he looks happy like I've never seen him before." She smiled. It kind of made me wish I had siblings.

"Where do they go to school?"

"Jimmy's at Boston U studying engineering. Mark's a junior at Penn State majoring in art or something. And Paul's going for a law degree at NYU."

"Dang."

She smiled. "Underneath the hick, we're a family of semigeniuses.

Paul's, like, crazy-ass smart, but we couldn't afford to send him any-where too fancy."

She smiled again, happy for her brothers. A thought struck me. "Trish, what's your GPA?"

"Since when did you turn into Ms. Blunt? That's my job."

I blushed. "I'm sorry; I didn't mean to ask it like that."

"Don't be; it's not a secret. I've got a 3.95." I stared at her. "Oh, come on, we're in the middle of Stony Creek; the curriculum isn't exactly rigorous."

Since when did she use words like *rigorous*—or *curriculum?* And since when was a 3.95 something to shrug off? I barely had a 3.0 (thanks to my lack of enthusiasm for living and subsequent inatten-tion to homework), and it wasn't a walk in the park trying to bring it back up.

"Where do you want to go to school, after this?" I asked, unasham-edly curious.

Of all the reactions I would have expected, embarrassment was not one of them. "I don't know," she said, not meeting my eyes.

"Oh, come on, Trish," I said, reveling in being the one with the questions now. "You obviously have something in mind."

She glowered at me. "So what if I do? There's no way."

"If there's no way, then there's no harm in telling me."

She rolled her eyes and said, "Fine. I want to go to Oxford."

I blinked. "Oxford?"

"Yeah. Like, in England."

"I know where Oxford is. But—why?"

"Because it's one of the founding schools of English literature. Mr. Warren's trying to help me get a scholarship."

She wanted to go there to write? "You want to go there to write?"

She shook her head in a so-so motion. "Maybe. It's more about the history of the place. And I want to travel. I was thinking of getting a master's in literature, then going on to publishing or something."

It was like I was talking to a different person. I briefly wondered if Trish was schizophrenic, but she interrupted my thoughts.

"But that's a long way off. I got plenty of time to screw around and be a reckless teenager. Which is why we should get some homework done."

"Doing homework is reckless?"

"Nah," she grinned, "but making sure you have absolutely nothing to distract you from your night with Adrian is."

---

"I'm gonna take Caitlin home," I heard Trish tell her parents. They replied low enough that I couldn't hear. "Yeah, she's not feeling good. I'll be back for dinner."

I heard her climb the stairs so I grabbed my bag.

"You ready?" she asked, stepping into the room. I nodded and tried to look ill.

"Hope you feel better soon, Caitlin," Mrs. Fields called from the kitchen. She was cooking something on the stove that smelled deliciously like chili, and my stomach rumbled. I covered it with a grimace and said, "Thanks; I hope so, too."

We made it to the truck and Trish drove me five minutes down the road until we saw a black truck parked on the side. I thanked Trish again for covering for me and hopped out, sprinting to the truck to keep out of the snow.

"Hey," Adrian said as I closed the door.

"Hey," I said back.

We sat in semiawkward silence for another two seconds before Adrian pulled onto the road.

"How was your afternoon?" he tried again.

"Good. Got my homework done. Learned that Trish is a closet genius and dreams of going to Oxford. Had a cola. The usual."

He looked at me sideways. "Trish wants to go to Oxford?"

"Yep. Apparently all her brothers are really smart, too."

Adrian looked mildly surprised. "They always seemed kind of big and dumb to me. Of course, that was during my I-hate-humans phase, so I didn't think very highly of anyone."

I stared at him. "You had an I-hate-humans phase?"

He smiled and shook his head. "Just because I am what I am doesn't mean I didn't go through puberty like everyone else. I was a very angry adolescent."

"Why was that?"

He cleared his throat. "That's when I was told we're not allowed to get attached to humans."

"Aah," I said, blushing for some reason. "That must've sucked."

He smiled, and it was a little bitter. "It wasn't a great time for me. I wanted friends, but it wasn't allowed. Hating people made it easier to keep my distance. It finally made sense why I moved around so much when I was younger." He shrugged, but I could tell he was agitated. "I have to interact with regular, everyday people, but Mariana and Dominic don't. They've already forgotten how hard it is to be around humans, but constantly maintain distance from them."

My face crumpled up sadly as I looked at him. "So you never, like, spent the night at someone's house?"

He shook his head. "Nope."

That was awful. I mean, I'd had a sad childhood, in a way, but my parents had been awesome. They were smart and funny and wonderful and they'd always made sure I knew they loved me. Adrian's childhood sounded more like prison.

"How do I factor in, then, if you're not allowed to have human friends? We're alone together all the time."

"You are a loophole," he said, pulling through the gates that led to his house. "We endangered you, so we protect you in whatever fashion is necessary. Being around you, being alone with you, is vital to your safety. We had to let you in on it, because sooner or later you would've realized I was not who I said I was, or around you for the reasons you thought. We could have used our Jedi mind tricks to make you less suspicious, but that's another rule—only use Jedi powers in an emergency." He shook his head, lips set in a tight line. "I get 'permission' to be around you, to appear to be *in love* with you, but I'm forbidden from growing attached. And the penalties for disobedience are high."

"How high?" I blurted out before I could stop myself.

He gave me a look that clearly said I didn't really want to know.

We wound around the final curve in the road and parked. For a moment, he didn't move, just stared out the windshield at his house.

"Adrian," I said, staring down at a hole in the knee of my jeans. "When this is all over—are you going to make me forget?"

"No, I won't." But he wouldn't look me in the eye.

I peered at him closely. "Is someone *else* going to make me forget?"

He looked down for a moment, then back up at me. "Probably."

My heart surged in my chest. "And what if I refuse?"

He couldn't meet my eyes. "We don't operate under a democracy. If the Council orders your memories wiped, someone will do it. It's just a matter of who."

Part of me wanted to ask *What if we said no?* But I didn't. The more time I spent around Adrian's family, the more I realized I was a sort of glorified pet, not a guest. I could live my life fairly normally, but when push came to shove, I didn't have any rights, as far as they were concerned.

Adrian breathed in, let it go, and got out of the truck before I could ask more. I followed him clumsily, trying to process and walk at the same time. As soon as we were through the front door, I heard a soft whooshing sound and looked up at the curving marble staircase to see Lucian sliding down the banister, face-first. Just when I thought he'd crash, he pushed himself up, hopped off the pedestal at the end, and jumped onto Adrian, who caught him effortlessly, and without any show of surprise. Lucian scrambled, squirrel-like, until he was sitting on Adrian's shoulders, his chin resting on Adrian's head as his arms dangled in their usual lifeless fashion.

"Hey, nutcase," Adrian said, looking up.

"Hello," Lucian replied.

"What's for dinner?"

"Chicken." He overexaggerated the syllables so that it sounded like "ch-ihh-cken."

"Did you take your medicine?" Adrian asked seriously.

Lucian nodded.

"You shouldn't let him do that," a voice called from somewhere above us. I looked up and saw Julian—in a pair of silk pants and no shirt—on the third-story landing, leaning against the railing with a look of bored disapproval on his face.

"Why?" Adrian called up, eyes narrowed. "He's my brother."

"You're so"—Julian's eyes flickered over to me—"naive."

Adrian smiled darkly. "I'll take that as a compliment."

It looked like Julian was about to respond, but Adrian looked at me, then back at his older brother. "Later." Julian glanced at me again before disappearing into the third story hallway.

"Did I do something wrong?" Lucian asked, looking dejected.

"No, Frankie; you didn't do anything wrong."

"Frankie?" I asked.

Adrian turned as if he'd forgotten I was there. "Oh, yeah. Just a little nickname I gave him when he came home. Short for Frankenstein. Come on, let's go eat."

I followed him into the adjoining dining room (where a small feast was laid out), contemplating the logistics of brotherhood among a thirty-five-, eighteen-, and eleven-year-old. Throw in the fact that they weren't human, they drank blood, and they lived indefinite lifespans, and I guessed some awkward tension might arise.

"Caitlin; it's so good to see you again," Mariana said, bringing a huge silver platter of some sort of meat in from the kitchen.

"That smells delicious," I said, quite sincerely.

Mariana just smiled. A part of me couldn't help but wonder if it was because she thought it was cute that I had complimented her cooking. Of course, considering that she'd had over a hundred years to perfect her recipes, perhaps she had a right to be confident.

"Let's eat."

Julian and Dominic materialized out of nowhere, it seemed, and everyone sat. I was between Lucian and Adrian while Julian, Mariana, and Dominic sat across from us. Dishes were passed silently, except when Lucian dropped a green olive. He scooped it up quickly and shoved it in his mouth, but aside from that, everything moved with machinelike efficiency. Everyone, even Lucian and Mariana, had taken three times as much as I had, each staring at his or her own plate of food. It was weird.

A few minutes later, as if on cue, everyone stood up and walked their dishes into the kitchen, plates empty of even the smallest scrap of food. I brought my half-full plate with me and set it on the counter. Thankfully, Adrian took me by the elbow and led me back to the front hall.

"That was tense," I said, finally feeling like I could breathe.

"You see why I like your house?" Before I could respond, he shook his head and said, "Never mind. Let's go."

We climbed the winding stairs and got off at the second floor. At the end of the hundred-foot hall, lined with majestic paintings and expensive wall sconces, we stopped and Adrian opened at a door to our right.

"This is your room."

# 13

## INTERVIEW WITH A VAMPIRE

The only light came from two bedside lamps and the flickering glow of the fireplace. There was a queen-size, four-poster bed complete with awnings and a mountain of red silk pillows, and it didn't even take up half the room. I'd probably need a stepstool just to get in it. An old-fashioned gold-brocade lounge chair faced the fire, covered with a deep red throw. French doors led to what I assumed was a deck, although in the gloom outside, I couldn't really see much. I walked up to the bed and ran my fingers over the fabric reverently. I would kill to work with material like this.

"There's a bathroom through there," he said, pointing to a door to the left of the fireplace. "If you need anything, you can either call my phone or push the third button on the intercom, which will connect you to my room."

"You're leaving me?" I asked, a little alarmed.

"I'll be one room away." He smiled and patted his pockets as if making sure he had nothing left to give me. Finding nothing, he said, "All right, well, good night."

"Night," I called as he stepped out and closed the door with a soft click. I stood alone for a moment in the large, extravagant room, somewhat lost. Finally, I grabbed my bag and went into the bathroom, then stopped dead. I guess I shouldn't really be surprised by the de la Mara grandeur anymore, but the bathroom was *huge*. Tall ceilings, archways, the whole thing made out of warm, honey-colored marble illuminated by soft lights. Rather than take a shower, I filled the claw-foot tub with hot water and poured in expensive, spiced Parisian bubble bath, and stepped over the edge. The tub was so deep that I could float in it. I bunched my hair into a messy bun and leaned my head against the backrest, letting my arms hang over the edge of the porcelain.

This was certainly heaven.

I soaked until I felt thawed out and boneless. If I was going to stay in a room like this, I was going to make the most of it.

When the bubbles were mostly gone, I got out and took a quick shower, threw on some pajamas, and went back into the bedroom. Looking around to make sure no one was there, I used the brocade couch as a runway to somersault onto the bed. It was stupid and childish, but I figured if I was about to suffer from a horrifying nightmare, I'd squeeze in all the stupid, childish fun I could get.

I crawled between the cool sheets, switched the lamp off next to the bed, and nestled into the mound of pillows. I was asleep in seconds.

The first thing I noticed was a gentle rocking motion. It seemed vaguely familiar, like stepping into someone's house you haven't been to in years and remembering the smell of it. Blue sky and green tree branches waved above me in a friendly, lazy sort of way. As I looked around, more details settled into place, like graphics loading in a video game. I realized, finally, that I was sitting on the floor of a fishing boat. And with sudden clarity, I knew exactly where I was. In fact, I'd been here many times.

And I absolutely didn't want to be here now.

My throat was already tight with tears as I looked up. And there he was, sitting on an old folding chair in a flannel shirt and jeans, looking out over the water. He noticed I was awake and looked over at me with a wide smile.

"Hey, care bear, how was your nap?"

I blinked my way past the tears to look at his face.

"Dad?"

The smile disappeared. "Hey, what's wrong?" He stood up and came over to me. "Why are you crying, honey?" He knelt down and wiped a tear off my cheek. Then his expression cleared and he smiled sadly. "You're a little bit surprised to see me, I bet."

I nodded, not trusting my voice.

"You grew up so beautiful. That's all your mother's doing, of course." He turned to look back the way he'd come, and I looked with him. There, at the end of the boat, I saw my mother, sitting in a chair with a book and a cold soda. She looked over at us, sliding her sunglasses down the bridge of her nose.

"Is she awake?"

"Yep," he called to her.

She set down her things and picked her way over to us, looking young, thin—beautiful, even. Like they'd been frozen in time from when I was five years old.

"What's going on?" I asked, waiting for them to keel over dead or start talking in demonic voices. They looked at each other and back at me.

"We're going fishing," my dad said. "Like we do always do."

"Mom never came with us."

"I came a few times, when you were younger," she explained. "You two always seemed to enjoy it more than I did."

I looked at my dad. He was thirty, maybe thirty-five, with laugh lines and boyishly tousled hair. He looked so . . . alive.

"Come on, Cait; let's fish."

He grabbed my hands and pulled me up. My mom smiled encouragingly and went back to her chair and her book. Still somewhat bewildered, I followed him over to the rail where two chairs were set with fishing poles.

"It's so good to see you, sweetheart," he said quietly. "Did you miss me?"

I took in a shaky breath. "Yes."

He looked out over the water and swallowed. "I'm sorry about the way I left. There was nothing I could have done, but still, I'm sorry."

I couldn't take it anymore; I let my pole drop against the deck and flung myself onto his lap. He wrapped his arms tightly around me.

"It's okay, Caitlin," he murmured as I cried into his shirt.

"No, it's not," I sobbed. *"I grew up without you."*

He didn't reply, just tightened his hold on me as the sun played in golden waves over the lake. I felt exhausted and heavy, like all my mass had settled to one side of my body, pinning me with gravity.

"Caitlin," he said quietly, "I wanted more than anything to live. To be with you and your mom and see you grow up, because I love you more than I've ever loved anything in my life. But it doesn't work that way. I couldn't come back."

My lips trembled as a few more tears trailed down my cheek. "Why not?"

He kissed my forehead, but didn't say anything.

I closed my eyes and listened to the steady beat of my father's heart. He seemed so real.

"You're exhausted," he said finally. "Why don't you sleep?" I started to protest, but he hushed me. "I'm right here. It's okay."

He smiled, so I smiled and laid my head down again and closed my eyes, and soon the sun and the waves rocked me to sleep.

When I woke up (which was a weird thing to do in a dream), the sun was gone, and the stars were out. I stretched and murmured incoherently.

"What time is it?" I asked with a little yawn.

"Almost midnight."

I froze.

No.

I looked up slowly and saw that the arms that were holding me did not belong to my dad. They belonged to Adrian.

"No," I whimpered.

He looked sad. "I'm sorry, Caitlin. Your dad had to go."

"Please bring him back," I begged.

"He told me to look after you. I promised him I would."

The whole world tilted upside down, the stars rocked wildly in the sky, and I felt dizzy and nauseous. Slowly, everything stopped spinning, and I realized I was lying back in bed. A large, dark shape was half sitting and half lying next to me.

"Caitlin?"

I didn't answer, just closed my eyes and let the hot, miserable tears trickle down my face in silence. I could feel the sheets and blankets rustle as Adrian slid into bed beside me. Large arms wrapped around my shoulders and I turned and buried my face in his chest, misery winning out over embarrassment.

"I'm sorry," Adrian said after a moment. "I couldn't wake you up."

I rubbed enough tears out of my eyes to look up at him. "What?"

"You slept fine for a few hours—then I could tell." He sounded concerned. "I tried to wake you up, but I couldn't."

I didn't say anything, just held on to him as tightly as I could, the dream still vivid in my mind.

"Do you want me to take it away?"

I thought about it. "No. Not this time." I didn't know if that meant he'd leave, but I hoped he'd stay.

He tucked me against his side, drew the covers up, and wrapped his arms around me like he wasn't ever going to let go. And I let him, because it was him, and because I was tired, and because, in the middle of everything, being next to him felt like the safest place in the world.

———○

"How was quality time with Mr. Man over there?" Trish asked lightly as I closed the door to her truck. Ahead of us, Adrian pulled back onto the road. I'd wanted to show up at school in Trish's car just in case Norah saw me and reported back to her parents that I'd come to school with the wrong person.

"It was nice."

Trish rolled her eyes as she pulled onto the road and headed for school. "I said it once and I'll say it again: You are the worst story-teller on the face of this planet."

"What do you want to know?" I asked, settling back into the seat, feeling more rested than I had in days.

"Oh, I dunno; how about *did you sleep with him?*"

I chewed my lip thoughtfully. "Yes."

Trish's eyes popped open wide before she noticed the grin on my face. Her eyes narrowed. "Let me rephrase: Were you sexually active with one Adrian de la Mara on the night of the eighteenth of December?"

I smiled at her. "Nope."

"You're such a killjoy," she muttered at me.

"You know, what I don't understand is why everyone's so inter-ested in whether or not I have sex with Adrian. It's not like we're not the only couple in Stony Creek."

Trish gave me a dry look. "Mystic, it's *Stony Creek.* There's liter-ally nothing else to talk about." She turned left. "Besides, I don't think you understand how much of a *thing* Adrian is here. I mean, first his aunt and uncle show up out of nowhere about ten years ago and hole themselves up on the mountain and hardly ever talk to anyone in town, and then Adrian shows up out of nowhere about two years later and gets chauffeured to fifth grade in a brand-new Mercedes, and he's this awkward, cute kid that never talks to anybody, and then high school hits and that boy turned from cute to forest-fire-in-the-middle-of-a-dry-July *hot* and didn't give a single girl the time of day, and then you show up and suddenly wham-bam-thank-you-ma'am, you're together twenty-four/seven and *not* trying to lick each other's faces off every five seconds—which you should be because you're both too hot not to—so you understand if we're all a little curious as to *why.*"

I stared at her. That was the longest sentence I'd ever heard in my life.

She saw the look on my face and sighed. "Let me make this simple: You and Adrian are magical strangers in the land of Stony Creek. All the dull little woodland creatures want to understand the smallest details about the magical strangers, but the magical strangers keep to themselves, thus building up their own mystery and allure. That curiosity built and built until everyone imploded, creating a black hole that sucked the entire universe into the size of an eyeball, which burned a hole right through space and dropped straight down into hell, where it was incinerated. You basically just killed everybody, Caitlin; are you happy now?"

I just kept staring at her. "I . . . don't think so? But it was fun to listen to you talk. I just thought you should know that."

Trish rolled her eyes and parked. We got out of the truck to head to first period—as usual, I sat on Trish's left and Ben sat on her right. He was a foot taller than both of us, with short brown hair, huge arms and shoulders, and the kind of face that would look stern if it wasn't constantly lit up with a smile. When I'd met him that first day of school, he'd looked kind of caveman-ish. As I was observing him discreetly, he reached out and took Trish's hand in his own; neither of them looking at each other, intent on the lecture Mr. Warren was giving. They were absolutely adorable, and I felt a strange surge of happiness.

"Miss Holte?"

I jerked and looked at Mr. Warren. "Uh—transcendentalism?"

He smiled dryly. "Try 'manifest destiny.'"

I nodded, embarrassed, and promised to pay attention the rest of class.

After that one night at Adrian's house, I never dreamed of my dad again, although my mother was a frequent visitor in her various forms of decay. Adrian told me neither Mariana nor Dominic had ever heard of something like this, but if it was connected to their father, it must mean two things: He had, at some point, touched me, and he was currently nearby. The only thing I could think of that made sense was that the shopper dude at the mall that I'd bumped into had been him—which scared the shit out of me, because he'd seemed so normal. With the nightmares coming night after night, and with me unable to fall asleep again afterward, the lack of sleep became a consistent exhaustion that rode around with me like a second skin. Adrian couldn't stop them, I couldn't stop them, and there was no way to avoid them besides not sleeping in the first place, which, well, really wasn't an option.

It was the last day of school before Christmas vacation. I jerked awake when my boots slipped off the bookshelf in the school library and I just about fell off my chair. Adrian automatically reached out a hand to catch me, and I grabbed it, heart racing, startled from the abrupt end to my nap.

He cleared his throat and released my hand. "You okay?"

"Yeah." I felt the fatigue wash over me all over again as I laid my head on the table to stare blankly at the wall. "Just tired."

On the opposite side of our ridiculously tiny table, Adrian lay down so he could be eye level with me. We lay in silence for almost a full minute before he finally said, "Hey."

I responded with a monotone "yo."

We both smiled.

He traced a scar in the table for a moment before letting his hand drop to his side. "I guess now would be a good time to tell you we've come up with a temporary solution, to help with the nightmares."

I blinked at him, unable to dredge up the energy to show more enthusiasm than a sleepy "yay." At least I smiled while I said it.

He was beginning to blush a little, so I perked up. It was always adorable when Adrian got flustered. It also usually meant something really awkward was about to happen.

"So—when you stayed at our place, I couldn't stop the nightmare," he began. "But you slept fine the rest of the night?"

I nodded horizontally at him, since my cheek was still glued to the table.

"We think that physical proximity to us helps sever, or at least interrupt, the connection between you and the source of the nightmares. The Council has decreed that one of us should, uh . . . stay with you, at night. In your room."

I couldn't help but let a short burst of laughter escape. Then I realized he was serious. "Wait—really?"

"Yeah," he said, looking amazingly uncomfortable. "As far as the Council is concerned, it could be any one of my family. I convinced them I was the best choice." He looked at me quickly. "I mean, I thought Mariana or Dominic wouldn't exactly promote peaceful sleeping. But if you want one of them instead, or Julian, that can be arranged."

"No," I shook my head vigorously at him. "But how will you get in?"

He waved a dismissive hand. "Getting in isn't a problem. Although theoretically I could be outside the house and still be effective."

"That's dumb—you're not sitting outside the house."

Adrian smiled at me softly, and it lit up his face in a way that was entirely too endearing.

"Well," I continued, "this sounds like a recipe for amazing levels of awkwardness, but a full night's sleep sounds fantastic."

"Should we try tonight?"

I nodded, heart suddenly jumping into overdrive. Adrian sat up, as though he could hear it—which, I remembered, he could. I buried my face in my arm, embarrassed, but within moments I fell back asleep.

That night, the whole family watched a movie together to celebrate the start of Christmas vacation. We had hot spiced cider and gingerbread cookies and watched *It's a Wonderful Life*, which I'd somehow never seen before. I fell asleep twenty minutes before the end and only woke up when Norah threw a gingerbread man's foot at me. I ate it and announced I was going to bed.

Once I was upstairs, however, I realized that Adrian was going to appear at some point during the night. He'd said he'd come over after everyone was asleep and that I shouldn't wait up for him, although *how* he'd know when everyone was asleep I wasn't sure—another freaky vampire mind thing probably. My room wasn't a total disaster, but I spent a good twenty minutes picking things up and spraying Febreze around the room. It didn't smell bad in the first place, but I was paranoid. I also usually took a shower in the mornings, but I hopped in and washed my hair and double-brushed my teeth to be on the safe side. He probably wouldn't be anywhere near me, but I had no desire to smell like anything but mint and sunshine, just in case.

I sent a text off to Adrian saying that I was going to bed, then crawled under my covers and immediately fell asleep.

And entered into one of the more horrendous dreams I'd had yet.

I was in the woods at dusk. I couldn't see myself, but I knew I was naked and barefoot, since rocks and thorns were digging sharply into my feet. Someone was chasing me, but I didn't know who. I didn't know where I was going, or where I had come from, only that I had to get away, and I had to get away *now*.

There was a presence behind me, I could feel it, though I some-how knew—in that way you know certain things in dreams—that even if I turned around, I wouldn't see anyone. The world strobed, like a glitching movie, information lagging. By the time my eyes caught up to my momentum, it was too late to avoid the gully that seemed to stutter into place out of nowhere. I flew out over the ledge, tumbling down the ravine. When I came to a stop at the bottom, I sat up slowly, even though my brain was urging me to *run, run, for God's sake, run!* and pushed the hair out of my eyes with my hand—then screamed.

Half the flesh on my palm was gone.

I glanced down and discovered that huge rolls of skin were sim-ply missing from various parts of my body. I looked back up the hill and saw little globs of flesh sticking to the rocks that I'd hit on my way down. As revolting as it was, I didn't actually feel any pain, and I had to move. I scrambled up the opposite bank, the soles of my feet growing bloodier with each step, losing skin, as I fought a rising tide of panic. The light was fading. But if I could reach the top before the sun was gone, I'd somehow be okay.

Of course, I didn't.

With mere feet to go, the light abruptly shrunk back into total darkness, and the monster was upon me.

I woke up to find a hand covering my mouth, so I reacted pretty naturally—I punched the owner of the hand in the face.

There was a soft "ow," and then, "Caitlin, it's me."

I stopped struggling and sat up. Adrian let go of me, perched on the edge of my bed.

"Sorry about the face thing," he whispered. "You were starting to scream, and I didn't want you to wake up your family."

My racing heart didn't seem like it was going to calm down anytime soon, so I leaned my head back against the wall and closed my eyes, trying to breathe.

"Was it bad?"

I nodded.

It was too dark in the room for me to make out anything more than his vague silhouette, but I knew it was him—it sounded like him, like what he would say. Part of me remembered the Green Thing nightmare and urged me to verify his identity, but the rest of me was too tired. Adrian settled onto a pile of throw pillows on the floor by my fireplace and waited. Knowing he was right there, I immediately dozed off.

And woke a half hour later from a second nightmare, shaking uncontrollably.

"Sh-shit," I gasped, looking wildly around the room. "*Shit.*"

Adrian was instantly at my side. "What happened?"

"Another n-nightmare," I said, teeth chattering. "What do you t-think happened?"

I was being short with him, but I was scared out of my mind. Adrian was there—I wasn't supposed to have another nightmare if he was there. Right?

"Why didn't it work?" I asked, clutching my arms to my chest. It was so cold. I couldn't remember the dream at all, but I think it had something to do with hypothermia.

Adrian's eyes bloomed light in the darkness. "Hey," he said, cupping his hand to my cheek. I looked at him, and his eyes pulsed, swirling. Tears leaked down my cheeks as he did his vampire thing, and suddenly, I wasn't afraid anymore. Cold, still, and shaking, but no longer afraid.

"How do you feel?" he asked, searching my eyes. His were still silver, but they were motionless.

"Tired," I said, taking stock. "But fine."

We were whispering pretty quietly, but I thought I heard a creak from somewhere in the house. Adrian instantly tensed, turning to listen. We stayed frozen like that for a few moments, before he relaxed.

"House settling," he concluded. His hearing was better than mine by a ridiculous margin, so I trusted his conclusion.

"What did we do differently?" I asked. "Why didn't it work?"

Adrian opened his mouth, then closed it. "I don't know. Unless—" He paused, thinking. "The nightmares started right after you went to the mall, right?"

I nodded.

"And that man—did he touch you?"

I nodded again. "Briefly, just my wrist."

"When you were at my house sleeping, after the nightmare, I was next to you. Maybe to interrupt the connection, which was established by physical touch, that's exactly what's required to block it."

I stared at him. "What does that mean?"

He shifted slightly on the bed. "I mean I think I can't just be sitting on the floor." He looked down, and though it was too dark to see if he was blushing or not, his voice definitely made it sound like he was. "I think I have to be touching you to make this work."

I laughed, suddenly. "I'm *really* glad Mariana or Dominic or Julian didn't volunteer for this."

He smiled, but I could tell he was embarrassed. "I guess I could just hold your hand?"

I yawned mid-scoff. "You need to sleep, too. I'm not going to make you kneel by my bed all night holding my hand." I looked at him and pushed back my covers. "Just get in already."

My bed was a twin, barely long enough to fit Adrian. It wasn't even pushed against a wall, so there was a good chance that one of us was going to fall out. He crawled in beside me and sat. Side by side, we both hung out over the edge slightly.

"You have the tiniest bed I have ever seen," Adrian said after we'd both sat there for a minute trying to figure out what to do next.

"Yeah. Came with the room."

Still mostly blind in the dark, I poked his knee, then felt along his calf, trying to figure out what he was wearing, since I couldn't see him. I patted his six-pack, too.

"Sweatpants and a T-shirt. You came well prepared."

"Figured I might as well be comfortable."

"Well, get ready for some ultimate snuggling. You're gonna be the little spoon."

"I am not going to be the little spoon."

I stared somewhere in the vicinity of his face sternly. "My bed, my spoon rules."

He sighed, which I interpreted as a sigh of resignation, and I pushed him down—which I was only able to do because he let me—and snuggled up behind him. I could feel him pull the blankets over both of us, tucking it in around my shoulders, before settling onto his side. Mostly because there was so little room—but also because I wanted to—I pressed my forehead into the middle of his back and closed my eyes. And then I realized something.

"Wait, do you think there has to be actual skin-on-skin contact?"

After a moment he replied, "That would actually make sense."

I nodded, and slid my arm over his waist, heart racing mutinously. I knew he could feel it, because my chest was pressed to his spine. After a moment, though, he put his arm over mine, moving my hand until it lay flat against his heart. He covered it with his own, and we lay like that for a long moment, our breathing too loud for the deep silence of the house.

"Caitlin," he murmured. "If you tell anyone I was the little spoon, there will be consequences."

I laughed into his shirt. "Admit it—you like being the little spoon. I'm a fantastic big spoon."

He just snorted and threaded his fingers through mine. Finally, I gave him a little squeeze, burrowed closer into the space between his shoulder blade and the pillow, and fell fast asleep.

When I woke up, Adrian was gone—which was disorienting, even though I'd known he would have to leave before my aunt and uncle were up. When I went downstairs for breakfast, I was extra careful to check if Joe and Rachel had any inclination that someone had been in my room last night, but they appeared to be completely oblivious. Maybe Adrian and I could pull this off, after all.

As restful as my night had been, I'd still gone through two nightmares before we'd figured out how to effectively block the dreams. Backlogged with sleep deprivation, it was only eight p.m. when I said good night to everyone and headed back up to my room. I fell asleep immediately—but everyone else stayed up much later than normal (since it was the holidays now), which meant Adrian was delayed in coming over, which meant I had another nightmare.

When I woke up gasping, Adrian was sitting beside me, eyes already glowing.

"Hey," he murmured. "You all right?"

I sat up, took in a long, shuddering breath, and leaned my forehead against his shoulder.

"Every time," I mumbled. "Every time, nothing I do can change what happens. I always lose."

"What do you mean?"

I rubbed my eyes into his collarbone, frustrated. "In the dreams. It doesn't matter how much I fight or struggle or run or scream, something bad happens, and I can't stop it. It's pissing me off."

He wrapped his arms around me in a hug, and I let him. After a moment he pulled back, eyes flickering to silver. "You ready?"

I looked at him—and then shook my head. "I know that helps. But it feels wrong. It feels like I'm cheating, somehow. Even though it sucks, I feel like I need to be able to *feel*." I looked up at him, hoping I hadn't hurt his feelings. He was frowning, but he didn't seem angry.

"I understand," he said, after a long moment. "I actually do understand. No more Jedi mind stuff."

He smiled and I smiled, and it was awkward again. I patted the bed and he crawled in next to me, stretching his arm out underneath the pillow. I guess he was going to be the big spoon tonight. I didn't argue, just fit myself along the contour of his body and pulled the blankets over us. He rested his arm on my waist, and in a mirror of the night before, I wound my fingers through his. His breath was soft and warm on my neck and I heard him murmur, "Good night, Caitlin."

I smiled, glad he couldn't see me.

"Good night, Adrian."

Adrian came over every night, sometimes crawling in beside me while I was still asleep, so that the moment I woke up, he was there. I'd grab his hand and squeeze it for as long as it took for the dregs of the dream to slip away. Sometimes he got there early enough that I didn't have a nightmare at all. Usually we didn't say much. Most of the time I woke up in the morning and he was gone. Occasionally, though, we were so entangled that he had to physically move me to get out of bed. I'd murmur something incomprehensible, he'd laugh (very quietly), and bundle the blankets back around me so I didn't get cold. And it really only took a few nights before it wasn't awkward at all anymore. It felt sort of . . . right, actually, to be sleeping next to him. And for that to be all we were doing. It was peaceful.

And before I knew it, it was Christmas Eve.

The insistent buzz of my annoying comes-with-the-phone ringtone startled me awake. I groped for it blindly on my nightstand and brought it to my ear, answering with a grunt instead of actual words.

"You're always so eloquent in the morning."

"Nmphmm."

"When can you be ready by?" Adrian asked. It was funny talking to him on the phone knowing that he'd been lying next to me only a few hours before.

I searched my brain groggily. "A few years? I don't know. For what?"

"It's Christmas Eve. We're supposed to go to my place?"

"Oh, yeah."

Thank goodness I'd already told Joe and Rachel a week ago. They'd had time to get used to the idea.

"Julian's been a pain in the ass lately. Do you mind if we go somewhere else?"

To be honest, I didn't really want to be around Adrian's family, either. They were kind of party poopers. "Sure," I yawned into the phone. "Where you wanna go?"

"We own a cabin a ways up the mountain. I was thinking we could go there and just hang out?"

"Sounds good," I said sleepily. "Give me an hour to wake up and five minutes to get ready."

He laughed. "I'll pick you up at eleven. And do you mind if I bring Lucian along? I want to get him out of the house, and he seems to like you."

That surprised me. "No, I don't mind."

"All right, we'll pick you up in an hour. Dress sort of warm; it'll take a while to heat up the cabin."

"Okay," I yawned again. "See you then."

I hung up and buried another yawn in my pillow, then forced myself to get up. At 10:48 I'd managed to shower, dress, and make myself breakfast. I was spitting a mouthful of toothpaste into the sink when I heard Norah yell her usual mantra up the stairs.

"I'll see you guys later," I said as I headed toward the door.

"Be careful," Joe grunted in my direction.

"Call us if you need anything," Rachel offered.

I waved and headed out the front door. Rachel and I still didn't exactly chat, but we'd unofficially declared a cease-fire for the holidays. Maybe I was finally getting used to this place. The rage that had once been a natural part of my day had quieted, and sometimes I even felt downright happy.

Through the window of the truck, I could see Lucian bouncing up and down excitedly. When he saw me, he climbed over Adrian and pressed his face and hands against the window. I smiled and waved at him; he grinned back, lips squished to the glass.

"Hello, Lucian," I said as I climbed into the passenger seat.

"Hello," he replied, squirming with excitement.

As we pulled out of the driveway, Lucian leaned forward, cranked the volume on the stereo to an almost painful level, and sang.

"Jesus is just all right . . . something! Jesus is just all right, oh yeah! Jesus is just something something! Yeah, yeah, yeah, yeah, yeah, yeah, yeah!"

I stared quizzically at Adrian. "You got him hooked on The Doobie Brothers?"

He shrugged helplessly. "Ever since he heard this song, he can't stop singing it. I have no idea why."

We listened to Lucian's broken, half-filled-in lyrics for the next four and a half minutes. I'd never seen him look so energetic. He bopped his head along to the fast-paced beat and sang boldly. I was actually a little impressed. When the song was finished, he leaned back against the seat with his usual blank expression and listened passively to the variety of songs that shuffled through. Two playlists later, we pulled up to a log cabin and the landscape looked vaguely familiar.

"Remember when we went sledding?" Adrian asked as he parked the truck. "That was part of this property, about a half a mile northeast of here."

That would explain it, then. We climbed out and Adrian led the way to the cabin. A fire was roaring in the stone fireplace of the main room.

"I came up here earlier to start warming it up," Adrian admitted, looking shy.

I smiled. Of course he had.

He disappeared into a side room and came back without the small lunch cooler he'd brought with him.

"Would you like a tour?" he asked.

I shook my head at him, smiling. "There are three things in this world that require tours: museums, castles, and de la Mara private properties."

He rolled his eyes and took me by the arms. "Come on; it's a short tour today due to grumpy tourists. This," he said, turning me in a slow, 360-degree circle, "is the main room. Notice the shabby-chic sofas, the Stony Creek original area rugs, and the Fields dining set."

I stared at the dining room table and the six chairs that sat grouped around it. "Are those really Fields?" Trish had told me once that her grandfather had been a carpenter, and a ton of the furniture around the county had been handcrafted by him, once upon a time.

"Yep. Mariana and Dominic thought it would be best to have something that represented the spirit of the town. They actually lived here for a while, while the house was being built."

"Doesn't have enough marble to seem like their style."

"And you've managed to sum them up in one sentence. On with the tour."

He walked me straight forward toward two open doors. "In door number one, we have a bedroom! Door two is a bathroom. Over there is the kitchen. That's it."

I was surprised. "Really?"

"The cabin was already here when they moved in; otherwise it would have a six-car garage next to the well out back."

I suddenly realized Lucian was missing. "Where's your brother?"

Adrian sighed. "Frankie?"

"Alejandro!" I heard a small voice call from the kitchen.

"He's recently discovered YouTube. Lady Gaga particularly fascinates him."

"Ah." In a weird way, that made sense.

We walked into the kitchen and discovered that Lucian had taken a jar of green olives out of the fridge and was thirstily drinking the juice from it. I shuddered.

"Why is he doing that?" I whispered as Lucian drained the jar and started popping olives onto his fingers.

Adrian leaned in. "Salt content is comparable to blood. It's one of the ways we're trying to help him with withdrawals. He's down to two blood bags a day."

I blinked. "Oh."

"You're gonna get a stomachache, buddy," Adrian warned. Lucian stared at his brother and slowly chewed an olive off his pinkie finger.

Adrian shrugged. "All right, but don't say I didn't warn you."

We walked out as Lucian contemplated the remaining olives.

"Still think he's cute?"

I looked back at the door. "He's adorable. Strange and slightly terrifying, but adorable."

"You're the only one who thinks so." Adrian sat down on the couch and stared blankly into the fire. For a moment, he kind of looked like Lucian.

"What do you mean by that?" I sat next to him and drew my knees up to my chin to keep warm. Adrian grabbed a blanket from the back of the couch and handed it to me.

"I don't know," he said, propping his feet up on the coffee table. "He just has such a limited world. He's not allowed to interact with anyone outside our family—besides you, of course, and I had to pull strings to even allow that—and no one in the family pays any attention to him. Which seems so stupid after we went to all the trouble of getting him back. Sometimes I feel like . . ."

He closed his eyes and leaned his head back against the couch. "Sometimes I feel like the only reason he's important to us is so we can say we won. Julian sure as hell doesn't care about him, and Mariana and Dominic are so wrapped up in their own lives that they don't even realize he's there half the time. I try to help, but he needs more than me. He needs structure and discipline and love—he needs *parents*." He smiled bitterly. "We all need parents."

I'd never heard Adrian say that much about his personal life the entire time we'd known each other.

"What was your childhood like?" I asked, a bit abruptly, hoping to keep him talking.

He blinked at me a few times and shrugged. "I was born in Greece, so I lived with a family there until I was eight. Then I was sent to live with Julian in France for four years. Since we were related and similar in age, they thought it was a good idea to pair us together."

"Aren't you guys, like, seventeen years apart? And who's this 'they'?"

"The Council—they decide where we live until we come of age. And, yeah, we're seventeen years apart, but that's very unusual for siblings; most are centuries older than each other. A demon can only get back to earth in a physical body once every couple hundred years—it simply requires too much energy. My father got through a century and a half ago, created a body, and had Mariana. We destroyed his body and sent him back to hell, since he can't really be killed."

"I still don't understand that," I said, leaning forward. "*Everything* can be killed."

"You can't kill something that's not real," he explained, then shook his head, as if he knew that didn't make sense. "I mean, they are *real*, but not like we think of things being real or imaginary. They're ideas; individual units of energy that happen to have some sort of consciousness. It would be like trying to 'kill' light—you can cover a light source, stars can implode and go dark, but you can't end the life of something that was never really alive to begin with. Honestly, we don't understand what they are. That's why we call them demons— they're the stuff of nightmares." A dark look passed over his face. "In your case, literally."

He leaned back against the sofa. "Anyway, he got through again thirty-six years ago and had Julian, which was honestly pushing how quickly we thought demons could regroup their power. Then, some-how, he broke through less than twenty years later and had me. Which should have been impossible."

Adrian's eyes narrowed as he glared into the fire. "He's smarter than the others, or stronger. More adaptive, somehow. Seven years go by and he gets Lucian's mother pregnant and manages to steal him from right under our noses before we even realize what's hap-pened. It was an embarrassment. I remember listening to my Greek 'parents' talk about it at night when they thought I was asleep. I was only seven, but I knew it was important to get him back. It's only recently become clear to me that it was to save face, not to save Lucian."

The firelight hit Adrian's glowing eyes and turned the silver dark, almost black. He was angry; I didn't need an internal emotion sen-sor to tell me that. Lucian seemed to be a very delicate subject for Adrian.

"When I was at your house, you let Lucian climb on your shoul-ders," I said slowly, "and Julian said you shouldn't do that. What did he mean?"

Adrian's face twisted into a scowl. "Julian's a jackass. It literally doesn't compute with him that I actually give a shit about Lucian, because Julian doesn't give a shit about anything." He blinked and scrubbed a hand over his face, letting out a long, slow breath. "My older brother," he tried again, "is dissatisfied with his role in life. He thinks the Council's rules are stupid. I do, too, but for different reasons."

"Which rules, in particular?" I prompted. "You have a lot."

Adrian looked disgusted. "Celibacy with humans. He could care less about having friends or truly getting to know someone, but he's seriously pissed about not being able to have sex with whomever he likes. Since we're sterile and can't receive or pass on diseases, there should be no issue with taking full advantage of his . . . natural assets. I, on the other hand, could care less about sex. Well"—he paused, blushing slightly—"let's just say it's not a priority. But I want *friends*. I'm in high school, for God's sake. But the same rule applies to both of us: no intimacy with humans. No friends. No spouses. No one-night stands. I couldn't even join the math club."

He glanced over at me and shrugged. "There aren't that many of us, and we've survived this long by hiding, placing ourselves apart from the rest of the world. That level of isolation is too hard for most of us to handle. Immortality becomes far easier to cope with when you stop caring. The couple Julian lived with as a kid basically ignored him for ten years. When he sees me actually trying to be a brother to Lucian, I think he gets mad that he never had that growing up. I understand why he's an ass, but it's still hard not to hate him."

I huddled in my blanket, afraid that if I so much as blinked, Adrian would stop talking. "So why don't you ignore Lucian, like Julian ignored you?"

He laughed, which I wasn't expecting. "Honestly? The library. Books. Harry Potter. I couldn't be friends with real people, couldn't interact with my classmates beyond academic necessity, but as long as I told Mariana that the books were for school, I could read as much as I wanted. I consumed fiction like it was food. At home, I had no real concept of compassion or brotherhood or loyalty or bravery—I learned about all of that from books."

He smiled suddenly. "You know Mrs. Goode, the office lady at school? She used to be the town librarian. She was probably the closest thing I had to a friend. She'd always pick out new series that she thought I'd like, and call the house to tell me that my 'research materials' were available. I felt like a spy." He grinned and shrugged happily. "Once I realized that I could choose to be different, that I could *love* people, even if they didn't know it, I promised myself I would find a way to live a different life. I would be nothing like Julian or Mariana or Dominic. I wouldn't grow bored with the world. And once Lucian came to live with us, I promised myself that I would do my best to make sure that he knew he was loved. He exhausts me, and he's kind of insane, but he's my brother." He paused, a hard look stealing over his face. "I've accepted what I am, but I will not accept that my existence is meaningless or that I can't be inherently good despite my lineage." He glanced over at me. "That's why you're . . ."

He trailed off and swallowed hard. "That's why you're unique," he finished after a moment. Adrian stared at a stain on the old plaid couch, tracing it with his finger. "I am so sorry that all this has happened to you, with my dad," he said finally. "It's awful. It's terrible, and it's unfair. But I can't help but be happy, in a way." He looked up at me slowly, eyes dark, rimmed with firelight. "You are my excuse to be the person I've always wanted to be," he murmured almost to himself, searching my face as if he'd never seen it before. "Every moment I spend with you is stolen time, and I don't care. I will never have someone like you again. I will protect you with my life, I will keep you safe from my father—but what truly terrifies me is the thought that, when this is all over, you won't remember me at all."

I stared at him, dumbstruck.

There were so many words, so many feelings and impulses building up inside me that I could hardly breathe. Before my stuttering brain could come up with anything even resembling an elegant reply, he blinked, as if coming out of a daze, and stood up.

"Are you hungry?" he asked abruptly, heading toward the kitchen.

I wasn't, particularly, since I'd eaten breakfast less than an hour ago, but he returned from the kitchen with Lucian under one arm and the cooler under the other and set his brother on a chair and the cooler on the table. I shuffled over with my blanket and sat down, and we ate silently. It was Mariana's cooking, so it was delicious, but I didn't really notice because I was distracted by everything Adrian had said. Lucian finished eating in record time, and produced a deck of cards out of thin air.

"Can we play?" he begged Adrian.

A tiny wave of what could have either been irritation or tiredness passed over his face before he smiled and said, "Sure."

"I'll clear the dishes." I picked up everyone's plates and carried them into the kitchen to wash them by hand in the glacier-cold tap water. A few minutes later, I had the dishes laid out on the drying rack and crept to the door to listen, peeking through the sliver where the door didn't quite meet the jamb. They were sitting on the rug in front of the fire.

"Go!" Lucian said excitedly.

Adrian picked up a card from a pile between them.

"Do you have any Jacks?" Lucian asked, holding his cards awkwardly close to his chest so he wouldn't reveal them to Adrian.

"Go fish."

Lucian's face fell and he picked up a card from the pile, but as soon as he saw it, he grinned and laid down four matching cards.

"I win!"

There was still a huge pile of cards sitting on the floor between them, but Adrian folded his up and said, "You sure did."

I decided to walk in then and join them on the rug.

"Would you like to play?" Lucian asked me as Adrian began shuffling the deck again.

"Sure," I said, pretending innocence. "What are we playing?"

"Go," he announced.

"It's Lucian's version of Go Fish," Adrian explained and dealt out cards to us. We played a few rounds where whoever got the first set of four 'won' the game. It was amazing to see how Lucian's normally blank face would light up when he thought he played well or got a good hand. After Lucian won his fourth game, Adrian gathered up the cards. "Do you think that's enough for one day?"

Lucian said, "Okay," but looked pretty bummed.

"Why don't we open presents now?" I suggested.

Adrian looked at me. "You brought presents?"

I shrugged as I stood up and went to my messenger bag. "Nothing much." I sat back down and handed the first package to Lucian. His eyes got wide behind his aviator goggles. "Open it."

He reverently untaped the paper and slid it off. When he saw what was inside, his mouth formed a round O of surprise.

"What'd you get there, Lucian?" Adrian asked.

"*The Adventures of Frankie the Boy*," he replied in an awed voice.

Adrian looked at me and I shrugged shyly. "I got the idea from when you said he liked stories. So I made him that."

I wasn't exactly an illustrator, but I drew fashion designs all the time—it hadn't been a huge stretch to try and capture Lucian's quirky mannerisms in some simple sketches. As far as the dialog was concerned, I'd mostly taken that from actual conversations we'd had.

"Adrian, look!" Lucian demanded, crawling onto Adrian's lap and turning the hand-cut pages slowly. "That's me! I'm in the library hanging upside down like I'm not supposed to, and there I am jumping out of your truck, and that's me on your shoulders, and there's me and the lady, and there's me *dreaming!*"

Adrian looked attentively down over Lucian's shoulder at the colored pages, making appropriate "mm-hmm" sounds when necessary. I thought maybe he didn't like it until I realized his eyes were a bit shinier than usual. Not vampire glowing, but kind of glassy. As Lucian babbled on, Adrian leaned his forehead against his little brother's hair. I looked down at the carpet, not wanting to intrude.

A moment later, I heard Adrian say, "Tell Caitlin thank you for the book."

I felt a small pair of arms latch around my neck at the same time I heard Lucian exclaim, "*Thank you!*"

I hugged him back, tightly. "You're very welcome. I'm glad you like it."

I peeked over Lucian's shoulder at Adrian. He mouthed the words *thank you*. I shook my head in an it-was-nothing sort of way and smiled.

"Do you want to see what I got your brother, Lucian?"

He instantly let go of me and sat on the floor to look at Adrian. I picked up the other package and handed it over.

"Merry Christmas," I said, feeling suddenly shy. "This is from me and my family."

He took the package and opened it just as meticulously as Lucian had, then frowned curiously when he saw the box inside.

"I know it says Folgers, but it's not that," I assured him.

He smiled at me, opened the box, and pulled out a pair of lamb's wool slippers.

"My uncle makes them every year for everybody, and since you're kind of family now, he wanted to make you a pair, too." I shoved a second package at him before he could say anything. "This is from me."

He took the second, smaller package and unwrapped it. Then he stared.

"*Interview with a Vampire?*" he asked, and I couldn't tell if he was amused or disgusted.

"It seemed funny at the time," I said, feeling completely and utterly lame. It had been half off on Amazon, so I'd bought it. I heard an odd noise, and looked up to see that Adrian was laughing so hard he had to lean against the couch for support.

"Are you okay?" Lucian asked, concerned.

"Yeah, I'm all right; Caitlin's just a very odd girl." He wiped his eyes with the back of his hand and let the laughter trickle off into chuckles.

Before I could respond, Lucian hopped up and said, "Caitlin, will you read to me?"

"Lucian, I don't think—" Adrian began, but I cut him off.

"No, it's okay. I'd love to read to you; come up here on the couch."

He scrambled immediately onto the sofa and crawled onto my lap, holding his prize book in his hand.

"'*The Adventures of Frankie the Boy*,'" I began reading. "'By Caitlin Holte. Once upon a time, there was a boy named Frankie, who loved to do strange things . . .'"

He made me read it three times, and by the middle of the third reading, he'd completely zonked out, and I wasn't far behind. The repetition of the story, the warmth of the fire, Lucian, and the blanket, and my constant exhaustion combined to throw both of us into a mid-afternoon nap. Lucian was hanging limp in my arms.

"You want me to take him?" Adrian asked quietly from his place on the floor.

I yawned. "No, I don't want to wake him up. He can stay with me, I don't mind." I propped the two throw pillows against the arm of the couch and slowly tilted so that we were both lying down, facing the fire. He stirred and snuggled closer to me. In minutes, I was deeply asleep, and for once, I didn't dream.

---

"Shh, we don't want to wake her up."

"Why not?"

"Because she's very tired. We should let her sleep."

"Oh. Okay."

---

I slowly opened my eyes to see Adrian leaning back on his elbows and Lucian kneeling on the rug in front of the fire, concentrating very hard on making an elaborate, multideck card castle. I watched them for a few minutes as I slowly began to wake up. Unfortunately, I couldn't keep a small yawn from escaping, and Lucian whipped his head to look at me.

"She's awake," he said in a stage whisper to Adrian, who smiled and nodded.

"What time is it?" I asked sleepily.

"Just after five," Adrian replied.

I stretched and yawned again on the couch. "When do we have to go back?"

One corner of his mouth tilted up in a sad smile. "Soon."

I looked at Adrian. He looked back.

"Is it dinner?" Lucian asked, unable to mask his excitement.

"There's a Snickers bar for you in the cooler," Adrian said, not taking his eyes off me. Lucian darted into the kitchen in search of his treasure. I blinked out of necessity, but kept my gaze level. The sound of Lucian searching for the Snickers bar escalated, but I almost didn't hear him because nothing was so important in the world as this moment, here, with Adrian. Just then, Lucian ran back in, prize in hand. I blinked and sat up, folding the blanket to give my hands something to do.

"Caitlin," I heard Adrian call my name. I looked up. "I left your present in the other room. Lucian, we'll be back in a few minutes, okay?"

"Okay," he said, happily chewing on the candy bar.

I stood up slowly and followed Adrian through the bedroom door, which he closed behind us. A single lamp shone from the nightstand. My heart was beating too fast, and I couldn't seem to breathe right.

"Caitlin," he murmured, and backed me up against the door. I stood perfectly still, half afraid I was asleep. He closed his eyes, leaned his forehead against the door and his cheek against mine and whispered my name again, like it was sacred.

I slid my arms around his waist and murmured, "Merry Christmas."

He breathed quietly against my neck. Slowly, as if afraid I would disintegrate in his arms, he gathered me into a hug that lifted me off my toes.

"Merry Christmas," he whispered. Slowly, he let me down again, and finally let me go. He shook his head and cleared his throat. "I suppose you want your present?"

I cleared my throat, too, feeling weird and emotional. "I didn't expect you to get me anything," I told him as he went to the other side of the bed and picked up two large boxes.

"I know. But I wanted to." He set them on the bed, and they made a huge indent. "Open them."

Cautiously, I went over to the first box and unwrapped it. Inside was the sewing machine my mom had bought me, the one with the broken pedal cord.

I looked at him. "You fixed it?"

He shrugged, blushing. "I thought you might want to use it again."

I felt tears racing to my eyes and I turned, blinking rapidly to bat them away. "Is this other box for me, too?"

He nodded.

I scowl-smiled at him as I ripped off the paper. Underneath was the packaging for a brand-new Brother serger.

"Adrian—is this what's actually in there?"

"Yes."

I tried to breathe again. "I can't accept this. This is very expensive."

"If you don't accept it, I'll just drop it off at your front door with a note to your aunt saying it's an anonymous Christmas present for you."

"Adrian," I breathed, "I can't—"

"Yes, you can. Please."

He almost looked anxious. I rubbed my hands over my face. "No one's ever gotten me anything this nice before."

"Then it was about time," he said with a small smile. I looked at him again. He seemed determined.

"Thank you," I said finally. "They're perfect. I don't know where I'm going to put them, but they're beautiful and perfect."

He blushed a little. "That's already taken care of."

"What do you mean?"

"I converted one of the offices into a studio for you. You can come over and use it anytime you want."

"Adrian," I began to protest again, but he cut me off.

"It's already stocked with some of the fabrics you'll need to start making your designs."

I stared at him. "What are you talking about?"

"Remember when I borrowed those sketches of yours after Thanksgiving?" I nodded warily. "I sent copies of them to a contact in New York. He agreed to supply you with fabric and materials. He also said that if your work is as good as your sketches, there's an internship waiting for you when you graduate—assuming you don't mind moving to the city, of course."

I continued to stare at him, unable to comprehend the words coming out of his mouth. "What are you saying?"

He shrugged. "You said you wanted a job."

"That's a career."

"It's a foot in the door."

"I'm seventeen."

"You're talented." And with that, he picked up both boxes—which probably weighed eighty pounds combined—and headed for the door. "Come on, I need to get Lucian home before Mariana and Dominic have a hernia."

I followed him back into the main room, still in shock. Lucian had finished his card castle and was staring at it in triumph.

"Come on, Lucian; we're going home," Adrian said to his little brother.

He sighed. "Okay."

We packed up in a few minutes and headed out to the truck. Lucian fell asleep, his head against Adrian's chest and his feet thrown over my legs. Adrian had his arm stretched out over the back of the seat, his hand wrapped around my shoulder, as Christmas music slowly drifted over the radio. I closed my eyes and breathed in. As the shock of his presents started to wear off, I realized one very simple, awful thing:

I loved Adrian.

# 14

# TWO WORDS:
# SLUMBER PARTY

On Christmas morning I woke to fluffy, white snowflakes floating sleepily past my window, and my first thought was that
this would be the first Christmas without my mom. But if I
wanted to make it through breakfast and presents and being around
other people, I couldn't think about that. Not yet.

I groped around for the slippers Uncle Joe had given all of us
the night before and followed the scent of coffee out of my room,
then stopped short at the balcony. Rachel was downstairs on the
couch dozing lightly against Joe's chest. He was reading an old, yel-
lowed paperback Western, but put it down after a moment and simply wrapped his arms around his wife. It made a lump slide up the
back of my throat until it was hard to breathe. It also made me wonder if my parents had ever been affectionate like that. I honestly
couldn't remember.

I went back to my room, intent on giving them a little while longer to themselves. Still fighting the throat lump, I checked my e-mail and saw I had a new message from Trish. It was, predictably, short and sweet.

Mystic!
Merry Christmas. Don't forget to tell Adrian what we told you to tell him.
—Trish

I shook my head but smiled. I didn't know how someone could be infuriating and endearing all at once, but Trish managed it. After the Green Thing incident, I'd decided to save money and give her and the rest of the girls in our class these two-by-two-inch hand-embroidered pictures. My mom always made me one as a stocking stuffer, and just last year taught me how to pencil in the design straight onto the muslin and stitch over it. Flowers and butterflies were easier to do, but I was always easily bored with patterns, so I made stylized sketches of what everyone reminded me of. Trish's was, of course, a bear. I stitched red mittens for Stephanie, a mountain range for Jenny, Red Riding Hood's cape for Meghan, and a stack of books for Laura. They took forever, so I made them small, but everyone really seemed to like them, and it made me feel close to my mom, to carry on that tradition. But I couldn't think about that now—I couldn't think about her.

And I couldn't think about Adrian—not after last night, not after that moment in the back room of the cabin where he'd whispered my name. Someday soon I wouldn't be a target anymore, and then he and I would have to break off our fake relationship—which had never felt all that fake to begin with—and then my memory would get wiped and I wouldn't remember that I'd ever felt anything about him at all.

A while later, Rachel called up that breakfast was ready. Shoving all the emotions back down into the pit of my stomach where they belonged, I headed downstairs. We ate a huge pile of waffles with the strawberries cooked right into them, and bacon. I went through several cups of coffee, and then we headed into the living room to open presents. Joe, Rachel, and Norah all seemed appreciative of my somewhat pathetic gifts, although Rachel overdid it, feigning so much enthusiasm that I had to pretend to go to the bathroom to avoid the bear hug she was trying to give me. Norah got me a cool old sketchbook she'd found at an antique store with a metal lock-clasp and faded purple velvet cover, and Rachel bought me a couple sweaters in different shades of funky greens. I really liked the gifts but it was hard to sit there with them, like this was normal, like there wasn't someone missing.

I slipped up to my room after presents and wrapped myself up in the quilt. After staring at my closed laptop for a few minutes, I finally opened it, clicking through to find the pictures I'd buried so deeply in subfolders I wouldn't ever be able to stumble across them by accident. It was hard to see her face and not be immediately overwhelmed by all the feelings I'd spent so long trying to not feel. That was the only way to do it, really. That was the only way to get through every day and not just break down crying. I couldn't let myself remember her, I couldn't think about her, or miss her.

But it was Christmas. It had been almost three months since she'd died, and I felt guilty—not for moving on, but for forgetting. It was easier to forget, and selfish, and cowardly, and it was time now, finally, to acknowledge that she was gone.

I started way back, back to the baby pictures, back to when my dad was still around. My mom was thin then, my dad looked healthy, I was all round blubber and wispy hair. The sad thing was, there weren't all that many pictures to look at. My dad had always been the photographer in the family, and when he died, my mom just stopped taking them. All the ones I had of the two of us were from my grandma's really awful point-and-shoot. But there were a few scattered moments from early childhood: Mom and me at Thanksgiving baking pies, Mom helping me into my coat last year before prom, just three days before she would go to the hospital and never come home; Mom and I eating Jell-O out of little plastic cups in her hospital room the day before she went into the surgery that would give her the infection that would kill her. And that was it—that was the last one. She'd said she was too ugly from the chemo, she didn't want any more pictures taken of her until she was feeling better. But she never felt better, and she was never going to—and she knew that. We all knew that. And I didn't realize she would fade so quickly from my memory, and these photos would be all I had of her, and they wouldn't be enough. How was I supposed to hold on to an entire life with so few pictures? She was just an idea now—a lovely thought, faded at the edges, like my dad.

A long time later I shut the computer down, buried my face in my knees, and cried. I'd meant to go back downstairs to be with everyone else, but I couldn't, and I think they understood because they didn't come knock on my door. Eventually I fell asleep as the light faded and the snow stopped.

As usual, I woke up from a nightmare.

In it, I walked through Adrian's silent mansion, but all the angles were slightly off; the floor was sloped, the door frames were crooked, and the walls were just the tiniest bit caved. I walked from one room to another, but the rooms never ended. Always, I would eventually end up in the main foyer.

I walked for hours until I felt tired and sore and the floors felt sticky. I looked down and saw that I was standing in a spatter of blood.

The blood was dripping from twin puncture marks all over my arms. I looked up and realized that my footprints were scuffed through a trail of blood that led both behind and in front of me—I must have been walking in it the entire time.

As all these realizations descended, the spatter of blood became a trickle, although it didn't seem to be coming from me anymore. Suddenly, the trickle became a flood, and the flood started rising to my ankles, my knees, my hips, my waist, my chin, and then I was floating in it, being carried up to the ceiling, and it was warm and thick and smelled like copper. I reached the ceiling and still the ocean of blood kept rising until there was no more air, just blood.

For once, Adrian wasn't awake—when I sat up sharply, he did, too, though his eyes were mostly closed and he looked extremely confused.

"What's what?" he asked, blinking as he scanned the room. "S'ome happening?"

I planted my face against his chest angrily. "Nightmare," I said. "Go back to sleep."

Adrian sunk back into the pillows and rested his hand on my back. Still not really awake, he mumbled something I couldn't understand before going still and quiet once more. I lay awake for an hour looking at him—not because I was afraid of another nightmare, but because I didn't understand how I could be so happy and so sad and so angry all at the same time. Several times Adrian's arm tightened around me, and I wondered what he was dreaming of.

---

"Two words, Mystic: slumber party."

It was the day after Christmas and I was trying to brush my teeth and talk to Trish on the phone at the same time.

"Who, wha', whe', where?" I asked around my toothbrush.

"Are you brushing your teeth?"

I spit into the sink. "Yep."

"Gross. Anyway, it's at my house, junior gals, tonight. Be there or suffer my wrath."

I headed downstairs and found Rachel sitting at the table. "Can I go to a slumber party at Trish's tonight? If I don't, I will suffer her wrath."

She thought about it a moment. "Sure."

I pulled the phone back up to my mouth and said, "Yes. What time?"

"Dinner's at six, and we're making Sloppy Joes. You need a ride?"

I chewed my lip, thinking. I hated asking Trish to come all the way out to get me, I didn't want to bug Joe or Rachel, and I felt stupid asking Adrian to take me to someone else's house. I had my license, but there was no way I was driving any sort of vehicle through snowy mountain roads on my own.

"Errr . . . ," I said, stalling.

"Do you need a ride to Trish's?" Rachel asked.

"Errr . . . ," I said again.

"I can take you; it's okay," Rachel assured me. "Y'know, I've been so used to having Adrian pick you up that I've forgotten you have places to go. What time?"

I looked at her, feeling torn. "Trish says dinner's at six?"

Rachel nodded. "Okay. You'll be there at six."

I smiled at her. "Thanks, Rachel."

She smiled and returned to her paperwork.

"You in?" Trish asked.

"I'm in."

"Mystic! You made it." Trish took my bag out of my hand and dragged me inside. I waved good-bye to Rachel as the door began to close.

"Just to warn you, my brothers are home for Christmas, so it'll be kinda loud until they pass out."

She dumped my stuff in her family room and led me into the kitchen/dining room, which was jam-packed with people. I noticed Meghan, Stephanie, Laura, Jenny, and Trish's parents. But there were also three guys I didn't recognize.

"Yo, Paul, Mark, Jimmy, say hi to Caitlin."

As one they turned to face me, and though I instantly saw the family resemblance, my stomach clenched with dread that anyone of them might be Adrian's dad. They seemed nice enough, and they didn't have glowing eyes or anything. I told myself to chill.

"Jimmy's on the left there, Paul's in the middle, and Mark's on the right," Trish clarified.

Jimmy was easily the shortest of the three, maybe five ten or eleven. He had medium brown hair and broad shoulders and kind of just looked like he was happy all the time. Paul was at least six foot and stood with a lazy sort of grace. I wondered if he'd picked that up in law school.

Mark stood a little shorter than Paul, and had the same hair as Jimmy, except longer and gathered into a messy, hipster ponytail. If I remembered correctly, he was the art and music guy.

"Hot Sloppy Joes coming through!" Trish's dad warned, setting a huge platter in the center of the table.

"Wait your turn, Jimmy!" Mrs. Fields exclaimed. "Ladies first."

Jimmy withdrew his hand sheepishly. Out of the corner of my eye I thought I saw Mark staring somewhere past my shoulder with a curious expression, but I couldn't tell what he was looking at.

"Dig in," Trish said, breaking my thoughts and taking a burger for herself. "Also, how was everybody's Christmas?"

"Aka what loot did everybody score?" Meghan translated and then dug into her burger.

The conversation revolved around the table until the food was completely gone, and we dragged ourselves off to the family room, which had been designated as Girls Only for the night. We unrolled our sleeping bags and spread them across the floor, flopping down amid bowls of chips and candy that Trish had brought in earlier.

Meghan popped in a horror movie (which made me cringe—it would just add fuel to the fire for my nightmares) and we munched on the snacks until eventually I heard the rest of Trish's family wander off to their respective rooms.

"Come on, Mystic; you gotta watch this!"

"No," I said stubbornly.

It was the last twenty or so minutes of the movie, and I had my face covered resolutely with my pillow.

"Ronnie, watch out!" Meghan called to the main character's best friend right before I heard what sounded like a metal baseball bat connect with his skull.

"Oooh!" Meghan and Trish groaned in unison.

I peeked to my left and saw Laura sitting with a horrified expression on her face as she systematically ate popcorn one buttery piece at a time. On the fringe of our little circle sat Jenny, who sat looking at the TV with her usual passive expression. I almost wondered if she was asleep, except she blinked. Stephanie was clutching her pillow to her chest, looking extremely concerned.

"Caitlin, Caitlin, he's about to find the"—but she was cut off by a loud crashing noise, a splash, and Shia LaBeouf screaming in revulsion—"dead bodies," she finished a moment later.

I shuddered. I was not a horror-movie person, especially not the last couple weeks.

"Tell me when it's over," I called from underneath my pillow.

"Is that *Disturbia*?" someone asked from across the room. I peeked out and saw Trish's brother Mark. He was leaning against the door frame with his arms crossed across his chest.

"What part of 'girls only' do you not understand?" Trish asked, eyes glued to the screen.

"I'm not technically in the room."

Trish rolled her eyes, but didn't say anything else. Fifteen minutes later, the movie ended. Finally.

I took my head out from underneath my pillow and saw that Mark was still standing in the doorway, but sometime while I'd been hiding under my pillow, he'd changed into sweatpants and a white V-neck with a loose flannel shirt over it.

"Good night, Mark," Trish called to her brother, her tone a warning to leave.

He turned to look at the rest of us, and for a moment, his eyes flickered to the corner of the room. "Good night, ladies. I'm right upstairs if anyone has bad dreams."

He flashed a smile and disappeared.

Meghan turned to Trish. "Since when did Mark get hot?"

She looked back blankly.

"Oh, come on! I always remembered him as this quiet, out-of-the-way guy, and now he's got this really sexy starving-artist thing going on and I like it."

Trish stared at Meghan like she was an alien. "Are you serious?"

"He's quite attractive," Stephanie supplied with a shy smile.

"Paul's more my type," Laura said, "but I could see how people might find Mark appealing."

"Guys," Trish warned, "he's my brother. Ew, okay?"

Meghan leaned forward eagerly. "Is he dating anyone?"

"Not that I know of. But he's old!"

She rolled her eyes. "He's only a junior. We're juniors! It's practically the same thing."

Laura shook her head vigorously. "That's not the same at all."

"Besides," Meghan said, leaning back on her elbows with a satisfied smile, "I like older men."

"Meg, you are sick." Trish didn't really look angry, more morbidly puzzled.

"And he's yummy," Meghan added with a grin.

"I *really* don't think he's your type."

"He's totally my type!"

Trish looked at her skeptically. "I thought you wanted to be a hair stylist."

"What's wrong with that?"

"Nothing," she replied with a shrug, "I just think Mark wants to do different things. He's doing a semester abroad in France next year, to study at an art academy."

Meghan looked like she was about to drool. "I like cultured men."

Trish shook her head, disgusted. "Culture for you is eating a microwaved croissant."

"I'll learn French. We'll live there and make French love and have cute little French babies."

Trish looked horrified. "Dude, just—no."

"When are they leaving?" Jenny asked suddenly. As always, it surprised me when she spoke.

"Abou' a wee' af'er New Year's," Trish said around a mouthful of popcorn. She swallowed thickly. "We're having a little shindig here and you're all invited, by the way."

"I claim dibs on Mark for the New Year's kiss!" Meghan exclaimed. I happened to be glancing at Jenny and was startled to find an irritated expression cross her face as she stared at Meghan.

"I'm not sure you can really claim dibs on a human being," Laura replied dryly. "That's, like, slavery. Or prostitution."

"You guys are so melodramatic." Meghan sighed, leaning back against her pillows.

I decided to try and break the tension. "Hey, Trish, do you mind if I bring Adrian?"

She grinned at me. "Hell no, I don't mind! I'm bringing Ben." She looked at the other girls. "That's an open invitation; if y'all have dates, bring them along. Everybody should get a little midnight action."

The conversation spun off from there, and we stayed up until two in the morning talking. I conked out the moment we decided to call it a night.

Two hours later, I was awake again after a ferocious nightmare involving a thousand binoculars like the ones from the movie staring at me as I posed naked for an art class that was meeting in the Eiffel Tower.

It was mostly just creepy, but I woke up feeling like I was being watched. When I looked around, everyone was deeply asleep.

Except that Jenny's sleeping bag was empty.

Through the crack under the door, I saw a faint light. Trying not to step on anyone, I made my way over and peered through the sliver where the door wasn't quite closed.

There, sitting at the kitchen table, was Jenny.

And . . . Mark?

I could see two mugs sitting in front of them, like they'd been there so long they'd needed refreshments. Jenny had her chin cupped in her hand, white-blond hair draped around her, and was actually looking Mark in the eye, something I'd never seen her do with anyone else. Mark was murmuring something quietly to her and I strained to hear.

". . . talking and saying nothing. People don't understand the power of words. I love talking to people, but I can't stand it when they have absolutely nothing to say." He chuckled in a self-deprecating sort of way. "Which is ironic, because I'm doing all the talking."

Jenny smiled. I'm not sure I'd ever seen her smile before. "I like listening."

"Then you're pretty damn different from every other girl I've ever met."

They regarded each other for a few moments in silence.

"When are you going back?" Jenny asked finally.

"Two weeks."

She looked down at the table.

"But I'll be back this summer. Four whole months." He leaned forward, resting his arms on the table. "I'm going to bring all my supplies and start a new series. It's an idea that's been floating around in my head for a few years and I've been looking for a model, but no one on campus is right."

Jenny looked up at him from underneath her lashes, but I couldn't read her expression.

"I was wondering—well, to be honest Jenny, you're stunning. I was wondering if maybe you'd like to model for me? I mean, I know that sounds weird, but it's totally clothed, it wouldn't creepy or anything. I can't pay you much, but I do have some money set aside."

I could see Jenny immediately tense. "I'm not sure it's a good idea."

He looked surprised and a little hurt. "Why?"

Her eyes fluttered wildly around the room, reminding me of a trapped bird. "Meghan's into this sort of thing. Go talk to Meghan. I'll go get her."

She stood and made a bid for freedom and he simply put his hands on her waist and prevented her from moving.

"Jenny," he said, backing her toward the fridge with his sheer overwhelming presence. "If I wanted Meghan, I would have asked Meghan. I asked you."

For a moment, I thought they were going to kiss, which was crazy, they'd just met a few hours ago. Well, they'd probably known of each other their entire lives, but I doubted they'd ever really talked much before tonight, unless there was something I didn't know, but it didn't seem likely from the tone of their conversation.

But they didn't kiss. They stared at each other for a long moment and then Mark stepped back. "Just think about it, okay?" Jenny nodded.

I made my way back to my sleeping bag and crawled in, completely flabbergasted by what I'd just witnessed. I briefly considered telling Trish, but discarded the idea. She'd either kill Jenny or kill Mark. Probably Mark.

Besides, it was absolutely none of my business.

But it was very interesting.

---

"You sleep like the dead," Trish commented, pouring herself a bowl of Cap'n Crunch. It was ironic, because I'd had a nightmare in which I'd died quite grossly from some sort of flesh-eating bacteria. I was happy to be awake. The rest of the girls were lounging on their sleeping bags, munching on bowls of cereal and watching cartoons. It felt like I was in second grade again. It was awesome.

Trish held out the Cap'n Crunch. I grabbed it and sat up, glancing over at Jenny surreptitiously. She seemed more relaxed than usual, and maybe it was just my imagination, but she looked like she had some color in her cheeks, too. In my head, the whole scene last night seemed kind of surreal, but then I remembered the fact that

I was dating a vampire who wasn't allowed to love me and couldn't die and revised the level of weirdness for Jenny's situation.

People started wandering off after breakfast. Aunt Rachel came to pick me up at one, after I promised Trish that I'd come back for her New Year's party, and bring Adrian. Meghan made a special point of saying she'd come back if Mark was going to be there.

At the very least, it would be an interesting New Year's.

I hopped in the shower once I got home and threw on one of the new green sweaters Rachel had gotten me for Christmas. I could hear my phone ringing from my bedroom, and hurried in to answer it.

"Hello?"

"Hi, it's me. Just wanted to let you know your studio is all set up." I blinked. "Already?"

"Did you want to come over tomorrow and see it?"

I breathed for a moment. I hadn't made anything since well before my mom's funeral, besides the little embroidered pictures for the girls, and those didn't really count. He seemed to sense my hesitation.

"It's just a tour. Don't feel pressured to use it anytime soon."

I let the breath out. "Yeah, I'd like that." I was about to say goodbye when I remembered—"Oh! I promised Trish we'd go to her New Year's Eve party. Is that okay?"

He sounded amused. "Sure."

"Good. There's something I want your opinion on once we get there; it's too hard to explain now."

"Now I'm curious."

"Then you know what it feels like to be me."

He laughed. "Fair enough. I'll see you tomorrow."

"Don't you mean tonight?"

"Yes," he conceded. "To be fair, though, I see you every night. I don't always see you tomorrow."

I laughed at him and we said good-bye and hung up.

I couldn't tell Trish about Jenny and Mark—but I could tell Adrian. He was a master of discretion, and more importantly, he was impartial. I'd tell him what I'd seen, and then have him observe Jenny and Mark at the party, and see if Mark's intentions were pure. Part of me was freaked out that maybe Mark was not Mark, and that Mark was Adrian's dad, and that they'd gotten it all wrong and Jenny was the one in danger, somehow, not me.

For now, I settled on reveling in Christmas vacation. First: bake cookies. Second: eat them all. Repeat as desired.

———————◦

"I'm nervous," I said the next day as we were driving to Adrian's house. "Tell me not to be nervous."

"Don't be nervous."

We pulled up to the wrought-iron gates surrounding his property. He pushed a button on his key ring and they swung silently inward. Once again, I was reminded of how his mansion looked like it was pulled straight out of a fairy tale, especially with the weeks of accumulated snow on the grounds. He parked and we dashed inside to get out of the cold.

"Caitlin!" I heard a small voice say at the same time I felt something latch on to my waist.

"He finally learned your name after reading it on the cover of the book about fifty times," Adrian said, hanging up my coat.

I hugged Lucian's shoulders and looked down at him. "Are you gonna come see my new room with us?"

He looked over at his brother, who nodded, and then back at me, smiling happily.

"It's upstairs," Adrian said, leading the way. Lucian and I followed him to the third floor and down the hallway, all the way to the end. Adrian stepped behind me and put his hands over my eyes.

"You ready?"

"Sure," I said, unconvincingly.

"Lucian, you want to grab the door for me?"

I heard rustling and the soft turn of the handle and then Adrian was nudging me forward until we were inside the room. Slowly, he lowered his hands. I opened my eyes. I blinked.

"Holy shit."

Belatedly, I clapped my hands over Lucian's ears.

The room faced the front of the house, so the roof angled steeply to the floor, studded with huge windows. A cutting table was set up against the far wall and my serger and sewing machine had been set up back-to-back on a short table in the center of the room. The walls were lined with shelves, already partially filled with bolts of fabrics.

"They sent some samples based off the sketches you did. I know it's not everything you need, but it's a place to start."

I stared at the room. "I can't even contemplate how much this cost you."

He shrugged. "It didn't really cost *me* anything. Besides, when you make it as a famous designer, you can pay me back with free clothes."

I continued to stare at the room in complete shock. It was not sinking in that this was all mine to use anytime I wanted. I sucked in a deep breath and went to the wall of fabric, running my hands lightly over the cloth.

"Your sketchbooks are on the table and the drawers over there are full of scissors and needles and threads and . . . stuff," Adrian said, looking a little lost as he pointed to rows of dark, wood-paneled drawers. I peeked inside—professional equipment. Top of the line.

"Adrian," I said, feeling a little dizzy, "I can't ever repay this."

"It's a gift," he explained. "You're not supposed to."

I turned back to him. He was standing with his hands in the pockets of his jeans, wavy dark hair framing his face; his gray eyes soft and warm even in the cold, blue light coming from the windows. I rested my face against a bolt of silk and closed my eyes.

"I'm happy."

I heard a small *whap* a few moments later and opened my eyes to discover that Lucian had jumped on one of the mannequins and was currently riding it around the room like a horse.

"Frankie," Adrian said in a warning tone. "This is one room you can't play in, okay? This is Caitlin's room."

He climbed off the mannequin immediately and sheepishly wheeled it back to the others. Overcome with a giant bubble of happiness, I danced over to Adrian and threw my arms around him in a hug. "You're the best," I murmured. "Thank you so much."

I heard a low whistle from the door and looked up to find Julian leaning against the frame, staring at us. Adrian instantly pulled away from me.

"I'm dying to know how you justified this to Mariana," Julian said, taking in the room. His eyes settled on me speculatively. "Caitlin, my dear, I feel it's my duty to inform you that extravagant gifts are my brother's absurd version of foreplay."

Before I could even blink, Adrian had crossed the room and slammed his brother violently against the wall. "Shut up," he demanded him in a voice so low I almost couldn't hear.

Julian just rolled his eyes, looking bored. "This is exactly what I've been talking about."

Adrian looked livid, though his voice was calm. "Do not threaten me."

"I don't need to threaten anyone." Julian laughed. "I don't need to say a word. You'll see how this ends, eventually. The difference between us is that I don't disillusion myself about this shit."

I felt someone grip my hand. It was Lucian. Adrian's eyes flicked over in our direction for a moment, and then back to his older brother. Finally, he released him. "You're pathetic."

Julian adjusted the neck of his shirt. "And you still don't understand. You really don't. The day's gonna come, bro, and it's going to suck." He winked at me over Adrian's shoulder. "No pun intended."

Adrian pointed at the door. "Get out."

Julian looked at me over Adrian's shoulders. Finally, he left.

I let a few moments pass as Adrian stood silent and still. "Adrian?"

He didn't turn around. "Do not talk to me right now," he murmured, voice was shaking with rage.

I took a step back like I'd just been slapped.

"Damn it, Caitlin; stop *feeling* that!" He whirled toward me, eyes blazing silver. "This isn't about you."

"I didn't say it was," I replied, blinking back sudden tears. "I didn't say anything at all."

Adrian glared at me a moment longer, then leaned forward with his arms against the table, head bowed. Lucian hugged me, his face pressed into my waist. We stood there like that for an entire long, silent minute. Finally, he stood up, refusing to face me, eyes normal and gray again. "Come on; I'm taking you home."

I didn't move. "Adrian, please talk to me."

He headed for the door. "There's nothing to talk about."

"What just happened?" I asked, trying to sound resolute although I was terrified. I'd never seen him angry before, and it reminded me how very not human he was.

He leaned his forehead against the door and breathed. "Just Julian being an ass, as usual."

It was a vague answer, but it was an answer. I wasn't going to push him. "Okay."

I walked up to Adrian and stood there. He turned slowly to face me. "I'm sorry," he murmured, and brought his hand up like he was going to brush his fingers through my hair, but thought better of it and lowered his hand. He blinked and repeated his apology. "I'm sorry. If you can, just forget what you saw. It's not important."

I searched his face, but he wouldn't meet my gaze for more than a moment.

"Adrian," I began, but didn't know how to finish.

He looked agonized for a moment. "You feel . . ." He seemed to search for the right word, but couldn't find it. He closed his eyes. "I can't do this."

"What do you mean?" I whispered.

He opened his eyes. "Nothing. I mean nothing. Come on, I should get you home."

He reached for the door and I reached for his arm, stopping him. "Will you tell me someday? What this is about?"

He finally met my gaze. "Maybe. One day."

I nodded, and let go of his arm.

Adrian turned back to his little brother. "Frankie, why don't you stay here this time?"

Lucian looked sad, but didn't protest.

We drove back in silence, without even the sound of the radio to distract me from the weird stress emanating from Adrian. When we reached my house, he parked and leaned back, closing his eyes.

I turned in his direction, careful not to touch him. "I'm sorry if I've caused any tension between you and Julian."

"Caitlin, you have absolutely nothing to apologize for," he replied without moving a muscle.

"In that case," I continued, "I apologize on behalf of life." He opened his eyes and peered at me strangely. "For dealing you cards from a completely different game than the rest of us," I clarified. "It's kind of impossible to win that way."

It was a weird way to put it, but he seemed to get what I was trying to say. I opened my door, but he stopped me before I could actually get out of the truck.

"What time do you want me to pick you up for Trish's party?"

I tried to plaster a happy smile over the unease I felt. "How about nine?" I suggested. "I think the party starts sometime after that."

He nodded. I closed my door. Once he pulled away and I was back inside, all I could think was, *What the hell just happened?*

# 15

## FIVE MINUTES TO MIDNIGHT

"Please be careful," Rachel said for the hundredth time that evening. She was determined to dress me up for the party, so I was currently sitting on the toilet seat waiting for her to finish curling my hair.

"I will," I promised her. Again.

She began curling another piece distractedly. "I know it's just Stony Creek, but people still drink on New Year's Eve and the roads are very slick."

"I promise we will not be drinking tonight."

She bit her lip, looking very mom-ish and concerned as she fussed with my hair. "I know, but other people might be."

"Adrian's a very careful driver," I reassured her. "If someone looks like they're driving all crazy, he'll pull over."

I felt like I should be annoyed, but I kind of liked that she was worried about me.

Rachel released my hair from the curling iron and picked up another strand. "You and Adrian seem to be pretty happy with each other." It was more of a question than a statement.

I shrugged. "Yeah. We are." Just not in the same way most couples were, since we were not, in fact, a couple.

Rachel tested the strand of hair with her finger and decided it wasn't quite hot enough yet. "So how serious are you two?"

I frowned. "We're not about to get engaged, if that's what you mean."

"Well, I mean more . . . are you two . . . *together?*"

I stared at her, trying to figure out where she was going with this. "We're dating."

She took a deep breath and looked way more awkward and nervous than I'd ever seen her. "Okay, let's go for the blunt approach. Are you two having sex?"

I blinked.

I blinked again.

And then I burst into laughter. I had to dab at my eyes before my mascara got all smeared.

"I know I'm not your mom," she said, looking flustered, "and I'm not here to cast judgment on you if you are . . . doing . . . that, but I just want to make sure you're being safe."

"Is this, like, *the talk?*" I asked, trying not to giggle, and totally failing. I decided to spare her the embarrassment of having this conversation. "No," I said adamantly. "We are not having sex. I will let you know if we do."

She still looked kind of awkward and nervous, but relieved, too. "Good. You have your whole life to live without worrying about being physically intimate with another human being."

I nodded gravely but on the inside I was laughing again—Adrian wasn't exactly a human being.

"There," she said, releasing the last strand from the curling iron. She ran a comb through my hair, twisting the individual strands into larger, more elegant curls. "You're all set."

I hopped off the toilet cover and stood in front of the mirror. And had another Green Thing moment. I forgot that underneath normal, plain Caitlin was a more sophisticated, somewhat less-plain Caitlin. It also helped that Rachel had done my makeup; she was wicked good with eyeliner. As much as I was interested in fashion, I hadn't exactly mastered makeup yet—Mom hadn't worn any, ever, so I'd tried to copy what I saw in magazines and *Vogue* shoots, to very, very limited success. Most of the time I went really simple: foundation, mascara, ChapStick. Tonight, though . . .

Norah passed by in the hallway, stopped, backtracked, and looked in. "Is prom early this year?" she asked, staring at me.

"Is it too much?" Rachel asked her daughter, looking worried.

"No," Norah said. "I've just never seen Caitlin look so . . ." She trailed off as if the reflection in the mirror spoke for itself.

"Thanks, Norah," I said, and meant it.

"Adrian's here," Norah said suddenly, turning. Wow, how had she heard that?

"Hurry up and get dressed!"

I ran into my room and threw off my bathrobe. Careful not to mess up my makeup or frizz my hair, I tugged the dress over my head and looked at myself in the full-length mirror hanging on the inside of my wardrobe. It was a knee-length black dress with a square-cut neck and sheer, wrist-length sleeves. I slid on my Halloween stilettos and contemplated what coat to wear. My regular jacket would look awkward over this outfit.

There was a knock at the door. "Come in," I called, rifling through the wardrobe a little frantically.

"I thought you might not have anything to wear with that dress, so I dug this out," Rachel said, stepping through my door. In her hands was a black, floor-length wool coat.

"That's gorgeous," I breathed.

"I bought it on a whim when I lived in the city," she said, holding up the coat to me. "Don't have much use for it now." I slid my arms through the champagne-pink satin lining.

"You lived in New York?"

She smiled. "A long time ago. I'd won a few beauty pageants in high school; thought I wanted to be a model."

I had not known this. "Why'd you leave?"

Her smile grew. "I met Joe. My car broke down in Stony Creek on my way to visit a friend and he happened to be the only one around for miles. I fell in love with the town, and I fell in love with him. After that, I didn't want to be anywhere else."

"Rachel," I began, and she looked at me. I didn't know exactly how to say this. "A while back, Joe mentioned that he knew why you and my mom stopped talking. If there's really a reason why I never met you guys before my mom died, would you tell me, sometime?"

She pressed her lips into a thin line, and I couldn't tell if she was sad or angry. After a moment, she smiled. "Yes. But not tonight. Now go on, I bet Adrian's waiting."

She pushed me gently out the door and I tried not to trip going down the stairs wearing the high heels and the bulky coat. I reached the bottom, looked up, and realized that Adrian was standing there, next to the door, watching me with a small smile on his face. He was wearing his usual understated designer jeans, but he'd put on nice shoes and beneath his coat I could see a collared shirt. I was glad I wasn't the only one who'd sort of dressed up.

When I reached him, he bent down and kissed me on the cheek, whispering, "You look beautiful."

I blushed and mumbled, "Thank you."

"I expect you to take care of Caitlin," Joe warned.

Adrian leaned back and met his gaze. "I will. I promise."

For a moment, I was sucked back into the nightmare—the one where I'd fallen asleep in my father's arms and woken in Adrian's; the one where he'd promised my dad the exact same thing he'd just promised my uncle.

Joe nodded gravely. "I'll hold you to that. Remember, I know where you live." Rachel smiled and dug her elbow into her husband's ribs, hard. He sighed. "All right; get out of here and have fun."

"Good night!" I called out over my shoulder and shut the door behind me. It was snowing and despite the heavy coat, I shivered. "Sorry about that."

Adrian held out his arm and I latched on to it as we picked our way to the truck. He opened the passenger door and helped me in.

We listened to Frank Sinatra on the way to Trish's house without saying a word. It was surprisingly pleasant to just lean next to him in the dark, in silence. Soon, we reached Trish's house. Before I even had time to knock, it flew open.

"Happy New Year's!"

Trish enveloped me in a bear hug and invited us in. Music was playing from somewhere in the house and streamers were hung from the ceiling. I saw all the girls, plus Ben and a few boys, as well as Trish's parents and brothers. We took our coats off and Trish threw them in the downstairs guest room. When I turned back, Adrian was staring at me.

"What?" I asked, looking down at my dress, horrified that I'd spilled something or that my underwear was showing.

"Nothing," he said, and looked quickly away. "You thirsty? I'm thirsty." He steered us over to the snack table and poured me a glass of punch. Trish was passing by and I caught her arm.

"This isn't . . . special punch, is it?" I muttered so only she could hear.

She grinned. "Sadly, no. My parents would kind of notice if I spiked the refreshments."

I smiled and let her go. When I looked at Adrian again, he was refilling his glass.

"Are you okay?" I asked, touching his arm.

He glanced down at my hand, then back up at my face. "I'm fine."

"Okay," I said, puzzled.

"Caitlin?" a voice behind me asked. I turned and looked at a girl standing in a midnight-blue dress, her white-blond hair pinned back in a French twist.

"Yes?" I asked.

She blinked. I looked at her again more closely.

*"Jenny?"*

She smiled a little. "Trish helped me get ready."

Not only was she wearing a dress instead of a washed-out, thrift-store sweater, she was also wearing makeup, jewelry, and heels. She was Jenny, but she was *Jenny.*

I gave her a startled hug. "You look amazing!"

She blushed.

"Hello, Caitlin," I heard someone say behind me. It was Jack, Jenny's twin. He nodded to Adrian in greeting.

Before I could reply, someone else joined our group.

"Hey," Mark said, standing in slacks and a rumpled, paint-spattered shirt with his hair pulled back in a loose French braid. He looked like a scoundrel, in a romantic way, and Jenny blushed at the sight of him.

"Mark, right?" Adrian asked.

"That's right. And you're . . . Abram? Ayden?"

"Adrian."

He nodded as if he remembered now. He looked at me, then Jenny, then Jenny's brother. "I've already met Caitlin and Jenny, so you must be Jack." He stuck out his hand. "I'm Mark."

Across the circle, I could see Jenny turn even redder. I even held my breath a little.

Jack shook Mark's hand. "Thanks for inviting us."

"It was all Trish's idea," he said. "I just live here. Speaking of, I have to go help my dear mother with the hors d'oeuvres. Enjoy the party."

He made a quick exit, but not before making eye contact with Jenny for a split second.

"Jenny!" Stephanie called excitedly from across the room.

"See you later, Caitlin," Jenny said, and escaped to the safety of a group of girls. Jack nodded at us and wandered off.

"What was that all about?" Adrian asked.

Not wanting to be overheard, I said, "Quick, hug me."

He seemed to hesitate, but a moment later, I felt his arms circle my waist. I put my hand on his neck and pulled him down until I could whisper in his ear.

"When I was over here the other night, Jenny and Mark were up at four in the morning talking together in the kitchen. He asked her to model for him this summer. You're objective. I was wondering if you could watch them tonight and tell me what you think."

"You want me to spy on them?"

"Not spy so much as observe."

"Why do you care?"

"I'm paranoid he's your dad."

Adrian turned sharply to look at Mark's retreating figure, and I pulled his face back. "Don't look now! You're the worst spy ever."

"I'll check it out," Adrian murmured.

"Movie's starting!" Trish called.

"What're we watching?" someone called out.

"*Moulin Rouge!*" she yelled back.

People started congregating in the family room, so we followed. Somehow in the chaos of trying to seat that many people in that small of a room, Adrian and I ended up sitting together on the love seat. Way off in the shadows of the room sat Meg, Steph, Laura, and Jenny. Jack had gotten stuck sitting next to Paul and Jimmy on the floor.

I wondered where Mark was. Just as the movie started, I saw him slip into the corner. Jenny didn't react, but for a moment she closed her eyes. I looked at Adrian and saw he was surreptitiously glancing over at the corner every now and again.

I settled into the love seat more comfortably, curling up next to Adrian (because people would expect us to look all lovey-dovey, especially on New Year's Eve) and he put his arm around my shoulders, but like earlier, he seemed to hesitate. I didn't have time to think about it because Ewan McGregor went into a spitfire narration about the children of the revolution and bohemians and narcoleptic Argentineans.

I watched the rest of the movie feeling like I had a little golden ball of happiness inside me that was engulfed by a cold, crushing mass of sadness. It didn't help that Ewan McGregor was singing every five minutes about how great love was and all you need is love and we should be lovers forever and ever and all that sentimental crap that somehow seemed so sincere coming from him.

And of course, she dies—even after they defeat the creepy-ass duke, she dies anyway. He couldn't save her. Love didn't win.

I wasn't the only girl who was teary-eyed at the end of the movie. Who the hell's idea was it to watch *Moulin Rouge!* anyway?

As we let the melancholy credits roll, Trish solemnly announced that it was almost time. I hadn't realized the movie was that long— but here we were, five minutes from midnight.

Trish switched the channel to a news station and the TV host talked animatedly about the upcoming countdown. Everyone perked up and got chatty as Trish passed around champagne poppers and kazoos. I closed my eyes, afraid my face revealed how upset I was.

"Caitlin?" I heard Adrian ask, sounding mildly concerned.

I turned my face toward his and smiled. "I'm just tired," I told him, which was true, if not the truth, per se.

"One minute!" Trish yelled. The excitement in the room rose tangibly.

"Are you sure you're okay?"

I nodded and kept the smile plastered on my face, trying to make it look relaxed and natural. I was going to have to get better at lying to him. Which would be a trick, considering he could read my emotions.

I guess I'd have to get better at lying to myself.

"Thirty seconds!"

Somehow over the course of the movie I had pretty much wriggled my way onto his lap. I leaned my head back against the armrest and looked up at him; his dark, wavy hair partly shadowing his face. I reached up and slowly brushed it back.

"Ten seconds! Nine!"

I slid my hand down his jaw, over his chest, and splayed my fingers over his heart, listening with my fingertips to the incredibly slow beat.

"Eight! Seven!" the crowd yelled on the TV. "Six!" everyone in the room shouted. "Five!"

I wanted to tell him. He had to know, it was *important* that he know—

"Four! Three! Two! *One!*"

—I was done pretending.

"Happy New Year!" a dozen voices cried out as an avalanche of confetti burst onto the TV screen and filled Times Square.

But I barely heard them.

I leaned close—so close my lashes brushed his cheek—and waited, giving him a chance to pull away. But he didn't. He tilted his face toward me a fraction of an inch—

And I kissed him.

It was soft and still, like one breath would break us both. He drew in a sharp breath and pressed his lips to my temple, eyes flared into their luminous silver. He pinched them closed, resting his cheek against mine. I slid my fingers through his hair and let my cool hand rest on his warm neck, slowly folding him into my arms. He buried his face in my shoulder and hugged me tightly.

We didn't say anything.

I held on to him as long as he would let me, and then I let him go.

As we were leaving, Adrian intentionally bumped into Mark while helping me on with my coat, to get a better "read." When we got into the truck, he told me that Mark was definitely human—he could actually sense his emotions and they all felt "light," which I guess was a good thing. Basically, there was no way he was Adrian's dad.

When we got to the ranch, Adrian walked me to the door and popped inside to say good night to Joe—who'd waited up for me—before driving home. I wondered, not for the first time, how he got back over every night, and how he got past the locked front door. He couldn't dare take the truck, because Rachel and Joe would be able to see it from their bedroom window. Did he walk? It was a mile each way. Which really wasn't that far for someone like him, but still, it was every night in the snow and the dark.

I didn't wonder long, though, because I was asleep the moment my head hit the pillow. When I woke up, Adrian was just kicking his shoes off to climb into bed. I sat up to give him enough room, then realized I hadn't set my alarm for the next day. Unfortunately, I'd left a half-full mug of coffee on my nightstand right next to my phone, and when I groped blindly for it, I knocked the mug over. It crashed to the floor, spilling coffee all over my pillows—and Adrian's white shirt.

It was a mark of how distracted he was that his first thought was to take care of the stain—instead of listen and see whether anyone else had heard the noise.

He'd just pulled his shirt over his head when the door burst open and the light flipped on. Norah stood there with a fireplace hatchet and a sleepy look on her face.

"I heard a—"

But she stopped dead when she saw Adrian sitting next to me in bed, half-naked.

We all froze in a moment of mutually stunned silence.

And then, of course, Joe came in behind Norah.

"What's going on?" he asked, eyes still adjusting to the light as he squinted into the room. It didn't take him long, however, to notice who was in bed with me.

Without a word, Joe took the hatchet from his daughter's hand.

"Norah, go back to bed."

Shit. That was Joe's serious voice.

Norah slunk off immediately, although I would've bet money she had her ear pressed to the door. I'm pretty sure she had rushed in here with the hatchet to protect me from whatever it was she'd thought had been attacking, but Joe looked like he wanted to use it for other purposes.

And then Rachel walked in.

It took her a split second longer to take in and process the scene before her.

I knew I should speak up and explain what was really going on, but—how? For once, Adrian was just as tongue-tied as I was—and probably just as scared.

Joe finally pointed at Adrian with the hatchet. "You—out."

Adrian pulled his still-damp shirt back over his head and stood, grabbing his shoes.

Joe didn't move, so Adrian had to shuffle sideways to get through the door. Joe and Rachel shared a look before Joe followed Adrian, and Rachel stepped into my room, closing the door behind her.

"Would you like to tell me anything about what just happened?" Rachel asked. I could see a vein beating in her temple.

I didn't say anything. Honestly, what could I say that she would believe? There was no way to defend myself.

"I'm disappointed," Rachel continued after I didn't speak. "You told me earlier tonight that you and Adrian weren't . . . together. You lied to me."

I could feel my face burning, not in embarrassment, but in anger. This was unfair. She didn't know it was unfair, but it was still unfair, and it made me really, really angry. I already knew what was coming next.

"Consider yourself grounded until further notice," Rachel said. "Joe and I will discuss this with you in the morning." She turned to leave and then stopped, looking back over her shoulder. She opened her mouth, as if to speak, then closed it again. Finally, she left, turning off the light behind her.

In the darkness, I sat very still. If I moved, all of the rage would leak out somewhere, and I'd do something rash, like yell, or slam my door, or run out in the night to go scream and throw rocks at birds. I stayed still until I started shaking, and then I lay down and stared blankly at the wall, and didn't fall asleep until dawn.

———o———

I wasn't allowed to see Adrian anymore. Rachel drove me to school every morning, and picked me up every afternoon, as if afraid I'd make a run for it.

They couldn't keep me from seeing Adrian on campus, but that hardly mattered—he seemed to be punishing me as well, though for *what*, I had no idea, because he refused to talk to me. At lunch, he'd walk me to the picnic tables and even sit next to me, but he wouldn't speak or make eye contact unless someone started acting suspicious. If necessary, he'd put his arm around my shoulders mechanically or kiss my hair.

After lunch, we'd walk hand in hand to my fifth-period class— silently. In study hall, if I asked him to help with algebra or chemistry, he would. Other than that, we didn't talk. I convinced Rachel and Joe that without Adrian, I'd be failing my classes, so they occasionally let him over to the living room to tutor me, but they'd be sitting in the same room with us, chaperoning. I made a habit of shoving my hands into my coat pockets so no one would see that they were shaking. The rage of several months ago came back in full force, drenching every moment.

The one thing that surprised me was that Rachel and Joe let me hang out with Trish—in fact, they encouraged it. Maybe they figured if I hung out with my friends more often, I'd forget about Adrian. I went over to Trish's three or four times a week for the afternoon, and often one of the others would come, too; mostly Meghan, but sometimes Stephanie with Laura or Jenny. Ben was also over at Trish's a lot. He never interfered with us hanging out with her, but he was always nearby, and I often caught the two lying side by side on the floor or sitting next to each other on the couch, holding hands, as if that simple expression was all they needed to say how they felt about each other. I felt so happy for Trish, and for Ben too, I suppose, but mixed in was a stupid bitterness. The most complicated thing that would ever interfere in their relationship was whether or not Trish made it into Oxford. I could picture him gladly going with her. I could picture them getting married. I could picture them with big, fat babies, and grandbabies. They would eat scones and start saying "poppycock!" and they'd be happy.

I tried to push the bitterness down.

I tried—but most days, I failed.

# 16

## FAIRY GODMOTHER

Rachel dropped me off at school and I shuffled, eyes mostly closed, to homeroom. I got all of three steps before tripping over the curb, landing on a piece of ice, and going straight down in a flail of limbs. Adrian was walking ahead of me down the sidewalk and must have done his vampire thing and rushed over, because I never actually hit the ground. Holding me, he sighed—an angry sound—and put his arm around my waist as he half dragged, half led me to Mr. Warren's class. Trish met us at the door and stared curiously.

"Can you help her inside?"

"Sure."

Surprisingly, she didn't ask any more questions, just slung my arm over her shoulders and helped me walk through the door. After she deposited me in my seat, the bell rang, and I knew Adrian would be long gone.

"What's wrong with you?" Trish whispered, leaning close before Mr. Warren took roll.

"I'm tired," I replied bluntly. My cheek was stuck to the desk and my eyes were cemented shut.

"You look like you haven't slept for a week."

"Mphm," I replied. More like two weeks, but whatever.

"What's wrong with Duchess de la Mara?" Meghan asked. I'd made the mistake of looking at her face; she wore lipstick so bright it seemed to pierce my eyes.

Mr. Warren saved the day. "Rise for the Pledge of Allegiance, please. You, too, Ms. Holte."

Trish grabbed my arm and all but dragged me up. I mumbled the pledge and fell back down into my seat when we were done, dragging my sweatshirt hood over my face and propping my chin on my fist to appear awake. It seemed to work; Mr. Warren didn't bother me the rest of the class, and Trish raised her hand to answer whenever he looked in our direction.

As the bell rang and we headed to math (a class I had trouble staying awake in anyway), Trish glowered at me. "Mystic, something is seriously not right with you."

I laughed, a little hysterically, because it was funny.

"See?" she demanded. "This is weird!" We took a seat as far back in the old brick classroom as we could. "Not to mention that you and Adrian have been acting funny since New Year's." She looked at me suggestively, and I wasn't exactly sure why.

Leaning my face on my arm, I closed my eyes. "As far as me acting weird, it's honestly just because I'm tired." To make lying to her simpler, I decided to tell her the truth. Part of it, anyway. "I've been having these nightmares a lot, and they keep me awake. If I'm with Adrian, I can usually get back to sleep." I yawned hugely. "But my aunt and uncle grounded me"—Trish had already heard this story, and found it equal parts hilarious and awful—"and Adrian's been act-

ing weird, so I don't want to bug him right now. Family stuff, I think."
I opened my eyes blearily to gauge her reaction.

She was frowning, obviously displeased. "De la Dumbass is not taking care of you. And he should have stood up for you in front of your aunt and uncle." A mischievous smile spread over her face. "I'm gonna have to have a little chat with the stud muffin."

I thought about telling her no, she shouldn't, because he did take care of me (just not in the way she might think). But I didn't. Because maybe she could figure out why he was ignoring me and being so weird. Trish had a way of getting information out of people.

Second, third, and fourth periods passed slowly. When lunch rolled around, Adrian was waiting for me outside the art room, as usual. Before he could say anything, I reached into his jeans' pocket and snatched his keys.

"I'm gonna take a nap in the truck."

Trish walked up as I walked away. I could hear her exclaim, "Adrian! By golly, what on earth are you doing here? Y'know what? I was just thinking about you . . ."

I smiled as I opened the door to the truck and climbed in. I really shouldn't let Trish interrogate him. But she deserved to have a little fun, and he deserved to be uncomfortable for twenty minutes. I set the alarm on my cell phone, laid my head down on the seat, and immediately passed out.

"I got to hand it to you, Mystic, that boy is not easy to read," Trish said, plunking her book on her desk after lunch. "I mean, I never really *knew* Adrian, but I've had more animated conversations with brick walls."

Thank God, I wasn't crazy then.

"What'd you talk about?" I asked, feeling weirdly excited, or maybe nervous, or maybe afraid. Probably all three.

"Trish?" Mr. Warren called out, looking up from his roll sheet.

"Here," she answered, looking up at him. She turned back to me briefly. "Sixth, 'kay?"

I nodded, and tried to stay awake. Mr. Warren was an interesting teacher, but even the most violent, bloody Civil War lecture wasn't going to keep my brain functioning on the amount of sleep I'd been getting.

Forty tired and uncomfortable minutes later the bell rang and we headed off to choir where we could pretty much talk as much as we wanted. As long as some kids had some sound coming out of their mouths, Mrs. Leckenby was satisfied.

"So?" I prompted once we'd sat down in the back.

Trish frowned. "He said you've been dealing with a lot and haven't been able to sleep well."

She paused, and I asked, "Is that it?"

"I also mentioned that you two had seemed kind of distant, and asked if everything was okay, and he said something like 'every relationship has its ups and downs' and that it was none of my damn business."

I stared at her, shocked. "He told you it was none of your damn business?"

"I know!" she whispered as Mrs. Leckenby looked in our direction. "I've never seen him so riled up before. It's like all this time he's been pretending to be a really attractive teddy bear but he's actually a porcupine I poked in the eye with a stick."

"Well, what'd you say?"

She looked pleased with herself. "I told him you were my friend first and it was sure as hell my business to see that you were happy and being taken care of and if you weren't, there'd be some answering to do and I had three brothers and a boyfriend who'd be happy to take care of the questioning."

I stared at her in shock again, this time because I wasn't sure Adrian had ever been talked to like that before, outside of Julian or me.

"Well, wow," I stuttered, "thanks, Trish. For sticking up for me, I mean."

She shrugged. "You'd do the same if Ben were neglecting me."

Actually, Ben kind of intimidated me. He was, as Trish had once put it, a sweetheart, but he was a massively built sweetheart with arms the size of fire hydrants. I still couldn't believe Trish had gone up against Adrian. Adrian was slimmer than Ben, but just as tall and, well, ripped. And he was a vampire. She didn't know that, but still.

It suddenly struck me that Trish was really my friend. Not just the girl that had treated me nicely when I'd shown up as an orphan, but a real friend; somebody I'd think about fondly ten years from now; somebody I'd try and keep in contact with if either or both of us went off to college; somebody that was there for me without my asking her to be.

"You okay, Mystic?"

I broke out of my reverie. "Yeah."

"You tell me if he needs to be slapped around a little. I'll take care of it."

The great thing was she was totally serious.

I grinned at her. "I might just take you up on that."

———⊙———

"Mystic!" Trish called to me happily as I sat down next to her in first period.

"Morning," I mumbled. I felt glued to my chair. I was so tired my arms and legs didn't even want to work.

"Trish Fields," Mr. Warren called out in a voice that did not belong to Mr. Warren.

My hackles rose.

I looked up. He was wearing his loafers, his khaki pants, his collared shirt, and sweater vest. But he had dark, wavy hair and piercing silver eyes.

"Present," Trish responded, smiling.

He took a few steps toward her, returning the smile. "I just received word that Oxford is willing to offer you a scholarship, on one condition."

Trish looked ecstatic. I tried to warn her, but I was so tired, so heavy, I could barely move.

"What is it?"

"Nothing much." He shrugged. "Just a little blood."

I managed to let out a mangled curse. Mr. Warren/Adrian glared at me. "This is none of your damn business."

He took another step toward Trish, who tilted her neck to the side happily. He grabbed her by the jaw with both hands and twisted sharply. I heard the sickening crack of her spine splintering. Unbalanced by her head, attached only by limp folds of skin and muscle, her body fell over sideways, the mangled bones crunching as they hit the floor.

I screamed, mutedly, in outrage, unable to move. He turned to me again and leaned down, looking me in the eyes with a sick smile. Then his mouth crashed against mine. He pulled back a long time later.

"Consider her a down payment," he murmured intimately. "Your cousin is up next."

I tried to punch him, but I couldn't move. He kissed the tip of my nose and smiled.

As usual, it was a relief to wake up.

My right shoulder ached oddly, and I realized that I had, in real life, been trying to punch the nonexistent Mr. Warren/Adrian hybrid, but had prevented myself from doing so by the simple fact that I had been asleep. I rubbed my shoulder and looked at my phone. It was three a.m.

I turned on my bedside lamp and waited for morning, knowing that if I closed my eyes, I'd see him breaking Trish's neck over and over again. Even if I did manage to fall asleep, I'd simply have another nightmare. Most nights I woke up and started crying because I was so tired. Lately, I'd gotten so tired I couldn't even cry.

When my alarm went off, I got up and took a hot shower, wishing the steam would refresh me somehow, but it didn't. When I got out and looked in the mirror, I almost didn't recognize myself. I looked *old*. Purple bags hung under my eyes and my cheeks were downright gaunt. My sweater hung off me like it had been made for my uncle. I hadn't even realized that I'd started wearing belts to keep my jeans up.

This was getting ridiculous.

I pulled my makeup bag out and actually took the time to put on foundation and blush to hide the fact that I looked like I had an eating disorder. It did a fairly good job of masking the signs of exhaustion, but there wasn't much I could do about the fact that I looked thin to the point of anorexic.

I blinked rapidly as tears threatened. My emotions were on such a tightrope and the smallest things set me off. I was tired of being tired; tired of worrying; tired of living like this.

At lunch, Trish looked at the full two feet of space between Adrian and I, then stared at him pointedly. In response, Adrian scooted marginally closer and kissed me briefly. Without even thinking, I stiffened. He frowned as he pulled back.

"You could look a little happier," he muttered in my ear.

I wanted to hit him.

"Sorry," I said quietly, and dragged a smile out of somewhere, pasting it on my face.

He stared at me and flinched.

I sat through my classes with all the muscles in my body clenched to keep from exploding. I had to keep my atoms together by force of will so they wouldn't float off. I had to keep myself together.

Trish asked me if I was okay. I smiled. I said I was great, just tired.

Eventually, inevitably, the bell rang again, and I had to go to the library for study hall. When I arrived, Adrian was already sitting, working on homework. At least I didn't have to make eye contact with him.

Five minutes before the end of class, he looked up. "I've arranged to have you spend the night at Trish's. I'll pick you up as soon as you get there. You can stay in the same room as last time."

He looked down at his homework again. I looked down at mine.

End of discussion.

Never before had it been driven home so bluntly that what we had was a business arrangement. What I had to remember, what I absolutely had to hold on to, was the knowledge that it hadn't always been like that, and it didn't always have to be. Whatever the hell was going on with Adrian, I'd figure it out. I'd get him back.

I had to.

Trish and I had a few hours to kill before I snuck over to the mansion. I was staring blankly at an essay I was supposed to be writing while Trish was on Pinterest browsing for winter formal dresses.

"Are you and Adrian even going?"

I blinked, snapping out of my daze. "I don't know. Probably not."

Trish shook her head, irritated. "I don't get him. I mean, I've never really gotten him, but I especially don't get him now."

"Me, either."

Trish stared at me for a moment. "Y'know, Mystic, if you're unhappy, you could dump him."

I laughed, suddenly—because the truth was, I couldn't. Not when the mysterious Council decreed that we should still be dating. I wasn't just worried about what they'd do to *me* if I refused—I was really worried about what they'd do to Adrian. What had he said? "The consequences for disobedience are high"?

"I love him," I deflected. "But it feels like he's lost interest in me, and I have no idea why."

Trish frowned. "That sounds like a very good reason to no longer be dating someone."

I shook my head. "I don't want to break up with him. I just want him back, the way it used to be."

Trish nodded, looking thoughtful. "Well, then, you can call me fairy godmother from now on, because I've got an idea."

I shook my head. "I'm not having sex with Adrian to get him to like me again."

"Um, duh, that would be dumb. I'm talking about visual stimulation."

I stared at her, confused, and automatically lifted the can of soda to my lips again. Caffeine was having less and less effect on me, but it helped some.

"What you need," she continued, "is a Cinderella moment."

I stared at her. "You want me to talk to mice and scrub pots?"

"No," she said, rolling her eyes. "Look, if you don't want to break up with him—which I think you should still strongly consider—you need to remind him why he waited all those years of not-dating until you came along. You changed something for him. I saw it, *everyone* saw it. He just needs to remember." She glanced at her Pinterest board, grinning. "You need a dress."

"For . . . the dance?" I asked, slowly.

"Yes. A Cinderella dress. The kind of dress where you walk into the room and everyone stops and stares at you like you're the heroine in a Disney movie."

I considered it a moment, then shook my head, defeated. "I'm so broke right now it's not even funny." I threw back the last sip of soda and burped halfheartedly. "I'd still like to come help you guys pick stuff out in Queensbury, though." But then my brain, sluggish though it was, started churning. "Trish, wait—" I began, staring off into space. "I could *make* a dress."

She raised a brow. "Out of what, bedsheets?"

I shook my head. "No—Adrian bought me a ton of fabric, and set up a sewing studio for me in his house. I haven't had a chance to use any of it because of the craziness with the Shirtless Encounter."

A gleeful smile began to take over her face. "Can you make it in time? Winter formal's in three weeks."

I chewed my lip, thinking. "I can—but I need your help. Rachel and Joe won't let me go over to Adrian's anymore. Could you cover for me so I could use the studio?"

"Dude," Trish said, grinning at me. "Yes. I am so down with this. Do you have a design in mind? How does that even work?"

I thought through all my sketches, the books full of ideas, scanning through them mentally. I quickly decided they wouldn't work, because I hadn't designed them for me. I needed something brand-new. I reached into my backpack and pulled out my sketch pad and rubber-banded bunch of watercolor pencils.

"I don't know," I said, smiling. "Let's find out."

I shut the door to Trish's truck and walked over to where Adrian had parked on the side of the road. My family once again believed I was spending the night at Trish's. The next day was Saturday, so whenever I woke up he would drop me back here, and she would take me home.

As soon as we walked through the front door, Lucian ran to meet us, sliding breathlessly to a halt. He looked up with a smile that slowly faded as he looked first at Adrian, then at me, then back at Adrian, then again at me.

He didn't know who to hug first.

Adrian made the decision easy—he walked into the hall leading to the east wing, leaving us behind. Lucian stared after him.

"Wanna come help me?" I asked, to distract him.

He turned and half smiled at me. I gave him a quick squeeze and ruffled his hair like Adrian always did and we headed upstairs to my studio. Pulling out the sketch I'd designed (and Trish had approved), I ran my hands over the bolts of fabric until I found the one I was looking for. It would be insanely hard to make, mostly because the fabric was difficult to work with. If you messed up, you had to cut it off and start all over. That's just how velvet was.

I pulled the bolt and laid it on the cutting table, envisioning the pieces in my head. If I was careful, I would have just enough material to pull this off. Nervous, I set the velvet aside and pulled out the dollar-a-yard muslin instead, planning to create the pattern with it first in case I messed up. Usually I had my mom at my side, harping about aligning the grains and offering alternative stitches and little tricks she'd made up over the years. All of that was tucked away safely in my head, and I could recall her voice perfectly from the hundreds of times we'd done this together. It felt right to be working on something again. It felt, almost, like she was with me.

A few hours later, Lucian and I headed downstairs to have dinner with Mariana and Dominic and, of course, Adrian. A sumptuous meal was laid out, but simply being in this house made me lose my appetite. I picked at my food while everyone else cleaned the supersize portions off their plate.

"Are you feeling all right, Caitlin?" Mariana asked as she was finishing up.

"What?" I asked, looking up. "Oh, yeah. I'm fine."

"You're not eating very much," she persisted. I wasn't sure if she was concerned about me or irritated because I was dissing her cooking abilities.

"I'm fine," I said tightly.

Mariana didn't look convinced. I stood up to clear my plate. As I was leaving the kitchen, I could hear Mariana speaking to Adrian.

"Why aren't you taking care of her?"

"What do you want me to do?" he asked, sounding angry. "I watch her every day; what the hell more do you want? This isn't my problem."

"We understand that the burden of her safety rests heavily on you," Mariana said in a reasonable tone, "and that it is the responsibility of us all to see that she remains safe, but it must be you that oversees her well-being. She looks sick, Adrian."

"You're blaming me for her *immune system?*"

I didn't want to hear anymore, so I hurried upstairs and got another hour's worth of work done on the dress. Literally falling asleep at the sewing machine, I finally called it a night and used the ridiculously deep bathtub to soak for another hour. I stumbled into my pajamas and collapsed into bed, falling asleep the instant my head hit the pillow.

When I opened my eyes, everything was white. I knew I had a body, but it was so bright I couldn't see anything. The only other thing I knew for certain was that I was falling. There was absolutely no sound, like I was in space where sound didn't exist, but I could feel the air rushing past my body, I could feel my hair whipping up behind me, could feel my eyes water as they were buffeted by the wind. And I continued, silently, to fall.

And fall.

And fall.

I woke up when I hit the ground.

When I opened my eyes, Adrian was sitting in a chair next to my bed. I looked at him, feeling as though my entire body were broken, like I actually *had* hit the ground from a great height. Every muscle was triple-tied into knots. Adrian's eyes were glowing softly, providing the only light in the dark room.

Turning my back on him, I let the tears slide down my face, too tired to even cry properly.

But a moment later I felt the mattress next to me dip as Adrian sat on it. And then my hair was being brushed aside and he was rubbing my neck and it felt amazing. He didn't say anything, just started on my shoulders, painfully working out the knots, and I kept crying because there wasn't anything left to do but cry.

He worked a long time, making his slow and methodical way

down my back until every point of tension was deliberately, pain-fully erased. When he was done, I felt like mush. He pulled back the covers and settled in next to me. Then I was being rolled over until I rested with my face against his shoulder and my arm tucked life-lessly against his chest. I fell asleep instantly.

# 17

## IT COUNTS FOR TWO VOTES IF YOU SAY IT LIKE A PIRATE

**W**hat's the theme this year?" Meghan asked, popping a cheese puff in her mouth. We were all crammed into Trish's room for an emergency dance-planning session.

"Winter Neverland," Stephanie replied. Laura looked less than excited, but Neverland was right up Meghan's alley.

"Hold the train," Trish interrupted. "I know who I'm going with, and I know who Caitlin's going with, but before anybody buys a dress, I need to know who everybody else is going with—that way I can approve purchases based on scandalicity."

"I don't suppose Mark will be back in time?" Meghan asked.

"Hell no."

She sighed. "Too bad. Such a nice body."

"Tim asked me," Stephanie broke in.

We all turned to stare at her.

"*Tim* Tim?" Laura asked at the same time Trish said, "Emo-Punk Emerson?"

Stephanie blushed, smiling. "Yeah."

"Whoa, whoa, whoa; are you two, like, *dating*?" Meghan demanded, forgetting Mark in the wake of juicy gossip.

Stephanie blushed even further. "Well, I don't think so."

"What's that supposed to mean?"

"He only asked me to the dance."

"This explains so much!" Meghan said with a look of epiphany. "He just got a haircut, and I haven't seen him dye his hair in a month!"

"He said he wanted it to be normal for the pictures," Stephanie defended him, her cheeks a bright pink.

"Wow," Meghan said in genuine awe. "He must, like, love you."

"I don't think—" Stephanie began, but Laura cut her off with, "Just because a boy lets his hair go back to its natural color doesn't mean he's in love. Maybe it was just getting too expensive to dye."

"Or maybe he's in love," Meghan countered, and I could sense a battle on the horizon.

"Who're you going with, Laura?" I asked.

She blinked at me. "Daniel."

"*Kane?*" Meghan asked in pure disbelief.

Laura frowned. "Do you know another?"

"He's a senior."

"It's not unheard of to go with someone outside your own grade."

"Damn," Meghan said, "pretty soon there's gonna be no one left." She paused with a cheese puff halfway to her mouth. "Who *is* left?"

"Andrew and Eric are taken," Laura said, naming senior boys I didn't know very well. "And Adrian, of course. I think Luke's available."

"He's taken."

We all looked at the corner where Jenny usually hid.

"You snagged Luke?" Jenny nodded and Meghan groaned. "Great; *now* who am I going to go with?"

"Jack's available."

Meghan looked thoughtful. "He's not bad-looking."

"Right," Laura said. "Because that's all that's important."

"I didn't say that."

"We're all still going shopping this Saturday?" I piped up.

"Hells yeah."

---

All day long the girls were talking about our impending shopping trip until I was sick of hearing the words *dance, dress,* and *date.* Adrian caught a whiff of our conversation at lunch and looked like the proverbial deer in the headlights.

He leaned over. "Do you want to go?"

I answered around a bite of peanut butter and jelly. "Well, since I've been working on a dress nonstop for two weeks, it might be a good idea to have something to wear it to."

"Ah," he replied, and cleared his throat. "Am I supposed to ask you officially, then?" I stared at him. He took that as confirmation. "Will you go with me to winter formal?"

I narrowed my eyes and looked thoughtful. "I was actually thinking of going with one of Trish's brothers."

I was teasing, of course, but for a moment, I could have sworn I saw Adrian's eyes flash silver. Could have been a trick of the light, I suppose; the sun was actually out for once.

"Of course I'll go with you," I said quickly, and he relaxed.

He nodded and went back to his sandwich, which sucked away all my enthusiasm about the dance. At least I had a full night of sleep to look forward to—Trish and Adrian had coordinated another fake sleepover so I could crash at the mansion.

I grew out of my funk during choir when Trish spent the entire class playing Obscure Hangman with me on the back of an old math test. She said she and her brothers made it up one time when they were stuck in the car.

"'Jellybeans must die'?" I whispered when I was down to one leg.

"Damn straight."

And that's why it was called Obscure Hangman.

I left with Trish after school got out. Adrian picked me up about a mile away from her house.

"What were you two giggling about during choir?" he asked when I got in.

"What? Oh, nothing. We were just playing Hangman."

He looked at me, and I felt like a five-year-old. "What's Hangman?"

I realized he hadn't ever been a five-year-old. Well, at least not like everybody else had been a five-year-old.

"It's a kid's game," I said, trying to explain. "You guess letters and try to figure out the phrase or sentence the other person has written down. Except in the obscure version, the phrase is . . . obscure. Like 'please tickle my earlobe with yarn.'"

We blinked at each other.

"I'll show you when we get to your place," I said, giving up.

When we arrived, I felt, as usual, that the sign that read PRIVATE PROPERTY should instead read ENTERING DE LA MARA–LAND, or WELCOME TO A HOUSE THE SIZE OF A SMALL COUNTRY, or even THE ENTIRE *LORD OF THE RINGS* TRILOGY WAS FILMED IN OUR LIVING ROOM.

He parked and we headed inside.

"Time to connect with your inner child," I said, dragging him into the library. We sat down on the couch near the humongous fireplace and I pulled out a sheet of paper and scribbled a stick-figure gallows, thought a moment, then underlined the spaces I wanted for my phrase. "All right, guess a letter."

He looked at me. "Which one?"

I stared back. "Any one."

"How do I know which one is right?" he asked seriously.

"You don't," I replied. "That's the point of the game. If you guess wrong, I draw in a body part."

"Excuse me?" He looked appalled.

"Just guess a letter."

He looked down and contemplated the blank spaces on the paper.

"*E*," he said finally, looking up. "It's the most commonly used letter in the English language. I'm assuming this is in English?"

I stared at him in disgust. "You *would* know that. And yes, it is." I bent down and filled in four *E*s. He looked entirely too pleased with himself.

"*A*," he said.

I wrote in two *A*s.

"*O*."

"Sorry, my friend." I drew in a head at the end of the noose. "No *O*s."

"What does that mean?" He pointed at the head.

"That means that you have a spine and four limbs to go before you lose."

He stared at me. "This is a children's game?"

I nodded. He shook his head. "*I*."

"Two Is."

He contemplated the paper. It read: _ _ i _ _ _ _ _ _ ea_ _e_ _ie_ _ea_ _.

He guessed a couple more letters, all correct, before saying, "G."

"No G." I added a spine to the hangman and wrote the letter G off to the side. Adrian narrowed his eyes, his competitive edge starting to come out.

He guessed a few more rounds, ending up with two spare limbs and the phrase "c _ i _ _ _ n _ s eat refried _eans."

"What on earth?" he whispered under his breath. I grinned. "U," he said finally, and I knew it would be a matter of seconds before he got it. He stared at it a moment longer, then looked up at me slowly. "'Chipmunks eat refried beans'?"

I smiled, filled in the rest of the letters, and said, "Yay, you won."

He stared at me in disbelief. "Those were the two least productive minutes of my entire life."

"Yeah, well, it's supposed to be fun." I was already wishing I hadn't shown him the game. He was spoiling everything lately.

"You guys played this for forty-five minutes?"

"We had some good phrases," I said, feeling suddenly tired. "Trish started with 'jellybeans must die' and then I had 'silver socks sing sadly' and then she came up with 'Polly Pocket picked Peter Piper's peppers,' and then I had 'cliff-hanger kisses carabiner,' and then she ended with 'denim stole my soul' because the bell rang. It kind of turned into Hangmen of Alliteration, but that's okay."

"Lady loves Lucian," a voice said from somewhere behind me. Lucian slipped over the edge of the couch and slid beside me with a smile. I gave him a hug and said, "Yes, lady loves Lucian." I sighed. "Unfortunately, lady also has homework that lady must do before shopping with other ladies tomorrow."

"Should I go?" Lucian asked. I knew a few months ago he would've just sat there staring blankly. Slowly, he seemed to be adjusting and picking up on social cues. I was so proud of him.

"You can stay as long as you're quiet," I said. Then I looked up at Adrian. "That is, if your brother doesn't mind."

Adrian shrugged. "He can stay."

Lucian looked happy, which made me happy, which gave me the energy to start the essay that was due Monday for Mr. Warren. We worked for a few hours, together but separate, as the fire cracked and popped. When we went to dinner, Mariana had cooked steaks, and I filled up on the Japanese "Wagyu" beef that was, Mariana explained, the most elite of steaks. I didn't even know it was possible for meat to be elite, but whatever, it tasted good, so I ate it.

It was still early when dinner was finished, but I knew I'd actually have to wake up in the morning, so I took my (now) customary soak in the tub, a hot shower, and snuggled into the monstrous four-poster bed in my favorite pajamas; content that I'd gotten a first draft of the essay pounded out, I had food in my stomach, and as soon as my nightmare was over, I'd sleep like a baby.

I floated slowly down into the dream, and when the nightmare hit, it literally hit. I staggered back from a punch to the jaw and fell hard against the ice. Blinking to get the black dots out of my eyes, I realized I was sprawled out over the frozen pond Adrian had taken me ice-skating on back before Thanksgiving. I looked up just as someone pounded down on my stomach with what felt like a steel-toed boot. My body convulsed in and then snapped back sharp enough for me to know that bones had broken. Not only that, but the kick had driven all the air out of my lungs and I couldn't breathe.

I stared up at the bright blue sky listening to my attacker circle me as I lay gagging. He grabbed my hair and pulled me up so my toes just barely scraped the ice. I finally sucked in enough oxygen to scream before I was thrown to the center of the pond. It cracked instantly and I fell down into the dark, freezing water. The current sucked me away from the hole in the ice and scraped me along the underside of the frozen lake until my face was raw and bleeding. When I opened my eyes the water pierced them, it was so cold. I hadn't gotten enough air before and now the pain of the subfreezing water shocked what little air I *did* have right out of my lungs. I choked, sucking in water. I couldn't move my fingers, couldn't feel my feet; my eyelashes were crusted shut with ice and I was going to die.

I jerked awake, arching off the bed without an ounce of air; eyes wide in the darkness as my lungs stayed shriveled like popped balloons. I twitched, trying to loosen something so I could breathe, but every muscle was contracted, locked firmly in place. White dots were beginning to swim in front of my eyes when I felt two hands run quickly down my throat. One hand cupped the back of my neck and the other circled around my waist and lowered me back down against the bed, but I still couldn't breathe. Adrian was pushing on my stomach, my rib cage and sternum, my throat again, tilting my head back to let air in; and then there were lips on mine, breathing air into me, forcing it down into my lungs, and everything unlocked at once. I turned away and coughed, sucking in huge, wracking breaths.

Slowly, slowly, my breathing began to calm down. I heard him mutter, *"Peur de la merde de moi; je vais avoir une crise cardiaque, un de ces jours,"* which I didn't understand at all, but it sounded very lyrical and soothing. Then there was more muttering and rustling of sheets and I was being tucked very carefully into Adrian's very warm body and I murmured something like, "You speak French?" and then I was out again.

I swam through murky un-dreams for a few hours, heavy and a little restless, and when I surfaced back to consciousness, I expected to find myself alone. But I wasn't. I was lying on my side with Adrian's arm wrapped around my waist, his face pressed into my neck, his legs tangled up with mine. He was still there. And he was asleep, breathing so quietly that I could feel his unnaturally slow heartbeat against my back. He stirred, rubbed his face against my neck, tightened his arms around my waist, and settled.

It still amazed me how much I loved him.

* * *

"For Pete's sake, Meghan; that's the eighth dress you've tried on— I've been counting."

"Hold your friggin' horses," came the reply from behind the dressing room door. In the next stall over, Jenny was helping Stephanie with the zipper on the back of her off-white dress while Stephanie stood on her tiptoes and sucked in her stomach muttering the word *pictures* over and over again. The door flung open and Meghan stepped out in a low-cut, red satin dress.

"We've got a winner!" Trish said, giving her a thumbs-up.

"A winner with a chunky price tag," Meghan muttered.

Trish flipped the label and sucked in a breath. "Oooh."

"Winter formal comes but once a winter, however, and I have been saving."

Trish stared at her. "You—saving? *Money?*"

"I know, I know; Jesus must be coming back or something. Anyway, I've got enough to cover it."

"There!" I heard Stephanie squeak from her stall as Jenny finally got the zipper all the way up.

"Can you breathe?" Laura asked, peeking over her stall door.

"I don't need to breathe, I just need to get through the pictures. And I'll be losing weight before the dance."

Stephanie was popping out of her dress a bit in the chest area, which was rather scandalous for her, but on the whole she looked really nice. It was a creamy, off-white chiffon with a deep V-neck and a small trail. She kinda looked like a Greek goddess.

"Come on, Laura, what you got?" Trish said, waving at Laura who was peeking out from behind her door. She grimaced, disappeared, and then the door swung open and she was standing in front of us in a deep, plum-colored, square-necked halter with a side tuck that went halfway up her thigh.

"Yes," Trish said, granting her approval.

"You think?" Laura asked, looking doubtful.

"Definitely. Dan won't know what hit him."

Laura smiled, caught herself, scowled, and headed back into the dressing room. Trish had already bought a black dress at the last store, which amplified her naturally impressive bosom. I was sitting on a little plastic footstool thing in the hallway, watching the hubbub with a happy, tired sort of amusement.

"Are you going to try anything on?" Jenny asked me.

I shook my head. "I already got my dress. I'm just here for moral support." I noticed her hands were empty, and I couldn't remember her trying anything on in the past six stores we'd been to. "What about you? Are you getting anything?"

She shrugged, and I could tell she was upset.

"Hey," I said, standing, "you've gotta try at least one dress on."

"There's nothing I like," she said simply.

I grabbed her by the arms and made her sit. "Let me pick something out. I guarantee you'll like it."

She rolled her eyes but didn't protest. I darted through the clothing racks, not entirely sure what I was looking for other than something in a deep, rich color. Jenny was too pale for pastel. And then—

"Get in there," I said, hauling her into an empty stall and handing the dress in after. I stood there for a good five minutes while Jenny muttered what might have been obscenities, but it was Jenny, so I couldn't hear her half the time anyway. By now, everyone else had changed back into their regular clothes and was waiting for the big reveal. Finally, the little metal door handle squealed and swung open.

I raised my hand, which Trish immediately slapped in a slo-mo high five. "I win."

Jenny scowled, clearly uncomfortable being the center of attention. I pulled her into the hall and stood her in front of the three-way mirror.

Damn. I was good.

Remembering how amazing her New Year's Eve dress had looked on her, I'd chosen a deep blue, floor-length dress. In place of sleeves, it had a dozen thin straps on either shoulder that met at the waist in the back.

"Oh, Jenny, you look gorgeous," Stephanie said, the last to step out of her dressing room.

Jenny stared at the mirror. "I look naked."

"There's plenty of material in the front," Trish scoffed. "All in favor of Jenny buying this dress, say 'aye.' It counts for two votes if you say it like a pirate."

There were three normal ayes and two pirate ayes (I was one of the pirate ayes), so I guess that counted as seven votes against her. She smiled in an excruciatingly shy way, and stared at the floor.

"Fine," she said, giving in. Trish and Meghan cheered in victory.

Everyone made their purchases and we piled into Stephanie's mom's Suburban and drove back to Stony Creek in high spirits. I sat down next to Jenny as Meghan blasted pop music from the stereo.

Afraid I'd overwhelmed her, I asked Jenny, "How's it going?"

Oddly enough, she blushed. "Good."

I raised my eyebrows.

"Really good," she amended. "There's this boy. And he sent me this for my birthday." She held up her wrist and I saw a delicate silver band around her wrist with a single deep blue stone set in the middle. "He said it matched my eyes."

That would've sounded cheesy if it weren't for the fact that Mark (I assumed it was Mark) was right—they were almost the exact same shade. I grinned at her and she covered it back up with her sleeve. We got sucked back into the general conversation and the ride back passed quickly. When I got home, I could smell dinner cooking and realized I hadn't eaten anything since breakfast at Adrian's.

"Hi," Rachel smiled tentatively as I came through the front door. "Did you find a dress?"

"Yeah—I left it at Trish's."

It was a weird excuse, but since I was still working on my real dress, and that dress was at Adrian's, I couldn't have Rachel ask to see what I'd bought.

Before Rachel could question why I'd left my dress at Trish's, I was saved by Joe dragging Norah in through the front door, smelling strongly of horses.

"Five more minutes!"

"You've been out there since dawn."

"And it's still dusk!"

I glanced out the window. It was pitch-black.

"You've still got a week to practice for the semifinals," he said, setting her down as he closed the door, "but dinner is now."

Since it was already a habit of mine to go over to Trish's three or four times a week, it wasn't difficult to trick Rachel and Joe. It was actually so easy that I almost felt bad about it—almost. I'd go home with Trish after school and she'd tell her parents we were going out to study, or to Jenny's or Laura's or Meghan's or Stephanie's. Then she'd drop me off at Adrian's and I'd get in several hours of work on the dress. Adrian drove me back over to Trish's, who drove me home. It was ridiculous and convoluted, but I slowly made progress. If I totally ignored homework for the next week (which, to be fair, I couldn't concentrate on anyway with the sleep deprivation), I'd get the dress done in time for the dance. I knew my priorities were totally backward on that one, but, well, I was literally not thinking straight.

A bizarre event happened a few days before winter formal as I was working in my studio. Lucian had just run out to tell Adrian something, a story or an idea, I can't remember, and I thought he had come back, but when I looked up, it wasn't Lucian standing there, and it wasn't Adrian—

It was Julian.

He stopped just inside the doorway, hands in the pockets of his thousand-dollar jeans, shirt loose and open at the chest. I remembered my first impression of him that day in the library—he'd seemed confidant and chiselled, but not as beautiful as Adrian. Adrian was simpler, adapted to Stony Creek, content with blending in—as much as he could, at least. Julian expected attention.

I sat paused with two pieces of velvet in my hands, waiting for him to speak. He didn't look friendly, but he didn't look angry. More . . . perturbed. Puzzled, maybe.

"Are we going to stare at each other, or can I get back to work?"

He gave me a brief, wry smile. "Mind if I come in?"

I hesitated—he and Adrian were still not on good speaking terms (although I wasn't sure if they'd ever been on good speaking terms), and I didn't want to add to it. At the same time, I didn't know much about Julian.

Curiosity won.

"Sure," I said, and pointed at one of the many padded stools around the worktable. He took a seat and rested his chin on his hand. I wondered if he knew it looked like he was posing.

"Is there something I can help you with?" I asked, since he didn't seem to feel the need to speak.

Now that he was closer, I could see that his eyes were that strange, celestial mix of deep blue and amber. It reminded me of a compass for some reason, or a globe. He stared at me a moment longer, a small crease marring his forehead as he frowned in thought.

"Your boyfriend hates me."

I was a little startled, both by what he said and the fact that I had begun to get a little lost in the colors of his eyes. "You mean your brother?" I deflected.

He shrugged dismissively. "Same thing."

I snorted. "Um, no. He's *actually* your brother. He's pretending to be my boyfriend."

He looked amused, glancing around the state-of-the-art studio. "This is pretend?"

I blushed. "Adrian has an overdeveloped sense of guilt, for whatever reason, and tries to pay it off by buying me expensive things he thinks I need." I didn't want to talk about that anymore. "And he doesn't hate you."

"Perhaps," Julian conceded. "But he doesn't think very highly of me, does he?"

I couldn't really argue with that one. "Why is that?"

Julian cocked his head to the side and stared at me as though trying to work out a puzzle. "Adrian isn't like the rest of us," he said finally. "He tends to want too much."

I scowled. "You're being intentionally cryptic."

He snorted. "Couldn't properly call myself a vampire if I wasn't."

I looked at him—I mean really looked at him, probably for the first time. He was incredibly beautiful, but there was a blankness to him. Less than Mariana and Dominic, but it was there. Like he was fading right before my eyes. "Why are you really here?" I asked finally. "I have things to do—and I was under the impression you didn't like me all that much."

"Don't flatter yourself. I don't care about you enough to dislike you."

I laughed, too tired to be offended. "Someday you are actually going to care about something, and you won't have any idea what to do about it. I should get you a puppy," I mused. "I can't see you being mean to a cute little puppy."

"Don't you know?" he asked, leaning back with a dry smile. "I drink the blood of innocent puppies for breakfast. Right after my corn flakes."

"Nice try." I turned back to my sewing machine. "I already know you guys only drink people juice."

"Ah," he sighed, "the secret's out."

Was it weird that I wasn't hating this conversation? Regardless, I only had another twenty minutes to work on the dress before

Adrian had to take me back to Trish's, so I ignored Julian and examined the edge I was about to sew. Before I could put my foot back to the pedal, I thought I heard him mutter, "Why you?"

I frowned at him. "Why me, what?"

He leaned close, as if inspecting a funny little bug. "Why *you*? There's nothing special about you. All this fuss," he murmured. "The Council is in such an uproar over a passing vision about tiny, insignificant Caitlin Holte. You're not intelligent, you're not clever, you're not beautiful. You're not going to change the world. You're going to grow up and live a tired little life, and then you're going to die. That's what people like you do. That's what people like you are good for. Filling space."

His words stung so sharply I couldn't breathe.

"And yet," he continued, "the world—for now—revolves around you. A dull, common star in a bright, massive galaxy. You hypnotized my brother. You terrify my sister. And I'm the only one who's sane enough to wonder *why*."

My heart hammered up into my throat, a heady mixture of fear and rage, but the rage, as usual, won out. "You're right," I whispered finally. "I'm not special. I know that. And I admit I've had a rough year. I have not been at my best. I've been vindictive and petty and immature and angry, but I still *care*."

I laughed, suddenly, as I realized that Julian didn't scare me anymore. Julian didn't scare me and Mariana didn't scare me and the Council didn't scare me, because I was worn out and they were all so blind.

"I love your brother," I admitted for the first time out loud. "I love him. You deign to exist, Julian. You don't love anyone or anything, and that makes your life pointless. It's so sad—and you don't even know. So wonder away, poison Adrian against me, do your worst.

I've already lost everything I ever cared about, and I'm still here. I haven't given up. So fight me, or get the hell out of my face because I've got shit to do."

Julian sat still for a long, long moment. Finally, he stood, looming over me. "Very brave. I will give you that. But my eternity isn't the one you should be concerned about. Remember—Adrian is going to live forever, too. Think about that. Think about what that means."

And he walked out of the room.

I sat very still. Outside, the snow fell in the soft afternoon light. It would be dark in an hour. I laid my head on my arms. I felt like crying. I felt tired. I felt confused. A small hand touched my back. I lifted my head and saw Lucian standing there, looking concerned.

"What are you doing?" he whispered.

I tried to smile and couldn't. "I'm crying. Again."

He tilted his head. "What's that?"

"It's something people do when they're very sad."

"Why are you sad?"

I managed a weak smile. "I don't understand your brothers." But he still looked confused. "You know how you get rid of tears?" I asked. He shook his head. "You find somebody you love and you hug them."

"Love?"

"Yeah. Somebody you care about."

He nodded. "Who do you want me to find?"

"I think you'll do."

His eyes widened. "You love me?"

"I sure do, kid."

He thought about it a moment. "I love you, too. I think."

I smiled a big, watery smile; on the verge of tears again because in the midst of all of this, he was so great.

"You're still crying," he pointed out.

I laughed and wiped a few tears off my face. "That's because you haven't hugged me yet."

Lucian immediately wrapped his arms around my neck. A few moments later he leaned back to peer at my face.

"They're still there," he whispered.

I smiled. "Sometimes it takes a while for them to stop."

"Lucian," I heard Adrian call from the doorway, "leave Caitlin alone."

Lucian immediately pulled away from me and scampered into the hall.

I glared at Adrian, my emotions on their last frayed rope. "Why did you do that?"

He stared at me impassively, arms crossed over his chest. "I told you we aren't allowed to love humans. You know that."

Rage bubbled up through my stomach. "He's a kid, Adrian."

"He's one of us."

"Since when are you 'one of them'?"

He smiled, but it was cruel. "Since the day I was born."

I was so angry I couldn't speak for a moment. "Funny. I thought I heard you say that you weren't anything like them. My mistake."

His face tightened. "What do you want from me?"

"I don't want anything!" I cried, eyes brimming with frustrated tears. "The sewing machine, the studio, your protection, I never asked for *any* of it. I didn't ask you to save me, you just *did*. You did that on your own. You made me love"—I caught myself just in time—"Lucian. You made me love Lucian." My voice faltered. "How could I not love him?"

He stared at me. I concentrated on keeping my voice level.

"I don't know what you feel. I can't. And I don't understand what you're doing. Why things are different than they were be-fore. But I will not sit here and let you forbid me from loving any-body. You're a vampire, not a god." I stood up. "Now either get out or I'm calling my uncle to tell him that you're scaring me."

He closed his eyes but didn't move. I'd never been this angry at him before. Actually, I'd never been *angry* at him before. Not really.

"Adrian, I swear to God I will call Joe if you don't leave right now."

He turned around and walked out the door, closing it quietly.

I stared at it for a moment, then sank to the floor and sobbed.

# 18

## CINDERELLA MOMENT

I hated this part.

It wasn't so much the act of primping, it was the waiting; the time it took to get ready. I was wrapped in an old bathrobe feeling awkward and hot in the cramped bathroom. Norah was painting my toes, which were separated by those uncomfortable pink foam things, and Rachel was pinning my curled hair into an elaborate *Pride and Prejudice*—esque updo with an armada of black bobby pins. My makeup was done (courtesy of Rachel), my dress was hanging in my room along with the stilettos (which were getting their money's worth of use this year), and I'd already vigorously brushed my teeth—twice.

I was beyond amazed that Joe and Rachel were letting Adrian pick me up for the dance. It had been almost a month since the Incident in the Bedroom, and they seemed to have cooled off somewhat. Maybe the fact that I hadn't argued about being grounded swayed them in my favor. I'd brought the dance up to Rachel, Rachel and Joe had discussed it, and they'd decided I was allowed to go— although I still wasn't allowed to have Adrian over for anything but homework sessions. The past few days I'd barely seen Adrian at all when I went over to use the studio. The fight had been pretty bad.

"Stop fidgeting," Norah warned from her place on the floor. My foot was propped up on her knee and she had the concentration of a surgeon as she applied the pale gold gloss. Five minutes later, she was done. Ten minutes later, Rachel finished, my nails were dry, and I was running out of time. I ran into my bedroom, threw off my robe, and very carefully slid into my dress, trying not to smudge my makeup or catch any of the pins in my hair on the fabric. I slid my shoes on and opened the wardrobe to look at the mirror hanging on the in-side of the door.

Rachel was a miracle worker. I don't know how she did it, but I looked complete down to the last detail. I had on dangly earrings, but with this particular dress, a necklace would have been too much, so I spritzed on some body spray and threw on Rachel's borrowed wool coat, buttoning it all the way down so only the hem peaked out underneath—there was no way I was letting my aunt and uncle see the back of this dress before I left the house. Or the front, for that matter.

"Adrian's here!" Norah yelled, her voice muffled by the heavy wood door.

I breathed in and out, suddenly nervous.

It was just a dance. Get it together.

I opened my door and headed carefully down the stairs, con-centrating on not breaking my ankle in the shoes. For the first time in a long time, Adrian was smiling that slow, warm smile that al-ways made me happy for a reason I couldn't quite put into words. I reached him and he took my hand and slipped the corsage on—a grouping of perfectly white snowdrops. It was elegant and lovely and different.

A flash went off and I looked up to see Rachel holding a camera. Norah handed me Adrian's boutonniere and I put every ounce of concentration into not poking him while I pinned it to his lapel. More flashes. I felt my cheeks burning—if we were at Adrian's, no one would be taking pictures.

Finally, I had it pinned so that it at least wouldn't fall off. Norah clapped sarcastically.

"Eleven p.m.," Joe warned, looking very unhappy and scary as hell. "I'll be waiting."

Adrian didn't say anything, just shook Joe's hand like a man, nodded at Rachel, and then we were out the door.

"Sorry—" I began saying, and then stopped dead. For a second, I was terrified I was stuck in a nightmare and everything was about to go horribly wrong because what I was seeing shouldn't be where it was.

Adrian took my arm and walked me to the passenger side of a silver Aston Martin.

"1961," he explained. "Dominic restores classic cars, remember?"

Holding on to his arm, I folded down into the black leather interior and buckled myself in automatically.

"You own an Aston Martin?" I asked as soon as he got in the car. Car? *Car* didn't even begin to adequately describe this thing—it was money personified.

"We own three," he said, and started the engine. It purred as he pulled down the driveway. I sat in dumbfounded silence. They owned three Aston Martins. I didn't own so much as a skateboard.

"Dominic tours them around at shows, picks up a few prizes, and then sells them off. Some of them stay in our private collection, or get shipped to others of our kind worldwide. He just finished this one, so I borrowed it for the night. Normally we don't like to flaunt our wealth—it kind of sticks out."

"No kidding."

We hit the main road and Adrian switched gears manually, going forty, fifty, sixty, seventy, and then eighty miles an hour. My heart was freaking out—I knew Adrian had driven this road thousands of times, but I'd never seen him go above the speed limit and I didn't really know what mood he was in.

I glanced over. He looked calm as he twisted through the mountains, around curves and down slopes, but I saw the ghost of a smile tugging at the corner of his mouth.

It took eight minutes to reach town. Normally, it took twenty.

Abruptly, he slowed down, switching gears with lightning speed. Ten seconds later I saw a cop parked on the side of the road who stared at the car as we passed—more in awe than anything else.

"How'd you know he was there?"

Adrian just tapped his temple. Ah. Emotion radar. Sweet.

We pulled up to the school and parked. I could see the walkway to the gym lit up with strings of soft white lights. We headed inside, passing a few other couples on the way. The walls were drenched in shadows, making the cinder block all but invisible. In fact, the place was surprisingly well decorated with Chinese lanterns, soft lights, and tea candles. The floor was even covered in a giant gray tarp so you couldn't see the basketball court lines. I spotted Trish sitting at one of the circular tables and we walked over. I unbuttoned my coat, suddenly nervous, and felt Adrian slip it off my shoulders. When I turned, his face was frozen in an expression of pure shock as he stared at my dress.

I'd decided to go with a deep, luxurious green velvet, to match my eyes. The bodice was fitted to the hips, then flared out softly, ending in a slight train in the back. I'd spent hours hand-sewing various shades of iridescent glass beads to the halter strap in an abstract flower formation.

As for the back, well—there was no back. Between the top of my neck and the base of my spine, there was simply no fabric. This lack of dress was what Adrian had initially been staring at. But now, he was unabashedly staring somewhere else.

"Is that . . . ?" Adrian asked, nodding at my cleavage.

I nodded, blushing. Yes, it was the Green Thing, peeking out from underneath the dress. I'd designed the sweetheart neckline an inch lower than I normally would have so the beaded edge of the corset could show through.

Adrian blinked. And then blinked again. "I'm gonna go . . . get . . ." He trailed off, turned abruptly, and walked away.

That was not quite the reaction I'd been hoping for. Trish, however, whistled. "Mission accomplished," she grinned. "That boy can't even see straight right now."

I sat down carefully. "I don't know," I muttered. "He didn't exactly sweep me off my feet."

"Give it a few minutes," Trish said. "He probably needs to go adjust some things in the pants department."

"Trish!"

Before I could scold her more, Ben came and sat next to us, holding two flutes of sparkling cider. "Hey, Caitlin," he said.

I returned the greeting with a smile. The table was only big enough for three couples, and I saw Jenny and Meghan headed our way with their dates. Jenny picked up the pace subtly, reaching us first. Meghan made an awkward detour and tried to pull it off like she'd intended to go to the neighboring table all along.

"You look gorgeous," I whispered as Jenny sat down. The deep blue satin caught the light and shimmered, making her look like a mermaid. Her hair was curled elegantly and she'd done her makeup.

"Thank you," she whispered back. "So do you."

All around, I could see guys glancing over and doing double takes. They weren't used to seeing Jenny look hot—heck, they weren't used to seeing Jenny at all. She had a habit of blending into walls, posts, trees, whatever happened to be behind her. Luke, her date, still looked shocked that he'd invited the weird, pale girl from the junior class and shown up with what looked like her supermodel alter ego.

Adrian came back with drinks, handing me a glass. I immediately took a sip in order to keep my hands busy. So did Adrian. Eventually, we all started talking and the tension around the table eased a bit. There was a little three-tiered thing in the middle set with tea-light candles, chocolates, and little snacks and we munched on them while we waited. Eventually the Muzak crap that had been playing as we walked in was replaced by current pop songs, and Tim, Stephanie's date, announced that the dance had officially begun.

I'd only gone to one dance before, and my date had been a very sweet, but very bad dancer. I had no idea if I was any good at it because I'd spent the entire evening wishing I hadn't gone in the first place.

I felt a hand on mine, and looked up. Adrian was standing there in a form-fitting Armani suit, lit softly by hundreds of candles, wavy dark hair brushing the collar of his jacket, gray eyes deep and calm.

"Would you like to dance?"

He looked so beautiful, all I could do was nod.

He held my hand, lacing our fingers as we walked slowly to the center of the gym. Three or four other couples had braved the dance floor, and we melded in with them, Adrian's gaze sweeping up and down my dress slowly.

I rested my hand on his shoulder. We danced apart for a moment before he pulled me closer. I was afraid to look at him. His fingers were on my waist, tracing the edge of the velvet slowly. I wasn't entirely sure if Trish's Cinderella-dress plan was working, or if he was mocking me. *Look how well I can pretend to love you.* I desperately hoped the moment was sincere. But in all honesty, I couldn't tell.

As the song began to fade, Adrian wrapped a loose curl around his finger, then slowly drew it out, scraping his knuckles softly down my shoulder. I was so hyperaware of his touch that I had no idea if we were still dancing or not.

"Did you really make this?" Adrian asked, running the tips of his fingers across the beading on the neck of my dress. All I could do was nod. "It's beautiful," he murmured. "It's incredibly beautiful."

He pressed his palm to the dress-less small of my back and I shivered. As other couples folded in around us, his lips skimmed my shoulder and my knees buckled. He tightened his hold on my waist to catch me, which was not good because it meant we were pressed even more tightly together. I made the further mistake of looking up at him and our eyes caught and held and we just breathed, teetering on some invisible edge and I honestly didn't know which side I wanted to fall on. This had to be real. This *felt* real.

"Adrian—"

Someone bumped into us and I mentally said *thank God* at the same time I was thinking *damn it.* Adrian cleared his throat, and since the song was faster paced than before, we separated and looked away from each other and got swallowed up in the crowd that had finally gathered. Adrian excused himself to go get drinks and I didn't realize he never came back. Some time later—I don't know how long because the songs just kept coming one after the other and Trish was amazingly good at keeping us all herded on the dance floor and waving our arms dorkily in big, group dance moves—Tim went back on the mic and we all wandered back to our seats, sweaty and exhilarated. I found Adrian at our table, checking his phone. I scowled at him and he slipped it back into his pocket.

"All right," said Tim when everyone had finally settled. "The court of Winter Neverland proudly presents its just-now-voted-upon leaders. Beginning with the least important, this year's court jester is"—he paused and opened an envelope, then laughed abruptly, blushing—"uh, well, this year's court jester is actually me." Everyone laughed as he put a paper Burger King crown on his own head. "Okay, I have the results for the king and queen in my hand. Drum-roll please." A few boys beat the tables rapidly. "Thank you," Tim said dryly. "Now I know why we don't have a school band. All right, all right, your Winter Queen is . . . Jennifer Adams!"

We all looked over at Jenny, who was looking around as if unaware that her name had just been called. Trish nudged her. "Go on up there!"

Luke stood quickly and pulled her chair out, stunned that his date had turned out to be Winter Queen. Jenny walked in an adorably dazed fashion to the front, where Tim placed a laurel crown on her head. She glanced nervously back at us and everyone at our table gave her a thumbs-up and hollered at her obnoxiously.

"And the moment you've all been waiting for. Your Winter Court King is . . .." He dramatically double-checked the piece of paper in front of him. "Adrian de la Mara!"

I looked over at Adrian as everyone clapped and hollered. He looked uncomfortable, then resigned, and stood up, weaving through the tables. "Your Winter Court King and Queen, ladies and gentleman!"

Half a dozen flashes went off as Adrian and Jenny posed together for pictures, and I felt my gut twist. Seeing him stand next to her and smile—even if it was only for the cameras, even if it was only Jenny—highlighted the fact that we were never meant to be together. I clapped along with everyone else, cheering for Jenny because she deserved it, and then took a sip of cider to cover the sudden lump in my throat. My hand was shaking and I set it down.

"New York State of Mind" came on and everyone cheered and flooded the dance floor. I guess even out in the boondocks, there's state pride. Before Adrian could make his way back to me, I stood and walked over to Stephanie, suddenly not wanting to be near him for a few minutes.

"Caitlin!" she said when I reached her table. She and Tim were the only couple there, so I took an empty seat and sat down.

"Nice announcing, Tim!" I gave him an exaggerated high-five.

He grinned back. "Thanks." I noticed that he was looking very nice in a traditional suit, and his hair was a normal, natural brown instead of its usual stark black. Stephanie seemed to glow with happiness.

"That is a gorgeous color on you, Steph," I said. "Really compliments your hair. Don't you think so, Tim?"

Tim blushed and mumbled, "Yeah."

"And Tim, seriously, nice job with the mic tonight; they couldn't have picked a better announcer. Right, Steph?"

She blushed and nodded.

"Well," I said, mission accomplished, "Adrian's getting lonely without me. You two have a nice night."

As I stood up to leave, they were both blushing and smiling and adorable. I went back to Adrian feeling happy—

—which all vanished the moment I saw him sitting with his arm strewn across the back of my chair, a frown darkening his face as he was very intentionally *not* talking with anyone else at our table. With the Armani suit, the low light, and his natural chiseled-ness, he looked like an asshole. I saw Ben ask him a question, and Adrian flat out *ignored* him. It was suddenly so obvious that he was only here because he had to be, because it was part of our grand lie. He was a great actor. He was an incredible pretender. And none of it was real. Whatever that thing had been at the cabin, at Christmas, that moment when he'd whispered my name—that was gone.

And just like that, I wanted to be home. Not ranch-home, not bedroom-home, but *home*. Mystic. Connecticut. The ocean, my mom, my house, my *life*.

I walked up to Adrian and stopped abruptly. "Can we go?" I asked the back of his head, not wanting to sit.

He looked up at me, then checked his watch. "I think we should wait another twenty or thirty minutes."

I was going to cry, damn it. "I'd like to leave now," I said again, struggling to keep my voice from catching.

Without waiting for a reply, I waved good-bye to Trish, grabbed my coat, and headed for the door. I hadn't even had time to put it on before Adrian caught up to me in the parking lot.

"What is going on?" he demanded, pulling me to a stop.

"Nothing," I said, wrenching away so he wouldn't see that I was crying. "Let's just go, please."

"For God's sake, I did everything right," Adrian said, throwing his hands in the air. "I got the corsage, I wore a suit, I borrowed the car, we danced. Why are you upset with me?"

I just stared at him, tears mutinously coursing down my cheeks. "This isn't a game, Adrian. It's not a show or a play, this is my *life*. This is the dance, this is high school, this is us, and you're not *here*."

He looked at me like I was insane. "I'm here. I'm here every day. This was the setup, this was how we decided to play it—you're the one who came up with the rules, that stupid chore chart. If you're not happy with all of this, you have no one to blame but yourself."

I sucked in a sharp breath, trembling.

That was cruel.

There was no way I could justify his response, or explain it away for him. He was being mean, and I was done.

"Adrian," I whispered after a long moment. "I'm breaking up with you."

He stared at me. "You can't do that."

I stared right back at him. "Yes. I can."

Leaving him speechless, I walked back into the gym and found Trish. She saw the tears on my face and immediately pulled me into a dark corner where I bawled my eyes out on her shoulder. She and Ben immediately packed up and drove me home. I had to lie to Joe— again—and say that Adrian'd had a flat tire, so Trish had given me a lift. I told them the dance was wonderful, and that I was tired and going to bed.

But of course it wasn't over. Breaking up with Adrian didn't mean it was over.

So cue the nightmare.

It felt like the first one. Where I'd woken up in a dark room, unable to move. Completely paralyzed. A light formed somewhere overhead, growing slowly brighter. In front of me, a shape materialized in the darkness until I saw it was a person. Scratch that, a kid.

It was Lucian.

He was sitting with his head bowed forward so that his curly light-brown hair fell over and shadowed his face. It took an eternity for the light to brighten enough to see that he clutched my book in his hands, *The Adventures of Frankie the Boy.*

Suddenly, his head rolled back.

His aviator goggles were gone. His eyes were wide open, and they were completely black.

He was dead.

Out of the darkness, a white figure slowly approached. Nearing, I realized it was my mother, dressed in the World War II nurse's outfit she'd worn before. She knelt by Lucian's chair and smiled at me sadly with her bright red lipstick. I didn't know what she was doing here, but I knew it was bad. She slid Lucian into her arms like he weighed nothing. I watched helpless as the book slid out of his fingers and fell to the ground. She walked away into the darkness, taking Lucian with her, until they disappeared completely.

# 19

# FINALS

A week after winter formal, I woke up to the clatter of pans, the patter of feet running up and down the stairs, and the calls back and forth between Norah, Rachel, and Joe. It was seven in the morning, and I'd managed to get in about five hours of sleep—three before my nightmare and two after, once the sun was really up. It was a school day, but we were leaving at ten to head for Richmond, Virginia—the site of the East Coast Equestrian Finals, where Norah was about to kick ass—so Joe and Rachel had decided to just let us stay home until we left rather than pick us up early from school.

I was grateful, because I couldn't handle much more whispering and hushed conversations about the breakup. Adrian hadn't called me over the weekend, he hadn't fought for me or talked to me or so much as looked at me at school. Which was fine, except it was very obvious to the rest of the student body that Adrian and I were no longer a thing. Even through my exhaustion, I could tell that little else was being discussed at the lunch tables. On the supernatural side of things, I'd heard nothing from Mariana or the Council. Which was fine with me—as far as I was concerned, they could go be miserable and ancient all they wanted if they'd just leave me alone.

Groaning, I rolled out of bed, wrapping myself in my green quilt like a mummy, and headed downstairs to snag a cup of coffee before I took a shower. I could hear the washing machine and dryer going and bet Rachel was trying to do some last-minute housekeeping before we were gone for the weekend. Norah was running around with various pieces of clothing in her hands looking frazzled, and Joe was conspicuously gone—probably outside checking on the horses—where it was quiet.

I actually took the coffee with me into the shower, setting it on the window ledge above the spray of the nozzle. Halfway through rinsing my hair, the water gushed violently, then immediately relented, drizzled, and stopped altogether, then spurted on again, but lukewarm, and then cool, and then ice cold. I yelped and shut it off. A knock sounded on the bathroom door.

"Caitlin?" Rachel called, her voice muffled.

"Yeah?" I replied.

"We had to shut off the hot water."

"What happened?" I called back.

"The water heater's leaking and the laundry room flooded."

Even through the door she sounded like she was about to cry. Not only had she had a load in the wash that was half finished, but we were supposed to leave for Virginia in less than an hour and it was the weekend, so getting a plumber to come all the way out here would be a nightmare.

"Hold on," I told her. "I'll be out in a minute."

I dried off quickly and threw my clothes on. I'd gotten most of the shampoo out of my hair, toweled off the rest, then twisted it up into a bun and stuck a pencil in it because I was pretty sure Norah had stolen all my hair bands. When I stepped out of the bathroom, Rachel was gone, but I could hear someone in my aunt and uncle's bedroom, so I peeked inside. Rachel was on her laptop searching for plumbers. Norah sat beside her looking dazed. Joe came up the stairs without any shoes on, but his socks and the bottom of his jeans were soaked. Rachel looked up as he came in, but he just shook his head.

"Hello?" she said into the phone. "Yes, um, our hot water heater is leaking." She listened for a few moments. "The laundry room flooded and it's spreading into the hall." She listened again, eyes glistening. "I don't know. Joe?" she asked, looking up at her husband. "Is there corrosion?" He nodded. She repeated the information into the phone and listened again and then choked when she said, "Not until five?"

Norah looked like she was going to burst into tears and Joe sat beside her on the bed. "Are you sure there's nothing before then?" Norah looked hopeful for a moment, but I knew in that Murphy's Law sort of way that there wouldn't be anyone here to take care of this before we had to leave.

"Rachel," I said, trying to get her attention. She looked up at me distractedly.

"Just a minute, Caitlin."

"No, Rachel," I said again insistently.

She looked at me again and said, "Hold on, please," into the phone.

"I can stay," I told her. I knew she was going to protest, so I bowled over and kept talking. "Look, I really want to go see Norah, but if we have to wait for someone to show up, then we're not going to make it in time anyway, so either way I wouldn't see her compete. If I stay, I can let them in, clean up enough of the mess so that the floor doesn't get completely ruined, and then spend the weekend at Trish's. She won't mind. And that means you guys can leave on time."

"Caitlin," Joe began, "it's a very nice offer, but—"

"It's really not that big of a deal," I broke in. "And aren't they going to be broadcasting the events, anyway? I can still watch her on cable."

This was all half true—but mostly I just wanted some time alone to decompress from everything that had happened with Adrian, and to be out from under the suffocating watch of Joe and Rachel. And honestly, I really, really didn't want to spend ten hours in the back-seat of the truck.

Rachel was stuck with the phone against her ear and her eyes on Joe.

"I've seen Norah ride," I continued. "And it's amazing. She should go."

And I left it at that.

Joe and Rachel looked at each other, and then Rachel's eyes flicked to her daughter.

"Okay," Joe said. Rachel looked at him a moment longer, then at me.

"Send someone over at five," she said into the phone. They talked a moment longer, and then hung up. Norah hugged me as soon as her mom set the phone down, actually knocking me back against the bed.

"Thank you, Caitlin!" she exclaimed. "You're the best cousin ever!"

"It's no big deal, really," I replied as she grabbed my face and placed a loud kiss on my forehead. "Don't you need to finish packing?"

She let me go and dashed out of the room. I could hear drawers being opened and closed recklessly.

"Okay," Rachel said. "The plumber should be here around five. Only the water to the heater is turned off, so you can still use the bathroom." I nodded. "There's food in the fridge and the Stevensons are coming over in the morning to take care of the animals, so don't worry about that." She bit her lip in worry.

"I'll be fine," I told her. "Everything's gonna be fine."

Rachel nodded, smiled, and wrapped me in a hug and then Joe stood up and wrapped the both of us in a hug—I resisted the urge to wriggle away. Finally he set us down and Rachel went back to packing. Joe and I went downstairs and laid towels over the portions of the floor that had gotten wet and then set up a few rotating fans to blow in an arc and opened the front door and the downstairs windows. It was still snowy outside but there wasn't much of a choice—I'd just bundle up in every coat I owned and then close everything up once the sun set or the plumber showed up, whichever came first.

"It's ten!" Rachel called up the stairs from the kitchen a while later.

There was a muffled "ready!" from Norah's bedroom and then she was bounding down the stairs and everyone was gathered in the kitchen. Norah gave me another hug and whispered "thank you" in my ear and then everyone was stuffing last-minute things into the truck and then stuffing themselves into the truck and starting the engine and waving good-bye and driving away.

I had a few empty hours staring me in the face and I was going to use it to nap like a pro. I curled up on the couch under three blankets and conked out.

I woke up to a metallic clunk from outside. Sitting up, I brushed the hair out of my face and realized the sun had almost set—I must've been asleep for a while. Although, for once, no nightmares, which put me in such a good mood, I didn't stop to wonder why.

"Hello?" someone called out.

Stuck in the blankets, I bunny-hopped to the door and opened it, shouting, "Over here!"

I saw a utility van parked near our house and a guy in a light-blue shirt and brown jacket walking my way.

"This the Master residence?" he called out.

"Yeah," I said, holding my hand out as he reached me. "I'm Caitlin."

He shook my hand with a smile. "I'm Tommie. I hear your hot water heater's leaking?"

"Yeah, part of the downstairs got flooded."

He nodded and wrote something on his clipboard, then adjusted his hat as he looked at the house.

"This it?" he asked, nodding toward the front door.

"Yeah, come on in."

I led him to the laundry room where the hot water heater was located. He whistled when he saw the mess. "Looks like I got my work cut out for me." He bent down and poked around the base of the heater with his pen and then looked up at me again. "I'm sorry, what'd you say your name was? Carly?"

"Caitlin," I repeated.

"Caitlin. Sorry, I'm horrible with names. Anyway, it looks like whoever called us earlier was right; you've got a corroded valve here, and just looking at this thing, I can tell it is way past its prime. Probably been waiting to bite the dust for a few years."

I frowned. "So what does that mean in terms of fixing it?"

He laughed and took his hat off, running his fingers through his hair as he stood up. "There's no fixing it; you'll need a new one. Now I don't have a spare water heater just lying in my van, but I can remove this one for you."

"Is that really necessary?" I asked, blanching. "I mean, you really can't fix it?"

He gave me a sheepish half smile. "'Fraid not."

I sighed and rubbed my hands over my face. I didn't know a lot about water heaters, but replacing one had to be expensive.

"How much will all this cost?"

He stuffed his hands in his pocket, looking embarrassed to be talking to a girl about money. "Well, for me to remove it today and take it away will be about two hundred. To replace it could be anywhere from seven hundred to a thousand depending on what unit you get."

I choked. He looked embarrassed. "If it could be avoided, I'd tell you that, but this sucker's dead."

I sighed. "Well, all right. You said you can remove it?"

"Yes, ma'am; just show me where the water controls and power breaker are."

"It's just Caitlin," I said, leading Tommie into the hallway to show him the master panel.

"Caitlin," he repeated with an embarrassed smile, and I couldn't help but smile back. He switched off the power to the laundry room.

"I'm just gonna go get my toolbox," he said, and headed out the front door.

While he was gone, I texted Rachel and Joe to tell them the plumber had arrived and that he was working on the water heater. Rachel texted back and said that they were still driving, and thanked me again for staying behind.

Tommie came back in with a big metal toolbox. "Can you go through the house and turn on all the hot water spigots?" he asked, sliding his jacket off. "It'll relieve pressure in the tank, and then we'll run a hose in here and drain all the excess water outside."

I nodded and went through the house to do what he'd asked while he went back into the laundry room, and then I went back down to watch him work since it somehow felt rude to just ignore him. He was crouched on the floor, reaching behind the water heater with both arms, the short-sleeved utility shirt straining across his back and shoulders, and I had to admit there was something to be said for working men.

"Do you need any help?" I called.

"Nah, I'm fine; just trying to locate your drain valve. And I think"— his voice trailed off and then came back—"I got it."

He turned around to face me with a triumphant smile. "All right; let me just go grab a hose from the van and we can start draining."

He hurried back to his truck and returned with what looked like a garden hose, and attached it to what I assumed was the drain valve he said he'd located. I ran it through the open window to the snow-covered lawn outside.

"You ready?" he called.

"Yep."

I heard a gurgling sound, and then hot water poured from the hose into the snow, causing it to melt and steam.

"This'll take a few minutes, then I can get started on disconnecting the pipes."

I nodded, and my stomach rumbled loudly. "Sorry," I mumbled, embarrassed.

"That's all right; I'm getting hungry myself."

"You want some dinner? I was going to make something anyway, and it seems like this'll take a while."

He looked torn. "Well, that's real nice, but I don't want to be a bother."

I shrugged. "I'm cooking anyway. It's not hard to make a little more."

He hesitated a moment longer. "All right; I'd like that."

"Do you eat meat?" I asked, then realized that sounded rude. "I mean, are you a vegetarian or anything? I was going to make burgers."

He laughed. "No—definitely not a vegetarian."

I headed into the kitchen, pulled out the frying pan, and started cooking bacon. Periodically, I heard clunks and clanks from the laundry room, and occasionally saw him step out to his truck. Every time he passed he'd smile and do this funny little half bow.

While the burgers were finishing up, I pulled out the bread and a bunch of condiments and plates and silverware and set the table, figuring we could be at least somewhat civilized.

I went over to the laundry room and leaned against the door frame. "How's it going?"

He was lying on his back with his hands reaching under the water heater, a determined look on his face.

"This is a really old unit. I've never seen one this ornery before; these screws are practically melted to the frame."

His arms strained and his whole body seemed to hum with tension as he tried to turn a wrench at a very awkward and uncomfortable angle on the underside of the heater.

"Would you like a break? Dinner's just about ready."

He let his arms fall on his stomach and smiled up at me. "Sounds great."

I smiled back as he heaved himself up and followed me into the kitchen. It was well past dark now, and I went to close the front door and the windows. "There's cold soda and other drinks in the fridge; grab whatever you'd like."

He turned to the sink and washed his hands and then poured himself a glass of orange juice from the fridge. I closed the last window and came back, flipping each bacon-and-cheese-covered burger onto a bun. He waited until I sat down before he allowed himself to sit, and then took his hat off out of politeness. I couldn't help but smile.

I was about to eat when I saw him close his eyes and bow his head, so I waited for him to finish praying.

We ate in silence for a few moments. Finally, he cleared his throat. "So what are you studying?"

I looked at him strangely. "Lots of things . . ."

Now he looked at me strangely. "Where do you go?"

"Warren County," I replied.

"Oh," he said, looking surprised. "I'm sorry; I assumed you were in college. You don't look like a high school student."

"Oh, well . . ." I trailed off, feeling kind of embarrassed and flattered at the same time. "Where do you go?"

"Schenectady Community College, part time. I do this to pay for tuition. Do you have any plans after high school?"

I shrugged. "I'm not sure, exactly. I might have an internship waiting for me, but . . ."

"What?"

But with Adrian and I no longer "dating" I had no idea if the internship was still available. And it felt pretentious to say that I wanted to be a clothing designer, at least here where manual labor was the norm.

"Come on, it can't be that embarrassing."

I rolled my eyes. "All right, I want to be a designer."

"Really?" He looked surprised, but not in a condescending way. "Are you any good?"

I shrugged. "I'm not sure. My mom was really good, and she taught me everything I know."

"Was?"

I smiled in that way people smile when someone doesn't realize they've asked a touchy question. "Yeah, she died a couple months ago."

"Oh," he said, looking mortified, "I'm so sorry. I didn't mean to—"

"It's fine," I interrupted.

"Even so, it's none of my business. I'm sorry."

"Seriously, it's all right," I said, throat tight. I was still so tired that I was on the verge of tears pretty much all the time. "Let's just talk about something else. What do you want to be?"

He twirled his fork. "I'm not sure, exactly. I mean, I'm good at plumbing—sort of a family trade—I could make a living off it if I wanted, I just don't really think it's what I'm supposed to do, you know? And my dad, he really wanted me to take over the business, and I feel like since . . ." His voice trailed off and he looked far away for a few moments.

I stared at him. "You all right?"

"What?" He looked back at me like he'd forgotten I was there. "Oh, yeah. I just . . ."

I frowned. "What?"

He cleared his throat. "Well, I feel weird saying this after you mentioned your mom, but my family, uh . . . died. In a car accident, just before Christmas. My mom and dad and my little brother. It was snowy and this idiot tourist . . ." He shook his head. "I don't normally think about it, because if I think about it, it's just too hard. Like if I remember how it used to be, I can't move. Just sort of caught me by surprise there. Sorry."

"No," I breathed, feeling the lump in my throat grow, "I'm sorry."

"Don't be. They're in a better place now. And I get by. It's all right."

He smiled and I noticed his food was gone.

"You done?"

He nodded, swallowing a few times.

I reached for his plate, but he stood up quickly and grabbed mine. "You cooked dinner; the least I can do is clear the table."

I nodded, and then started washing the frying pan and utensils as he brought everything over to the sink. We worked side by side for a few minutes in silence. When he didn't have anything else to do, he stuffed his hands in his pockets and I turned to him.

"Tommie, I'm really sorry. About your family."

He smiled a sad half smile. "I am, too. For you."

My eyes were watering so I turned to the sink and continued washing plates. He passed behind me and went back to the laundry room. I followed him a minute later, since weren't that many dishes to clean. Tommie was hard at work on the water heater, concentrating on the pipes. He looked up when I walked in.

"You need anything else?" I asked.

He stood up slowly, his eyes fluttering from me to the water heater and back. He cleared his throat. "Y'know, I may be forward by asking this, but I honest to God haven't touched anyone since my parents and Jake died. I've forgotten . . ." He laughed nervously, but it was a sad sound. "I've forgotten what it feels like. Could—that is, would you mind if I hugged you?"

A part of me thought the whole situation was absurd, but the larger part of me knew what he was talking about. I'd felt this exact way after my mom died. I nodded and he took a step forward. Slowly, he raised his arms, placing them gently around my shoulders like I'd break. He let out a breath and let the weight of his arms pull me closer, resting his cheek lightly on top of my head. I hugged him back because I knew the price of a hug when there was no one you could depend on to hug you freely. I hugged him back because he wanted to hug me. I hugged him back because it felt good.

He pulled back a little and I looked up at him to say something dumb and sympathetic, but then his lips were on mine and I was dizzy

and confused and we just stood like that for a moment, barely touching. He pulled away.

"I'm sorry," he whispered, and cleared his throat. "I didn't mean
to do that."

"You didn't mean to kiss me?" I asked, still in shock.

"No. Well, I mean, I definitely wanted to, I just didn't mean to
actually do it."

But he was still holding on to me. And I was still holding on to
him.

He looked at me again, and for some reason, I didn't look away.
The moment became heavy, and he leaned down once more.

And once again, I didn't stop him.

He pulled me gently against him and I returned the kiss very, very
slowly. Far away, I could hear my phone ringing. I ran my hands up
his back, feeling the rippling muscles that came from hard labor, from
real work, and he kissed me again and backed me up against the wall
and held me pinned there with his body and I didn't mind because
this was what I wanted, this was what I'd always wanted. My phone
stopped ringing.

He picked me up, wrapped my legs around his waist, and we
crashed back against the wall and his lips were on my neck, my jaw,
my mouth. Somehow, we were walking and we were kissing and he
set me on the couch and leaned down over me, and my nerves were
on fire and I was unbuttoning his shirt and *damn* he looked good and
I wondered if there'd ever been a time I'd ever wanted anything else
and then I stopped wondering because his hands were sliding under
my shirt and lifting it over my head and it felt so nice to have my
skin pressed against his skin and I was glad I'd worn a cute bra today.
Then his lips were skimming down my throat and chest and stomach and buttons were being unbuttoned and zippers unzipped and
I was happy because I'd been waiting for this, for him, and here we

were. My jeans were beginning to slide slowly down my hips and I whispered *"Adrian"* against his lips. There was a small breath of frigid air and the *click* of the front door opening, which I couldn't spare any brainpower to think about, but a voice was calling my name, which caught my attention enough that I opened my eyes.

And there was Adrian, standing in the open front door.

Oh. Shit.

One moment Tommie was above me, the next moment he was gone, and there was the sound of something very solid hitting the utility van outside. I blinked, and looked down at myself. My shirt was gone and my jeans were halfway off.

There was another metallic *thunk*, and muffled shouting.

I shoved my jeans back on, threw my shirt over my head and ran to the doorway. Just as I stepped outside, a hand—not Adrian's, because I could see Adrian picking himself off the ground ten feet in front of me—clamped over my mouth and I screamed. Before I could figure out what the hell was going on, Tommie threw me over his shoulder and dragged me into the trees, his shoulder biting into my stomach with each step. Moments later, we were in a clearing and I was thrown to the ground, my knees crunching in the snow, and then jerked back with a fist wrapped in my hair. Adrian was two seconds behind us and stopped abruptly. We all stood very still.

"You can't kill her," I heard Adrian call from the edge of the clearing, still hidden in the shadows of the trees. "It's forbidden."

"True," Tommie said in a friendly sort of way. "But *killing* her isn't what I had in mind."

He was pulling so tightly on my hair I was afraid it would rip right out of my head while my mind was still trying to figure out *what the fuck was going on.*

"I will kill you if you hurt her."

♥   345   ♥

"You need to work on your technique, son—couldn't even seduce one little human girl. I show up and give her everything she wants—an older, tragic man. She couldn't keep her hands off me."

I let a hard breath escape as it finally dawned on me just exactly who Tommie was.

"You didn't try very hard to make her fall in love with you—" he said, then paused, considering Adrian. A slow smile spread over his face. "Which makes me think you don't know who she is, yet."

Adrian didn't respond for a long moment. "Whatever plans you have for Caitlin, they are done. She is under my protection."

"Before you go all white knight, let's talk."

"I'm not interested in talking. Let her go."

Tommie suddenly lifted my arms into the air behind my back, pushing my face into my knees and I screamed because if he pulled another fraction of an inch, things in my shoulders would start tearing.

"Don't make me rip her arm off," he said pleasantly. "She'll be fine without an arm, for my purposes. And I know how thirsty you are."

"Caitlin, stay calm," I heard Adrian call to me. "He's feeding off your fear. Don't give him more than you have to."

Great, not only was I scared shitless, I was feeding the enemy. And if Tommie—or whatever his real name was—tore my arm off, I would, y'know, bleed profusely. And Adrian was thirsty.

Which meant if the injury didn't kill me, Adrian probably would.

"Son," Tommie tried again. "Let's talk."

"I'm not your son," Adrian replied quietly, but I could hear the rage underneath his self-control.

"No?" Tommie asked, wrenching my arms until I screamed.

"Stop!" Adrian yelled, panicked. "Just—what do you want?"

Immediately, Tommie lowered my arms to a bearable height and I sucked in huge gulps of air.

"So you do have manners; I'm so glad your sister was able to teach you something."

Even though my view was limited to my knees, I could just make out Adrian's shoes moving closer in my peripheral vision. "You're not worried the Council will destroy you for this?"

"Not really." He sounded almost amused. "The Council has failed repeatedly at stopping me."

The Council.

Mariana, Dominic, Julian—where was Julian? New York, where he always was. Where was Adrian's sister? Couldn't they feel what was happening? Why was Adrian alone?

"There's a lot you don't know, son. There's so much that they've kept from you."

"I am the product of your psychological rape, but I will never be your son," Adrian replied calmly. "You are incapable of love—you can't even feed off it."

The way he said it was strange, slow and deliberate, like he trying to tell me something. But he took a step toward us and I couldn't think about it because Adrian's dad dug his fingers into my arm like a vise and I screamed.

Tommie was silent a moment. "Then tell me why they haven't told you who she is. Tell me why she wasn't better guarded."

Adrian didn't reply.

"Tell me," he murmured, "why they assigned a boy to guard this girl's life. They were hoping you would fail. They were *hoping* I would kill her—because *they know what she is.*"

"You're lying."

Tommie laughed, sounding genuinely amused. "Your Council is

so moral, so predictable. If I got her pregnant, if she gave birth to another vampire bastard and died in the process, it would be so convenient for them. Adrian—you were intended to let her die."

Tommie suddenly let go of my arms. I fell forward with a cry of pain, the blood draining back down into my limbs. He bent down, wrapped his arm gently around my waist, and pulled me up, holding me pinned against him.

"She could love you," he said, staring furiously at Adrian. "You know how to make that happen." He tilted my head back and breathed in the scent of my neck. "But if you don't want her—"

Adrian stepped forward. "I want her."

I didn't understand what was happening anymore. I had no clue what was going on.

"Take her, then," he said, lips murmuring over my neck. "If you want her."

My head was still tilted back, but out of the corner of my eyes, I watched as Adrian walked slowly in our direction; the silver of his eyes rivaling the stars.

He stopped a foot away as his father kept a tight grip on my waist. Adrian reached out and touched my cheek, his irises burning like suns. I searched his face desperately, looking for a sign, a clue as to what was really going on, what I was supposed to *do*.

Staring me straight in the eye, he was in compulsion mode, I could tell. Jaw set in a hard line, he whispered, "Kiss me."

Shit, he was really doing it—he was really *forcing* me to do this. Immediately, despite the situation, despite everything, I strained forward, unable to resist his command.

With a delighted laugh his father let me go and I rushed at Adrian, crushed my mouth against his as he pressed his warm body against mine in the cold, dead night, holding me tighter than he'd ever held me before, tangling his hands in my hair, completely unrestrained, and then—

"Stop," he ordered, and I froze, because I had to. He slid his lips near my ear and whispered, almost too low for me to hear, *"I'm so sorry."*

But as soon as he said it, he kept moving, lips gliding down my jaw, my throat, across my shoulder, my arm, finally pressing a kiss against my wrist. I winced involuntarily because my arms were a mass of fresh bruises. He held my hand in both of his and turned it, examining my skin in the moonlight.

"She's bruised," he said lightly, like he was commenting on a bad piece of fruit. He looked up calmly at Tommie.

And then Adrian punched his father in the face.

His head snapped back, unprepared for the blow. Before I could process this bizarre turn of events, Adrian swung, kicking his father in the face with his motorcycle boot with a sickening crunch.

Blood sprayed everywhere as Tommie shook his head. Recovering quickly, he feinted, tackling Adrian to the ground. They rolled halfway across the clearing, kicking, cursing, until Tommie lifted Adrian by the shirt and slammed his head back against a tree stump with a sound that made me gag. I was frozen in place, still in shock, or maybe Adrian's command was keeping me from moving, I wasn't sure. There was a sudden, intense flash of light coming from Adrian's eyes—somehow he'd pinned Tommie. But the man only laughed.

And with that he blasted Adrian twenty feet into the air, though *how* I couldn't see. Before Adrian could hit the ground, Tommie made a pushing motion with his hands and smashed Adrian into a tree with a blast of air. He crashed against the trunk, fell to a heap on the ground, and lay still. Tommie advanced slowly, and I knew that unless

I did something, Adrian was about to die. I searched the grass around me desperately. Where was a rock when you needed one? No rocks. No rocks?

Shit.

Finding my legs again (maybe compulsions didn't work once he was unconscious?), I ran toward Tommie and screamed, "I want to go with you!"

Adrian's father looked up. I knew he could feel my fear, absorb it, but I also knew he could tell I was being honest—at least to a degree. If going with him meant saving Adrian's life, then yes, I wanted to go with him.

Out of the corner of my eye, Adrian was still. I wasn't sure if he'd actually passed out or if he was acting. Either way, I was not going to lose him. Not like this.

"Adrian," Tommie called. "It appears your human doesn't want you." He turned his back on his son and smiled. "But she's going to have to convince me."

I was kind of amazed at myself in that moment. Amazed that I wasn't crying. Amazed that I wasn't shaking. Honestly, I was amazed that I was even standing.

I put my hand on his neck and whispered, "Come here." He searched my eyes, was satisfied with whatever he saw there, and inclined his face so I could reach him. I closed my eyes. I was calm. I could do this. Adrian was going to die; I could do this.

I brushed my lips against the corner of his mouth.

And then I stabbed him.

I pulled the pencil out of his neck and stabbed him again. I put every ounce of terrified adrenaline I had into it, pushing it halfway through his throat. I'd felt the pencil poking me in the back of the neck where I'd stuck it in my hair after I got out of the shower, as

Tommie carried me through the trees. Now, blood dribbled and then spurted from the wounds, and I'd bet money I'd hit an artery.

Furious, he slapped me. I flew three feet and crumpled to the ground, the world going in and out of focus as I struggled to remain conscious.

Gasping in air, I looked up and saw that Adrian, far from being knocked out, had hooked his fingernails into the punctures I'd made in his father's neck. I looked down again just as he jerked his hand, but I couldn't stop myself from hearing the skin rip away in a flopping, juicy mass. Terror made me open my eyes again and watch. Neck half *gone*, his father still managed to grab Adrian by the throat and lift him off the ground.

"Idiot child," Tommie roared. "You don't even know what you're fighting for."

He held his hand out and Adrian flew into the air. The trees whipped into a frenzy and I felt a massive wind pulling at my hair, tearing at my clothes. It shrieked toward Tommie, diverting at the last second to push up against Adrian, to hold him in the air.

Tommie looked up at his son, expressionless. "I suppose you won't know what you're dying for, either."

My mind was perfectly blank—I didn't have the faintest idea what to do. I had no idea Adrian's father was capable of these kinds of things—I had no idea that *any* of this was possible.

My brain sputtered into action, sluggishly sorting through options. If I threw anything at Tommie, it would just get sucked up into the vortex and hit Adrian. If I stayed still, eventually Adrian would be killed. If I got too close, I would get swept up into the same weird wind tunnel that was holding Adrian immobile in the air. There was nothing I could do. As always, there was absolutely nothing I could do.

And that seriously pissed me off.

I was sick of being helpless. Sick of watching the people I loved die quickly or slowly but always painfully. Sick of standing by.

I was enraged—familiar, beautiful rage.

But then Adrian's voice came back to me, dancing in the back of my mind—something important, something *crucial*. What had he said, about Tommie? It was only a few minutes ago. What had he *said*?

Something about love. Tommie . . .

Tommie couldn't feed off love. He wouldn't use it.

But Adrian *could*.

Rage was useful, rage had seen me through a lot, but at the moment, it was literally fueling the psychopath who was hurting one of the only people I really cared about.

So I let it go.

And instead, I remembered.

I remembered my mom, and how much she'd given up for me. I remembered how happy my dad had been, how full his life was. And I remembered Adrian. I remembered meeting him, in the library. I remembered when he brought me home and made me toast and tucked me into bed. I remembered night after night sleeping next to him, feeling for the first time in my life that I was completely and utterly safe.

Adrian's eyes, flickering dimly, suddenly flared back into life.

"I love you," I whispered, looking straight at him, forgetting about Tommie altogether. He was forty feet away, he couldn't possibly hear me, but he looked at me as if my voice was as clear as day.

The silver blossomed into a flood of light so bright that everything faded and lost color. I continued to stare at Adrian suspended in midair and whispered again, "I love you."

There were no shadows. Everything was white. I couldn't see the stars or the grass or my hand in front of my face, even though my eyes were wide-open.

"I love you so much, you stupid boy."

The roar of the wind faded until it was completely silent, with nothing but the ringing in my ears and the cold sting of the snow beneath my hands and knees to remind me we were still on earth.

And then—abruptly—it was dark.

I felt someone rush past into the forest, the stench of burning flesh trailing after them. My eyesight lagged, strobing under the disorienting glare of the stars overhead. I looked toward where I'd last seen Adrian, but white dots took up most of my vision, and for a panicked second, I couldn't find him.

Then my vision cleared, finally, and landed on a dark, motionless figure in the grass. I ran, but it felt like a dream, like the distance between us could never be crossed.

But I did reach him. He was facedown in the snow, completely still. The back of his skull was sticky with congealing blood. Shaking uncontrollably, I grabbed his shoulders and rolled him over. His eyes were closed, his face was drenched in blood; more was trickling out of his mouth, and his black shirt was wet.

Trembling, I gently pulled it up.

And then I turned my head and threw up.

His torso looked like ground meat.

Dozens of jagged wounds littered his chest, ranging from pinpricks to holes an inch wide. Rocks, or debris of some kind, must have gotten caught up in the wind tunnel and shot at him so quickly they'd gone straight through his body, like tornadoes that drive flimsy pieces of straw straight through tree trunks. Vampire or not, there was no way someone could survive these kinds of injuries. Adrian had said he wouldn't *die*, and I realized now he meant he wouldn't die of natural causes, of old age or sickness. He was hard to kill—but he *could* be killed.

"Adrian?" I whispered. He didn't so much as twitch. "Adrian, please." But he remained silent, still.

My fingers hovered over his chest. I could feel heat seeping from the jagged wounds like it was his life itself floating away.

I kept expecting him to wake up, to open his eyes. I kept waiting for him grin and give me a lecture on antibodies and how awesome his immune system was and that he'd be fine, just give him a minute.

But he didn't—he just lay there.

Because he was gone.

I let out a sob, then slapped my hands over my mouth. I fisted my hands in my hair and sat back on my heels. The stars burned on above us, silent. Feeling like I might puke again, I stood and walked in a short circle, then collapsed, digging my fingers into the snow. I was afraid, though, that he would disappear, if I couldn't see him. Panicked, I crawled back and cradled Adrian's body against my chest, finally letting loose the scream I'd held in for so many months.

What did it matter now? No one was listening, anyway.

# 20

## IT IS FINISHED

H is body wasn't just cold, it was *frozen*. When I touched his skin, it seemed to suck the warmth out of my fingertips.

My jaw hurt, not just because I'd been slapped, but because I'd spent the last two hours gritting my teeth in shock—the hour before that had been spent crying uncontrollably, and now my throat was raw and I'd lost my voice. The snow around us was picturesque, the sky above was clear as glass, and I'd long ago become dangerously numb.

Alone in the clearing, I felt once again like I had when Adrian stripped away my sense of self, to hide me from his father during the storm. I felt like nothing. I felt like I had never been.

Congratulations, God, universe, demons, Council, whatever. You won.

They would all pay. Mariana, Dominic, Julian, Tommie—they would all pay for this.

I tore my gaze away from the empty sky and down to Adrian again. He was so beautiful, even now, blown halfway to hell. I'd scrubbed the blood off his face while it was still fresh, but there wasn't anything else I could do. I couldn't lift him, couldn't carry him, couldn't call for help; didn't even know which way led back to the house. But it didn't matter.

I had loved him. That still amazed me. I'd gotten the chance, however briefly, to love someone.

There weren't any clouds. Brilliant stars, though. I wondered if Adrian was up there. Was he looking down? Was he in heaven? Was he in hell, because of what he was? Or did he just not exist anymore?

I hoped he existed somewhere. Even if it wasn't here, I hoped he was somewhere. He should be somewhere beautiful. Where somebody loved him.

Except I loved him. So he should be here.

"Adrian, *you promised me*," I whispered for the hundredth time.

For the hundredth time, he didn't answer. The meadow smelled like blood.

I was tired. I was going to sleep. I laid my head down on his icy chest and closed my eyes and it didn't take much to let everything drift away.

I slept hard. So hard that even being asleep felt dark, black. Like the bottom of an abyss, perfectly silent and still.

I was alone.

---

I found it odd that I didn't have a nightmare. I figured I should have one. I deserved to have one. My punishment for allowing Adrian to die. But the fact that the entire night had been a waking nightmare perhaps canceled the need for a regular one. Either way, all I did was sleep, and came up slowly, like rising to the surface of a pool after letting all the air out of your lungs. You become heavier, somehow; less able to float. Waking was like that—something you have to do because you can't stay under forever, but not something you want to do. It's peaceful with the sound and light muted and the pressure pushing in on you from all sides equally. Water was good like that. It was fair.

I heard my heartbeat pounding sluggishly in my ear. For a moment, I'd forgotten where I was, why I was, why he was the way he was. My heart was loud, and the beat was awkward. Maybe I was having a heart attack.

Huh.

It was *really* loud. I raised my head off Adrian's chest to check my pulse, and the sound went away.

Every muscle in my body froze.

I laid my head back down on his chest and waited.

And waited.

Three minutes later: *tha-thump (thump)*.

I took my head away again. Again, the sound disappeared.

I made myself examine his face. His eyes were still closed, face still pale and bluish, lips slack.

Trembling, I reached for the hem of his shirt and lifted it up. Still dozens of holes—but they were pink, and closing before my eyes, slowly, chunk of tissue by chunk of tissue like some reverse-motion time lapse.

I was going crazy. I must be. I had been out here for hours.
*Hours.*

He had been *dead* for hours. I was going crazy.

"Adrian?" I whispered. Did I see his eyelids move, just the tiniest bit? "Adrian, honey, if you're there, come back," I whispered, holding his face in my hands. "Come back. Please come back. I'm here. Please come back."

He frowned, very slightly.

Oh my God.

I put my fingers under his jaw, trying to feel for a pulse. An artery pressed very lightly and very slowly against my fingers.

"Oh my God," I sobbed, hot tears splashing down my cheeks.

He frowned again. I laughed, clapped my hands over my mouth, and watched him. I was going nuts. I was going absolutely nuts. Joe and Rachel would commit me—they'd find me out here with Adrian's body two days from now and they'd see me laughing and crying and talking to him and they'd commit me and I wouldn't blame them.

He sighed a tiny bit, the creases in his forehead deepening.

"*Wake up,*" I whispered.

I rubbed his arms vigorously, thinking that maybe he'd get warmer or something. Maybe I just wanted to touch him. Maybe I was so scared that I couldn't keep my hands still. Maybe I was going into shock.

His lips parted and he sucked in a thin, raspy, awful breath.

I held the side of his face, leaned down over him, tried to gather him as close as possible, keep him warm with my half-numb body. He coughed weakly, then violently, and frowned.

"*Come back,*" I warned him. "You promised me."

He took in another breath. It sounded excruciating. It sounded like half his insides were torn up. I told him to breathe again.

He did. In and out, irregular and hoarse and slow and it was hard to listen to, but I stared at him like if I looked away he'd disappear.

He coughed up blood. I wiped his lips off with my sleeve. His eyes were racing back and forth behind his lids.

Finally, he opened them.

But as he stared up at the sky, it seemed as though he couldn't see anything. Like the stars *were* his eyes and he was looking down at himself, at me, at the blood-spattered clearing, from an entire galaxy away.

"Come back to me," I whispered.

And a few moments later, he did. His eyes twitched, unfocused. Then he turned, and saw me, recognition lighting up his face. Tears leaked out of his eyes and ran down his bloodstained skin.

We stayed like that for a long time. Staring at each other as he tried to breathe, coughing occasionally as his insides knit themselves back together. I ran my hand under his shirt to feel his injuries. They were raw and sticky, but closed.

"Caitlin?" he whispered in a harsh rasp.

"I've got you. Don't talk, okay? I've got you."

He couldn't even nod, just stared at me, his eyes blurred with tears, hardly even blinking, as his breathing slowly became less and less jagged. Eventually it became regular, a clear, consistent sound.

"What?" I asked, when a tortured look passed over his face. "What do you need?"

His face contorted into an expression I didn't understand. All he said was, "No."

I brushed his hair back from his face, thinking he was delusional. "What do you mean no? No what?"

He shook his head weakly. "Go away."

I pulled back. "What?"

His eyes snapped open, blazing silver. "*Go away.*"

I shook my head violently.

"Caitlin," he whispered, looking panicked, "I will hurt you. *I won't stop.*"

It finally dawned on me. He'd bled for hours—he'd been thirsty before his father had even shown up. He convulsed, sweat rolling down his temples, teeth clenched.

"It's okay. It's going to be okay." I propped him up against my knee, pulling my hair away from my neck.

"*No,*" he whispered, gritting his teeth on the word, writhing in my arms like he was on fire.

"Shut up," I said, and leaned over him.

He let out something between a groan and a snarl and then there were teeth in my skin, slicing through it.

And it hurt.

Oh my God, it *hurt.*

I held back a cry because if he heard it, he'd stop, and if he stopped, he'd die.

He tried to be gentle. Still it felt like someone was twisting scalpels in my neck. I grew light-headed as the blood that should have been pumping into my brain was now draining into Adrian. As he grew stronger, he reached up and held my face with his hand and I closed my eyes and concentrated on breathing. Just breathing. Everything else was starting to fade away.

I don't know how long it went on for. I only knew the pain was constant and sharp; the only clearness in the fog of existing. I had no real concept of time, but eventually, blessedly, it stopped. He pressed his trembling lips to my skin in a kiss.

"You promised me," I murmured, on the thin edge of consciousness.

"I know," he whispered. "Open your eyes."

I did. He met mine and murmured something in that funny language of his—and I could feel the teethmarks in my neck closing back up. I should really ask him about that language sometime. Probably not now, though.

I fell back against the snow, drained. In my mind I laughed because I'd never used that word literally before. I felt Adrian crawl slowly over me. He touched my cheek, my eyes, my lips. He whispered my name brokenly against my heart.

And then I didn't feel anything.

———◯———

I used to chew on pennies when I was teething, or so my mom always told me. She'd have to hide all of them on the top shelf so I couldn't find them. I remember they tasted like copper.

I woke up in the clearing and the world was copper. The trees, the grass, the clouds, my tongue—all copper. I would never be able to get that smell, that taste, out of my head.

I realized something heavy was covering me from head to foot.

Ah, yes.

That would be Adrian.

I muttered and shifted. He woke up, blinking sleepily. Our eyes met and we stared at each other for a long time. And then I reached up, stiff from the cold and dried blood, and put my arms around his neck and hugged him because I still didn't believe he was alive—I wanted to, but wasn't I crazy? Crazy people thought their dead, fake ex-boyfriends were alive. I didn't know anymore. His arms felt warm around me—real. As long as they held on, I didn't care if I was crazy. That was fine.

"Adrian?" I whispered against his cheek.

He buried his face in my hair. "I'm here."

"Okay."

I drifted off again.

"Caitlin," he murmured into my hair a while later.

"Hmm?"

"We need to go back."

"There's no going back," I mumbled.

"We need to go back," he repeated. "We have to get to my house. I need to call Mariana and Dominic and Julian. We need to get warm."

Warm sounded good.

Half letting go of me, we stumbled to our knees, and then, after many shaky attempts, we made it to our feet. I was so dizzy. The clearing smelled of copper. Adrian smelled like copper.

We took a step, and then another. Holding on to each other for balance, we staggered across the meadow and into the trees, the bright starlight dusting the path enough for us to see our feet on the white ground. We walked for so long. Everything in me begged me to stop, to fall into the snow and sleep, but I ignored me, and thought about clean clothes, a hot bath, hot chocolate, a fire, food, protein, food, a blanket, sleeping in a bed, sleeping anywhere.

The house came into view. The utility van was gone.

"Adrian," I said, pulling him to a stop. "I . . . smelled him. It was like—like charred meat. What did you do?"

He paused before saying, "I honestly don't know. Whatever it was, I've never done that before. I didn't even know I could."

We went inside the open front door cautiously, listening. The house was silent, a few lights burning on into the darkness.

"Grab some clothes, whatever you need for a few days," he said as we headed up the stairs, checking every door as we went. There was no one there. As I packed, he went back downstairs and started raiding our fridge. I moved sluggishly, limply placing sweatpants and shirts and socks into a duffel bag, paying little attention to what I grabbed or if it matched. I headed downstairs again. Adrian looked better, more awake—more *alive*.

"You ready?"

I nodded.

"Lock the door, and we'll come back tomorrow."

We headed outside and I locked the door. My phone beeped anxiously in my bag. I fumbled onto the motorcycle and unlocked the screen. I had a text message from Rachel asking how I was doing over at Trish's. I texted her back: *sry was watching movie marathon. im good, going to bed now.*

I shoved my helmet on and Adrian pulled down the driveway, onto the main road, toward his house. Ten minutes later, we were there, the massive wrought-iron gates swinging open. He parked, and I tapped my phone again and sent a text off to Trish: *can u cover me? im with adrian; rachel & joe think im with you. thx.*

I could only hope that Rachel hadn't already called Trish or her parents and asked how I was. Since I'd never called Trish earlier to tell her I would be coming over, she wouldn't know that I hadn't gone with them to Norah's competition like I was supposed to. Oh hell, I hope the police hadn't been called. I shoved my phone in my pocket, too tired to think through the possibilities, and followed Adrian inside. We went up to Adrian's room and he found his cell phone where he'd left it. I sat on the floor, not wanting to get blood on any of the furniture. Some insane part of me found it amusing that the last time I'd been in this room, I'd been drunk and Adrian had been a pirate.

"Mariana?" he asked a moment later. "Come home now. He came back." He listened for a moment, then glanced at me. "At the house, with me. I'll fill you in when you get here." He listened a moment longer, then hung up.

"Why didn't they help?" I asked. "Why were you alone?"

He shook his head. "They were in D.C., following a lead about our father. It was a setup. He planned this whole damn thing." He ran a shaky hand through his hair, then grimaced when he realized it was matted with blood. "I need, uh—you need food." He helped me up and we stumbled downstairs and into the kitchen where he flipped on a few lights.

"Eat these," he said, handing me a plate of chocolate chip cookies. "It'll hit your system fast."

I popped one into my mouth and chewed mechanically. I loved chocolate chip cookies, but I honestly couldn't taste them now. He opened the fridge and reached into a drawer, pulling out a plastic IV bag. I watched, fascinated, as he ripped off the stopper and drained the blood in one long swallow. I was on my second cookie when he reached for another bag. I figured I should be nauseous, but I wasn't. He wiped his lips, threw both bags in the trash, and reached back in the fridge, pulling out a covered Tupperware container. He popped the lid, slid something onto a plate, and stuck it in the microwave.

"What's that?" I asked around my fourth cookie.

"Spaghetti; lots of carbs. Can you handle that?"

I nodded. "Do you have any milk?" I was eating chocolate chip cookies. I needed milk.

"Milk? Yeah . . ." He grabbed a gallon from the fridge, poured me a huge glass, and set it in front of me, hands shaking.

"Keep drinking," I told him.

He saw me sitting there, munching on my fifth cookie, then went back to the fridge and pulled out his third bag and began sipping at it slowly. The microwave dinged. He held the IV in one hand and handed me the plate of spaghetti with the other, then set a knife and a fork in front of me.

He'd been dead an hour ago.

I twirled some pasta on my fork and ate it. Mariana's cooking. Good.

"Why aren't you in Virginia?" he asked finally, voice neutral. "You were supposed to be in Virginia."

I blinked. "Our water heater broke. I had to wait for the repairman."

Tommie. The repairman. Adrian's father. So stupid.

"Why didn't you call me?"

I couldn't tell what he was thinking. I couldn't tell if he was angry.

So I shrugged. "We broke up. I didn't want to call you."

He bowed against the island we were both sitting at, his face in shadow. "We thought you would be gone all weekend," he muttered. "We had someone in Virginia on standby to keep an eye on you. We let our guard down—Mariana and Dominic went off, Julian was in New York, and I stayed here with Lucian. I could feel you at your place, but I assumed it was residuals. I didn't *think*."

I swallowed my bite of spaghetti. "If you thought I was gone, how did you know what was happening?"

He looked up and I couldn't read his face. "You—felt something—that you don't normally feel. Well, you don't . . . feel it all the time; only—it shouldn't have been there, not if it was residual. You don't feel like that when—when you're away from me."

My stomach clenched into a slimy ball of curdled cookies and spaghetti. I knew what he was talking about.

"Adrian," I said, eyes watering, "I got all messed up."

"We don't have to talk about this now." I couldn't tell if he was offering me a way out or just didn't want to hear about how I'd made out with his father.

I felt sick. Adrian had *died* because of me.

I let the fork clatter to my plate as I stumbled to the garbage can, barely getting the lid off before I violently threw up. There were hands on my back pulling my hair away and I just kept going until there was nothing left, and even then I couldn't stop for a while. Adrian handed me a paper towel.

"Thanks," I mumbled, and he helped me sit on the stool again because I was shaking too badly.

"Caitlin," he murmured, "he's a demon. I know you don't like that word, I know you don't believe it, but you've seen him now. You have to understand that he has means of persuasion beyond your control."

"I don't care about *him*. I care that I almost got you killed," I whispered.

"No," he said tightly. "I almost got *you* killed. Twice."

"I let him into my *house*."

He met my eyes levelly. "You were waiting for a plumber. A plumber came."

He blinked, and swallowed tightly.

"Did you get enough?" I asked, nodding at the empty IV bag.

"Yeah," he muttered, voice rough and thick. "We should get cleaned up."

I looked tiredly at the hall, which led to the stairs, which led to another hall.

"I don't think I have enough blood pressure to make it that far."

He put his arms around me, lifting me off the stool. I listened closely to his heart as he carried me up the stairs to what had sort of become my bedroom. He nudged the door open with his foot, walked across the plush carpet into the bathroom and turned the lights on low, then set me on my feet. Reaching into the medicine cabinet, he pulled out two brand-new toothbrushes and a tube of toothpaste. We stood, trembling, at the dual sinks and brushed our teeth, not making eye contact.

He finished first and went to the giant claw-foot tub and began to fill it with hot, foaming water. When he came back, he frowned, perhaps really seeing me for the first time since we'd gotten to the house.

"You're covered in blood," he said bluntly.

"Yeah, well, it's all yours," I replied. "And his. And you have more of it on you than I do."

"I also have more of yours *in* me than you do," he muttered to himself. "Are you awake enough to take a shower?"

Honestly? Probably not. I nodded, though.

He looked around, pointed at the towels as if to say, "Hey, there's towels," and then actually said, "I'll be right outside."

I almost let him go. But the thought of being alone again after everything that had just happened, even for a moment, was out of the question. He turned to leave and I caught his hand. He stared down at it for a long moment before looking at me. I wasn't really thinking, just moving on instinct. I pulled him with me into the shower, turning it on without letting go of his hand. His face was a question mark even as I closed the glass door behind us. It was big enough to fit six people, but with just the two of us, it somehow felt impossible small. It must have looked kind of funny, both of us standing fully clothed in a giant marble shower, covered in blood. I kicked my shoes into the corner. Already the steaming water was running in little red whirls toward the drain.

I let go of his hand to reach for the hem of my blood-drenched shirt, but I was so weak I got it halfway off and it got stuck. After a moment, I felt Adrian's fingers brush my skin as he pulled it the rest of the way off. For the second time that day, I was glad I'd worn my cute bra.

A long moment passed. Adrian's lips were parted, his eyes dark and silver. Beads of water clung to the ends of his hair, building and falling, building and falling. I reached for his shirt, but before I could do more than touch it, he put his hand over mine. I flinched, waiting for the inevitable rejection. Instead, he ran his hands lightly up my arm, a pained look crossing his face as his fingers slid over the black-and-blue bruises that littered my skin. After a moment, he grabbed the shirt himself and tugged it slowly over his head, tossing it in the corner with my shoes.

Even in the clearing, I hadn't been this terrified.

He kicked his shoes into the corner with the rest of our things. I looked slowly up from the waistband of his jeans, up, past the dozens of raw scars on his stomach and chest and the field of purple-green bruises, up to his eyes. He was staring somewhere past my shoulder, and he was perfectly still, as if trying to hold himself together by force of will.

Blood was caked in his hair, on his neck, his chest, his hands. I reached up and dragged my thumb lightly across his jaw, rolling away a gunky strip of blood. He closed his eyes and turned his cheek into my palm. I wasn't thinking, really. I just wanted to wash everything away. I wanted to start over.

"You're too tall," I murmured.

He looked at me a moment, then sank slowly to his knees, arms hanging limply at his sides as he looked down at the blood-tinted water swirling down the drain between us.

I washed his hair, the bubbles turning bright red, then pink, then fading, finally, to white. He winced, once, when my fingers went over the bump on the back of his head—I'd forgotten he'd cracked his skull, too. Even when there were no more bubbles to rinse, I slid my fingers through his hair a few more times. He looked up at me when my hands finally went still.

His eyes were burning a low silver, swirling in lazy circles. He stood slowly, too close to me, and reached for the button on his jeans, pausing to see if I'd follow his cue. I reached for the button on my own jeans, which were irreparably stained with a mixture of muddy snow and vampire blood. We slid our jeans off and added them to the pile. He was wearing a pair of black boxer briefs, and nothing else—I'd seen him this unclothed once before, after the Halloween party, but it had been dark, and I'd been drunk, and my memory did not do him justice. I swallowed, heart hammering.

It was the wrong thing to say, but before anything happened, if anything was even going to happen, I had to tell him.

I looked at him, eyes already watering. "I'm sorry," I whispered.

He flinched.

Like that, the mood was gone, and I felt lost and disgusted and ashamed. I turned away from him, wanting suddenly to be anywhere but here because everything was messed up and I couldn't fix it and he wouldn't talk to me. And then his hand was on my shoulder, lightly, as if afraid I'd shrug it off. He pulled my hair to the side, running his knuckles down my spine in an echo of the dance we'd shared only a week before. And then he was scrubbing the blood off my arms and neck while I stood there shaking. When we were both finally clean, he picked me up, nudged open the shower door, and carried me to the nearly full bath, and I let him because I was so tired. He stepped in carefully, lowering us both into the steaming water. At least the bubbles covered up the wounds on his chest—at least they covered up the most obvious evidence of my guilt.

I finally got up the courage to murmur what had been on my mind since I realized who Tommie was. "Please don't hate me."

He tensed, I could feel the reaction course through the muscles in his arms. "Caitlin—*stop it*. Stop apologizing."

I didn't want to be touching him anymore, not if he wouldn't listen to me, not if he wouldn't *talk* about this—but when I tried to pull away, he wouldn't let me.

"I can't breathe," I said, beginning to hyperventilate, and he instantly let go. I clung to the edge of the tub with both hands while he brushed the hair back from my face.

"Cait," he whispered again, "it's over now. It's okay. We're safe. Why are you crying?"

I turned to him, tears spilling down my cheeks. "Because I'm *mad* at you!" I sputtered, not realizing it was true until I said it out loud. "Because you say it's okay, and it's bullshit, because it's *not* okay."

I could feel it, all of it, weeks of things I shouldn't have left unsaid, all pouring out now in an unstoppable flow. "You've been such a dick," I said, as if trying to explain something to a third-grader. "You pushed me away, you just shut down weeks ago, and you didn't tell me why, and it wasn't fair. I hated it, and you didn't care. I'm m-mad"—my voice caught on a fresh wave of angry tears—"because I should have known better, I should have *known* it was him. I just wanted to feel close to somebody again, and it didn't seem like too much to ask. I mean, come on! Normal people don't have to deal with this shit! Normal people can date someone and then decide their boyfriend's a jerk and break up and *move on* and they don't have to worry that the person they move on *to* is going to be a psychopathic demon that wants to impregnate them! This whole thing is stupid. This situation is *stupid*. No shit I kissed Tommie—*of course* I kissed Tommie. I'm *mad* at you."

I crouched back against the far edge of the tub. "I officially re-sign from the supernatural shit. I'm done with this—I'm done with all of it." Adrian sat staring at me with a dumbstruck look on his face. "So we're here," I continued, "and we've gone through all this, and you died, and then you un-died, and so you tell me, clearly, to my face—tell me how we're going to fix this. Tell me how we're going to be okay."

I let the silence draw on for five impossibly long seconds, but he didn't answer, because he was Adrian, and God forbid Adrian answer any question, ever.

I nodded. "Okay."

I stood, then, to get out of the tub, suddenly grateful I hadn't made a total ass of myself by getting completely naked in the shower. Bypassing the towels, I headed straight into the bedroom to find my sweatpants, trailing bubbles onto the carpet as I went. I was calcu-lating how long it would take Trish to come pick me up and decided it was too long. I'd just walk. If he wasn't completely dead, Tommie was very nearly dead, so I probably didn't have to worry about him, and if a bear tried to eat me, I'd just slap it across the face with my shoe. I'd just found my sweatpants in my bag when the little hairs on the back of my neck stood on end. I turned and found Adrian coming at me through the bathroom door.

He stopped, looking about as angry as I'd ever seen him. "*Fine*," he said, pointing a finger at me. "Here it is, here's all the stupid, ran-dom, *infuriating* shit that's been going through my head the past cou-ple months."

He took a half step toward me, then whirled back toward the bathroom, shaking. Finally, he turned and faced me again, eyes burn-ing uncontrollably silver.

"Do you know how *fucking hard* it was to lie next to you every night for *weeks* and do *nothing?* Do you have any idea how difficult it was to convince my family I didn't have any real feelings for you, whatsoever? Caitlin, you have no clue what would happen if they found out—"

"If they found out *what?*" I exploded. "As far I know, I am the same level of importance to you as the bag lady at the grocery store!"

"God, Caitlin!" He whirled in a circle, running his hands through his hair. "There are *rules.*"

"*We do not live in the Middle Ages,*" I sputtered. "This is *America*. This is a *democracy*. You are not obliged to do every tiny little fucking thing you're told!"

He laughed and shook his head bitterly. "You really think it's that simple?"

"It *is* that simple," I countered. "All you've told me from the beginning is that you want to be different, you want to be better, you want to be your own person, and every time you could have stood up for yourself, every time you could have stood up for *me*, you didn't. And all this shit just happened, and it's shitty, it's so insanely *shitty*, and I'm *mad*, so I'm only going to ask this once: Do you want to kiss me, or not?"

"Fine!" he said, and started toward me.

"Too bad!" I yelled, dancing around the end of the bedpost. "I don't *want* you to kiss me anymore!"

He closed the space between us, and in a sudden burst of childlike panic, I scrambled onto the bed to snake across to the other side. He caught my ankle and I fell flat on my stomach, scrambling for pillows, throwing them over my shoulder at his face. Finally, he dragged me toward him.

"No!" I said, struggling. "You're not allowed to kiss me anymore! My lips are *off limits!*"

We were face-to-face, both of us breathing hard.

I glared at him. He stared angrily back at me at with his upturned brows and his silver, dancing, stupid eyes.

We reached for each other simultaneously, hands diving into hair, lips crashing. I wrapped my legs around his waist as he dragged me off the bed, but he instantly tripped over a pillow and we went down. He grunted, hauled me up, and kicked open the door, stumbling into the hall, and then over to his bedroom between unpracticed but enthusiastic kisses. It was dark, lit only by moonlight and stars, like the last time I'd been in here, but I wanted to see him. I wanted to be seen.

"Turn a lamp"—I started to demand, but interrupted myself by kissing his face again with my face—"on."

He scrambled for the lamp, yanking the cord before accidentally knocking it to the floor. He left it there and staggered over to the bed, dropping down and rolling until I was pressed beneath him. He pulled back and stared at me a moment, both of us breathing hard, chests heaving. His mouth was set in a hard line, his damp hair was wavy and dripping onto the comforter. He opened his mouth, closed it, then opened it again, staring angrily down at me. "I love you." The expression on his face was somewhere between bitter and bewildered. "I love you, and I'm not allowed to, and I'm sorry for being a dick."

His face softened, slowly, muscle by muscle, until he simply looked tired, and sad, and totally worn-out. "I'm so s-sorry," he said, voice catching. "I love you."

At the words, my eyes instantly burned with tears. I hadn't cried this much in one day since my mom died, and it felt good. It felt necessary. I cradled his face in my hands. "Why is that always so hard to say?"

"I don't know, but I think it's your turn to say it."

I smiled, the wild energy all used up and gone. "I love you, too. But we got shit to talk about. Later. When I've spawned more blood cells or whatever, and can think straight."

He smiled, but it was kind of a miserable smile, so I pulled him toward me and pressed his face to my shoulder, wrapping my arms around his back as though I could be the one to protect him for a change. He breathed sharply, trembling, but I knew he was listening to my heartbeat, and he slowly relaxed. I ran my fingers lightly down his naked back and within a half a minute, he was fast asleep, and I wasn't far behind.

———◦

Adrian woke me up every few hours, pressed his ear against my heart, and listened. I'd stroke his hair and eventually he'd fall back asleep. That was how Julian found us. He opened the door quietly and stood there in his designer jeans and a fur coat, the light from the hallway casting him into a silhouette. He opened his mouth and I shook my head.

"Let him sleep," I whispered.

He ran a hand through his hair and down his face, looking tired. For a moment, I swore I saw his eyes flash blue and gold in the darkness. He backed out quietly and closed the door. I felt both safer that someone else was in the huge, empty house, and edgy—caught with the weird sense that Julian's presence both confirmed and denied everything that had happened that night.

The next time I woke up, I smelled coffee. It was disorienting for a moment; the smell of it reminded me of Rachel and Joe and home. There was a heavy but comfortable weight on me, and I realized Adrian was still there, still asleep—although so was one of my legs.

I looked over and saw a tray with two mugs, a small bottle of hazel-nut creamer, and a note. Pinned under Adrian, I groped awkwardly for it. Adrian murmured and I ran my hand up and down his spine absently as I read.

Caitlin,
Mariana and Dominic will be here in an hour.
Don't let them see you with Adrian.
                    Julian

My initial response was anger. Then I realized he wasn't warn-ing me to stay away from Adrian—he was warning me to not let Mar-iana and Dominic know. And he'd brought us coffee.

I didn't understand Julian at all.

"Coffee?" Adrian mumbled against my collarbone.

"Yeah," I said, brushing the hair back from his face as he stretched and looked up at me blearily. "Julian brought it."

His brow furrowed in confusion. "Julian?"

"He came back a little while ago."

He blinked. "*Julian* brought us coffee?"

"I know."

We disentangled and slowly sat up. My arms looked even worse in the morning light, and I was glad it wasn't summer, because I had no idea how I'd hide the bruises from Joe and Rachel without long sleeves.

Adrian sucked in a sharp breath, and I looked at him. He placed a hand softly on my jaw and murmured, "Shit, that looks bad."

I winced at the touch. I'd almost forgotten Tommie had hit me hard enough that I'd nearly blacked out.

"I can't heal all your injuries until I've had more time to recover,

♥  375  ♥

but I'll take care of that before you go home," he said. I nodded, and he cleared his throat.

We sipped at the coffee for a while in silence. I glanced over at Adrian, suddenly realizing we were both very nearly naked, and that things had been said, and that we'd definitely really, really kissed, for real last night. When I looked over, I realized he had also chosen that moment to look over at me, and we both immediately blushed and buried our faces in our coffee cups. We could fight demons together, but we couldn't make eye contact after making out. But there was something even better than eye contact, and that was Adrian's hand finding its way to mine, and holding it. I knew I had a big sloppy grin on my face, so I pressed my forehead to his shoulder so he couldn't see me smile, and we sat like that for a long time.

"Adrian," I said after a while. "The things that your dad said, about me—were they true? Were they really hoping that I would die?"

Adrian's hand tightened painfully around mine, then relaxed. "I don't know. He's a liar—but that doesn't mean he wasn't telling the truth."

"So what do we tell your sister about what happened? What do we tell the *Council*?"

He ran his thumb over mine slowly. "The truth—or part of it. We say that my father came, and tried to—" He paused, swallowing. "He tried to hurt you. I fought him. I scared him off. We came here."

"Okay," I whispered. "But what do we do if your dad wasn't lying? What if the Council wants me dead?"

Adrian shook his head. "It doesn't make sense. None of this makes sense. You're Caitlin, from Connecticut. You're—"

"Nobody?"

He looked at me seriously. "To them? Yeah. At least, you should be."

"I don't understand this. I don't know who to trust."

He found my gaze and held it. "Me. You can trust me."

I wrapped my arms around him, hiding my face against his neck. "Please don't leave me again," I said, trembling. "Please don't shut me out."

He hugged me to him tightly. "I thought I was doing the right thing. I thought it would be easier if you hated me."

I pulled back, searching his eyes. "*Why?*"

He closed his eyes and pressed his forehead against my shoulder. "Julian made me see something I didn't want to see. And it didn't occur me to try and find another way."

"What does that mean?" I whispered.

He looked up at me, pained. "Caitlin—starting now, at eighteen, my aging is reduced by ninety percent. By the time I *look* thirty, I'll stop aging completely. I will never grow old. Do you understand what that means?"

I did, but I shook my head, because I didn't want to know.

"We'll figure it out," I said, tears spilling down my cheeks. "We can figure that out."

He kissed me. "We will. I know we will. But when I realized that you would die someday, like everyone has to—like everyone *should*—I got overwhelmed. I can protect you from my father, I can protect you from the Council, but I can't do a damned thing about time. And I could never give you k-kids," he whispered, voice breaking.

"Shh," I murmured, holding him. "We don't have to talk about this now."

I kissed his hair and his arms tightened around me. We stayed locked in that embrace, and I was terrified. I was terrified that even if he loved me, even if there was no Council handing out laws and rules and restrictions, he was right—I would grow old, quickly. I would die.

And he wouldn't.

"I don't want to talk about this now," I repeated, sliding off his lap and onto the bed. "Can you just . . ."

I looked at him and he somehow knew what I meant. He pulled back the covers and we crawled in. I curled up next to him as close as I could get, and he wrapped me up in his arms. I must have dozed off, because the next thing I knew, Adrian's alarm was going off. I looked over blearily and saw that it was 10:50—and according to Julian's note, Mariana and Dominic would be back in less than ten minutes.

Beside me, Adrian sat up to turn off the alarm. Despite the heaviness of our recent conversation, I smiled at him. I couldn't help it—shirtless Adrian was such a nice view.

I could feel his gaze sweep over my face, down my shoulder, across my chest. A smile tugged at the corner of his mouth.

"Adrian," I warned. "If you keep staring at my breasts, we're going to get into trouble."

There was some sort of guttural grumble sound deep in his chest, and it immediately made me flush with goose bumps. He leaned toward me, eyes igniting into silver. As much as I wanted to kiss him, I really, *really* didn't want his sister to walk in on us.

So I defense-tickled him.

He jerked away with a surprised laugh, arms crossed over his six-pack. "Did you just tickle me?"

I grinned at him. "Yes, I did."

He tickled me back and I shrieked, trying to escape, but he grabbed me and rolled, pinning me beneath him.

Well, it was never a perfect plan.

He was propped up on his elbows, but other than that, we were flush together.

"I have coffee breath," I warned.

"That's nice," he said, kissing the noninjured half of my jaw.

"My hair's a mess."

"Such a mess," he agreed, twining his fingers in mine and stretching them slowly above my head.

And then a thought occurred to me. "Can Julian . . . *feel*, what we're doing?"

Adrian stopped dead. "He can feel what *you're* doing. Shit. Maybe he thinks you're . . . y'know . . . entertaining yourself."

I burst into laughter, then stopped. We looked at each other, both going red in the face, and I burst into laughter again. Then he sighed and kissed me anyway, mutual coffee breath and all, and nestled his face into my neck like a cat. "Caitlin," he said, voice muffled in my hair a full minute later. "We'll figure it out."

My heart jumped in my chest, beating heavily. "Promise?"

He propped himself up to look at me. "I promise."

I smiled, but it was a scared smile. He kissed my cheek, and my forehead, and my chin, and then my mouth. It could have turned into something more—I *wanted* it to turn into something more—but then he muttered, "Julian," and pulled back.

He slid out of bed and walked to his dresser. I propped my chin on my hand to watch him, trying to keep the mood light even though my chest felt tight and heavy.

"Adrian?"

"Yeah?" he asked, looking for a pair of pants.

"I have the utmost admiration for your backside. It's really nice." He looked up at me, cocking an eyebrow, and I shrugged, smiling. "Just thought you should know."

His jaw worked, fighting a smile. "Stop being cute, or I'm going to come back over there."

He blushed, and I blushed, and then he threw a pillow at me and I laughed, wrapping his blanket around me and standing with a yawn. He was wrestling his way into a pair of pants, and I bit my lip to keep from smiling. We had a lot of shit to deal with, but he was here, and I was here, and it was something.

I got up and slipped into my room to get dressed. A few minutes later, Adrian knocked on my door. "Breakfast?"

I nodded and followed him into the hall. He paused a few doors down and knocked on Lucian's door.

"Hey, bud, time to wake up! Breakfast!"

But there was no reply. Adrian frowned and knocked again. When there was no answer, he carefully opened the door, letting light spill into the room.

My eyes adjusted to the darkness enough to tell that the bed was not only empty, it was still made; sheet tucked in, pillows in place.

I frowned. "Is he already downstairs with Julian?"

"I doubt it," Adrian said, though part of him was considering it. "He always waits for me to wake him up."

Not saying anything more, Adrian hurried to the stairs and descended. I followed as quickly as I could. When we reached the kitchen, Julian was eating Cap'n Crunch and playing Angry Birds on his phone.

"Is Lucian down here?" Adrian asked, coming to an abrupt halt.

"Nope," Julian said, not bothering to look up from his phone.

Adrian went very still, then whirled and fast-walked back to the hall and up the stairs. I couldn't quite comprehend what was happening. Adrian opened the door to my studio.

"Lucian?" he called.

No answer. He ran back out, opening the next door. "Frankie?"
No response.

I took one side of the hall and he took the other. Every room was empty. Every hair on my body stood on end.

"Shit!" Adrian yelled, slamming his fist against the door frame.

"He's gotta be here somewhere," I said, on the edge of panic.

Adrian gave me a look that chilled my skin. We headed downstairs and checked the second floor room by room, calling his name loudly. Julian finally wandered out of the kitchen. "What's going on?"

Adrian threw Julian a dirty look. "Our brother is missing."

Julian paled.

We ran down to the first floor, to the east wing with the pool. It, too, was empty and silent. We raced through the dining room, the kitchen, the offices, and finally into the library, calling out "Lucian!" Even Julian looked a little panicked.

There was no one there but us. Adrian dropped to his knees, looking like the wind had gotten knocked out of him.

Lucian was gone.

———————⚬———————

Mariana and Dominic got home a half hour later. Julian was having a conversation with someone in spitfire French, and Adrian was still in shock. He'd scoured the grounds, calling Lucian's name, asking me to stay in the house as a precaution. Since Lucian was a vampire as well, Adrian couldn't sense him—they were all blank spots to one another—"voids," as Mariana had called it. The only way to find Lucian was to stumble across him, and that was becoming less likely by the hour. Mariana and Dominic had us recount the story over and over, picking apart details, analyzing the events—although we very carefully left out the bits and pieces we'd decided we didn't want the Council to know.

In the end, they concluded that Tommie must have come back here to the house while Adrian and I had been in the clearing. They didn't know how he'd gotten past the security measures—unless, of course, Lucian had simply opened the front door. He was the only one of the siblings that had anything close to affection for their father. It wouldn't be beyond reason to think Lucian has simply chosen to go with him.

Julian stayed that night while Mariana and Dominic made an emergency trip back to D.C. for some sort of Council meeting, which meant Adrian and I had one more night together before life got complicated again. But the joy of that morning was gone, the playfulness, the *something else* was put indefinitely on hold.

Adrian and I were sitting on the edge of his bed. It was three in the morning, and he had been silent for a long time. Norah had competed earlier that day, but I had no idea how she'd placed. It didn't seem that important right now.

Lucian was gone.

I felt numb. I felt like I'd felt everything it was possible to feel, the past few days, and now I was exhausted.

It was late, though, and we needed to sleep. I pushed Adrian down and pulled the covers over us. He stared at the ceiling blankly. I wrapped my arms around him, and pulled him close.

"My brother is gone," he murmured.

I didn't know what to say at first. Finally, I settled for, "We'll get him back."

"Little brother."

"We'll get him back," I repeated. Because we would.

He buried his face in my neck, wrapped his arms around me tightly. "I almost lost you."

I kissed his cheek softly. "But you didn't."

"Don't go."

"I won't."

"We'll get him back."

"We'll get him back."

Sunday morning, Adrian, Julian, and I were working our way numbly through bowls of cereal when the backup arrived. They walked into the kitchen, assembling regally in a semicircle, and I had the weird, passing thought that they seemed like they'd be more comfortable in armor than the array of designer clothing they were currently dressed in.

"For those of you who don't know," Mariana began, addressing the newcomers, "these are my brothers Julian and Adrian. And this is Caitlin."

Apparently they didn't need an explanation of who I was, and why I was there. Three days ago, I would have been intimidated, but I'd now faced far worse than a bunch of well-dressed European vampires.

"This," Mariana continued, pointing to three men, "is Javan, Vincent, and Farrar." She turned to the two women. "This is Sabine and that's Kalare."

"You're Caitlin?" Sabine said in a thick Parisian accent, looking me over with an expression that was borderline hostile. I'd just been introduced, so I didn't really know how she could already have a problem with me, but making enemies of authoritative women seemed to be a specialty of mine.

"The one and only," I replied tightly.

Javan looked sternly at Sabine before stepping forward, and

though he didn't look particularly older than any of the rest of them, he *felt* older. He nodded at me in greeting.

"We are the war council."

I hadn't checked my phone since before we'd passed out at three a.m., so I didn't see the text from Rachel saying they'd decided to drive through the night and they'd be back by eleven Sunday morning, and could Trish please drop me off around noon. It was now two and I also hadn't noticed the multiple missed calls and texts asking where I was. Apparently she'd driven over to Trish's herself to pick me up, and I hadn't been there. Suffice it to say, when I did finally pull up, on Adrian's Harley no less, my aunt was livid.

"Where the *hell* have you been?"

Even in my emotional stupor, it caught my attention that Rachel had just sworn. I'd literally never heard a bad word out of her mouth before. She stalked up to the bike as I swung off, and glared at me.

"You can't *do* this, Caitlin! You can't just go off anywhere you want and not *tell* me! We're your family, we are responsible for you, and you *have* to listen to us."

She took a step forward and for a moment, I thought she was going to slap me. Instead, and to my great surprise, she hugged me so tight I could barely breathe. There was a moment of silence, and then she let me go.

"Excuse me, Mrs. Master—" Adrian began, but Rachel cut him off.

"You are in trouble, young man. This is the last straw. I am calling your aunt and uncle."

Joe came out, finally, and I could see Norah looking on from the kitchen window.

"Mr. Master," Adrian tried again, "please, let me expl—"

Joe shook his head. "Don't push it, son."

"Guys," I interrupted. "Adrian's brother is missing."

There was a moment of silence.

"My family was out of town for the weekend while I stayed home with my little brother," Adrian explained, carefully dancing his way through the truth. "Lucian's got . . . .special needs. I think he got confused, and wandered away from the house. I called Caitlin, because I didn't know who else to call. She came over to help me look for him. I'm sorry for not asking your permission, I just—I wasn't really thinking."

Rachel looked stricken. It was Joe who finally spoke. "Do we need to call the police, or your family?"

Adrian shook his head. "Police have been called. My family's back now. We searched the house and the property and even the surrounding woods. He's gone."

"I'm sorry I didn't call, Rachel," I said, turning to my aunt. "It was an emergency."

"No, it's okay," she said, looking oddly emotional. "Is there a search party? We can get our coats and boots and call some of the neighbors—"

"My family hired some investigators," Adrian said, cutting her off. "But thank you."

Rachel bit her lip, nodded, then pulled Adrian into a hug. He was surprised, but he let her hug him.

Adrian went home shortly after, but not before giving me a quick kiss—directly in front of Rachel and Joe. I guess that was his way of saying, to at least one set of authority figures, that things were going to be different now.

After he left, Rachel hugged me again. And for the first time since

I'd moved in with them, I hugged her back. Maybe she hadn't been there for me, once. But she was here now. And I needed my family. I needed them more than I needed to be angry.

I was saving all my anger for someone else.

I was going to get Lucian back. I was going to find a way for Adrian and me to be together. I was going to hurt Tommie, in whatever form he took, in whatever dimension he was hiding in.

And when all of this was over, I was going to take Lucian and Adrian and go to New York and do my internship and design beautiful things and somehow find a safe place for us all. Because I had something to live *for* again—not Adrian, not my career, but all of it: I had a future, I had a *family*.

And that meant I had hope.

# ACKNOWLEDGMENTS

## Alexis

It's pretty obvious that *Velvet* would not have been written without you. Not only did you come home from class every day asking to read the next chapter I'd managed to crank out, you were the only person able to coax me out of my hermit cave / bunk fortress to go outside and interact with the rest of the world. We went to the *Twilight* midnight premieres together, even when you moved three hours away, you gave me notes on *Velvet* five years after I first wrote it in our dorm room, and you are an incredible and dear friend.

## Beta Readers

Kim Wilcox, Tony Sands, Greg Dember, Nicholas Limon, Audrey Ney, Kristen Rea, Alexa Riddle, Mel Case, Shelby Etcheson, Ashley Oczkewicz, Elizabeth Stoker, Jeffrey Holmes, Rosalie M. Town, Dan Marchant, and everyone else I guilted into reading *Velvet*. Your criticism, enthusiasm, and time were critical in getting *Velvet* to where it is today.

## Mr. Bratt

I still can't call you by your first name, even though it's been six years since I was your student. Your classes were spectacular. Doing homework for you was a privilege (which sounds insincere and brown-nosey, but I'm completely serious). You treat your students like intelligent, thoughtful adults, which made such an incredible difference in my reception of my own education. In your classroom, I realized that my decisions were my own, and I had within me the power to think critically about the world, to observe it and decipher it and understand it, rather than accept it at face value. The way you presented literature to a bunch of fidgety teenagers was nothing short of remarkable. I blame you for my love of archetypes.

## Dad

In addition to sneaking me food and gas money over much of the last five years, you also instilled in me a love of fantasy literature. Reading *The Chronicles of Narnia* every night before I fell asleep allowed for the story to percolate in my dreaming brain. You never minded when I wandered off on literal bunny trails when we went hiking and camping, when I borrowed your longbow for target practice, or when I appropriated your scrap supplies and tools to make failed Rube Goldberg projects. Whatever independent spirit I have, I learned from your love of wilderness, beauty, and elbow grease. You're an incredible dad, and I love you more than I can properly express.

## Deborah Halverson

When I was 19, I sent *Velvet* out to dozens of literary agents, and one of them passed me along to you. You took it upon yourself to give me 13 pages of notes on my (at that point) 150,000-word manuscript. All you asked for in return was that when I published my novel (which you knew I would), I pass it forward by advising another young author. I have no idea if you remember this encounter, but I do, and I wanted to let you know that I intend to fulfill my promise.

## Lonnie & Jess

I commonly refer to you two as either my mentors or my second set of parents, and both are apt descriptions. Whether it was a novel, a screenplay, or a pilot, you never failed to be both excited and supportive of my project, and wholly convinced of my potential, often when I was in extreme doubt. You've invested so much time and love into my life, and have been a steadying hand in the years when I felt lost and alone. Thank you for remaining a constant source of wisdom even when I moved a thousand miles away.

## Michael

If Lonnie and Jess are my second parents, you are my Obi-Wan Kenobi. For the past six years, any time a career decision came up, any time I wasn't certain what to do or where to go creatively or professionally, you were the first person I consulted. You are one of the most intelligent people I have ever met, and I owe so much of my development as an artist and a writer to you. I could not have asked for a better mentor, and I am proud to call you my friend.

## Mrs. Madison

I only had you as a teacher for seventh grade, but over a decade later, I still remember what you did for me. Besides being a generally fantastic educator—funny, intelligent, and just a little bit sarcastic—you unknowingly confirmed my decision to become a writer. We had to submit a short story for your class and I was in such a rush of excitement that I turned one in on ripped-out notebook paper, scrawled in my completely unintelligible handwriting. You enjoyed it so much, you gave it 21 out of 20 possible points. Getting extra credit from you, simply for telling a good story, was the moment I knew for certain what I was going to do with my life. So, y'know, thanks for the being the catalyst for that semi-pivotal moment.

## Mom

As my English teacher in both junior high and high school, you held me to a higher standard than your other students because you believed, well before I did, that I was going to be an author. You gave me your life savings so I could go to college, you sat across the table from me during the edits for this book and pointed out comma splices and laughed out loud at lines you thought were funny, and you inspired me to try the path less taken by living your own life outside the boxes others might have been expected you to stay put in. You are an incredible, brilliant woman, and I am proud to call you my mother.

## Nathan

I can't imagine how annoying I must have been as a kid, following you around all the time. But you never seemed to mind as I perched on the back of the couch and watched you and your friends play video games for hours (*Final Fantasy VII* still holds a key place in my heart). My interest in sci-fi and fantasy grew in direct proportion to yours, as I would often steal the books off the shelf in your room after you'd finished them. Without you, I would never have discovered Robert Jordan, Terry Brooks, or Brandon Sanderson (although I claim credit for introducing you to Scott Lynch). It is one of my greater joys to Skype you and geek out over *Doctor Who*, brainstorm plot options for our various novels, and discuss our mutual love of bacon. I respect and admire you greatly, and miss you like crazy.

## Rachel

My entire life, I've looked up to you in the best possible way. I took my fashion cues from you (and your hand-me-downs), my love of all things vintage and antique, and my appreciation of beauty even in the midst of disappointment and pain. When I was in high school, you convinced your editor to let me write a guest article for the newspaper, and it was the first time I saw my name in print on a professional publication. This past year, you let me stay in your guest room so that I would have the financial freedom and mental focus to see *Velvet* through to completion and publication. You are the best big sister I could have asked for: beautiful, intelligent, inspiring, and kind.

## Red Twig Cafe Baristas

For keeping me well-supplied in vanilla lattes while I took over the corner of your cafe every week while editing *Velvet*. For asking me how the book was coming along every time I came in. For sneaking me free coffee. And for having awesome beards. I mean truly, they are fantastic (especially yours, Steven).

## Holly West

My dear Holly, I must thank you for a lot of things, beginning with your patience. I had a bizarre list of questions (What are pass pages? What is this squiggle mark on the copyedit? What should I be doing to promote the book?), which you answered promptly, and a bizarre list of fears (What if someone points out something I forgot to answer in the book? WHAT IF EVERYONE HATES IT AND I SUCK AT WRITING?), which you assuaged many, many times. More importantly, thank you not only for helping me craft *Velvet* into its best form, but for being so darn *excited* about it. Your enthusiasm was infectious, and it made me believe that perhaps I had a story worth telling after all.

## Swoon Reads

When I wrote *Velvet*, I mostly wrote it on a whim. While I, of course, dreamed about publication, I thought about it in the same way one thinks about what one would do if one won the lottery (say that five times fast). In short, I never really believed it would see the light of day. Thank you for providing a platform where my work could be seen, and thank you for believing in *Velvet*.

## Swoon Reads Readers

I owe a huge debt to everyone who read, reviewed, and rated *Velvet* while it was a baby manuscript on the Swoon Reads site. Thank you for investing your time in a no-name book from a no-name author, and for providing such great feedback.

Turn the page for some

Sw♥♥nworthy

Extras...

# A Coffee Date

with author Temple West and her editor, Holly West

## *"About the Author"*

**Holly West (HW): Let's start with my favorite question. You can take a second to think about it. If you were a superhero, what would your superpower be?**

Temple West (TW): Oh, I already know that. Flight. I have always wanted to be able to fly. Just Superman-esque. Anywhere. No wings or anything. I don't want extra appendages, I just want to be able to fly.

**HW: You're stranded on a desert island. Who would you bring for company?**

TW: I feel that Johnny Depp would be a really good person to take just because, I mean, after that many *Pirates of the Caribbean* movies, he's got to know how to get off an island.

**HW: That is very true.**

TW: Plus, it's Johnny Depp. So, the company would not be bad.

**HW: Also, very true. Other than writing, do you have any hobbies? Since writing can't really be considered a hobby for you anymore, what with you being a published author.**

TW: I do. I have so many hobbies, it's a little overwhelming. I love sewing. That's part of why I wrote *Velvet*, because my mom was a decorator sewer for about ten years when I was growing up, so that was a part

of our lives. That's how she made an income for a while. I can't sew half as well as she can, but I really enjoy doing it. But I hate patterns, so I just make things up, and they don't always work, but I really enjoy it. So, there's that. And I like, tangentially, knitting. My art teacher in high school taught me how to knit. And weaving. I built a loom a couple of weeks ago because I was bored. I'm weaving a rag rug. I also like book art, which is where you actually carve images into the pages of a book, so it becomes a three-dimensional piece of art. It's super cool. It takes forever, like 14 hours per thing for a simple design. So, there's that. And leatherworking. My grandfather was into leatherworking and I discovered a box of his tools in the garage when I was a kid. I love being able to carve designs into belts and stuff. What else? Carving things. Swords and stuff out of spare wood. That was a weird hobby of mine as a child. And painting, I like painting. I like singing, but I'm not very good at it, so I don't do it in front of people. And just crafty stuff. I love crafty stuff. Making something that wasn't there before, or taking supplies and making something beautiful out of it. That is my happiest time, just making something.

**HW: That is an impressive list. I thought I was vaguely crafty because I knit and crochet and occasionally costume and I've done some embroidery, but your list is a little bit more extensive.**
TW: I have to admit, I'm not very good at any of these things. I just dabble very lightly across a wide spectrum of activities.

## *"The Swoon Reads Experience"*

**HW: How did you first learn about Swoon Reads?**
TW: From my mother. She saw an ad for it. I still don't know where (I think it might have been on Facebook or maybe one of her friends

had posted a link to it or something). I was actually at her condo sewing. I had totally taken over her living room with all her supplies out and was making costumes for something, and she said, "Hey, there's this thing called Swoon Reads and it sounds like it's right up your alley. It's a competition-based, young adult, romance novel division of a company." I said, "Yeah, that sounds great, but it's probably a scam." I didn't even look at the link until a couple of days later. I read the terms of service and all the finer points and I thought, "Oh, no, this sounds fantastic! I should submit to this because I have a novel," and then I did.

**HW: Before you were chosen, what was your experience like on the site?**

TW: Really good. It was really fun to be able to see the other community members, not only what they were writing, but what they were doing. Like what their backgrounds were. Were they a stay-at-home mom, were they a college student, were they in high school? Just to see the different people who were attracted to Swoon Reads and to these types of stories.

**HW: Are you going to have a big celebration when the books actually end up in your hands?**

TW: My plan is to go to the nearest Barnes & Noble or bookstore and grab every copy that I can and just kind of roll with them on the floor and giggle uncontrollably.

**HW: That sounds great. No, really, we need video of this!**

**HW: Where did you first get the idea for *Velvet*?**

TW: After reading *Twilight*. I had kind of been into vampires before. I thought that they were really cool creatures. A lot of creatures in mythology are part animal or so inhuman, they're a little bit hard to connect to, but vampires are basically humans with some teeth and some undead-ness, depending on which book you read. So, they seemed a lot more relatable. Then *Twilight* came out and it was this huge thing. The movies were just coming out as I was reading the books and my roommate was super into it, and that's kind of what sparked my idea of, "Okay, I want to do my take on this now. All the frustrations that I have with previous versions of vampire stories, I want to address those and make my perfect vampire, if you will, or my perfect vampire story." So, that's what I attempted to do with *Velvet*.

**HW: So, we selected the book and gave you the call, and then you got my huge edit letter with the "Don't panic, I love your book, really!" e-mail. What was that like?**

TW: I was really nervous. I was really, really nervous. While I had edited it as much as possible, I hadn't really touched *Velvet* in a long time, so I knew there were things about it that I wasn't satisfied with when I submitted it to Swoon Reads. I was really nervous to have your notes come in, knowing that there were things that even *I* didn't like about it. And then I actually read your notes, and I think I literally laughed out loud at the fact that I agreed with all of them and that they were so kind. I was expecting this scathing, "This is wrong, this is wrong," and it was just so sweet and kind. I won't spoil it, but your notes about adding that one scene to the ending, I know I literally laughed out loud and said, "Of course, yeah. That definitely needs to happen." I just thought it was so funny. So, it was a very good experience, the editing process.

**HW: When you get your edit notes, how does the revision process work?**

TW: What I like to do is read the notes, talk them over with you if I have any questions, and go through and just be like, "Page 147, go make that change. Page 287, go make that change," whatever it is, kind of spot-check it, and then go back and read through the entire thing cover to cover and make sure that those changes work. With some of the deadlines we had, I couldn't do that every time, but that's how I like to do it just to make sure that things are flowing correctly and that the old material works with the new material. A lot of times, it doesn't. The changes are good changes, but it's just not quite flowing.

## *"The Writing Life"*

**HW: Where do you write? Do you have a writing ritual, or have to be in a certain place?**

TW: That's a good question. When I wrote *Velvet*, I'd write it in my dorm room. My roommates and I had three people in our room, so the other bunk bed was just like bed-bed, but mine was like bed-desk, with the desk underneath my bed, so I had this little writing cave. I could pull my blanket over and make a space. It was awesome. I wrote *Velvet* there, at least the first draft. Nowadays, I try to write from home and it sometimes works, but I often get really

distracted, so if I really need to power through and get stuff done, I go to a café. And have coffee.

**HW: Coffee always helps.**
TW: It really does. I think it's like a Pavlovian response now. If I have coffee, I want to write, and if I write, I want to have coffee.

**HW: What's your process? Do you outline everything or do you just start at the beginning and make it up as you go?**
TW: I have tried to make myself become an outline person, but it has not really worked so far. Most of the time when I get an idea for a story, I just sit down and write for as long as I can on that spark of an idea. So for *Velvet*, I think that was like the first chapter. I think I wrote the first chapter in one go. Generally, it's a scene, a bit of dialogue, something. And then I'll stop and kind of think, "Okay, what genre is this in, what story am I telling, where is this going?" And I'll try to kind of think through it a little more and that'll generate more ideas and I'll write those into a scene. So, I kind of go back and forth between thinking about the story and just vomiting the story onto the page.

**HW: If you could give a piece of writing advice to someone, what would it be?**
TW: I would say study your favorite stories, whether it's a movie or a book or whatever, and figure out what makes that story work. Why do you like it? Why is it satisfying? What did they include in the story that makes it satisfying? Basically studying other stories, dissecting them analytically. And obviously just keep writing. That's a given, just keep writing all the time.

# Velvet

## Discussion Questions

1. Are *Velvet*'s vampires different from what you would typically picture for a vampire? If so, in what ways? Did you like them more or less than other vampire characters you've read about?

2. What is the significance of the title, *Velvet*? Would you have given the book a different title, and if so, what would it have been?

3. After Caitlin loses her mother, she's forced to move from her home in Connecticut to her aunt's house in New York. After such a terrible loss, do you think it would be better to get a fresh start somewhere else, or to remain in a comfortable and familiar place?

4. What did you think of Caitlin's reaction to Adrian's vampireness? How would you have reacted?

5. Is the explanation of vampire physiology/need for blood satisfying or distracting? Would you prefer to know or not know how vampires work?

6. Caitlin's friends go behind her back to buy the Green Thing for her to wear for Adrian. Do you think they were out of line? How would you have felt if your friends did that for you?

7. Adrian says he found solace in fiction, and that he learned about bravery, friendship, compassion, and loyalty from books. Have you ever had a similar feeling toward a book or books? Which one(s)?

8. In Chapter 16, Caitlin says velvet is a difficult fabric to work with because, "If you messed up, you had to cut it off and start all over. That's just how velvet was." How do you think this relates to the story?

9. Mariana is over a hundred years old, and has become a skilled cook in that time. If you could live forever, what skills would you want to perfect?

10. Have you ever played Obscure Hangman? If you haven't, go do that right now.

Want to host your own
*Swoon Reads Book Club Party?*
Download our *free* event kit at
*www.swoonreads.com / partykit!*

# What if you were fated to NEVER fall in love?

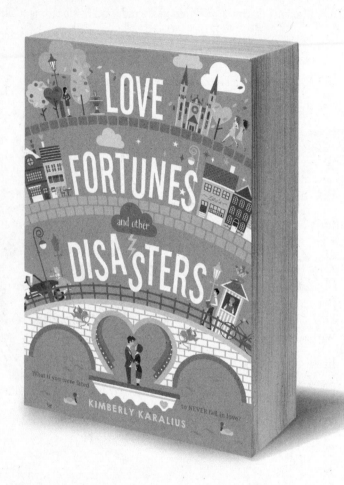

When Fallon Dupree's (100% accurate) love fortune from Zita's Love Charms says that she will never find love, she's devastated. But a rebellion is brewing and other students, including notorious heartbreaker Sebastian, are fighting back.

A LINE SNAKED THROUGH VERBEKE SQUARE, curving through a maze of café tables and around vendor stalls. The line began in front of Zita's Lovely Love Charms shop, the only shop in a row of old brick buildings that sold something other than lace.

Zita's shop had been painted a shade of pink lemonade with bow windows and a second story used only as a back-lit display of Zita's finest love charms that glittered with gemstones and gold. Sunlight made the shop gleam beside its drab companions. No one looked at the lace while they waited for their fortunes.

"Nico better be at the front of the line," Anais said. "My sandals aren't made for standing."

Fallon glanced at her friend's flat, faux-leather shoes. They looked cobbled together by a blind shoemaker, not a factory, and she doubted that the straps would last the walk back without breaking. "I'm sure he's got us a good spot."

The majority of the line consisted of Grimbaud High students. Tradition dictated that every high school student get a love fortune before the beginning of each school year. This particular love fortune was different than the other charms sold in Zita's shop: It foretold your romantic future for the entire school year. Zita's one hundred percent accuracy kept the townspeople coming back to her shop.

The line moved, releasing a smattering of students trying to process their fortunes. Some cried–good tears or bad– while others stared at their ticker-tape fortunes with stunned disbelief. The students with the best fortunes glowed like stars, one step away from dancing on the cobblestones. Nico stood in the middle of the line, twisting his damp shirt in his tanned fingers. He had brown hair burned gold from the sun and a sinewy body.

"Couldn't you have gotten here earlier?" Anais said, pinching his arm.

"Hey! It doesn't make a difference. The line's been here since dawn. Just be glad you're not in the back of the line," Nico said, "because I'm nice enough to let you cut me."

"Did you eat breakfast?"

"Nah. I can't stomach it." Nico rubbed the back of his head; his fingers paused over the thinning hair.

Fallon and Anais squeezed in front of Nico in line, much to the chagrin of the students behind him.

"After we all get wonderful fortunes," Anais said, "we'll have to indulge in a good brunch."

Nico pressed a hand to his mouth. "Please don't talk about food."

Fallon worried about the green tinge of his skin. "Sit down right now," she said, placing her hands on his shoulders. "Put your head between your legs."

Nico obeyed. He gulped down a few deep breaths before struggling to his feet again.

"Could you be seasick?" Anais teased.

"Not possible. Sailing the canals is nothing like the sea. The water's smooth, like gliding on mirrors."

"The better to see your bald spot with."

Nico rolled his eyes. "I'm just excited, okay? And out-of-my-mind nervous. This could be the year I get Martin's attention. Or not. Oh God, *or not.*"

"Deep breaths," Fallon warned.

"You don't understand," he said. "Martin broke up with Camille over the summer. I might have a chance."

Fallon had only known Nico for a month, having been introduced to him through Anais, but she already felt invested in his longtime crush on Martin Pauwels, the student government president. As a sophomore, Nico had secured the unwanted position of treasurer, enabling him to work side by side with Martin during the new school year.

Nico's full name was Nicolas Barnes, of the Barnes family that owned the most popular canal cruises in town and famous tourist attraction, the Tunnel of Love. Nico spent his days cleaning the boats, manning the Barnes booths spread throughout Grimbaud, and sometimes giving tours when the cruises were booked low. Over the weeks she got to know him, she had learned how to speak above the roar of boat engines. Nico had mastered that skill long ago and had no trouble bemoaning Martin's now ex-girlfriend and the fact that, to anyone's knowledge, Martin didn't like boys.

The line continued to move and each step brought them closer to the moment of truth. Fallon could see Zita's storefront now, adorned with slanted gold lettering. The windows revealed a shop lit with warm, round lights. Love potions in glass-blown bottles gleamed in the windows. A rack holding prewritten love letters spun like a carousel while charms molded like cupids sat in half-price baskets. Fallon tore her eyes away from the enchanting display.

The love fortune machine was built into the wall on the left-hand side of the shop. Like the storefront, it was painted the same shade of pink and rimmed with golden swirls. A series of cogs kept behind rose-colored glass moved each time the machine printed a new fortune on the paper strips. The boys in front of them shoved their coins one-by-one into the slot; Fallon heard Nico swallow loudly when the last boy, shouting with victory, brandished his good fortune and walked away.

"Who's going to go first?" Fallon said. Her hands shook.

Anais rolled her eyes. "Me. Otherwise, we'll be pelted for holding up the line."

She slipped her coins into the machine and placed her hand on the scallop-edged heart in the wall. The heart pulsed as the cogs turned. No one knew exactly how the love fortune machine worked, but it was clear that the heart read who you were—somehow. Fallon felt a slight tremor under her feet. As if Zita herself was underneath the cobblestones right now, reading Anais's heartbeat and scrawling her fortune.

The ticker tape slid out of the machine facedown. On the other side, written in red ink, was the fortune.

Anais squealed. "Good news for me. *'Your love life will be fruitful as long as you are true to yourself.'*"

Fallon let go of the breath she didn't know she was holding.

Nico frowned. "What does that mean?"

"If I'm myself, I'll get to keep Bear as my boyfriend."

"If," Nico said, "you actually let him see you in your work uniform."

"Never."

"What about the biscuit tins? I'm sure he'll think you're adorable when—"

"No way. No boyfriend of mine needs to know about that." Anais pushed him forward. "You go next."

Nico turned green when he put his hand on the heart. He shuddered so badly that the printing of his fortune seemed miraculous. Nico scanned the fortune, one, twice, and muttered, "Oh, no. Oh, no."

Anais plucked it before he could drop it. "*'Your love will go unnoticed by the one who matters.'*"

Fallon rubbed his shoulder, at a loss for words. "Nico . . ."

His eyes grew red with unshed tears. "No big deal, right? I expected this."

"Shut up," Anais said, drawing him into a hug.

Fallon wished she could tell him not to give up, but that wasn't how Grimbaud worked. Zita's love fortunes were always right. The red ink was clear enough; Nico would do better forgetting Martin once and for all. Easier said than done. Fallon squared her shoulders and stepped forward, taking her turn at the machine.

She placed her hand on the scallop-edged heart and closed her eyes. The cogs turned in a symphony of clicking and clanking. In that moment, Fallon swore the earth absorbed her heartbeats like sunlight and saw the truth in them. Her fate. She almost forgot to reach for the ticker tape as it slid out of the machine.

"Fallon, read it," Anais said, soft with new worry.

She opened her eyes and tore off the strip. The red ink made a long scar on the surface. " 'Your love will never be requited,'" she whispered aloud as she read each word.

Her stomach dropped out of her.

Nico rubbed his eyes, turning a new shade of green on her behalf. "Are you sure?"

Anais gently pried the fortune out of Fallon's hands and

read it herself. "It's true. It really says that. Fallon, have you been holding out on us? Is there a boy you like? Someone from your hometown, maybe?"

It took a few seconds for her throat to work. "No."

Anais cursed.

Fallon forgot how to breathe. The word "never" scared her. It held the weight of forever.

Her fate was sealed.

Looking for something else to make you swoon? Check out these other great *Swoon Reads* titles!

Fourteen viewpoints.
One love story.

Even her guardian angel
might have trouble
saving Cara . . .

Partners for life, or
just on the ice?

Words are strong.
Love is stronger.

# Temple West, debut author of the YA paranormal romance *Velvet*, is as nerdy in real life as she is on the Twitter. Armed with a very shiny English degree, she spent four months in Oxford holed up at the Radcliffe Camera amongst the hush of ancient books and the rich musk of academia. Returning to Los Angeles, she acquired a concurrent degree in film, mostly as an excuse to write essays about *The Princess Bride* and *Hook*. She can sew (poorly), drive stick (please fasten your seat belt), and mostly lift her feet off the ground while stuttering into first gear on a very small motorcycle. She currently lives in Nashville and is the proud mother to a one-year-old laptop and a vintage Remington typewriter.

ByTempleWest.com